High Praise for the Books of
MAX ALLAN COLLINS!

"Strong and compelling reading."
— *Ellery Queen's Mystery Magazine*

"Collins has an outwardly artless style that conceals a great deal of art."
— *The New York Times Book Review*

"Collins breaks out a really good one, knocking over the hard-boiled competition (Parker and Leonard for sure, maybe even Puzo) with a one-two punch: a feisty story-line told bittersweet and wry... Never done better."
— *Kirkus Reviews, starred review*

"Collins has a gift for creating low-life believable characters... a sharply focused action story that keeps the reader guessing till the slam-bang ending."
— *Atlanta Journal Constitution*

"The Nolan series by Max Collins is fast-paced and exciting. Plunk down some hard cash for this one today."
— *Prevue*

"Powerful and highly enjoyable reading, fast moving and very, very tough."
— *Cleveland Plain Dealer*

"Intelligent, witty, and exciting."
— *Booklist*

"Ingenious."
— *Publishers Weekly*

TWO *for the* MONEY

by **Max Allan Collins**

A **HARD CASE** CRIME NOVEL

A HARD CASE CRIME BOOK
(HCC-005)
November 2004

Published by

Dorchester Publishing Co., Inc.
200 Madison Avenue
New York, NY 10016

in collaboration with Winterfall LLC

ISBN 0-8439-5353-5

The name "Hard Case Crime" and the Hard Case Crime logo
are trademarks of Winterfall LLC. Hard Case Crime Books are
selected and edited by Charles Ardai.

Printed in the United States of America

Visit us on the web at www.HardCaseCrime.com

To Barb
For aiding and abetting

TWO FOR THE MONEY

BOOK ONE
Bait Money

Prologue

A woman was usually a night to a week in Nolan's life, yet this one had lasted a month and five days. But then, before it was different—before he'd never had so bad a need for one.

He sat up in bed, aware that the pain in his side was lessening, and scanned the room. He took in its drabness, and a slight smile came to his lips. Christ, had he really been staring at these four suffocating walls for over a month now? He closed his eyes, seeking not rest but relief from pink stucco walls and second-hand store furniture.

"Hi," she said. She was in the doorway, bundled in a heavy coat, a sack of groceries filling her arms.

He nodded hello.

"I'll just put these away," she said.

He kept nodding, said, "Okay," and watched her smile and leave the doorway.

He leaned back and reached out his arms while stretching his body. The pain didn't increase at all from the movement; the place in his side where the bullet had gone in seemed completely healed over. Quite a difference from even a week before, when his body had been one big ache, one long, slow, muscle-bone-gristle ache.

He got out of bed and caught, turned away from his reflection in the bureau mirror. He climbed into a pair of boxer shorts, shaking his head and muttering.

That damn face of his, high cheekbones, narrow eyes, widow's-peaked hair, that damn easily recognizable face, which both beard past and mustache present failed to disguise. At least the lean weeks had affected his body somewhat to the better. He felt drained, sure, but that roll of softness the years had put around his waist had disappeared.

"Hi," she said, in the doorway again, now wearing only bra and panties.

She had never been beautiful, he supposed. But she'd been better than plain, and nowhere near ugly. Now, after seven or maybe eight years of traumatic experiences—assorted divorces, abortions, affairs with married men—she was getting the kind of lines in her face that polite people say show character. Nolan saw the lines as too much age for too few years, giving her an air of having been taken advantage of emotionally, used once and thrown away like Kleenex.

"You look tired," he said.

She nodded, undoing the scarf that tied her black hair behind her head, letting the shoulder-length mane fall free. "I'm tired, all right," she said, "but not physically, you know, just mentally. I mean, the old mind really gets a workout waiting tables eight till five. It's a goddamn challenge."

As she spoke, Nolan watched bitter lines deepen in her face and then lowered his eyes to her breasts as she released them from her bra. The breasts were large, and though beginning to sag, were still quite good. Her nipples were like rose-hued sand dollars.

"How was your day, Nolan?"

"Long. Dull." He went back over to the bed and lay down again.

"How's the side?" She came and stood by the bed and leaned over him, her breasts swaying like hanging fruit.

"What?"

"Your side, how's it feeling?"

"Better."

"Do anything today?"

"Just slept."

"Oh? Now don't hand me that line . . . you haven't been sleeping more than nine hours out of every twenty-four since you been feeling better, and you had near that when I left for work this morning. So what'd you do today?"

"I watched television."

"Sure you did. The soap operas."

"That's right."

"Come on, Nolan."

"I read the paper."

"Do anything else?"

"No."

"Took you all day to read the paper?"

"Slow reader."

"All right, so be a bastard."

"That was an accident of birth."

"Smartass remarks don't make you less a bastard, Nolan."

"Okay, okay. I suppose I ought to tell you, anyway."

"Tell me what?"

"I made a couple long-distance calls."

"You did?"

"Yeah, I'll pay for them. I'm going to pay you back for everything you've done for . . ."

"Shut up, Nolan." She sat down on the bed, facing away from him and touching her face with her fingertips.

"What's the matter?"

"Nothing."

"What?"

"You don't owe me a damn thing, that's all. Do you understand?" Her voice was drum tight. "I am a lot of things, and I've been a lot of things, and I will be a lot of things in days to come. But I was not, am not, and will not ever be a whore." She was quiet for a few moments, then added, her voice hushed, "You don't owe me anything, Nolan. And if you try to give me any money, I'll tear your goddamn heart out."

He touched her shoulder.

She turned and rubbed her hand over his chest, twining her fingers in its hair. She made an effort and got a smile going and said, "I won't try to pry out of you what those phone calls were about—you don't have to worry about that."

He nodded, smiled.

"Did you do anything else today?"

"No. Just did some thinking."

"That's what I was afraid of. That's why those stupid damn phone calls put me on edge so."

"What do you mean?"

"Now you've started thinking."

"Thanks a bunch."

"You know what I mean. You've started thinking, and before I know it, well . . ."

"Well what?"

"Well, you'll be gone, damn it."

He didn't say anything.

"You *are* leaving," she said, "aren't you?"

"I didn't say that."

"You said you been thinking. Same difference."

"Sometime I'll leave. Everybody leaves sometime or other."

"You're half right. Everybody leaves me *all* the time."

"What is this, self-pity day?"

"You're goddamn right it is. Who else is going to pity me if I don't? You?"

"How old are you?"

"What? Why are you forever asking me how old I am?"

"Don't make me ask again."

"All right, all right, I'm thirty-one."

"What else are you? Besides thirty-one."

"Free, white, and ten years too many?"

"You're intelligent. Not bad looking."

"Beautiful is what I am. A funhouse mirror with sex."

"Shut up. You're a good-looking kid."

One side of her mouth smiled. "Maybe I should have pulled this self-pity routine before. I've never heard you talk so much—and compliments, too! Don't stop now."

He allowed himself a grin and said, "I'll grant you I don't talk much, but now I am, so listen, I got something to say: sling hash if you want to, or don't sling it."

She looked at him wide-eyed. "That's it? That's the big message?"

"That's it."

"Profound. Pretty fuckin' profound, Nolan. 'Sling hash or don't sling it.' Let me write that down."

He laughed and grabbed her arm. "Okay. You think about it. For now let's shut up and get on with it."

Her lips took on a wry smile, and she latched her thumbs in her panties and tugged them off. "You got yourself a deal."

They made love, slow, grinding love, and it was as good for them as it had always been over the past month of Nolan's recuperation. At the beginning, because his wound was serious, their lovemaking had been gentle, increasing in intensity as the weeks passed, each time different for them. Nolan was amazed that this one woman could seem to be so many different women. Never having bedded down longer than a week's time with the same woman, he had assumed a woman's sexual possibilities could be sufficiently explored in that time or less. It was a pleasant surprise to him to discover at this late date that he was wrong.

After several hours of sleep, Nolan and the girl awoke to darkness and, checking his watch, Nolan said, "It's nine, kid. What shall we do?"

"Hungry?"

"Yeah."

"What do you want?"

"How about breakfast?"

"At nine o'clock at night?"

"Yeah."

"Okay."

She climbed out of bed, slipped on her bra and panties, got into a houserobe, and went out into the kitchen.

Fifteen minutes later Nolan and the girl sat at the kitchen table, eating the evening breakfast of scrambled eggs, bacon, and toast in silence. Nolan's attention was on his plate of food, while the girl stared at him intently.

She broke the silence with, "Why do you ask me what my age is all the time?"

"Do I?"

"You did tonight, and I bet it was the hundredth time, too. Why?"

"To make a point."

"What point is that? Oh, I remember, don't remind me, that quote of yours that'll go down through the ages: 'Sling hash or don't sling it.'"

He looked up from the plate. "That's the one."

"There's got to be more to it than that."

"Maybe there is. You never bothered asking how old I was, did you?"

"No, I didn't. But then, you told me at the start not to ask you a lot of personal questions. For my own sake, you said."

"That's right. But you don't have to ask, I'll tell you. I'm forty-eight."

She was surprised. "I thought forty, maybe . . . but, hell, so what? I been had by older men, that's for sure."

"You never met anybody older than me. I'm a dinosaur who can't get it through his head he's extinct."

"What are you . . ."

"I'm forty-eight and I'm hiding out with a girl who spends her days slinging hash, and I'm living off her while I get recovered from a gunshot wound."

"You said not to ask questions, Nolan, so . . ."

"I know. You're not asking, I'm telling. You got time left. You got stuff left in you. I'm running out. Of time. Of stuff. I picked what I am, and I blew it. I got nothing left to do but make the best of the sucker choice I made a long time ago. Till it's over."

"I don't . . . don't follow you, Nolan."

"You don't have to. You got a life of shit here. Change it. Change yourself. You got time left to choose again. Me? My life's shit because I picked wrong. Too bad. Too late."

"I think you're feverish again."

"No, I'm not. Have you been listening to what I said?"

"Of course, Nolan, of course . . ."

"Sometime when you got nothing to do, think about it."

He wiped his mouth with a napkin and got up from the table. "Let's not talk anymore. I'm tired again."

They went back to bed, fell asleep quickly, then woke in a few hours and made love, hard, fast, violently. Then Nolan and the girl rolled apart and went back to sleep.

At five the next morning the phone rang them awake, and Nolan went for it, spoke a few times and listened for a minute-and-a-half without answering, said, "Yes," and hung up the phone. He went back to bed and pretended sleep, just as he knew the girl was pretending she hadn't seen and heard what had just happened.

At six-thirty the girl kissed Nolan on the cheek as she was preparing to leave the apartment for work. Nolan grabbed her, stroked her face, and smiled good-bye. Then he rolled back over in the bed and closed his eyes and she was gone. When she'd been away an hour, Nolan got out of bed, called the bus station to confirm his reservation, packed his bag, and left.

One

I

The drizzle felt good on Nolan's face. The night air was chill, though not enough to freeze the drizzle, and the light, icy sting of it on his skin kept him alert as he waited.

He was sitting on a bench in the parklike strip of ground that separated the Mississippi River from the four-lane highway running along it. The highway connected the Siamese-twin cities of Davenport and Bettendorf, whose collective reflection on the river's choppy surface vied for attention with that of Rock Island and Moline on the other side.

Across the highway was where Werner lived.

Werner's home was a white, high-faced two-story structure, nearly a mansion, complete with row of six pillars. Already bathed in light by the heavily traveled and streetlamp-lined four-lane, the house was lit on right and left by two spotlights set on either side of its huge, sloping lawn, which banked down gradually to the highway's edge. Even through the heavy mist, the whiteness of the overlit house made a stark contrast against the moonless night around it.

Typical Werner logic, Nolan thought, picking a place like that one: status plus prestige equals respectability.

Nolan had been waiting just less than an hour. His side of the road was darker, and the constant traffic flow and hazy weather seemed likely to obscure him from anybody who might be on watch over at Werner's. He hadn't seen any watchdogs yet, but he knew one would show sooner or later—a Werner-style watchdog, two-legged-with-gun variety.

He smoked cigarette number one off the first pack of the evening, second of the day. He was pleased when the drizzle didn't put it out. Just as he was getting number two going, he spotted Werner's man.

The watchdog came around from the back, walking slowly around the house, probing the thick shrubbery on both sides of it with a long-shafted yellow-beam flash. He was slow and methodical with his search, and after the shrubs had been checked, he headed for the paved driveway to the left of the house. He stood at the far end of the drive and let the flash run down over it, then walked toward the back of the house again.

Probably a garage back there, Nolan thought, the drive leading around to it.

Three minutes later the watchdog reappeared at the right of the house and began to move slowly over the sprawling lawn, crisscrossing it half a dozen times before angling down on the highway's edge. He stood there for a moment in the light of a streetlamp, and Nolan got a look at him.

Not overly big, just a medium-sized guy, wearing a hip-length black brushed leather coat, open in front to reveal a dark conservative suit, complete with thick-knotted striped tie. The man didn't look particularly menacing, but Nolan knew he'd probably been chosen for just that reason.

Subtle muscle. Typical Werner.

Nolan's hand in his jacket pocket squeezed down around the rough handle of the .38. He put on a smile and stood up from the bench. Stepping out into the stream of traffic, sidestepping cars, Nolan called out to the watchdog.

"Hey! Hey buddy . . ."

The watchdog had turned to walk away, and Nolan met him about a third of the way up the sloping lawn.

"Say, I think I've gotten myself lost. You couldn't give me some directions, could you?"

The watchdog had a bored, bland face that didn't register much change between glad, sad, and indifferent, although Nolan could read it well enough to rule out glad. The hand with the flash came up and filled Nolan's face with yellow light.

Nolan squirmed and held his free hand up defensively to shield his eyes, but he kept the smile plastered on. "Look, friend, I don't want to bother you or anything, I'm just a stranger here and got my bearings fouled up and thought maybe you could . . ."

"This isn't an information bureau," the watchdog said. "What this is is private property. So just turn your ass around and go back across the street and take off. Any direction'll do."

The flash blinked off, and Nolan could tell he'd been dismissed.

Nolan gave him a bewildered-tourist grin, shrugged his shoulders and began to turn away. Before the turn was complete, Nolan swung the gun in hand out of his pocket and smacked the .38 flat across the watchdog's left temple. The watchdog's eyes did a slot-machine roll and Nolan caught him before he went down. Nolan drunk-walked the limp figure up the remainder of the lawn, carefully avoiding the glare of the spotlights, and took him over to the left side of the house, dumping him between two clumps of hedge. He checked the man's pockets for keys but found none. He did find a 9mm in a shoulder sling, and tossed the gun into the darkness.

Subtle moves were fine for Werner and company, but right now Nolan hadn't the time or energy for them. The watchdog would be out for half an hour or more; plenty of time. He glanced out toward the highway, which by now seemed far away, and decided that there wouldn't be any threat from some public-spirited motorist stopping to question his handling of the watchdog situation. Thank God for mist and apathy.

He walked around the house in search of an unlocked window, trying not to let his out-in-the-open sloppiness with the watchdog bother him. He just didn't seem to have the patience to work things out smoothly these days. Making a mental promise to tighten himself up again, he tried the last of the windows.

Locked.

Well, there might be one open on the second floor, and a drainpipe was handy, but Nolan ruled that approach out: his side, while improved, was not yet in that kind of shape, and he was beginning to think it might never be.

He broke the glass in a window around the back of the house, seeing no need for caution since the neighboring houses on both sides were blocked by stone walls, and a large three-car garage obstructed the view from behind. A light was on in a window over the garage door, probably the watchdog's quarters, explaining the absence of house keys in the man's pockets. Nolan slipped his hand in through the glass-toothed opening in the window and unlocked it. Then he pushed it up and hauled himself slowly over and into the house.

He caught his breath. The room he found himself in was dark; after stumbling into a few things, he decided it was a dining room. A trail of light beckoned him to the hall, where he followed the light to its source, the hairline opening of a door.

Nolan looked through the crack and saw a small, compact study, walled by books. Werner was sitting at his desk, reading.

Several years had passed since Nolan had last seen the man, but their passing had done little to Werner: he'd been in his early twenties for twenty-some years now. The only mark of tough years past apparent in his youthful face was a tight mouth, crow-footed at its corners. The almost girlish turned-up nose and short-cut hair, like a butch but lying down, overshadowed the firm-set mouth. His hair's still jet-black color might or might not have come out of a bottle, though Nolan felt fairly certain that the dark tan was honest, probably acquired in Miami.

A rush of air hit the back of Nolan's neck, and he started to turn, but an arm looped in under his chin and flexed tight against his Adam's apple, choking off all sound. He felt the iron finger of a revolver prod his spine as he was dragged backward, away from the cracked door.

A whisper said, "Not one peep."

The watchdog.

Shit.

"That gun in your hand," the whisper said. "Take it by two fingers and let it drop nice and gentle into your left-hand coat pocket."

Nolan followed instructions.

"Now," the whisper continued, "let's you and me turn around and walk back into the dining room, okay? Okay."

The watchdog kept his hold on Nolan's throat and walked him along, each step measured. Once they were out of the hall and into the dining room, the grip on Nolan's neck was lessened slightly, though the pressure of the gun was still insistent.

"Keep it quiet and you'll get out of here with your ass," the watchdog whispered. "I'm only going easy on you because I don't want my boss in there finding out I let somebody slip by me. A window with some busted glass I can explain, you in the house I can't. So just keep it down."

They approached the broken window through which Nolan had entered, and the watchdog released him, shoving him against the wall by the window. Enough light came in the window for the two men to make their first good appraisal of each other.

Nolan had been right about the guy being tougher than he looked. The whole upper left side of his face was showing a dark blue bruise, and a still-flowing trickle of red crossed down from his temple over his cheek, but the man's expression remained one of boredom, only now it was as though he were bored and maybe had a slight headache. He'd shed the leather topcoat, and his suit was a bit rumpled, although the striped tie was still firmly knotted and in place.

"Sonofabitch," the watchdog said, "an old man. I got taken down by an old man. Will you look at the gray hair. Sonofabitch."

Nolan said nothing.

The watchdog's upper lip curled ever so slightly; Nolan

took this to be a smile. "Let's get back outside, and a younger man'll show you how it's done. . . . Come on, out the window."

The hand with the revolver gestured toward the open window, and Nolan grabbed for the wrist and slammed the hand down against the wooden sill, once, then again, and on the third time the fingers sprang open and the gun dropped out the window. Nolan smashed his fist into the man's blackened temple, a blow with his whole body behind it. The hard little man crumpled and was out again.

Nolan leaned on the wall and gasped for breath. Half a minute went by and he was all right; his side was nagging him again, but he was all right.

He undid the watchdog's shirt collar and untied the tie, then used it to lash the man's slack wrists behind him and picked him up like a sack of grain and tossed him out the open window, where he landed in the hedge. Nolan figured he'd stay there a while longer this time around.

When he returned to the door of the study, Nolan peered in through the crack and saw Werner, undisturbed, still at his desk, reading. With the .38 in hand, Nolan drew back his foot and kicked the door open.

Werner dropped his book and sucked in air like a man going down for the third time. "Nolan . . ."

Nolan waved hello with the .38.

Werner shoved the book off to the side of his desk. "Uh . . . shut the door, will you, Nolan?"

Nolan did. He walked over to a chair in front of the desk, turned it backward, and sat down, looking straight at Werner and leveling the .38 at him.

"It's good to see you, Nolan."

Nolan smiled. "Good to see you." He laid the gun down on the desk and stretched out his arm.

The two men shook hands.

2

"You didn't exactly make it easy for me," Nolan said.

"Oh, but I did." Werner smiled. "I usually have two men on watch here, one in, another out. I gave the guy who covers inside the house a night off. You only had Calder to contend with."

"Your boy Calder didn't seem to want you to find out I got past him."

The smile settled in one corner of Werner's mouth. "That's the way Calder's mind works, all right. He's a thinker. Thinks too much, really. As long as he doesn't ever stub his toe too bad, he's got a chance to make it in the business. Have much trouble with him, Nolan?"

"Some. Wouldn't have a few years back."

"Calder's a hard-headed little bastard."

"You're telling me."

Werner spread his hands. "I'm sorry to put you through this breaking-and-entering routine, but it's best to maintain certain appearances, don't you think, Nolan? If, uh, interested parties found out you and I still have connections after all this time, things could turn sour for me in a hurry."

Nolan nodded and said, "I know there's risk involved, for both of us. I didn't think I'd ever have to contact you again, till this came along." He patted his side.

"It has been a few years, hasn't it?"

"Five. That was when you said things had cooled down. You said, don't worry."

Werner shrugged. "I thought things *had* cooled down. Eleven years should be time enough to cool anything down. But it obviously wasn't. Even after that eleven years has gone to sixteen, it's like it started yesterday. Who'd ever think one of Charlie's dimwits would be able to recognize that ugly face of yours, after all those years?"

"He didn't seem to have much trouble."

"How're you feeling, anyway? How long'd it keep you down?"

"Just over a month. Feel weak. Never was much for getting shot."

"Hell, you don't look so bad. The bus trip okay?"

Nolan got out the pack of cigarettes and offered a smoke to Werner, who shook his head no. Nolan lit one up. "Trip was short, few hours is all. I slept all the way. I sleep a lot these days."

"Meaning what?"

"Meaning I'm getting old. Like everybody gets old, but sooner. Like you're getting old, but worse."

"Forty-four isn't old, Nolan."

"When you live the way I do it is, and for me it's forty-eight."

"Nobody forced you into being what you are. You could've had what I've got if you'd played it just a little bit different. Do you see this place, Nolan? Not bad. My life's a breeze, old buddy. Only time I ever work up a sweat is when I go down to the local gym for a workout."

"Yeah. Life's a regular Disneyland when you don't fall from good standing with the . . . what are you boys calling the Family now these days? Cosa Nostra? Too ethnic. The Outfit? Too vague. Better Business Bureau, maybe?"

Werner's smile twisted. "The term Family is back in fashion, among the insiders. We're back to calling it the Family again."

"Cozy."

Werner got up and went to the door and flipped the lock. In his blue Banlon shirt and gray slacks he looked like something that had walked off the front of a country club brochure. He strolled over to a line of bottles sandwiched between two quarter-rows of books on a shelf halfway down the wall behind the desk. He poured two glasses of Scotch, handed one to Nolan, and kept the other.

"You know, Nolan, killing Charlie's brother that time was a mistake."

Nolan lifted his shoulders, then set them back down. "Today it's a mistake. Sixteen years ago it wasn't."

"No, you're wrong." Werner's smile was gone now. "Even then it was a mistake. Maybe less of one, since you were young and had a chance and could live a running life without much sweat. But, now, the inevitable is starting to catch up with you, and it gets closer by the day."

Nolan nodded. "I'm old."

"You're not old . . . but you sure as hell aren't young anymore. Look, I got to admit that when you quit Charlie, you had no choice but to turn to what you did. I mean, a murder rap hanging over your head on one side, your ex-friends gunning for you on the other. And I'll give you credit . . . you turned out to be the most successful grand larceny artist I ever ran across. Racked up how much in those sixteen years? Near half a million?"

"Just over that."

Werner waved his hands. "More or less, what's the difference? It's gone now. All that's left for you is to decide what happens next. The money is gone, or as good as."

That was right.

Gone.

Nolan looked into his drink. When he'd called Werner from the girl's apartment the day before, he'd found little need to tell his old friend about what had happened: Werner'd already gotten most of it through the Family grapevine.

For sixteen years now, Nolan had made his way as a specialist in engineering institutional robberies. Through a number of sources, Nolan lined up other professionals, with their own specialties (drivers, strongmen, climbers, safemen, electricians, et cetera) and molded them into compact units of three to six, hitting banks, armored cars, jewelry stores, and firms on cash payroll. Occasionally, a well-moneyed individual would also feel the squeeze of Nolan's particular talents. He'd stayed away from places owned or controlled by what was now calling itself the Family, and he avoided Chicago and the surrounding area, where the local Family operation was helmed by his ex-employer, Charlie.

Over the years Nolan had kept in touch, off and on, with Werner, his lone Family friend who remained as such, though then only secretly. Eleven years after the incident that had enraged Charlie over Nolan, Werner told Nolan that Charlie's grudge had cooled. Cooled enough, at least, for Nolan to quit looking over his shoulder.

A month-and-a-half ago, considering the matter with Charlie past history, Nolan had consented to use the Chicago area as the planning base for a bank job three other pros had in mind for a little town some thirty miles out of the city. Nolan and the three others used an old hotel in Cicero while they hassled out the details of the job. A week before the score was to be made, Nolan was spotted in Cicero by one of Charlie's men, who recognized him and got off the shot that had caught Nolan in the side.

The other three pros he'd been working with split (and Nolan could hardly blame them: he'd likely have done the same in such a case), but he managed to get to the apartment of a girl he'd picked up just the night before, and she stayed by him and didn't ask questions. The only problem he had with the girl was convincing her a doctor wasn't necessary, since Nolan felt that as long as the bullet wasn't in him, had passed through clean, there wasn't anything to worry about.

The tragic part, as far as he was concerned, was that his cover was blown.

When he'd sent the girl to his hotel for his personal belongings, she had found that somebody (Charlie's man, Nolan assumed) had traced him there and had taken all his things. One of the things missing was a suitcase, and in it was a billfold and papers belonging to one "Earl Webb."

The Webb name was one Nolan had built for many years, a costly name, a name that had documents to prove its existence as a living being, a name that owned three restaurants and a miniature golf course and laundromat and a couple of drive-in movies, losing businesses purchased to keep on losing so that juggled books would keep the name's federal income tax returns looking legitimate.

A name that held over half a million dollars in banks around the U.S.

"If Charlie leaks the Earl Webb cover to any of the authorities," Nolan said, "all I got to do is try and touch a cent of my money and local cops and state cops and FBI'll swoop down on me like hungry birds. I got to find out whether or not Charlie's leaked it yet."

Werner shook his head from side to side. "The answer to that one I don't know. But I *do* know Charlie, and my guess is he hasn't let out a word . . . up to now. He's got this Earl Webb lead on you, and he'll try to find a way to use it himself before he gives up and lets it go to anybody else."

Nolan stubbed out his cigarette. "He won't be able to use it himself. Oh, he might track down a place or two I rented under the Webb name, places I stayed at between jobs sometimes, and maybe he'll get to some of the guys who run fronts for me. But there isn't anything or anybody connected with the Webb name that I'm about to touch or go near now. The only possible good he'll get out of the name is to expose it and screw me out of my cover . . . and my money."

"You're probably right, Nolan. And Charlie's had just about enough time to find this out for himself."

"You got any ideas?"

"Well, maybe one. But suppose I do have a good way out. Suppose I got things straight between you and Charlie and he got off your back for good. What then? Try and get in good with the Family again and shoot for an executive position? Or maybe just continue your present career without threat of Family intervention?"

"None of that," Nolan said. "I want to retire."

"Retire?"

"I couldn't work now if I wanted to. The word's out that the Syndicate people want me dead . . . and that doesn't exactly make me a desirable working partner in the circles I move in. Me saying things are clear with Charlie, if that could happen, won't make any difference. The people I work with would expect me to say that whether it was true or not."

"I see." Werner finished his drink. "You surely have more on your mind than just retirement."

"I do. I want to go back to what I used to do."

"Nightclubs, you mean?"

"That's right."

"It's been sixteen, seventeen years, Nolan, since you were managing clubs for Charlie. The whole nightclub scene has vastly changed."

"I can adjust. For twenty years, the last sixteen especially, I been going the fast pace. Been shot four times. Fires. Car wrecks. Can't remember all the times I got the shit kicked out of me. You name it, I did it, or somebody did it to me." He got out another cigarette and lit it. "It's not that I want to quit this life so much as it is I've burnt it out. I got to try something else, and clubs are the only other thing I know."

Werner looked away for a moment, as if weighing each word he was preparing to say, then said, "If things *could* get straight with you and Charlie, I might be able to use you in one of my clubs here in the Cities. Like I say, you been away from it a while, but I'd be glad to have a man of your caliber working for me."

Nolan got up and poured himself another drink. "I may take you up on that offer, Werner. But if I can get to my money, I can buy my own club."

Werner shrugged. "Well, the offer stands."

"That's generous as hell of you, and I appreciate it, don't get me wrong, but it won't be worth last year's calendar if I don't get this thing settled." Nolan leaned over with the bottle of Scotch and refilled Werner's drink. "You said you had an idea. Let's hear it."

"It's going to sound crazy."

"It'll have to sound crazy to be worth a damn. Go on."

"Well, all right . . . in a word, negotiate."

"What are you, crazy?"

"You got to understand, Nolan, things have changed since the days when you were working for Charlie. Things aren't handled the way they used to be. The violence, it's soft-pedaled now. The Family's into businesses now, Nolan, big ones, not just front operations, but big and on-the-up-and-up businesses. The old way of handling things is passé."

"How does that affect me?"

"Well, since the Cicero shooting, Charlie's probably been getting pressure from upstairs, pressure to cool it if and when he does find you again. They're not saying, 'Don't kill Nolan.' They're just saying, 'Careful and no mess.' Now, Charlie knows damn well you're not the kind who'll lay down and die like a good boy . . . with you, he knows there's going to be mess."

"So?"

"Take advantage of it. Offer to meet and talk. Charlie could come in from Chicago, it's just half an hour by plane, and I can have some place set up here in the Cities as neutral ground. You could tell him that the pressure of having him out for you these past sixteen years has finally got to you; that he really got you cold over in Cicero; that you're sorry you got mad that time and shot his little brother . . . tell him any and all the lies you like, but get it talked out."

"Seems to me this kind of thing doesn't get talked out."

"Maybe not, but remember—Charlie was probably just as upset about the twenty thousand you relieved him of as he was about you knocking off baby brother. Money means a lot to Charlie, and then there's his pride. He'd probably like to find a way to come out on top with you, without violating the 'cool it' orders coming from upstairs. You paying him off is a possible out for both of you."

Nolan didn't say anything for a few moments. Then he said, "It's worth trying."

Werner laid his hands out on the desk. "I'll make the contact tomorrow morning."

"You can do this without getting yourself up shit creek?"

"I think so. I'll just tell Charlie that you got me at gunpoint or something and proposed the idea and that it sounded good to me, so I thought I should let him know. He'll eat it up. Charlie always has been a melodramatic bastard."

Nolan nodded.

"Tomorrow I call him."

"I appreciate this, Werner."

"I owe you, Nolan, for a lot of times. No need to talk that end of it. Where you staying?"

"Nowhere, yet. My bag's across the highway behind a bush."

"There's a hotel of mine between here and downtown Davenport. Called the Concort Inn."

"Yeah, saw it on the way out here. Nice-looking place."

"I'll call over and have them get a room ready for you. On me. You'll be registered as Logan. Okay?"

"Good enough."

"You need any entertainment?"

"Female you mean?"

"What the hell you think I mean?"

"Tomorrow night maybe. Tonight I'll just sleep."

"You *are* getting old."

"That's right."

Werner unlocked the door to the study and walked with Nolan to a side door and let him out. The watchdog, Calder, was nowhere to be seen, and was probably still safely out of the picture, though Nolan was keeping his eyes open this time around.

From the doorway Werner said, "Nolan, we'll make this thing work. The shooting *has* to stop."

Nolan said, "Unless it's just starting," and turned toward the highway.

3

The phone rang Nolan awake.

He grabbed for the receiver, glancing at his watch: seven o'clock.

"Nolan?"

"Morning, Werner."

"I just got through talking to Charlie."

"Bet he was happy you called him this early."

"Delighted. When he got the screaming out of his system, he agreed to fly in tonight."

"I see. What about ground rules?"

"I'm supposed to check with you on that and call him back. If your terms are acceptable, then in he flies."

"Okay—you, me, Charlie. In my hotel room. No body-guards. No guns."

"I think he'll agree to that."

"Good. Call me back."

Half an hour later the phone rang again and got Nolan out of the shower. He wrapped a towel around himself and walked across the plush pink carpet to answer it.

"Nolan?"

"What'd he say?"

"Your ground rules are fine."

"Good."

"Nolan, this might just work out."

"Yeah."

"How do you like the room?"

"The bridal suite's appropriate, somehow."

"Thought you'd like it. Got any other needs?"

"Just the answer to one question. Does Irish still run that jukebox concession up here?"

"Cavazos? Yes, he does. I'm his silent partner, as a matter of fact, have been ever since you sent him around, seven or eight years back. It's a lucrative little piece of action."

"He still got the same sideline?"

"Now wait a minute, Nolan, you said no guns, in your own ground rules. . . ."

"This doesn't have anything to do with the meeting," he said. "All my personal belongings got stolen, Werner, back in that Cicero hotel a month ago. I need some traveling security."

"Well. I can understand that. Yes, he's still in the same sideline. He supplies all my men, for a start. What'll you use for money?"

"Put up my balls as collateral, I guess. About all I got right now."

"You need anything else?"

"Besides my balls you mean? No."

"Talk to you later, then."

"Talk to you later."

Nolan dropped the phone into its cradle and went back to his shower.

4

Since Nolan had neither a car nor enough cash on hand to rent one, he was grateful that the Concort Inn was only a few blocks from downtown Davenport. The modern seven-story hotel was perched on the edge of the city, a blue slab facing away toward Bettendorf, as if ashamed of keeping company with the couple of seedy blocks separating it from the Davenport business district. Nolan's destination was in the less seedy of the two blocks closest to the hotel.

The air was still late October brisk, but the sun was out, and there weren't many clouds. The one-way street Nolan was walking along branched off from the four-lane highway and angled into the downtown area, and though he had the sidewalk to himself, the street was heavy with traffic—women, mostly, on their way to some midweek shopping.

As he rounded the corner, his eyes were drawn to a window filled with three lines of huge lettering: QUAD CITY/JUKEBOX SERVICE/INCORPORATED, bright red print outlined in heavy black. The window fronted the bottom floor of a five-story warehouse-style brick building across the street in the center of the block. To the building's right was a narrow alley.

Nolan found a hole in the flow of cars and crossed the street, walking up to the window. Beneath the foot-high red lettering were smaller red letters outlined in black: HERMAN CAVAZOS, MANAGER.

Herman?

So that was Irish's real first name. Nolan smiled to himself as he moved over to the front door and tried it.

Locked.

He peered into the room beyond the window, peeking between the huge red letters. There was a waiting room in there, as wide as the building but not very deep, with a reception desk and a couch. The room managed to look both messy and unused at the same time. There was no one in it.

Nolan walked around the side of the building into the alley and found a side entrance, also locked, and a triple-size garage door with a row of head level windows running across it. He looked in and saw a huge cement-floored room. Coin-operated entertainment, new and old, was scattered across the floor: jukeboxes, pinball machines, cigarette vendors, and coin-run machines of many kinds.

Nolan tried the handle on the garage door and found it unlocked. He swung the big door over his head and walked in.

No one around.

Since this was Wednesday, it didn't really figure as a day off, but that was the only way Nolan could see it.

Of course, there were four floors above this one, and

somebody might be on one of them, so Nolan decided to give it a try. He yelled, "Irish!"

He didn't get an answer; he tried again.

After half a dozen tries, he got a response. A distant voice from behind a closed door yelled, "Who the hell's down there!"

"IRS!"

"In a pig's ass!"

"We tax those too!"

Footsteps came clomping down the stairs behind the closed door, which snapped open, and the figure that belonged to the voice appeared in the doorway.

He was a small man, a few inches over five feet, with a nut-brown complexion and carrot-red hair. Nolan had never questioned the strange racial mix: he'd been told the little man was called Irish, and he'd left it at that.

"Nolan!"

Irish stayed in the doorway for a moment, repeated "Nolan!" and began to cross the cement floor at a walk that was nearly a run. He grabbed Nolan's hand and pumped it.

"Nolan!"

"You dress good for a mick-spic jukebox jockey."

Irish was wearing a light blue cotton suit, the cut of which had not come off a rack, with a pale yellow shirt and a striped tie in shades of yellow and blue. His Latin complexion and the red hair, with shaggy red eyebrows hanging over deepset brown eyes, made startling contrasts with the pale colors of his clothing.

"And you," Irish said, "dress piss poor for an IRS man."

Nolan raised an eyebrow and said, "Some joke. Round now, a joke's the only place I can afford even thinking about the federal boys."

"You got trouble, Nolan?"

"Up the ass. Where is everybody? Don't you work all week like the other nine-to-five folks?"

"My guys are out today making their weekly run of service calls and deliveries—we do that every Wednesday. But what's this with you? Something happen, you have a job go sour?"

"Like month-old milk. Someplace handy we can sit and talk?"

"Sure. Upstairs. Come on."

They walked across the jukebox-filled floor, sidestepping machines, parts, and tools, and started up the rickety steps. They passed three doors on as many landings, going on up till they stopped at the fourth landing. The stairway and all the woodwork in the building looked poor, paint-peeling and seemingly rotting; and when Irish opened the final door, Nolan was stunned to see the room behind it.

"Like it, Nolan?"

"I take it Werner treats you well."

The room was large, lush. It had thick white wall-to-wall carpeting, with side walls paneled in rich, dark wood; the back wall was taken up by a bar and three shelves of booze behind it, against textured white wallpaper with red swirls. An open door in the middle of the paneled wall at the left revealed hints of a bedroom decorated in deep blues, and the other wall bore a large framed print of one of Dali's studies in soft washes. There wasn't much furniture, just a 26-inch Sony TV in the corner to the left of the door and console stereo stretched across a side wall. The only other furniture in the room, outside of a couple of stools at the bar, was a sofa, long, and fat and white, looking very soft and very comfortable, and reclining on it was a lovely young girl of twenty or so, dressed in blue lace panties, also looking very soft and comfortable. Her skin was the color of dark butterscotch, her legs long, breasts small but nicely formed. The breasts Nolan couldn't actually see that well, as her long black hair came down around both shoulders and partially covered them.

"Maria," Irish said, "wait in the bedroom, will you? This is a friend come to talk with me."

She got up. She was quite tall, five-nine at least. It figured, Nolan thought; Irish always did go in for big girls: his wife was practically six feet. Now that the girl was on her feet, her breasts didn't look so small, Nolan noticed. Her nipples were very pink against her dark skin.

She walked over to the door, flashing an ivory smile at Nolan.

"Go on, now, Maria, shoo," Irish said.

"Yes, Herman," she answered, bouncing attractively into the adjoining bedroom, closing the door after her.

"She makes friends easily," Irish said. "Maybe you'll want to take her out while you're in town."

Nolan laughed, softly. "Herman. Can't get over it. Herman."

Irish flashed a Cheshire cat grin as he slipped out of his sportcoat and tossed it on the stereo. "I knew you'd have something to say about that . . . you're lucky you got even 'Irish' out of me, I never got a first name out of you, you know." He went over to the sofa and sat down, gestured for Nolan to join him. "A well-kept secret, that name of mine, while I was still in the trade. But when I became a more or less legitimate businessman, I could hardly hang out a shingle saying 'Irish Cavazos.' "

"Suppose not."

"How about a drink?"

"No thanks. Haven't had breakfast yet."

"Nolan turning down free booze? Not changing in your old age, are you, for Chrissake?"

"The old age part's right, anyway. To be honest, Irish, my stomach gives me hell when I drink in the morning."

"Whatever happened to that cast-iron sonofabitch I used to know, name of Nolan? The one that hit that armored car with me ten years ago?"

"He's the same sonofabitch, Irish. Just ten years older, and pounded to tin foil. Are you forgetting who it was talked you into quitting the business?"

"I'm not forgetting it, Nolan. I owe you a hell of a lot for that. . . . If you hadn't sent me and my savings to your old buddy Werner eight years ago, chances are I'd be either in stir or under the ground."

"You were a clumsy bastard, Irish. Great with machines, but clumsy with everything else. It scared me when you worked a job without me."

"Yeah, well, you gave me discipline, Nolan, and when I was on a job with you, I was okay, you could make me feel at ease. But the biggest favor you or anybody else ever did me was you telling me to get out while I had my ass in one piece."

"So I did both you *and* Werner a favor."

"You know the way I owe you, Nolan . . . just like Werner owes you for a hundred times . . . and that's why I know I can ask you this and you won't take it wrong: what in the name of Jesus and Mary and any remaining Saints are you *doing* around here? You know what'll happen if anybody who knows you or that face of yours sees you? And reports to Charlie, who's minutes away from the Cities?" Irish stopped and half his mouth smiled, the other frowned. "Incidentally, Nolan, that mustache of yours won't fool anybody. You got a face worse than fingerprints."

"Tell me about it. I just got through healing up from a slug in the side. One of Charlie's boys spotted me in Cicero."

"Then what the hell are you doing still in the area?"

"Werner's helping me set up a meeting with Charlie. We're going to try to talk it out."

"Come on, Nolan, you don't really think . . ."

"I don't know, Irish. I'm getting old. So is Charlie. Because of him I can't get to any of the cash I've piled up."

"Jesus, what happened? You didn't get your cover blown, did you?"

"Right the first time. Charlie's onto my cover tag, so I got to get this thing settled before he starts giving it out to people like free samples."

"Why'd you come to see me?"

"Well, the ground rules set for this meeting say no guns, but I'm not about to go into this thing bareass naked. Werner didn't seem eager to tell me, but I finally gathered from him that you still got firearms for a sideline. Is that right?"

The shaggy red eyebrows knitted together and Irish nodded.

"I figure I can trust Charlie only with a gun in my hand. Can you fix me up?"

Irish got up from the sofa. "Come with me."

Nolan followed him out of the room and down to the floor below. Irish unlocked the door, and Nolan saw that behind it was a second door, a steel one with a combination lock. The little man dialed it till it clicked free, then eased the door open and they went in.

The room was the size of a small gymnasium, covering the combined space of the first floor's workshop and waiting room. The walls were padded with thick bulging tan canvas, as were floor and ceiling. Across the room a third of the way down was a wooden platform with a waist-high tablestand running along in front of it. Two metal cabinets were against the left wall, each as wide as a man with outstretched arms, and so tall they almost touched the ceiling. Covering the far end wall was a sheet of metal, which descended from the ceiling and slanted down into a catchbin; halfway down, a row of ten standard pistol range targets were lined across the metal sheet.

The two men walked over to the platform.

Irish said, "You still hot for .38s?"

"Smith and Wesson, if you got 'em. Four-inch barrels. Never could stand snub noses."

"Well, you can't always be picky. How many you need?"

"Several, at least."

"You want the kind of piece I think you want, no serial number and still in top shape, you take what's available. I got three Smith and Wesson .38s in stock, with four-inchers, and of the three, two are like new. The other one's been around, and it's got a pull to the left. I got a Colt Police Special that's a hell of a lot more reliable."

"Let's see them."

Irish walked over to the big steel cabinets, twirled the combination lock on one of them, and swung open the double doors. There were compartments and drawers inside, and after he'd done some fishing around, Irish came up with four guns and a box of cartridges. He scooped them all up in his arms, walked over to Nolan, and laid them on the tablestand in front of him.

"Don't sweat the noise. Soundproof as shit."

Nolan nodded, loading three bullets into one of the Smith and Wessons.

He tried all four guns. The Smith and Wessons were all good, but one of them did pull a hair to the left, and it was also slightly rusted. The Colt was fine.

"You're right, Irish. I'll take the two S and Ws and the Colt."

"You need three?"

"Got to be safe. The only gun I got is on me. I had a couple others that got lifted by Charlie's men in Cicero, along with a lot of other stuff."

"Got a job on the line?"

"I don't think so, Irish. I called Planner while I was healing up, and the only thing he had for me was a bad bet at best. Since Charlie shot my last job out from under me, nobody in the trade wants near me. Nobody worth a damn, anyway."

"Jesus. I hope you get this thing with Charlie straightened out."

"I will, Irish. One way or the other one."

"You want that drink now?"

"I'll pass again. Walk me down?"

"Sure. Let me put the guns in a box for you and wrap it up. Need any ammo?"

"Yeah. Better make it five or six packs. And throw some Three-in-One oil in, too, would you?"

"Okay."

Later, the two men stood by the open garage door downstairs and talked of jobs they worked together. After half an hour had gone, Nolan asked Irish how much he owed him for the guns and ammunition, and was his credit good?

"You don't owe me anything, Nolan. . . . I'm in to you for much more than money could ever repay. . . . I'm so goddamn lucky you got Werner to set me up. . . ."

"Werner's the lucky one. I never met a man who knows more about mechanical things than you. I don't care if it's cars or tools or guns or . . ."

"Or jukeboxes?"

"Yeah. Those too, I suppose. What exactly are you doing for Werner? The jukebox thing's a front, I assume?"

"Oh no, it's more than a front; you'd be surprised what a little moneymaker it is. We keep it crappy-looking around here sort of on purpose, so nobody official wants to spend much time nosing around. But the juke business is big. Got some thousand jukes in the area, another thousand-and-a-half pinballs, couple thousand cigarette machines, and then there's candy machines and gum, working out of our other place over in Moline. Got a whole building up the block just for trucks. I also service the slots Werner's got in the gambling room downstairs at the Maricaibo over in Milan. And, of course, I keep Werner's boys supplied in good clean workable gunware, and let 'em use the range upstairs for practice when they want. . . . For a sideline Werner lets me provide the same service to any of my old working pals, whenever they pass through the Cities. I only wish I'd been able to supply you sooner, Nolan."

"Thanks, Irish. You know I appreciate it."

"Forget it. Any time, anything."

"Say, you wouldn't know where I could line up a car, would you?"

"Sure. Phony registration and out-of-state plates and all? Fresh paint job to cool the heat? A cinch. Just give me a call, number's in the book. Friend over in East Moline can fix you up fine."

"Good. I got nothing going right now, but I may need a car later."

"Sure."

"Well, Irish, I better let you go back upstairs to your little girlfriend."

"Only not so little, huh? You're sure you maybe don't want to borrow her tonight? Maria's her name. Fantastic."

"How's the wife?"

"Oh, fine, pregnant of course. Jesus Christ, five kids we got. Why I had to be born Catholic I'll never know."

"Yeah, it's tough. I bet your priest looks forward to your confession."

"You crazy, Nolan? Think I trust those bastards to keep their mouths shut?"

"I'll see you, Irish."

"Good luck with Charlie."

"Yeah."

5

The first thing Nolan did after taking leave of Irish and his jukeboxes was walk on downtown to find a bank to get his hundred-dollar bill broken up.

Three blocks from the warehouse he came to the First National Bank of Davenport. He went in and scanned the faces of the five tellers at the five windows in front of him: two men, one wearing salt-and-pepper hair and dark-rimmed bifocals, putting the push on sixty, the other middle-aged with a brown butch and dimpled chin; and three women, two of them female counterparts of the men, the third an attractive young brown-eyed blonde.

Nolan opted for the blonde.

"Yes sir?"

"Break this into fives for me, will you?" He handed her the hundred.

"Of course." She pulled open her money drawer and counted out the fives, holding them out for Nolan to take.

Her brown eyes were large, long lashes fluttering around them. "Anything else I can do for you, sir?"

"Matter of fact there is. You could tell me how to get to the local YMCA."

"Yes, well, it's a YM and YWCA combined."

"I could get a room there, couldn't I?"

"I think so. If you stay on the male side."

"Do my best. How do I get there?"

"Oh. Yes. Well, walk down toward the river one block, till you get to Second Street, then take a right and go five blocks I think it is, five or six. Anyway, can't miss it, it's kitty-corner from the bridge."

"Thanks."

"Are you just passing through the Cities?"

"Business trip."

Salt-and-Pepper-Pushing-Sixty cleared his throat in the window next door, looking pointedly at the blonde teller over the tops of his dark-framed bifocals. There was a shrug in the girl's smile, and Nolan smiled back, folding his stack of fives in half and turning away from the window.

He paused for a moment before leaving the bank, pocketing the twenty splinters from his hundred-dollar bill. Must not be too ungodly old, he thought, if a pretty young girl like that teller can show interest. Encouraging.

Lingering by the door for a moment, he caught himself glancing around the bank's interior, casing the place almost subconsciously. A guard at the door gave him a fisheye and Nolan got himself quickly back onto the street.

Looking suspicious inside a bank was never good practice, Nolan thought, but especially not when he had a package under his arm filled with revolvers and ammunition.

As Nolan walked down Second Street, he passed by a Penney's store with a sign in the window reading "Close-out Sale on Men's Suits." He had a distaste for assembly-line clothes, more from the fact that he had a nonexistent suit size that fell between two standard ones than from anything else. Clotheshorse he was not, but as it stood now, his entire wardrobe consisted of what he had on—white shirt, black slacks, blue sportcoat, and brown corduroy overjacket. The bag back at his hotel room had nothing more in it than a safety razor, can of lather, toothbrush and paste, spray deodorant, and three or four changes of socks and underwear. No best-dressed-man lists this season.

Inside the store Nolan found a light gray suit that fitted him all right, a little tight in the shoulders maybe, and a couple of years out of style, but all right, and he cut his stack of twenty fives to thirteen buying it. Two sale ties brought the bills down to twelve.

With the second, less incriminating bundle under his arm, Nolan returned to the street and walked on.

The hundred-dollar bill had been a safety catch of his, a single C note pinned inside his inner sportcoat pocket to provide loose change in case his wallet got lifted or lost. Nothing more than a habit he'd picked up in those early years in Chicago, but a habit he'd hung onto. He'd never imagined the time would come when he'd be down to that hundred alone.

A hundred-buck stake, he thought. Christ.

The hundred and twenty-five he'd had in his wallet when the Cicero fiasco came up had gone relatively fast during the opening weeks of his month-plus recuperation at the girl's apartment. In the last few weeks of his stay, he knew, the girl'd had to dip into her personal savings. He almost felt guilty about not letting her know about the extra hundred pinned in his coat, but he'd known he'd need it to get him started when he was back on his feet again, so there'd been no choice.

Now the remaining twelve pieces of his shattered hundred were a folded lump in the same inner sportcoat pocket where the bill had been pinned. Nolan had asked for the hundred in fives because that way it looked like a lot of money without being as awkward as a stack of one hundred ones. Childish, he realized, senility setting in at last, but he hated like hell feeling broke. And anyway, he might find the need to make the remainder of his cash look like more than it was.

Down Second five blocks, the last two of which had gotten as seedy as the blocks surrounding Irish's place, and Nolan came to the YM–YW.

A huge parking lot encircled the building, separating it from its tenement neighbors on the left, and on the right from the busy street that led onto the Rock Island Centennial Bridge. Set apart like that, the building took on an aloof quality that Nolan couldn't link with recollections of YMCAs of his youth. The Ys in his memory were composed of crumbling brick and young sweat and old tennis shoes; this one was sheet glass and cement and scalloped steel.

Nolan edged his way through the packed car lot, went up the walk and into the building. The lobby was like the outside, only with carpeting. Over on the right was the reception desk, the kind you stand behind. This time Nolan didn't have a choice of personnel, there being only one clerk on reception duty, an unattractive girl in her late twenties. He paid her ten dollars for the room and didn't ask to see it.

Back out on the street, having waded his way through the lot of cars, Nolan winced at the dry, biting cold on his face and decided he wasn't up to the dozen-or-so-blocks walk to the hotel. He cut one of the fives in half with a cab ride back and finished off the other half with an eleven o'clock roll and coffee in the Concort coffee shop.

After breakfast, Nolan strolled out into the lobby and picked up a message at the check-in desk: "Call me at 555-7272, Werner." He walked to the phone booth next to the lounge entrance and put in the call. When the ringing stopped, it was replaced by the sound of a female voice saying, "Flaming Embers Restaurant, can I help you?" It was the kind of voice that went well with bedroom eyes.

"Speak with Mr. Werner, please?"

"Just a moment, sir, I'll ring his extension for you."

He heard the click of the button going down, and the ringing started in again, only to be replaced by another ultra-feminine voice, which asked for Nolan's name. Nolan said, "Logan," and after a thirty-second wait, Werner was on the line.

"Where you been all morning, old friend?"

"Bought myself a new suit. Never go to your own funeral poorly dressed, I always say."

"Funeral, hell. You're making a wise move. Charlie's ready to sit down with you. You'll get results with him tonight."

"What time tonight?"

"Eight o'clock's the set time. I'll be going out to the airport to pick him up at six-thirty or so. His plane'll be in at seven something."

"I see."

"It'll be just you and me and him. No bodyguards, no guns, just the three of us."

"A cozy Family scene. All we need is a fireplace."

"That's right. Nonviolence is in this year."

"I hope Charlie's heard about that."

"Don't worry about it. You'll be following your own ground rules, won't you, friend? My neck is out for you, you know. What about that visit out to Cavazos's you said you were going to make?"

"Pure social call. I don't have the money to buy fresh socks, let alone guns."

"Well, if you need anything, anything but guns, that is, I'll see you get it. We go back a few years."

"So do Charlie and I."

"Play by the rules, now, Nolan. You're the one set them up, after all."

"Right. See you tonight."

Nolan cradled the receiver and got out of the booth, headed back to the check-in clerk.

When Nolan introduced himself, the desk clerk—a short, dark, eager young man—spent a good thirty seconds assuring Nolan he would do "anything for a friend of Mr. Werner's." Nolan got out the roll of fives.

"Now, Mr. Logan, please, Mr. Werner said everything was to be taken care of, no charge whatsoever, Mr. Werner said . . ."

"Said I was an old friend of his," Nolan finished. "That's right, and I'm planning a little surprise for Mr. Werner tonight, as a matter of fact. I just hope he doesn't get wind of it. Hate for it to get spoiled for him."

"A surprise?"

"That's right. This is something kind of personal between Mr. Werner and myself. But you *could* help, if you're willing."

"Well, certainly, anything I can do."

"Good. I'll need another room."

"Is there something unsatisfactory about your present suite?"

"No. I need an *extra* room. It has to do with the surprise."

"Oh." The clerk leaned forward and smiled and said, "What is it, are you bringing in another old friend of Mr. Werner's? Or perhaps several? A surprise party, is that what it is? In that case you'll be needing a catering service, you'll need champagne and . . ."

"Just an extra room."

"Well, certainly . . ."

"Small. On an upper floor."

"I see."

"Which I will pay for."

"I see."

"Just see you don't see."

"I'll see that I don't."

"Fine. How much for the room?"

"Uh. Uh, thirty-five dollars."

Nolan counted off seven fives. "Can I have the key?"

The clerk reached behind and handed Nolan a key that said 714.

Nolan handed him another five. "And that's for your trouble."

"That's not necessary, Mr. Logan . . ."

"I insist."

The clerk took the money.

Nolan said, "You want me to sign the register or anything?"

"Oh, yes, yes, any name at all . . ."

Nolan took the register, smiled softly to himself and signed "E. Webb, Cicero, Illinois," then handed the register back to the clerk, who said, "And I'll do my best to keep from spoiling the surprise for Mr. Werner."

Nolan left the check-in counter, the two packages under his arm, and walked to the pair of elevators and pushed up. While he waited for his ride, he glanced down at the bill in his hand.

One five.

The big bankroll.

Several people got on the elevator with him, and a boy of around six years said, "Whatcha grinnin' about, mister?" Nolan pressed the last five into the kid's hand and waited for his floor.

6

The only method Nolan had ruled out completely from the number of ways Charlie might handle his visit was that of Charlie playing it straight. Oh, Charlie could conceivably fly in from Chicago, drive to the hotel to talk things over with Nolan, carrying no firearms and accompanied by no bodyguards and radiating good will.

And Christ might decide to make his second coming tonight.

Nolan wasn't counting on either. At the very least he expected Charlie to show up armed. Setting up those ground rules had been something Nolan had done because he knew Charlie expected him to ask for them. So he'd asked.

Nolan figured there were three courses of action, all similar, which seemed equally probable turns for Charlie to take.

First, a party unknown might arrive at the hotel in the late afternoon or early evening and go up to Nolan's room to kill him, with Charlie not even bothering to fly in.

Or, party unknown might go up to Nolan's room and get him at gunpoint and hold him for Charlie to execute personally.

Or, finally, party unknown might show up, take Nolan captive (maybe or maybe not beat the piss out of him), and hold him for Charlie, who would arrive later to discuss peace terms.

Any way he looked at it, Nolan figured he had company coming, and he spent the early afternoon getting ready for it.

Since he was going to be moving upstairs into that extra room, he packed his bag, which took ten seconds, and set it next to the Penney's box by the door, picking up the wrapped package from Irish at the same time.

He took the package into the bedroom, sat on the bed, tore the wrapping paper off and got out the guns. Then he added his bolstered .38 to the three from Quad City Jukebox Service and cleaned and oiled them. When he was done, he loaded all four and placed one of the fresh Smith and Wessons in his holster, an aging leather strapwork that looped around both shoulders with a band running across the back, so that from the front, if his jacket hung open, none of the rig was visible. The other guns he tossed on the bed.

There was a small table lamp with shade on the nightstand. Nolan unscrewed the knob atop the lamp and removed the shade, leaving the bulb and its spare metal framework exposed. He took a hanger and twisted it apart and bent it into a new shape, a spiral that would fit down over the bulb and its framework. He took one of the .38s and slipped the trigger guard over the curved end of the hanger. The gun hung there like a bulky Christmas ornament. He put the shade back on. He slipped his hand down in, found the gun, and brought it out, slowly. He did it again, quickly. The gun didn't show through the shade, nor did the butt poke above it. This would do just fine—as long as he remembered not to turn the damn thing on.

Then he dropped the other guns, one each, into his side sportcoat pockets, went over to the door, and grabbed up his bag and suit box. The elevator took him up to the next floor, where he used the key marked 714, and before he got half a look at his spare room he was sitting on the bed, revolvers next to him, doing his lamp-shade trick again. He pushed the lamp back so that it almost touched the wall, got up from the bed, and dug into his bag, getting out two clean hand-kerchiefs. These he wadded, knotting them to keep their bunched shape, and stowed them in the top drawer of the nightstand.

He had no special precautionary plan in mind for the leftover Colt—getting those three guns this morning hadn't been for Charlie alone, since he needed them on hand anyway—so he rather absently shoved the Colt behind the pillow of the room's single bed, enough of the Nervous Nellie routine for awhile.

He glanced around the room.

Room, hell, it was a closet with gland trouble, but that was okay by him. In a small room he could have control; he could see windows and door all at once. That suite of his downstairs was something else again—a vestibule and a living room and a bedroom and two cans and lots and lots of windows and no possible way to see all of it at once. In this room he could.

Nolan checked the window that took up most of the far wall of the crackerbox. It was locked, which was good. He noticed a fire escape beyond the window, going down into the alley, which was good and bad.

Then he showered again, making it cold to keep him alert, shaved, and got into his new suit. He slipped on one of the ties he had bought, a solid blue color, and strung on the shoulder-holster. The suit didn't show the jut of the gun too badly, and it fitted well for a rack cut, though it did pinch at the shoulders.

As he straightened his tie in the bathroom mirror, Nolan wondered if the man Charlie sent would appreciate his dressing to the teeth for him. Somehow he doubted it.

He left the room and took the elevator down to the lobby. At the check desk, the clerk smiled and said, "Well, hello again, Mr. Logan, is there something more I can do for you, sir?"

"There a phone in there?" Nolan motioned toward the entrance to the Concort Lounge across the lobby.

"Yes, there is, the bartender has a phone behind the bar so orders can be called in."

"Yeah. Well I'll be in there for a while. You suppose if anybody comes around and wants my room number that you could ring me over there and tell me about it?"

"I could just send whoever it is over and . . ."

"No. This has to do with that surprise we were talking about earlier. Give the guy my number, send him up to the room, *then* call me."

The clerk was puzzled but trusting, and said he'd be glad to do it. Anything for a friend of Mr. Werner's.

Nolan went into the lounge, pushing the saloon-style swinging doors aside, and walked over to the bar. He told the bartender about the call he was expecting, then went over and took a booth parallel to the swinging doors, where he could get a slatted but partially visible view of the check-in desk on the other side of the lobby.

He ordered a Scotch and water, charged it to Werner and looked down at his watch.

Ten after three.

He sat back and waited, nursing the Scotch with a patience he guessed was coming from old age.

At quarter till four, the first Scotch was gone, and he started on another.

7

At ten after five Nolan looked up from his third Scotch as the saloon-syle doors swung open and a tall, burly black man in a well-tailored navy suit shoved through them. The big man stood in the doorway for a moment, briefly ran his eyes across the lounge's half-dozen faces, then ambled over to the bar.

Though they'd never met, Nolan recognized him.

The hard face, with its rugged structure, nearly flat nose, close-set eyes, squared-off jaw, and forehead of solid bone, was unmistakable. And the six-foot-three, 270-pound frame, with its aircraft carrier shoulders, wasn't exactly commonplace, either.

His name was Tillis, and he'd played pro guard on an eastern NFL team a few seasons back, but was forced out in his third year of play because of knee trouble. The story Nolan had heard was that some mob guy fairly high up had been a fan of Tillis's team, and when Tillis had to quit pro ball, the guy offered him a job. A job with the organization that, as Werner had told Nolan, was calling itself the Family these days.

Nolan remembered seeing Tillis play ball a couple of times. He hadn't impressed Nolan as the most savvy lineman in the NFL, but when he didn't get faked out or double-teamed, he could be one mean, effective sonof-abitch. Set an unnecessary roughness record his rookie year, Nolan recalled.

Tillis was at the bar now, downing a shot of Jim Beam. He motioned for another, threw it down, then sauntered back out of the lounge.

Nolan got to his feet casually and went over to the still

gently swaying doors and glanced out over them toward the check-in desk.

Tillis was there, questioning the desk clerk, who was showing all the composure of a toastmaster who's just discovered his fly is open. When the clerk had told Tillis what he wanted to know, the black man walked over to the two elevators, jabbed at the button between them, and got his ride right away. As the elevator doors met behind him, Nolan stepped out from the lounge and walked over to the check-in desk.

The clerk was reaching for the phone when Nolan said, "Forget it. I'm here."

The clerk jumped slightly, then turned and motioned toward the elevators and said, "It's a big colored man," and Nolan nodded thanks.

Nolan took the same elevator Tillis had used when it came back down. It was self-service, and Nolan had it to himself. By the time he'd reached his floor and the doors had begun to slide open, he had his .38 unholstered and palmed.

His room was around the corner to the right of the elevators. When he got to the corner, he stopped and glanced carefully around it.

Tillis was at the door to Nolan's suite, trying a ringful of keys in the lock. When one key didn't work, he tried another, and just as he seemed to be running out of them, one got results.

Tillis gently prodded the door open, and behind him Nolan not-so-gently prodded the back of Tillis's skull with the side of the .38 barrel.

The big black tumbled like a small tree to the soft carpeting in the suite's vestibule and lay still.

Nolan shut the door and night-latched it. He was stepping around the bulky supine figure when a thick arm shot out, caught him behind the right ankle and jerked, setting Nolan down on his tailbone so hard that his spine did a xylophone imitation.

A beefy black fist rushed toward his face, but Nolan batted it away with the .38, and seeing that Tillis was on his feet, Nolan had a flash memory of the ex-guard's bad knees and drove a kick into the black's right kneecap that would have been good for a forty-yard punt.

Tillis landed on his side but started to spring back, and Nolan slapped him across the temple with the .38 barrel.

This time Tillis seemed to be soundly out, but Nolan was getting to the point where he didn't trust himself with knocking guys cold anymore. He leaned over cautiously, flipped open the well-cut navy suit, brushed aside the blue and white striped tie, and lifted a silenced Luger from a shoulder clip under Tillis's left arm. Backing up with care, Nolan pocketed the Luger, keeping his revolver trained on the man.

He needed something to tie Tillis up with; he knew he should have picked up some rope when he'd had the time earlier in the afternoon, but he hadn't, so now he had to improvise.

He tore off the nylon draw-cord from the drapes in the suite's living room, all the while keeping an eye on the reclined figure in the vestibule and a gun tightly in hand. Reluctantly he laid the .38 down on a nearby lampstand to use his pocket-knife on the nylon cord, cutting it into three lengths, two of them a foot-and-a-half or so each, the other a good three feet.

Some sounds came from the otherwise lifeless mass over by the door.

He slipped the lengths of rope in his belt and walked over to give Tillis a gentle kick in the ribs. "Wake up."

"Oh, shit . . . my fuckin' head . . ."

"Wake up."

The black man pushed himself to his hands. His close-set eyes zoomed in on Nolan and burned slowly. "You? You're Nolan? You were in the bar downstairs, weren't you, motherfuck?"

"That's right."

"I seen your picture once, but I didn't recognize you from it."

"I changed. You saw a picture maybe fifteen, sixteen years old."

"I didn't think I was gettin' sent after some goddamn senior citizen."

"And I don't suppose you thought you'd get knocked on your ass by one either."

A slight smile appeared on the black's lips, and he slowly eased himself into a sitting position. "Didn't have no mustache in that picture I seen. You had it long?"

"It comes and goes. It's the old age that sticks around."

"Jesus, man, you ought to give one of them retirement villages some thought."

"I got to say one thing for you," Nolan said. "You know what kind of games not to play. No pretending you can't understand why I clobbered you. No fake innocence, no claim of just accidentally getting into the wrong room or some such fairy tale."

The big head wagged side to side. "Why should I lie, man? I was sent to check you out, that's all, make sure you wasn't going to pull something."

"You mind, just for the record, telling me who sent you?"

"Shit, you know that as well as I do, man," the black said, grinning. "Mr. Charlie."

Nolan had to smile at Tillis's double meaning. Then the smile left his face and he said, "This visit was just a precaution, then? No beating? No bullet in the head?"

"Yeah, man, you know, like a social call."

"And the silenced Luger you had with you was a party favor."

"Oh, *that*. Just 'cause it had a silencer on don't mean I was going to shoot you or nothing, man. It's a habit of mine. Noise gets on my nerves."

"You used to go for the kind of noise a crowd makes, didn't you, Tillis?"

He smiled broadly. "Now ain't that shit. I didn't know

you by sight but you knew me. See me play ever?"

Nolan nodded. "You weren't bad. You weren't good either, but then we can't all make it onto the Wheaties box."

The smile vanished. "How would you like to wear your white ass around your neck?"

"How would you like your black ass shot the fuck off?"

The toothy smile returned, and Tillis said, "Yeah, you're some kind of motherfuck, you are."

"Let's keep my family out of this. I'd rather talk about yours. Family, that is."

"Clever motherfuck, too."

"You know, Tillis, there's no reason in the world why I shouldn't kill you right now. You coming up here with a silenced automatic . . . it's a finger pointing at Charlie sending you to kill me."

"Come off it, man, what you expect? You think Mr. Charlie's goin' to figure *you* to play by the rules? What kind of dumbass motherfuck are you, anyway?"

"A dumbass motherfuck with a .38 pointed at your thick black head."

Tillis laughed and the laugh had gravel in it. "You know something, Nolan, goddamn you? I like the way you think. You got a real logical way of looking at things."

"Thought you'd like it. Now, get on your feet, Tillis. We're going to the john."

"You mean me and the white folks are goin' to use the same one?"

"Cute, Tillis. On your feet."

The big man pushed up slowly, then his body tensed and he started to move forward. Nolan let him look down into the four-inch barrel on the Smith and Wesson, and Tillis's face split apart into his big white grin.

Nolan smiled momentarily, then waved Tillis on. Tillis moved slowly out of the vestibule and into the living room and followed Nolan's motions into the bathroom.

"Put the lid down on the stool and sit."

"What you doin', man?"

"Just do it, Tillis."

"Okay, okay."

Nolan tossed him the long strip of nylon cord. "Loop this behind the pot and tie your feet together. Firmly."

Tillis bent down and wound the cord behind the toilet and knotted it around his feet.

"Now make a couple fists and hold them out."

Tillis did so.

"I'm putting my gun away for a moment now, Tillis, so I can tie your hands. If you want to try something, go right ahead."

Tillis grinned. "Won't try no tricks."

Nolan stuck the gun in his belt and knotted one of the short strands around Tillis's massive wrists.

Tillis said, "Shove a smoke in my mouth for me, man?"

Nolan got out his cigarettes and held one out for Tillis to grab with his lips. Nolan picked a book of matches off the sink counter and lit Tillis's cigarette, then fired one for himself.

"Why you tying me up, Nolan?"

"Why d'you think?"

"Cause you hate niggers?"

"Does it show?"

Tillis laughed. "Ain't nothin' like an honest bigot."

Nolan laughed a little himself. "Don't hand me that shit. Not after your 'Mr. Charlie' cracks."

"Oh?"

"Don't play naive, Tillis. You and I both know why you're in this business."

The gravelly laugh echoed within the four close walls. "You're one smart motherfuck, aren't you, Nolan? It's just like football, right? Get paid by white men to beat on other white men."

Nolan said, "There's a lot of black guys in football, Tillis, and you knocked them around too. What if 'Mr. Charlie' had wanted you to work over a brother instead of me?"

Tillis shrugged. "Just like in football. My greedy nature just ain't that discriminatin'."

Nolan said, "Just so we understand each other. Okay. Now, I'm going to lean down and tie your feet again. If you try kicking me in the face while I'm down there, you're going to find yourself singing soprano in a gospel choir somewhere."

Tillis laughed again, but more softly. "Know something, Nolan?"

"What's that, Tillis?"

"You got style. You been around and all, and you're kinda old, but you still got style. Hope like hell I don't get orders to kill you sometime."

Nolan bent down and tied the short piece of nylon cord around Tillis's ankles, knotting it securely. "I feel sure you'll get over it, should the occasion arise."

Tillis's dark face was sober. "Hey, man, no shit. I hope it don't work out that way."

Nolan nodded. "I know what you mean."

The phone rang in the other room.

Tillis's grin came back. "That'll be Mr. Charlie, checkin' to see how well I got things under control."

8

The voice in the receiver said, "Tillis?"

"He's on the stool. Message?"

The receiver went silent for several moments, then the voice, which was a rough-edged baritone, returned. "Nolan?"

"Hello, Charlie."

"What happened to Tillis?"

"I told you. On the crapper."

"The years haven't changed you much for the better, have they, Nolan?"

He laughed. "And you, Charlie?" Nolan paused briefly,

then added, "Come on up. Bring Werner if you want. Any more men you got along, leave downstairs."

"You heeled, Nolan?"

"You mean is the wound better?"

"You know what I mean. You're the one said no guns, remember?"

"Well, hell, Charlie, Tillis was such a pansy, I just used my hands on him."

"For a man who wanted ground rules, you don't stick by them too goddamn close, do you?"

Nolan smiled into the mouthpiece. "It's your rules I play, Charlie," he said, and hung up.

The open area by the elevators was empty, so Nolan had no qualms about waiting there with the .38 in hand. The gun was in his palm facing inward, and if any of the Concort's other patrons wandered by before Charlie and Werner came up, chances were good they wouldn't notice anything.

The elevator doors parted like the Red Sea, and Charlie stepped out, Werner on his heels as though bearing a bridal train.

Charlie wasn't a large man, and he didn't look much like what a mob guy named Charlie should look like. His hair was short-cropped like Werner's, only stark powder white, and he had a deep Miami tan identical to Werner's. Resemblance between the two ended there, outside of the Brooks Brothers cut of their dark suits. The five-foot-nine Werner seemed to tower over the diminutive Charlie, even though he was standing behind him and trying not to. In spite of his size, or lack of it, Charlie was not a man Nolan planned to underrate. Nolan knew the little man was an old school tough, not remotely akin to Werner's businessman breed, and Charlie's use of acutely unsubtle muscle like Tillis was proof that he hadn't changed. Charlie was no parody of a hood, however; he had acquired, over the years, the look of a calm, polished executive—in advertising, perhaps, or insurance. But Nolan knew, too, that cement overshoes and one-way rides and machine gun executions would never be out of style as far as Charlie was concerned.

Nolan tilted his palm upward and let the two men get a look at the gun in it, then motioned them toward his suite. No one said anything until the door to the suite was shut behind them.

"Strip off the overcoats," Nolan said, "and then the suitcoats. And do it the nice, easy way you know I want you to."

The two obeyed Nolan's commands and let themselves be subjected to a fast but thorough frisk.

When he was through, Nolan said, "Well, can you beat that, you're both clean."

"Some people keep their word," Werner said, petulant.

Charlie's six-foot voice was heard in person by Nolan for the first time in sixteen years. He said, "Shut up, Werner."

"Let him talk, Charlie," Nolan said. "He isn't happy with me, so let him blow the steam off now and have it done."

"You've really put me on the spot, Nolan, do you know that?" Werner's face had a slight flush, his country club cool gone. "I urge Charlie to fly in for negotiations, and he's nice enough to accept your terms, and *you* show up waving a gun around in the air. Can't you understand this is business, and you can't handle business matters that way in this day and . . ."

"Jesus, Werner," Charlie said, "will you just shut up and let Nolan and me handle our differences ourselves?"

Werner clamped his lips together, and the slight flush was replaced by a slight pout.

"Okay," Charlie said, "you wanted to talk, Nolan? Okay. Then let's get started."

Nolan nodded. "Here on out, ground rules apply. This afternoon I checked out another room we'll use to do our talking. I'll leave my gun down here, locked in the closet, do the same with the one I took from Tillis. Then we go upstairs to the other room and talk."

Charlie lowered his head in acceptance.

"You got another room?" Werner said. "What the hell's

wrong with this one? Why wasn't I informed of this?"

Nolan didn't answer him, and Werner's pout evolved into a scowl, but disappeared when Nolan dumped his .38 and Tillis's silenced Luger into the closet, locking it with his room key.

Nolan opened the door for them. "Let's go, gentlemen."

Charlie said, "What about Tillis?"

"He really is in the can, alive and well; I tied him up in there. He'll be okay. Don't be hard on the boy, Charlie. He isn't really a pushover."

"He won't be so easy next time," Charlie said.

"There won't be a next time, remember, men?" Werner reminded them. "These are peace talks we're having."

"Just shut up," Charlie said. "This world doesn't need any more goddamn diplomats than it's already got."

"We agree on something, anyway," Nolan said, and gestured toward the elevators.

The trio again remained silent until they were shut inside the smaller of Nolan's two Concort rooms.

"You haven't exactly trusted me to the goddamn heights, have you, Nolan?" Charlie's mouth wore a sour smile.

Nolan pointed toward the bed. "Sit down, both of you." He pulled a chair over and sat facing them, his arm resting on the nightstand by the bed. "You didn't expect me to trust you, Charlie, and I didn't expect you to trust me, so let's forget all that now and get started, okay?"

Charlie again nodded assent.

Nolan got out his cigarettes, offered them around. Charlie refused, getting out a metal case of his own, and Werner also turned him down, mumbling that he'd quit. Nolan fired Charlie's cigarette and his own, then went on. "You know, Charlie, it would've been easy for me to kill you downstairs in the suite. Even had Tillis handy to build a frame around."

"Why so generous, Nolan?"

"Killing you's not the answer. Not at this point, anyway. Your boy Tillis had some influence on me, too, I suppose."

"Tillis? How so?"

"When I asked him if he was sent to kill me or just to check me out, he said the latter, and I believe him. I read Tillis as an open kind of guy, the kind who can't lie worth a damn."

Charlie nodded.

"If I figured you sent Tillis to kill me, you'd be dead by now . . . but I can't blame you for taking precautions when I did the same thing."

"And if Tillis had been sent to kill you," Charlie said, working an ominously bland tone into his voice, "he would've gotten it done."

Nolan smiled and said, "A strong possibility. He's a good man. Anyway, I think maybe you really are willing to talk, Charlie, and can see I am, too . . . so okay, so let's play peacemaker."

Werner said, "Now we're finally getting on the right track."

Charlie said, "Shut up."

"You know about my cover name, Charlie," Nolan continued. "Without it, there's a lot of money I can't get to. A decade-and-a-half of money."

"That's right, Nolan. Because all I got to do is let somebody know about that cover of yours . . . say, for instance, the FBI . . . and you'll be busted in every sense of the word . . . busted as in broke, busted as in iron bars."

"You got the cards," Nolan agreed.

"I hear you want to quit heisting. Want to shuck your evil ways and get back in the club business."

"You hear correct. Since your boys queered that job of mine back in Cicero, there isn't a decent heist man left who'll work with me. And I'm getting old, Charlie, and so are you. I don't know about you, but I'm tired of pretending I'm a kid."

Charlie sat up. "I'm getting old, Nolan, you're right on that count. And I've mellowed . . . I wouldn't be here tonight if I hadn't mellowed . . . but I can't let this thing between us die easy." He smiled; his teeth were white as a shiny sink. "Sixteen years of hate doesn't just turn to mist and drift off because we've had five minutes or so of goddamn chit-chat. There's one hell of a lot more to this than that, Nolan, and a certain grudging respect we maybe got for each other, just for living this long, doesn't change things for either of us."

Nolan drew on the cigarette and gave the smoke a go at his lungs. "What do you want, Charlie?"

"I don't want to kill you, Nolan, not really. My poor dead brother's been gone a long time now, and like the anti-capital punishment boys would say, your death won't bring him back. It's been said revenge is a fire that burns in a man, but all fires cool with time . . . besides, even I got to admit you had cause to shoot the damn fool like you did . . . and the money you took? A drop in the bucket." Charlie leaned forward, his eyes intense. "But do I hate you, Nolan? Do I hate you as I sit across from you like this, while the two of us chatter like a couple goddamn schoolgirls? Yes. I do, Nolan. Yes."

Nolan knew when not to say anything.

Charlie went on, his face a soft red. "Why? Reasons, Nolan. Reasons you never once had occur to you in these sixteen years past."

Charlie seemed to catch himself getting close to some self-appointed mark, and he stopped for a heartbeat and leaned back, trying to disguise his trembling. Nolan realized suddenly that the man had been working, working hard for restraint, to maintain a calm outer shell during these minutes of "friendly" conversation.

Nolan said, "What reasons, Charlie?"

Charlie forgot self-control and lurched forward, veins throbbing over his collar, letting loose words held in for too many years. "You made a *clown* out of me, Nolan!" He cupped his knees with his hands, and bones and veins on them stood out vividly. "You killed my brother, you stole my money, and then you got away with it! Everybody in the Family knew about it. Everybody knew a goddamn nobody in the organization, a goddamn club manager, had made a goddamn clown out of me! No, I don't have reason to hate you, Nolan, you didn't do anything but *destroy my life!* Because of what you did, I never rose an inch with the Family; sixteen years after your grandstand stunt I'm still stuck in the same goddamn spot I was in then. If you hadn't screwed things up for me, Nolan, Jesus, I might have made top man, I might be top man in the Family today!"

Werner said, "It's not like you were demoted or anything, Charlie."

"Shut up!"

Nolan stabbed his cigarette out in the ashtray resting beside the lamp on the nightstand. He repeated what he'd asked before. "What do you want, Charlie?"

Charlie's eyes slitted, and two small, penetrating coals glinted out at Nolan. Charlie had self-control back, and he had it in spades. He said, "I want you to sweat, Nolan. I want you to sweat blood."

"Talk sense, Charlie. You know I don't have your feel for the melodramatic."

The little man sat up, composing himself as though he were a family patriarch preparing to carve a holiday turkey. "All right, Nolan. We won't waste time with a lot of needless talk. I'll make it simple and spell it out for you. This is what I want, all I want . . . one hundred thousand dollars. That's all, Nolan. One hundred thousand dollars."

Silence held the room for a full minute.

Nolan sat back in the chair and got a fresh cigarette going and weighed Charlie's words. Werner sat leaning forward, mouth half open, trying to comprehend what was going on. Charlie sat straight, hands folded.

Finally Nolan cut through the silence.

"Okay, Charlie," he said, "it's a lot of money, but I won't bitch about it. We can call it interest on the twenty thousand I took from you sixteen years ago. All I need is your word you won't leak the Earl Webb name, and you can have your hundred thousand."

Charlie's features grew tight, seeming to converge toward the center of his face. "You miss my point . . . I don't want any of *that* money. That would be too easy. You got to go out and get *new* money for me."

"What?"

"You heard me, Nolan. Go out and get it for me. Earn it. Steal it. Counterfeit it if you can do a good enough job. But you got to be able to show me where you got it. I want to pick up the newspaper and see such-and-such jewelry store got hit, or so-and-so rich bastard was robbed. Don't even think about using any of the Earl Webb money to pay me off."

"Why the hell not?"

"Because I don't want you to. Because it would be too goddamn fucking easy."

"I can't pull a job, not now."

"Sure you can, Nolan. You're a pro."

"After what you did to me in Cicero, there isn't a decent man in the business who'll be willing to work with me."

"That's a problem you'll just have to iron out."

"This is insane. I've quit, Charlie, can't you understand that? I'm an old man and I'm not even fifty yet."

"You can quit. After this one. After this one last job."

"Yeah. And every guy I ever knew who tried pulling off one last big one with retirement in his head got it blown off trying."

"That'd break my fucking heart."

"What the hell's the difference? One hundred grand out of a Webb account is just as good as any one hundred grand I could come up with through a job!"

"Calm down, Nolan," Charlie said, his tone condescending. "I never saw you so upset before. What's happened to you?"

"Okay," Nolan said. "You want me to sweat blood for you. All right. I'll sweat it for you."

"Good," Charlie said, "good. We'll set a deadline . . . say one month from tomorrow? Pay the money, and you got your cover back and the funds that go with it. If you can't make payment by then, you're going to have to do your future dealing with the Chicago P.D., the FBI, the Treasury boys . . ."

"I think I get the idea."

"I thought maybe you would."

"What's my guarantee you won't expose the cover after I pay off?"

"You know there isn't any, outside of my word."

"Then why should I do it, Charlie?"

"Well, Nolan, as you pointed out, we're both getting on in years, myself even more so than you. I'm growing more sentimental in my old age and figure, why not settle this account with Nolan and have it over and done? But I can't just say 'Forget it.' The Family knows I've sworn to even scores with you, so I can't let it end with, 'Be seeing you.' Yet I've so much as been told not to kill you, so what am I to do? There's such a thing as saving face." Charlie let out a short laugh. "What I'm giving you is a *chance.* Sure, you can't be positive I'm leveling with you, but this way you *got* a chance of getting that cover of yours back. Any other way you got zero." He put his hands on his knees, but not so firmly as before. "That's my offer. Pay up a month from tomorrow . . . if you're ready sooner, just call Werner and tell him, and we'll set up a drop for the money. And then you can have your goddamn cover name back and retire a happy bastard."

Nolan reached over into the lamp, brought out the .38, and held its nose under Charlie's.

Charlie turned as white as his teeth, and small beads of sweat began making their way down his brow.

"Give me a reason," Nolan said, "why I shouldn't blow your head off and be the hell done with all this." He turned to Werner and said, "You can contribute, too, old friend."

"The Family would find you, Nolan," Werner said.

"Maybe. But then you'd be just as dead, wouldn't you, Charlie?"

Charlie said, "Put it away, Nolan."

"You haven't given me a reason yet."

"If I don't show up in my Chicago office tomorrow morning, kiss Earl Webb good-bye. That's a reason."

"Should I trust you, Charlie?"

"I won't renege on this, Nolan. Pay me and I swear the slate between us is clean."

"Clean?"

"Clean. Now put the gun away."

"No. I trust you, but not that much." He paused, then said, "Take off your ties and belts, men. Slow motion, please."

When they had, Nolan said, "Werner, take Charlie's tie and tie his hands behind his back. Tight as you can without cutting off the circulation."

Werner looked as though he thought Nolan was pushing what was left of their friendship a little too hard, but any argument he had ready died when the .38 barrel began to swing his way.

After Werner had tied Charlie, Nolan kept gun in hand as he secured Werner's hands in back, then bent down and strapped the belts around their ankles.

Charlie said, "I hope you know what you're doing, Nolan. Turning me down like this leaves you with nowhere to go."

Nolan said, "I'm not turning you down, Charlie. It's just I'm getting edgy in my old age. How do I know this summit meeting of ours hasn't been just so much bull to set me up for an easy kill? I figure this'll keep you boys away from the phone till I'm out of the hotel and gone."

Werner let out some pent-up venom. "Damn you, Nolan! Don't you know *yet* that we don't handle things that way anymore? This was a business meeting until you started to . . ."

Charlie said, "Shut up."

"Charlie," Nolan said, "I'm going to play your game. I'll dig up a job somewhere and you'll get paid . . . but back out, or cross me in any way, and you're going to die. A promise. You'll just die."

Charlie started to say something, but Nolan whipped

open the nightstand drawer and grabbed the two wadded handkerchiefs and shoved one into Charlie's open mouth. Werner started to say something, and since Charlie wasn't in a condition to shut him up, Nolan did it for him with the other wad of cloth.

Nolan holstered the .38, plucked the Colt from behind the pillow, and shoved the gun in his belt. He looked over at Charlie and thought about what a melodramatic sonofabitch Charlie was. Then he remembered his words to Charlie before stuffing the gag in his mouth, and glanced over at the lamp where he'd hidden the .38, and he had to laugh.

A couple of melodramatic sons-of-bitches, he thought, and headed for the door.

9

Downstairs in his suite Nolan unlocked the closet and got out the .38 he'd stowed there, jamming it in his belt. Tillis's Luger he left in the closet, leaving the door open. Next he removed the other revolver from this room's nightstand lamp and dropped the gun in his coat pocket.

No matter how silly precautions seemed in retrospect, Nolan knew only a dead man could afford not to take any.

He went into the bathroom and found Tillis, who was nodding off to sleep.

"Hey Tillis."

The big black shook his head and said, "Uh, what, uh, hey man . . . must've dozed off. What's happening? You kill Mr. Charlie or what?"

"No. Just fixed him and Werner so they'd stay quiet a while. When I get to where I'm going, I'll call the desk over here and have them send somebody up to untie you. Then you can go up and let Charlie and Werner loose. They're in room 714."

"Oh. Okay."

"You tell Charlie I'm going through with his offer. But tell him don't underestimate me."

"I'll tell him, Nolan. He can take my word for it."

"Your Luger's in the front closet. That's about it, Tillis. See you."

"See you."

Nolan walked out of the suite and took the elevator back up to the other room. He got one of the guns out before going in, though it was hardly necessary. Charlie and Werner were quite secure on the bed, hadn't budged: Charlie's eyes were bored, Werner's indignant.

Grabbing up his bag and dumping all guns into it save the one in his shoulder holster, Nolan went for the window and the fire escape beyond. He climbed down into the alley and started walking.

It was twelve blocks to the Y and that third room he'd rented.

Two

Planner sat behind the counter in his antique shop, puffing away at a Garcia y Vega and waiting for Nolan.

Planner liked cigars, liked them a lot, and always kept a box of Garcias under the counter and handy. Yes, he realized that smoking cigars hurt business—the air in a dust-trap antique shop did damage enough to customers' sinuses without the proprietor further polluting the atmosphere. And he supposed the image he presented of a lanky, balding old eccentric in red flannel shirt and baggy trousers didn't exactly boost sales, either.

But then Planner didn't really give a damn about selling antiques.

A real antique, he reasoned, wasn't for selling, since an antique's foremost value is its age; older it is, more valuable it gets. Sell today, take a loss tomorrow. For that reason, any time he ran across a genuine antique, he packed it carefully away in his back room.

He did sell some things, of course. Some people'll buy anything. Most of the junk that had been in the place when he bought it twelve years before, the old pots and kettles and china and beat-up furniture and the like, was long gone by now. Every time his junk-antique supply ran low, he replenished it with more of the same, picked up dirt-cheap at flea markets and yard sales around the state.

When other dealers or knowledgeable buyers came in looking, they'd find little of interest in Planner's shop, except for the buttons. The buttons were something else again.

Planner was a nut for buttons. He liked buttons better than cigars and almost as much as he liked money. Not coat or shirt buttons, but the kind that pinned on—political buttons, advertising buttons, sheriff badges. The political variety, especially, was a penchant of his.

He kept a display case of buttons up front, plate-glass and well locked. There were boxes of the less valuable ones in the back room, and a barrel of worthless ones in the front marked two for a quarter. Some of the real prizes were upstairs in his plush (if he did say so himself) living quarters, on the wall in frames, his Lincoln tokens and big picture-buttons of Hoover among them. He took real pride in seeing the looks on dealers' and collectors' faces when they saw the buttons in the case, the Wilsons, the Willkies, the Bryans; even the recent ones were relatively valuable, since during the past few presidential campaigns a person had to contribute five or six bucks to get a picture button of his or her man.

Of course it was an expensive habit, but it fitted in well with his antique shop front, which was a natural for faking the books for the tax boys. Because, after all, buttons weren't his only specialty; there was his business specialty, too, which was planning jobs for men like Nolan.

This one, though, this one he was going to offer Nolan today, would be a different case, since he hadn't worked this package out. Usually a job was completely planned down to number of men and list of suggested personnel, with detailed procedure and, whenever possible, blueprints of the target.

Not this job; this would be different, because at this point, Nolan was anything but a popular boy.

He hated, really, even having to offer such a low quality proposition to Nolan, but there wasn't a choice. And if it wasn't for his faith in Nolan and a vested interest in Jon, he wouldn't have had even this job to offer.

Jon was his nephew, his late sister's boy, and he, too, was a collector. Comics were Jon's field, strips and books. Planner was always keeping an eye open for comic strip tie-in items for Jon, things like Big Little Books and the counterpart Big

Big Books and rare comic books and radio tokens and Sunday pages from the '30s and '40s.

Jon and he had become even closer with Jon's mother gone and the boy living here in Iowa City and going to the University. Jon teased Planner about his name ("Planner" had been a trade nickname in the early, active days of his career, and when he opened this shop he'd taken the name as a permanent alias, prefacing it with "Edwin"). He said the name sounded like something out of Dick Tracy; but then everything was like something out of Dick Tracy to Jon.

Nolan could watch after Jon. There were few men left in the field like Nolan, men who treated the heist trade *like* a trade. A craftsman, Nolan was, one of the last going. Planner knew Nolan could help Jon along better than anybody.

The bell over the door jangled as it opened and Planner looked up to see if Nolan was there. No. Kids from the school let out across the street, in for three o'clock "penny" candy. Planner waited for the several minutes the kids took picking out their candy and gum from the double shelves by the door and accepted the coins they offered in return. The bell rang again as the door closed behind them and Planner flicked the ash off his Garcia and leaned back in his chair, puffing.

Planning jobs he'd always been good at. He had a knack for that sort of thing, but he'd been glad to get out of the active end and into a front like this one. The on-the-job stuff, the something's-gone-wrong-plan-on-the-job scene played hell with his nerves, and when he'd turned fifty he'd gotten this place and was glad of it.

His "buying" trips out of town, which were frequent, served to give him a cover that let him innocently case all sorts of business establishments and, as a kindly old eccentric antique dealer, ferret out all kinds of information about cash on hand and where it was kept.

The bell over the door jangled, and this time it wasn't kids.

A figure in a gray suit filled the doorway. The man stood

just over six feet and wore a lean, hard-featured, high-cheekboned face, with narrow eyes and a thick mustache. His hair was black, widow's-peaked, with only the hair along his sideburns completely given to gray. He dropped his bag to the floor and turned the OPEN sign around in the window, facing the CLOSED side out, then flipped the lock and drew the shade.

"How are you, Nolan?" Planner asked.

"All right. Getting cold, isn't it."

"Haven't been out today. Come by bus?"

"No. Didn't have the money. Hitched a ride in Davenport."

"Oh?"

"Yeah, struck up a conversation with a guy and convinced him I got wiped out gambling. Said I had to come here to get a stake."

Planner stabbed out his Garcia and reached under the counter for a new one. "Well? Isn't that true, Nolan, in a way?" He fired the fresh cigar with a wooden match and said, "Interest you in a Garcia y Vega? No charge, of course."

"No thanks. Cigarettes got first call on my lungs. You do still have that eight thousand I left with you last year, don't you, Planner?"

"Of course."

"Your safe in the back room?"

"No, upstairs in my wallsafe. Don't draw interest, but then it don't get taxed, either."

"Let's go up, then. I'll need the money whether or not I take this job you got for me."

Planner nodded, stepped from behind the counter, and guided Nolan into the backroom and then across it, through a pathway between its many boxes to the stairway at the rear. He led Nolan up the stairs and into the newly remodeled second floor. He smiled, showing off both his pine-paneled living quarters and his new teeth, and Nolan nodded appreciatively.

"You manage to live well, Planner. This must be the third time you remodeled since you moved in."

"Fourth. I like new things. I work all day downstairs with the old, so I live at night around the new. How do you like the modern furniture?" Planner had bought the stuff knowing that when he tired of it, he'd turn it over to Jon, whose one-room apartment was all but bare.

"It's okay," Nolan said, patting a white plastic armchair. "I hope it's kinder to my ass than it is to my eyes."

"Still the same old tactful Nolan. Drink?"

"No thanks. Could we get to the job?"

Planner motioned past the chair toward the circular couch, and both men sat. Planner said, "You still aren't much for conversation, are you, my middle-aged friend? Don't the years mellow you at all?"

"Grow mold on me is more like it."

"I looked older at thirty than you do at fifty."

"I'm not quite fifty yet, but if you don't mind, could the two old women cut the beauty-parlor age tally and get on with business?"

"In your own charming way you're trying to tell me how bad you need this job."

"Yeah. I'm anxious as hell for it, as a matter of fact. I only hope it's a good one."

Planner leaned over a transparent blue plastic coffee table and sprinkled his Garcia ashes into a tray shaped like the state of Florida, and said, "Jobs for you are a scarce commodity, Nolan. Any job, let alone good ones. You and I both know that the word is out you're in bad with the syndicate people."

"They're calling it the Family this year."

"I don't care if they're calling it Ringling Brothers, Barnum and Bailey, it's the syndicate and you're on their shit list."

"I'm glad you told me so I could find out about it."

"I only mention it so you know the position I'm in. You know I never sold you nothing but a good package, and now when I got to offer you a, well, bad risk, I want you to know why."

"A bad risk."

"I won't pretend that it isn't. It's something nobody else wants."

"Don't build me up like this, you'll only disappoint me."

"Oh, it gets worse, Nolan, don't let me fool you."

"Worse?"

"You'd be working with virgins. Three amateurs so green their biggest hit to date is maybe a cookie jar."

"It does get worse, doesn't it."

"It's two men and a woman. Or two boys and a girl, is more like it. The boys, who got less years between them than you got by yourself, have one score to their credit: a filling station last summer they took for a big sixty bucks. The girl never did anything wrong except maybe cheat on her boyfriend."

"An all-star lineup."

"Well, it's not quite as bleak as I've been painting it. I know one of these kids, and real well. He's my nephew, and a bright kid, smarter than hell, and strong. Went to nationals in high school wrestling at one of them medium weights. He found this job himself and had me check it out for him. If it goes right, it could be a big haul."

"What is it? Two filling stations?"

"It's a bank."

"A bank. Great. I could pick up a couple slobs from out of a bar and pull a smash-and-grab on a bank. I need more money than that. I got a debt to pay."

"This is better than smash-grab, Nolan. This is an inside job."

"How so?"

"The girl I mentioned. She *works* at this bank. Been there close to three months now. She's trusted. With that kind of inside help, you might be able to clean the place out."

"Sounds a bit more promising, I admit."

"Could run as high as seven hundred and fifty thou, you

hit it the right time."

"How planned out is it? You make up one of your regular critiques for me?"

"No. This is my nephew Jon's job. He has his own ideas about how to handle it. But he doesn't begin to understand the potential there, he's got no idea how big a take is possible in a case like this, if it's done right. But you and I do, Nolan. I figured you'd want to meet the people and work with them a while before making final plans. You know, weigh their capabilities and plan from there."

"Jesus. How much do you want for this dream package?"

"Not a cent."

"What? Since when does Planner run a charity house for heistmen on the skid?"

"Just look after my nephew, okay?"

"Goddamn. This must be one hell of a lemon."

"You can make it work, Nolan."

"Thanks. You having faith in me makes it all better."

"Some thanks I get. I got no other job I could give you, anybody else wouldn't give you anything at all."

"Yeah. It's a pisser. Well, I suppose I get the details from your nephew."

"Right. He's got a place downtown, an apartment over the Hamburg Haven. Know where it is?"

"Sure." Nolan got up. "I could use my money, Planner. I'll need it to finance this triumph."

"Sure," Planner said. He walked over to the frame that housed the two big Hoover buttons and lifted it off its nail to get at the wallsafe behind it. He twirled the combination dial and yanked the safe door open. He got out a manila envelope and, as an afterthought, took out a small white box.

He handed the envelope to Nolan. "Here you go. All there, eight thousand in hundreds."

Nolan peeked in at the money. "I wouldn't think of counting it, Planner, you know that."

"Yeah, yeah. And here, take this, too." He handed him the white box.

"What's this?" Nolan asked, giving the box a quizzical onceover.

"Something for my nephew, something kind of valuable I picked up for him the other day and haven't had a chance to give him yet. Thought maybe you wouldn't mind dropping it off."

"Sure. What is it?"

Planner let his face wrinkle into a sheepish grin. "A Dick Tracy Crimestopper badge," he said.

2

Iowa City depressed Nolan.

It wasn't the Midwestern atmosphere that bothered him, or even Iowa itself—he liked being left alone, which was basically what people did to each other in Midwestern states, as opposed to East Coast rudeness, West Coast weirdness and Southern pseudo-hospitality. Iowa City was a college town, and that depressed Nolan.

Or more specifically, college-town girls depressed him. Maybe it was this new awareness of what he was beginning to view as the onrush of senility. Or just an awkwardness that came from being around people he couldn't relate to. But these young girls, damn it, all looking so fuckable and at the same time untouchable, in their jeans and flimsy tee-shirts. . . . He guessed it was ego; he didn't like looking at a desirable woman without at least the remote possibility of getting in.

Not that he'd ever been much for playing the stud, that wasn't it; sex was a gut need to be filled when time and circumstance allowed. But with young girls like these, daughters and possibly granddaughters of the one or two generations of women he'd had intercourse with, he had no basis for rapport, no way, man, none at all to relate with such creatures. Conversation was enough of a pain for Nolan without having to struggle for whatever wave-length these children were on this week.

As he walked the blocks between Planner's antique shop and the Hamburg Haven, the thirty-above Iowa wind biting through his light suit into the healed-up wound, he had the strange feeling that this kind of sexual mind-wandering put him in the category of would-be child molester.

And he had to admit he liked the young look these girls had, the freedom of dress, long-flowing hair or mass of Shirley Temple curls or shortcut boyish; even those in grubby outfits managed to look fresh and clean, without appearing virginal, and Christ, where were the girls that showed it like that and had it to show when he was their age? Winter coming on and they weren't even wearing bras; he'd *never* get used to that.

As far as the young men were concerned, Nolan saw that their lifestyle reflected a similar freedom of dress and grooming, but they carried their lot of freedom around so conspicuously it might well have been heavy.

An idealistic bunch, Nolan thought, stupidly idealistic, perhaps, or maybe just stupid, but a different bunch than the one he had grown up a part of, and Nolan could almost feel an envy for these kids who were getting a shot at mistakes he'd only dreamed of making.

He approached the Hamburg Haven, a brick two-story in the middle of the block, its windows streaked with grease and other moistures, and ignored the main entrance, opting for the doorway to the far left which led up a flight of stairs. From the look of the stairs Nolan figured they could hold his weight for once up, but he wouldn't count on round trip. He took a chance and climbed them, knocked at the paint-flaked door at the top.

The door jerked open like a bad film cut and in its place was a five-feet six-inch figure in jeans and gray sweatshirt, with a mass of curly brown Harpo-like hair, intense blue eyes, and a little piggish turned-up nose in an otherwise well-featured face.

"Jon?"

"Mr. Nolan?"

Nolan nodded.

The boy seemed to be struggling to put the clamp on his enthusiasm, but Nolan could see the same look an eager puppy has jumping up and down in the bright eyes.

"Come on in, Mr. Nolan, come on in."

Nolan stepped in and closed the door behind. After he got a look around, he weighed going back out again as a strong possibility.

The room's crumble-plaster walls were practically wallpapered with posters, not the standard clever-saying type or famous movie star or once-the-rage psychedelic, but handdrawn posters depicting comic-strip heroes, and a few storebought movie posters of actors Nolan didn't recognize.

The posters were hung, four by two feet, uncanny recreations of Flash Gordon, Prince Valiant, Buck Rogers, Dick Tracy, Batman, and several other comic characters not familiar to him. The movie posters, fewer in number, were unrecognizable to him, with one exception: Buster Crabbe, playing either Buck Rogers or Flash Gordon, he wasn't sure which. Among the others was a gaunt-faced Western character with a mustache and pipe, dressed in black.

There was also a cot in the room, and next to it a drawing board with papers and pencils scattered on the floor around it. The room didn't have a kitchenette, just a hotplate on an old table and a tiny icebox. The can had both a stool and a tub, but no door. A closet, also doorless, contained skyscraper piles of comic books. Also in the room was a steel cabinet, an office file, which in the midst of the pop-art ruin made as much sense to Nolan as a naked girl in a church choir.

Nolan said, "Why the file?"

Jon said, "The top drawer is for my really rare comics. I collect them, uh, comics that is. It's my hobby."

"What're the other two drawers for?"

"Pardon?"

"In the file."

"Oh. The second drawer's for other rare things, you know, Big Little Books and daily and Sunday strips from old papers, stuff like that."

"Leaves a drawer."

"Clothes. That's where I put them, I put my clothes in the bottom drawer."

Nolan nodded. He looked around the room again, made an effort to suppress the gigantic sigh inside him wanting out, and reached in his pocket to get the white box Planner had given him.

Nolan said, "Here you go, kid. For the second drawer. Your uncle sent this over."

The boy took the box, opened it, and his eyes lit up as if he had a candle inside his head, his outer shell staying passive. "Uh, thanks for dropping this off, Mr. Nolan, thanks a lot."

"Yeah. Well. I got to be going. Nice meeting you, kid."

"Hey . . . hey, wait a minute!"

Nolan was opening the door. "What?"

"What about the . . . the, you know . . ." he dropped his voice, to a conspiratorial whisper, ". . . the robbery?"

"Forget it, kid."

"Bullshit. You came here to talk business. Now, now shut the door and come back in here and talk it."

Nolan hesitated and the boy reached over and slammed the door shut.

"Wait, don't tell me," Nolan said, "I just figured it out. We hit the bank, I take the cash, you take the dimes and we drop you off at a newsstand."

"You show both your age and your ignorance, Nolan. It's been years since comic books sold for a dime. I suppose you remember when they were a nickel."

"I remember when they drew them on cave walls."

"Listen, this is a big goddamn joke to you, isn't it? A little boy and his games? Okay, maybe I got a childish habit that isn't as mature and rewarding as booze or dope or something, but a cheap habit it isn't. I paid a hundred thirty-five bucks for the first 'Superboy,' a hundred for the first 'Captain Marvel Jr.,' and two hundred for 'Detective' thirty-eight."

"Thirty-eight?"

"That's the first appearance of Robin in 'Batman.' "

"Fine reason to hit a bank, fine. So you can build a comic book collection."

"Am I asking you what you want to do with your share?"

"No."

"Let me ask you something . . . you ever go to college, Nolan?"

"No."

"I'm not in this semester, going back when I can dig up the bread, but do you know what kind of grades I got?"

"No."

"I got a three point five average on a basis of four."

"Really? Well, that's fine, that's perfect. Sound credentials. Not only do you love comic books, you get straight As. Where's the note from the Dean saying what a swell heist artist you'll make?"

Jon walked over to the cot, lifted the covers that hung to the floor and pulled from under a barbell with massive lead weights on either end. He rolled it out into the middle of the room.

He looked at Nolan and said, "Try it."

"Step one in my test to earn you as a partner?"

"Try it."

Nolan finally let the sigh escape and dropped his bag to the floor and bent down and gripped the weight. His side burned as he brought the barbell to his waist, then jerked it up to his chin. He pushed to get it over his head, tried, tried, but couldn't make it. When he set the weight down, the room shook.

Jon laughed. "Bet that knocked a few hamburgers off the grill downstairs."

"Now," Nolan said, "I suppose you lift the weight and show me up, instantly creating a till-death bond between us."

Jon smiled and said, "Something like that." He leaned down, bending only at the waist, and quickly did an underhand curl with the barbell, shoving the weight over his head and switching his hands around in midair, then easing it back to the floor.

"Now what?" Nolan asked. "You kick sand in my face?"

"No," Jon said. "You and I talk about that robbery."

"If we were going to swipe a bunch of lead weights, those biceps of yours might come in handy."

"So it was a stunt," the boy shrugged. "It got your attention."

"This is a deadly serious business, you know."

"Sounds like you're the one reads comic books."

Nolan grinned. "Okay." He dug in his pocket for his cigarettes, got one out and lit it. "Best thing to do first off is meet with the other masterminds you got lined up for this once-in-a-lifetime score."

"Good enough. This afternoon too soon? We'll have to drive a ways. Fifty miles."

"Got a car?"

"Yeah."

"All right."

"I'll have to make a phone call."

"Go on."

"I don't have a phone. Have to use the booth downstairs."

"You need a dime, in other words."

Jon nodded, smiling.

Nolan searched his pockets, came up with two nickels and tossed them to the boy. "Just don't come back with a comic book."

"Be right back," the boy said, heading for the door.

Nolan was standing in front of the poster of the black-garbed Western figure with mustache and pipe, surveying it suspiciously, when the boy re-entered the room five minutes later.

"Lee Van Cleef," Jon said.

"What?"

"That's Lee Van Cleef. An actor. Looks something like you, don't you think?"

Nolan shook his head, smiled with half his mouth and jabbed a finger toward Buster Crabbe. "Flash Gordon's more my style. How long till we leave?"

3

Grossman didn't like beer: it was a liquid to be guzzled by simple-minded farmers who spent their evenings sipping its suds and listening to country-western music. He much preferred pot; in fact a friend of his who was a med school dropout had told him grass was safer than booze, maybe even good for you. But here in Junction he figured it was best to stay with beer, at least in a public place like this bar, where he and Shelly had already gotten more than their share of long looks.

He'd dressed as convervatively as he could, throwing an old green wool sweater over his usual tee-shirt with the Zig-Zag rolling papers logo on it, and jeans and a worn denim jacket. There was no way, of course, to do anything about the nearly shoulder-length hair, but even the hicks in a podunk like Junction ought to have seen long-haired men by now. In fact some of the younger farmers had beards and bushy hair themselves, in addition to bib overalls and duck-bill hats. Jesus.

The medieval atmosphere of the room gave Grossman a headache. From the booth in back where he and Shelly were sitting, he soaked in the tomb-like blackness of the place, which was highlighted only by the lengths of fluorescent tubing over the mirror behind the bar, and by hanging plastic beer ads lit up inside. The farmers at the bar, in their overalls and duckbill hats, were sneaking funny looks at the two of them—digging elbows into each other's ribs and making cracks, he supposed, about the weird-ass with the shoulder-length hair and/or the pretty little girl with the pretty little pink-sweatered boobies, and what was a pretty little girl like her doing with a long-haired weird-ass like him. The light from the plastic beer ads and fluorescent tubing hit their farmer faces angularly, making them look like stone gargoyles sprung to life.

And all the while in the background the jukebox retched country-western pickin' and a singin'.

One time out in Utah, in another podunk, Grossman had been sitting in a bar not unlike this one, listening to the same country-western slop dribble out of a juke, and slightly high on booze and grass, had stood up and said, not in a yell but in a controlled, firm tone of voice, "I knew an 'Okie from Muskogee' once and he was a goddamn fucking queer!" Before he'd sat back down, a couple of shitkickers in cowboy hats came over and lifted him up under the arms and hustled him out into the alley by the bar and beat the piss out of him.

That was bad enough, Grossman thought, but Jesus fucking Christ, of all the out-of-it states he'd been in in this out-of-it country, Iowa had to take top honors in the shit-kicking hick department.

Especially the podunks like this one, like Junction, dozens of which, Grossman felt sure, were scattered through each county in the Tall Corn State. Iowa City, where Jon lived, wasn't so bad; and Davenport, where Grossman was staying, was halfway decent; but Port City, the town of twenty thousand where Shelly had a job at the bank, was just a podunk gotten out of hand.

Junction, a one-tavern hamlet of two hundred, had been picked by Jon for the meeting because it was halfway between Iowa City and Davenport, and only twenty miles from Port City.

This meeting was something else Grossman didn't like.

He didn't figure they needed any outside help, some middle-aged bastard who thought age equals smart. Grossman figured he and Shelly and Jon could do just fine by themselves.

Shelly was sipping her beer, looking very calm, her blue eyes heavy-lidded and languid, and she laid her hand on top of Grossman's, stopping the nervous drumming of his fingers. Her touch felt cool, soothing.

Grossman rubbed his right temple and looked down into his glass of beer. "Where *are* those assholes?"

Shelly said, "It isn't time yet. Five more minutes."

Grossman nodded, gulping down a swallow of beer.

It would be okay, he thought. Just as long as he had Shelly. God, what a beautiful kid she was! Heaven, Grossman thought, heaven was Shelly and that musk-scented bod of hers between the cool sheets of a warm Canadian bed. All that long black hair, drifting down over creamy shoulders, and that pale ivory skin, the rose-petal lips, and those uplifted, brown-nippled breasts, the silken thighs, and that hot sucking warmth between her . . .

Grossman's back arched. He could feel the eyes of those shitkickers at the bar, feel them staring at him, gaping at her, peeling Shelly in their minds and with their words, and he wanted to rush over there and crack their farmer skulls open like melons on the hard mahogany bar.

And it wouldn't be the first time, either. That stagnated pile of shit called America was full of them, he knew, and it wasn't just the shitkickers, it was the "movement," too, and that was what made everything so hopeless.

A few years ago he had thought there was a chance. The fat-cat capitalists would get theirs, get it from the student revolutionaries, from the black militants, a cleansing bath of blood from the young and the blacks, that had been his credo.

Ever since he'd flunked out of that eastern junior college a thousand years back, when his loving parents (mom and hubby numero three) disowned him, he'd been campus-hopping, hanging around college towns and working with radical left groups, a pseudo-student, until he got bored or in trouble. Then he'd pick up and move on to another campus, helping the local revolutionaries stir things up there, pushing grass on the side to get the necessary bread.

Then at Berkeley he'd met Shelly, pretty, idealistic, intelligent Shelly. With horrible, smothering parents, giving her, giving her, giving her, suffocating her with guilt/love. Shelly wanted a new life, something simple, something fresh. And Grossman wanted her to have it.

He and Shelly connected about the time he was realizing that the "movement" wasn't what it once had been; he supposed he'd gotten aboard the train too long after it'd left the station. So many good people had been corrupted, swallowed into the straight world; what was left, among the older ones, were burn-outs and losers, and most of the ones his age or younger were into sex and drugs and rock 'n' roll, but in no political context. Talk of revolution had faded into trivialities like women's rights and nuclear power . . .

Take Jerry, for example. A Marxist whose idea of sharing the wealth ran to putting the make on Shelly. He'd caught Jerry forcing himself on Shelly in the backroom of the co-op bookstore, and had beat the living shit out of him. Shelly had cried. You're too trusting, babe, he'd told her; you're too gullible.

Then came the letter from that buddy of his in Colorado, who'd been "born again" and was living in a mountainside commune run by a Jesus cult. Back to the soil, a return to the land. Back to God. It was something new to try: Grossman and Shelly went.

They said they were children of love, those Jesus freaks, and they were children of love, all right, only when they said peace, they meant piece; and sharing food and lodging and Jesus was one thing, but sharing Shelly was something else.

He found one of the cult leaders "praying" in the high weeds with Shelly, taking advantage of her, taking advantage of her small size, her giving spirit, and Grossman lifted the guy up by the neck and threw him to the ground, and while Shelly cried hysterically in the background, he slammed his fist into the son of a bitch, kicked, kneed him, elbowed him, reached for the rock and smashed it down on the bastard's head and . . .

"Are you all right, Gross?" Shelly asked.

He breathed out. "Yeah. I was just thinkin'."

She shook her head. "Don't. Don't do that. Don't think backward, Gross, only ahead. Canada, remember?"

"Okay."

Canada.

Canada and bread. Canada where you could still buy some land and get back to beginnings. Canada and a nice fat bankroll to get them started *fresh*, Shelly and him, and leave all the phony idealism behind, behind in the land of the Red, White, and Blue, along with the shitkicking hicks and the fat-cats and the failed revolutionaries and all the other assorted American nightmares and dreams.

Revolution, Grossman had come to believe, was in the mind, and politics was a fantasy and nothing more. His personal purge accomplished, Grossman was ready, ready for years of lying on his back with his woman next to him, making love, getting high, living off the land; not bothering, not bothered.

Shelly said, "There's Jon. He's alone."

Grossman turned around in the booth. Jon was approaching them, winding his way through the shitkickers, looking nervous and a little excited.

"Hi, Jon."

"How ya doin', Shelly? How's it goin', Gross?"

"Jon. Where's the big man? We're here to meet the big man, aren't we?"

Jon leaned over the table. "Now look, Gross, let's start cool and stay that way, okay? We're lucky this guy's even willing to sit down and talk with us. I mean, he's been around a long time in a business where you don't stay around a long time, unless you're very, very good. And Planner says he's the best."

"You convincing me or yourself?"

"You're going to blow it, Gross, I just know you are. One talk with you and he'll be gone."

"Okay, okay. So where is he, this guy we're so lucky to be on the same planet with? Sees us by appointment only or what?"

Jon motioned toward the door. "In the car. Doesn't want to talk in here." He lowered his voice to a whisper. "Says we shouldn't be seen together."

"Christ. What does he think this is?"

"He'll probably ask you the same thing, Gross."

Shelly's soothing touch to Grossman's hand silenced his next response. She said, "Let's go out and talk to this guy. If he's as good as he's supposed to be, we'll profit by it, right, Gross?"

Grossman heaved a sigh, finally nodded.

Jon grinned. "Okay. Let's go out and talk to Nolan."

4

Nolan sat in Jon's decade-old Chevy II while the boy entered the narrow brick building, the outward-hanging neon in front already on, crackling now and then, glowing the words "Junction Tavern" listlessly in the cold late-afternoon overcast.

Reaching over by the driver's side to the dashboard lighter, Nolan punched in the button, stuck a cigarette between his lips and waited, trying to ignore his urge to laugh. Here he was, not forty miles from Werner and the Quad Cities where all this had begun, and scarcely more than two hundred miles from Charlie and Chicago, sitting in a beat-up old car in an Iowa village that consisted mainly of a tavern and a gas station, waiting for three punk kids to come out and tell him about the bank job he was going to pull with them. Ridiculous. It was a laugh.

Only it was Charlie's laugh: if Nolan fucked up, and died, or ended in stir, Charlie would just love it; and if Nolan did pull this off, Charlie would be a hundred grand ahead and would have saved face with the Family. Nolan would've appreciated the joke, but for the dull ache in his side from Charlie's last attempt to kill him.

The lighter popped out, and he yanked it free and lit his cigarette. Okay, he thought, on the surface it looked pretty bad, but at least he would have complete control. In the past, working with pros, he'd always been forced to compromise over certain points in the planning, because every individual pro has his own thoughts on how a heist should run. Nolan usually preferred Nolan's ideas, and when a job did go bad, he almost always could trace the failure to faulty, compromise planning.

Here he would be in charge, complete charge. Or else he'd just have to look for something different even if that something different was putting a bullet in Charlie.

The kid, Jon, seemed to have a good head. On the way to Junction from Iowa City they'd refrained from talking about the job, both of them thinking it best to wait for the other two. Nolan's initial scare over the boy's passion for such a triviality as comic books was gone now. A lot of people in the trade had crazy ideas; the business was full of unconventional dreamers who supplemented their dreams with heist money.

Jon had told Nolan of his plan to acquire a bookstore, where he would deal in rare comic books and strips while working on the side to get his start as a freelance cartoonist. His uncle Planner had heard of such a store in Waterloo, operated by an old guy whose health had started to fail. Jon wanted to buy the place and build it into a mecca for comic collectors.

It was a goal, and that reassured Nolan, because the best men in the business were men with goals. Cheap heisters, the kind who wanted a quick lift to an easy life, were bad risks; men like that spent as fast as they stole, could not be trusted. And it seemed like most of them lived life on a conveyer belt moving in and out of prisons. An intelligent heist artist would pick his jobs carefully, select co-workers carefully, and use his capital carefully.

Nolan had had a goal, too: he wanted to reach a state of financial independence by age fifty, so he could go through the rest of his years at a walk instead of a run, maybe operating a club or something to occupy his time. Now it looked like this job would be his last shot at fulfilling that goal.

The car door jumped open and Jon was there, saying, "This is Grossman, Nolan."

Standing beside Jon was a slouching figure of slightly under six feet, with a faint look of sour skepticism on his face and, hovering over his shoulders, matted, greasy hair that hadn't been washed any more recently than his faded jeans. At his side but behind him a little was a young girl of medium height, age nineteen or twenty, her face a strange but appealing wedding of innocence and sensuality. She was dressed in pink, her skirt tight, and she was slenderly but nicely built, her breasts tilting upward under her fuzzy pink sweater.

"And that's Shelly," Jon said, "behind Gross there."

Nolan nodded to her and she smiled hello, her eyes a warm and penetrating blue.

"Climb in," Nolan said, pointing his thumb toward the backseat.

Jon got in and sat behind the wheel as Grossman and Shelly slid in back. Nolan swivelled around in the seat and extended his hand to Grossman. The kid's handshake was sullenly limp.

"Why don't you pull the car off the highway and into the parking lot behind the tavern," Nolan said to Jon. "We don't want to attract undue attention."

"Okay." Jon started the engine and drove around the corner into the bar's cramped parking area.

"Leave the motor going," Nolan said. "It's cold, we can use the heat. Anybody want a smoke?"

All three accepted his offer, and after he'd fired everybody's cigarettes, Nolan said, "Who's going to fill me in?"

"Hold it a minute." Grossman leaned forward, his upper lip curling. "First I want to know just why the fuck *you* should be filled in at all."

Nolan said nothing. He could feel the eyes of the girl on him.

Jon jabbed at the air with a finger. Around him the windows were fogging up fast, and the car was already filled with smoke. "Look, Gross," he said, "this is *my* job. Mine. I talked it over with my uncle and he said we needed help to do this right, so he suggested we call in Nolan here. And I happen to think we're pretty goddamn lucky to have a professional like him willing to work with us."

"I suppose Captain America wasn't available."

"That isn't necessary, Gross."

"Oh?" Grossman did a little jabbing at the smoky air himself. "I think it's goddamn good and necessary, so we can cut through this pretentious bullshit and ask some questions. Such as, first off, why's Super-robber here want anything to do with an inexperienced bunch like us anyway? Why isn't he out hitting a mint with Willie Sutton or something?"

"Gross, I warned you about . . ."

Nolan said, "Jon, it's a legitimate question. Let me answer it."

Jon shrugged. "You shouldn't have to, Nolan."

"I want to." Nolan turned toward Grossman. "You're right. I'm not thrilled over the idea of working with virgins like the three of you. But I don't have any choice."

Grossman tapped Jon on the shoulder and said, "See?"

Nolan said, "Grossman, ever hear of the Family?"

Grossman shrugged, not understanding.

"How about the Syndicate? Cosa Nostra? Any of those ring a bell?"

Grossman nodded, slowly.

"About sixteen years ago I worked for the Family, which is the same thing. I ran a nightclub for them. I had a run-in with a brother of one of the Family higher-ups, and I killed him."

Grossman tried not to act impressed, but a twitch at the lower right corner of his mouth betrayed him. The girl was trying to keep her demure facial expression intact, but Nolan got a glimpse of her pink tongue flicking out over dry lips. Nolan continued, telling them briefly of the situation he was in with Charlie, but naming no names or particulars. He explained that the Family's interference with him while on a job had caused the word to get out in the trade that it was dangerous to work with him. And he told them of his need to make another hit to settle his Family differences by way of cash payoff.

Jon, who supposedly had heard the same story from Planner, gave Grossman a tense look and said, "Does that sound reasonable enough to you? Or does anything said by anybody other than yourself *ever* sound reasonable to you?"

Grossman shrugged.

"How many men," the girl asked Nolan, "have you . . . had to kill?"

Nolan turned to look at her and her blue eyes locked his in; where they'd been warm, they were now hot.

"A few," he said.

"How the hell do we know," Grossman said, courage regathered, "that this dude isn't just some washed-up stumblebum pal of Planner's, looking for a meal ticket and trying to snow us with his big Godfather fairy tale?"

"You don't," Nolan said.

"I wasn't talking to you."

The girl touched Grossman's arm and said, "I think he's leveling with us, Gross."

The long-haired youth slipped an arm around her shoulders and gave her a smile which was, Nolan felt, remarkably soft and obedient, considering what a rebel Grossman obviously pictured himself to be. "You think," he said, "we should give gramps here a chance?"

She nodded. "That I do."

"Anything you say, babe. Okay, old man, where do we go from here?"

"Where I suggested we go," Nolan said, "before you went into your tantrum. Somebody fill me in."

Grossman clenched his teeth and talked through them. "Now look, old man, only so much am I willing to take . . ."

"Hey, Gross, cool it, huh?" The girl touched his cheek with a pink-nailed hand. "You're the one dishing it out, right? Let's give him the chance you said you'd give him."

Grossman withdrew his arm from around her shoulders, folded his arms across his chest, and leaned back. "Okay, babe."

Jon said, "All right. I'll tell Nolan what's been going on."

Their plan, as Jon outlined it to Nolan, was fairly simple. Shelly had been working at Port City Savings and Trust for nearly three months now, using the name Elaine Simmons and false credentials courtesy of Planner, and was well trusted and liked at the bank. Jon's plan was to hit the bank, "kidnap" teller Shelly and, by having this ready-made "hostage," be able to make a clean, unhampered getaway.

"No," Nolan said.

The three kids looked at him, shocked. Jon started to say something and Nolan cut him off.

"No," he repeated. "It's lousy . . . the hostage idea is okay, but you're using it all wrong."

"I say dump the old man here and now," Grossman said, "and to hell with him! We don't need any fucking fourth wheel anyhow."

"Quiet," Jon said. "What's so lousy about the plan, Nolan?"

"You got in mind what's called a 'smash and grab.' That's a type of job a pro tries only when he's down and desperate for a stake, and with little or no planning, let alone this elaborate hostage thing you're setting up. You have an inside agent, a valuable asset on a job, which you plan to use in a next-to-useless way."

The girl moved forward in the backseat and said, "Why is that?"

"Look at it like this," Nolan said. "You'll already have pulled the FBI in on it, since the bank is covered by federal funds. Next you want to add a needless kidnapping charge which will just get everybody all the more upset, and probably get national coverage."

"But it isn't a *real* kidnapping!"

Nolan shook his head, smiling. "The FBI won't know that. Your object is to make everybody think the kidnapping's real, isn't it?"

Jon borrowed Nolan's cigarettes for a fresh smoke. "We figured with a hostage from the bank they would leave us alone, not wanting the girl to get hurt."

"No," Nolan said again. "Oh, you'd get away, all right. Tracked by more cars and helicopters than you ever knew existed. They'd know where you were at every moment, and they'd wait you out. You'd never shake them."

"Are you suggesting," Jon asked, "that we abandon the hostage angle? That's why we went to all the trouble of having Shelly establish herself at the bank as a clerk."

"Not abandon it," Nolan said. "Reshape it. There *are* a lot of advantages in taking hostage a person who's actually in on the hit, all of which I won't go into now. But . . . the getaway must be clean. You see, once you—or we, if you'll allow me to speculate—are safely away from the bank, we could split up in separate cars and, suitably disguised, make it away easy. Why? Because at roadblocks they'll be looking for three men and a woman, and they'll expect the woman to seem ill at ease since she's being held prisoner. Not, for example, two men on their way home from a hunting trip, or a married couple on their honeymoon. Which is what the four of us could easily become."

"It's good," Jon said.

The girl nodded and Grossman was silent.

"And there's still another reason," Nolan told them, "why you shouldn't handle this job smash-and-grab."

Jon's eyebrows arched. "Oh?"

"The half-assed way you had this planned is the way banks are hit all the time by semi-pros and amateurs. You read the papers. How much do you see banks usually get taken for?"

"I don't know," Jon said.

"A couple thousand at the most," Nolan said. "Four, maybe. And always marked bills."

"Bait money," Shelly said.

Jon wrinkled his face up. "What?"

"Bait money," Nolan said. "Banker jargon for the packets of marked bills each teller has at her window."

"That's still a thousand apiece," Grossman said.

Nolan crushed out his old cigarette in the dashboard ashtray, took his time getting a new one going. Finally he said, "Shelly, how much money would you estimate is in your bank on a Monday, in the afternoon, before the Brinks men come around Monday night to pick up the old bills and excess cash?"

She lifted her shoulders and put them down again. "Oh, offhand I'd say between five and seven hundred thousand dollars."

The mouths on Grossman and Jon dropped.

She stroked her chin with pink-nailed fingers. "Or maybe eight hundred thousand, on the right Monday."

Nolan said, "Like the first Monday in the month?"

She nodded. "Maybe a little more, even."

"November is less than two weeks away," Nolan said. "Anyone interested in doing some planning between now and the first Monday of the month?"

Jon laughed and seemed to be relaxed for the first time since the smoky dialogue had begun. "I sure am. What do you say, Gross?"

Grossman's head bobbed up and down.

"Shelly?" Jon asked.

"I'm with Nolan," she said, "all the way."

"Fine," Nolan said. He turned to Grossman. "I hear you're good with cars. Jon says you used to be a driver."

"Yeah," Grossman said, "I raced stocks when I was in high school and junior college, but gave it up a few years ago when I hit the road."

"But the car he's been hitting the road with still goes pretty good," Shelly said, rubbing the window beside her to clear a viewing spot in the moisture so Nolan could see the yellow Mustang a few spaces down from them in the tavern lot.

Nolan looked at Grossman. "That right?"

Grossman said, "It'll go."

The girl looped her arm in his and looked up into his face. "He handles it great, don't you, Gross? No matter how tough things have gotten, he's managed to keep it in shape. Souped up the engine himself, and tinkers around with it when he gets the chance."

"That's good," Nolan said, "we can use a driver-mechanic. But that's just one of a lot of details we have to work out. I got things to do to get ready before we start our planning sessions. I'll have Jon get in touch with you, Grossman, in a couple days."

Shelly leaned up and touched Nolan's hand. "What do you have to do?"

"Rent a house, with a barn or garage or something. Buy a car. Won't hurt me to do some thinking."

"Where's the bread going to come from?" Grossman asked him.

"Me. I'm bankrolling the job. I absorb all cost, then when we divide the take, we split five ways and I get two cuts."

Jon said, "Sounds okay to me."

Grossman unlatched the door on his side, shoved it open with his foot. "We'll see if the old man is as big as his talk." He pulled Shelly out after him, saying, "Let's go, babe."

"Two days," Nolan said.

The girl said, "See you later, Jon. Nice meeting you, Nolan."

The car door closed and Nolan and Jon sat and watched the two of them walk to the Mustang and get in, then roar out of the lot.

A few moments went by and Jon made a face and said, "I'm sorry about his attitude, Nolan."

"That's okay."

"All those goddamn insulting questions . . ."

"It's okay. At least they were the right questions."

"Well . . . what do you think?"

"The girl."

"What?"

"If we got a problem, she's it."

"What do you mean? Shelly a problem? You kidding, Nolan?"

"Hardly. Grossman has it bad for her, but she likes to sleep around."

"How in the hell can you say that?"

"It's a look she's got. Like she's got an itch in her pants and wants to have it scratched as many ways as she can."

"Oh, Nolan . . ."

"Grossman'll be okay unless she sets him off, but then it's going to hit the fan."

"I think you're miles off base, Nolan."

"Maybe so. But when you work with lovers, whether husbands and wives or a couple of gays or just a pair like those two doing the boy meets girl bit, jealousy's a very real problem."

"Well, I'll admit Grossman loves her."

Nolan put a hand on the boy's shoulder. "I don't want to shake you, kid . . . but if Shelly tried to fool around with one of us, Grossman could go off the deep end, and we might end up having to kill the poor bastard."

5

Jon pulled off the gravel road and guided his Chevy II down the half-mile drive leading into the circular cinder court that was shared by a ramshackle one-story gray farmhouse and matching barn. He halted the car in front of the house's rickety steps, grabbed the sack of groceries off the seat beside him, and walked up the steps, over the sagging porch and inside.

A mere forty-eight hours had gone by since the meeting at Junction; but they'd been an endless forty-eight hours for Jon, filled with Nolan's tedious arrangements and planning, most of which were left completely unexplained.

First, Jon had gone with Nolan to the real estate agent in Port City, who recommended the farmhouse and barn, which was on the Illinois side, fifteen miles and at least twenty minutes by car from the high bridge spanning the Mississippi downtown, that joined Iowa and Illinois. The agent called ahead for them and when they got there, an elderly farmer was waiting to show them around. Nolan's story was that he wanted to rent the place for a three-week duck-hunting vacation he'd be spending with his son, a role played for the occasion by Jon. The farmer explained he'd been renting the spread to satisfied hunters for years now, and said at a hundred and fifty bucks a week in advance, what with the pond and duckblind and all, it was a bargain. At that kind of money, Nolan later told Jon, it was anything but a bargain, though it did provide an ideal setup: a secluded place with plumbing and telephone, and a logical cover besides.

The coming night would be their first at the farmhouse, since the farmer had needed time to get the water turned on and the phone hooked up. Nolan had stayed at Planner's in

Iowa City the previous two nights, Jon's quarters being even less suited for two than for one.

In the early afternoon Jon had sat quietly and watched while Nolan got on the phone and began getting things going. One of the calls he placed was to a man named Werner, and judging from the half of the conversation Jon could hear, Nolan had contacted the man just to let him know he'd be working in the area. He also spoke to someone called Irish about getting a car. Nolan said he needed a station wagon with a good engine in it, one with solid pick-up, and also asked that its trunk-well be built into a special compartment large enough to accommodate two fully stuffed laundry bags.

For much the rest of the afternoon, Jon sat in a chair in the open-beamed, sparsely furnished living room, enjoying the nearby blaze of the fireplace that provided the house its heat. He'd borrowed a portable TV from Planner, but none of the daytime shows were worth the effort of turning the thing on, so he just lolled around with a drawing pad and sketched.

Most of Jon's sketches were of Nolan, who sat close by at a large, round poker table, appropriately poker-faced, scratching with a stub of a pencil at sheets of paper borrowed from Jon's supply. Nolan would wad spent sheets up every five minutes or so and toss them to the floor, then go on to a fresh page and start again. Every now and then Nolan would get up between pages and put in a call to Jon's uncle to ask him a technical question of some kind, or a word of advice on a particular aspect of the planning, returning afterwards to his paper-scratching.

Like Nolan's, Jon's sheets of paper were wadded up when spent and dumped on the floor. Every hour or so Jon would walk around and collect the balls of paper and pitch them into the fire one at a time, like a kid tossing pebbles in a pond.

When Jon entered the living room with the sack of groceries, he found Nolan still at the poker table, working at his latest sheet of paper.

"Hello, Nolan."

"Kid."

"I'll just go in and get these groceries put away."

"Okay."

"I got some beer and pretzels for the meeting."

"It's not supposed to be a picnic, but that's okay."

Jon went into the kitchen, with its rusty sink, dusty-shelved cabinets, faded white walls. The yellow formica table with its matching plastic-covered chairs and battered refrigerator and stove were 1950s classics. He unloaded the sack, filling one of the cabinet shelves with a dozen cans of vegetables, then transferred a wrapped package of hamburger, a small bag of potatoes, six six-packs of Schlitz and eleven TV dinners into the refrigerator. He left the box of pretzels on the table, then walked into the living room and sat in the chair by the fireplace. He picked up a brass poker and stirred the gently burning logs.

He had a queasy feeling, a mixture of fear and loneliness. He knew with Nolan in on this thing, it should go smoothly, but he and Nolan had spoken very little in the past two days, and that made him feel ill at ease. In Iowa City he'd had to sit by while Nolan discussed possibilities with Planner, and he tried to absorb all he could, but it was hard. And today, of course, he'd been hearing half conversations, the terse Nolan half—which was frustrating to say the least—and Nolan had spoke to him rarely.

"Kid," Nolan said.

"Yeah?"

"What time's Grossman and the girl going to get here?"

"When I called him I told him six-thirty, like you said to. It's ten after now."

"You make clear the instructions on how to find this place?"

"Clear enough. Gross'll find us. Those turn-offs on all those country roads are confusing, but he shouldn't have any trouble."

"Is that beer cold?"

"It was in the cooler where I got it, in that grocery store in the little town up the road, and less than a five-minute drive back."

"If that means it's cold, get me one, will you?"

"Sure, Nolan."

Jon was on his way back into the living room with two cans of Schlitz when the door buzzer sounded. He dropped the cans off with Nolan on his way to answer it and said, "They're a little early."

"Probably allowed extra time to find the place," Nolan said; but Jon noticed his right hand seemed to be drifting casually toward the revolver in the shoulder holster under his left armpit.

Jon opened the door a crack and Grossman shoved it open the rest of the way and came in, Shelly following behind him.

"Hi, everybody," Jon said.

Grossman nodded, throwing his denim jacket over a nearby chair. He was in his standard outfit of tee-shirt and worn jeans.

"How are you, Jon?" Shelly asked, Jon helping her out of her coat and hanging it on the rack by the door. "Is everything going all right?" She was wearing a baby blue sweater that accented the uplift of her breasts, and blue jeans that clung like a coating of cloth paint. As he helped her out of her coat, Jon brushed against those breasts ever so slightly and not entirely accidentally, but Shelly only smiled and gave him a warm look.

"Nolan's been working awful hard," Jon told her. "So I guess things are going fine."

Grossman walked over by the poker table, gave Nolan a half-nod, and stared into the burning fireplace. The girl walked over next to him, then turned toward Nolan and said, "How are you, Nolan?"

"Preoccupied. Sit down, will you? Everybody?"

Jon joined Grossman and Shelly and they all found places around the big table.

"Anybody else want beers?" Jon asked.

Grossman's grunt was affirmative and Shelly said, "I'd like that, Jon."

"Better bring the pretzels, too, kid." Was that sarcasm in Nolan's voice, Jon wondered, or just his own paranoid imagination at work?

Two minutes later Jon came back with the extra beers and the box of pretzels and sat down. Nolan spoke again.

"Okay," he said, "we got a lot to talk about. Before I say anything about the plan I'm working on, there's some incidentals to get out of the way."

Grossman gulped down a third of his beer in one multiple swallow, then wiped his mouth with his hand and said, "Such as?"

"Might as well start with you, Grossman."

"So now I'm an incidental?"

Nolan got his cigarettes out from his breast pocket, shook one free, and lit it, tossing the pack on the table for anybody else who might want one. "Jon told me you did some dealing in Iowa City. That so?"

"Yeah, big deal. You a narc all of a sudden or something?"

"What d'you push?"

"Just a little pot. Nothing hard. And I never got busted, if that's your next question."

"Smoke it yourself?"

"Do I smoke dope, you mean?"

"That's what I mean."

"Yeah, I smoke it. And I like it. So what?"

"So don't smoke it anymore. Not till you're out of my life."

"Why the fuck not? You think the noxious weed's going to turn my brain to cottage cheese or something? And you who supposedly been around."

"Christ you're stupid! What do you think it would do to this operation if you were to get busted for possession tomorrow?"

"I won't get busted."

"That's right. Because you'll be clean. If you got any stuff stashed in your apartment in Davenport, flush it down the stool when you get home tonight. I'm not shitting you, Grossman. After tonight, if I find one joint on you, I break you in half."

Grossman started to get up. "I don't have to take this kind of crap off you, old man. Come on, Shelly."

"Gross," Shelly said, "This is our last chance to maybe get *free.* Isn't that worth taking a little crap over?"

Grossman shrugged and said, "I guess you're right, babe." He sat back down, looked at Nolan. "I just gave up dope, okay, old man?"

"Good," Nolan said. "Now, something else. Have you been seeing Shelly in Port City, Grossman?"

"Some," he said.

"How much?"

"Some, I said."

"Once a week?"

"More."

"Daily?"

Grossman shrugged again, finally nodded.

"Do you mind explaining to me," Nolan said, "how the hell you expect anyone to believe that a girl could be taken hostage during a robbery by a guy she's been shacked up with for two months?"

Grossman reddened and Shelly, sitting between Jon and Grossman, leaned over toward Nolan and touched his hand. "Nolan," she said, "Gross has been very careful. If we go out, he takes me to Davenport for the evening, or Iowa City. Otherwise, he'll come up and spend time with me, alone, in my apartment. The girls at work know I have a boyfriend, but none of them have ever seen him."

"I take it you're living alone, Shelly?" Nolan said.

"Yes."

"Where's your apartment?"

"Above the Old Town Mill."

"What's that?"

"A restaurant. A bar."

"Downtown?"

"Sort of."

"Then somebody's sure to have seen you two together, as much as you see each other, with the apartment downtown and over a bar."

Grossman sat and thought about that.

Nolan continued. "You people have got to start *thinking*. There is a thing, a little thing, called common sense. It's too late to do anything about you and Shelly being seen together, Grossman, except work on an appearance change for you; and, of course, you'll stop seeing her."

"What do you mean?" Grossman slapped the table. "You're out of your fucking mind."

"You won't see her, except at these prearranged meetings. Starting today you're a priest."

"Look, Nolan, how about I just be careful, okay?"

"How about you just abstain."

Jon said, "It's only for a week or so, Gross."

Nolan said, "Shelly, I've got something for you to do, too, that'll put you to some trouble."

"Yes?"

"Today is Saturday. A week from today I want you to take a bus up to Davenport and get fitted for a short black wig. Be sure it's a good, expensive one. In the meantime, at work next week, tell your girlfriends at the bank that you're going to get your hair cut and styled, getting it cut short. On the following Monday, the day of the robbery, you'll wear the wig to work and tell everybody, well, your hair's cut, and how do they like it?"

Grossman said, "What's the point of that?"

"We have to be able to make a radical change in appearance after the hit if we expect to get away with it. After the robbery, our 'hostage' will slip off her wig and still have all her long hair, but dyed blonde. The FBI and cops will be on the lookout for a girl with short black hair."

"It sounds good to me," Shelly said, "but a wig can slip

when you're wearing it, and sometimes you have to adjust it. Besides, there's no guarantee a wig will fool everybody. Somebody at work is bound to notice it."

"That's okay," Nolan said. "It'll most likely be a girlfriend of yours who spots the wig, right? Well, you just take her into your confidence and tell her that when you got your hair cut the guy did a bad job, really butchered it, so you decided to buy this wig and wear it till your hair grows out again."

The girl nodded. "It's good. It's very good."

"I heard you and my uncle talking," Jon said, "about these appearance changes. Gross and I'll be having them, too?"

"Right," Nolan said. "In my case it'll be powdering my hair and mustache whiter. After the robbery I'll wash the powder out of my hair and shave off my mustache."

"When are you going to have the time to be doing any shaving?" Grossman asked impatiently. "You've been talking about a quick getaway."

"It's simple," Nolan said. "Standard operating procedure after a heist is usually one of two things. First, take off immediately and don't stop running till you get where you're going. Or second, hole up for a couple weeks some place nearby and wait till the heat's off, then go. We'll do neither. What we will do is get away from the bank as quick as possible and come here, taking an hour or so to make our changes. With our physical makeup different, and splitting up, we'll have no trouble with roadblocks or cops. With an hour gone, some of that initial heat'll be off. They'll assume we're either long gone or holed up."

"That makes sense," Grossman said, "but what's all this 'appearance change' bullshit?"

"Now personally I don't give a damn about anybody's looks," Nolan said. "This is only to help insure you get cash to spend, not time in jail."

Jon broke the ice for Nolan. "I heard you saying something to Planner about hair."

Grossman lurched forward. "Hair!"

"Hair," Nolan said.

"Let's get serious, old man."

"My sentiments exactly."

"I suppose I'm to cut it off?"

"That's right."

"Jesus fucking Christ!" Grossman pounded the table with both fists. "This is the only goddamn robbery I ever heard of with a fucking dress code!"

"Settle down," Nolan said. "I couldn't care less about your hair, a pony tail or a butch, it's all the same to me."

Grossman was still upset. "I don't get this. I don't get this at all."

"It's part of the plan I'm working on," Nolan said. "You cut it the night before the job."

"What the fuck for?"

"We'll get to that."

Jon was working on his beer, which was getting warm, and trying to ignore Shelly's leg, which was resting against his. He told himself she wasn't doing it on purpose, and her cool features weren't aimed his way, that was for sure; she was just sitting there innocently munching pretzels and listening. But when she did them, even listening and eating were sexy. Jon found himself almost wishing her leg was nestled against his because she wanted it there, but Nolan was talking again, and Jon had to make himself forget about that soft, warm thigh.

"Shelly," Nolan was saying, "have the bank examiners come around since you started working at Port City Savings and Loan?"

"Hey, old man, what are you getting at?"

"Quiet, Grossman. Shelly?"

"Bank examiners? Yes, as a matter of fact, they've come twice. Once each month."

"Once each month? Are you sure?"

"I'm sure."

"This could completely wipe out all my preliminary plans. Shit. I don't understand it, examiners usually make the rounds *once* in a nine month period. Why so often, Shelly? Do you know why the examiners have come twice in two months?"

"I think it's because of the changeover."

"The what?"

"The changeover. I think it's because of the changeover."

"What changeover?"

Jon couldn't believe it: Nolan was actually shook!

"The changeover," Shelly said, "from state to federal bank."

"Christ," Nolan said.

"Christ good or Christ bad, Nolan?" Jon asked. "What's the hassle, old man?"

"Hassle?" Nolan said. He smiled.

Jon felt butterfly-stomached; he'd never seen Nolan smile like that, it was a strange smile that Jon didn't know the meaning of.

"No hassle," Nolan said. "More like miracle."

Shelly was wide-eyed and wondering. "What's going on, Nolan? What's the big deal about changing over from state bank to federal?"

"Nothing," Nolan said, "except it's maybe our free pass to three quarters of a million dollars."

6

"Good job, Irish," Nolan said.

The small redheaded man leaned against the hood of the station wagon, a late-model Country Squire that looked strangely out of place in the midst of the jukebox-scattered cement floor. "He's an artist, this friend of mine," Irish said. "You'd never guess that wasn't a factory paint job, would you, Nolan? It was brown and white before it was light and dark green."

"It's good. How much do I owe you?"

"One and a half," Irish said.

Nolan reached in his pocket for a roll of bills and peeled off a pair of thousands. "Keep the extra for your trouble."

"No, Nolan, that isn't necessary . . ."

"Don't argue with me, you wetback bastard."

Irish grinned, ran a hand through his clump of red hair, put the money in his pocket. "Who's arguing, gringo?"

They shook hands and Nolan climbed into the driver's seat. Irish walked over and swung the triple-size garage door up and Nolan wheeled the car out into the alley. When Nolan had the station wagon outside the warehouse, waiting at the mouth of the alley to drive out onto the street, he rolled down the window next to him and yelled, "Irish! Thanks."

Irish came over to the open window and said, "Whatever it is that is happening for you now, my friend, good luck and God speed."

"You can have the God," Nolan said. "I'll settle for the luck."

Nolan guided the station wagon out of the alley and up the street, going a block and a half and pulling into a hardware store parking lot where Jon was waiting in his Chevy II. Nolan got out and went over to the Chevy and joined him in the front seat.

"That didn't take long," Jon said.

"Couldn't afford to let it take long," Nolan said. "Guy that runs that place is a friend. He could get stepped on if certain parties knew he was helping me."

"I thought this . . . what is it? Family? I thought this Family knew about what you're doing?"

"No. Just two people in the Family know, nobody else. If some other joker in the organization should spot me and decide to take things into his own hands, he could really screw us up."

"What would those other two guys in the Family think if something happened to you like that?"

"They wouldn't lose sleep."

"Oh." Jon cleared his throat. "Well. That sure looks like a nice car."

"Yeah. You'll like it, kid. It's got a secret compartment and everything. Just like in the comics."

"The Batmobile."

"Huh?"

"Nothing. You going back to the farmhouse now, Nolan? Going to follow me there in the station wagon or what?"

"No, I think I'll stay here in Davenport for a few hours and check up on our friend Grossman. See if our little talk last night sank in."

"I really don't think you need to, Nolan."

"I really think I do. Can you lead me to that head shop you were telling me about?"

Jon shrugged. "Suppose so."

Nolan returned to the Country Squire and followed Jon out of the lot. The little Chevy continued straight ahead on the same street, which a block later began a sudden angling upward, rapidly turning into a steep hill. Another four blocks up the hill, the Chevy II turned left and continued three more blocks, finally pulling into an open spot across the way from a one-story sagging building.

The building was covered in yellow pasteboard brick, and the front window had a stained-glass sign in it saying INNER LIGHTS. Painted on the window in black block letters were the words BOOKS, RECORDS, PARA-PHERNALIA. The head shop was one of the lesser struc-tures in what was obviously a low-income neighborhood, and the only commercial building in sight, though Nolan had noticed a grocery store and an upholstery shop the block before.

Nolan pulled in behind Jon and waited while the boy got out and came over to his window.

"That's it, Nolan. But I don't think you'll find anybody there today, let alone Grossman."

"Where's his apartment?"

"Three doors down, on the right."

"That white double-story with the busted porch swing?"

"That's the one, the real crummy-looking one. Top floor, number two."

"Okay. You go on back to the farmhouse and watch television or something. I'll be back later tonight."

"Okay."

Nolan sat back and waited for Jon to drive away. He lit a cigarette.

Today was Sunday, but it hadn't been much of a day of rest for Nolan and Jon, even though they had slept till noon. After a Sunday spread of frozen chicken dinners and Schlitz, Nolan had taken Jon out behind the farmhouse and let him take potshots at a tree with one of the Smith and Wesson .38s, to get him familiar with a handgun and create a few sounds to satisfy anybody who might wonder why the father and son duck-hunting team wasn't making any noise. Then Nolan took Jon inside and made him study the map of townships that fell between the farmhouse and the Illinois half of the Quad Cities. Nolan had gotten the map at the Port City Farm Extension office the same day he'd gone to see the real estate agent about the farmhouse, and it included all the county and country roads in the area, which a regular roadmap would lack. Even each and every farm between there and the Quad Cities was marked, including the one they were on. When the boy appeared to have memorized the entire route Nolan had drawn on the map, Nolan took him out to the car and let him have a try at driving the newly memorized route, for practice. Besides, Nolan was due at Irish's warehouse in Davenport at six to pick up the station wagon.

"Why are we going to the Quad Cities?" Jon had asked.

"To pick up the station wagon."

"No, I mean, why are we going there after the robbery? I figure that's what you're going to have us do, if you want me to memorize a route there."

"Once we've headed into Illinois, no one will expect us to cross back into Iowa, which is what we'll do at the Quad

Cities. Nobody'll be looking for us in Iowa. Not hard, anyway. You'll drop me off at a place in Davenport, then you'll take Interstate 80 home to Iowa City. Planner will help you with the money."

On the trip up Nolan and Jon didn't speak much, because Nolan was still very occupied with working out details and Jon was struggling with his memory to decipher the maze of country roads. Nolan knew Jon was wondering about the plan, which hadn't been completely revealed to any of the three, a fact which had pissed off Grossman the night before. But then, what didn't piss Grossman off?

As they entered the Cities, it had occurred to Nolan to ask Jon where exactly Grossman was staying in Davenport, and the answer surprised him.

"Up by the head shop," Jon had told him.

"The what?"

"The head shop. It's up on the hill, in sort of a black section. Couple of colleges are up there close by, and a lot of the college kids, the freaky ones especially, go over there and hang around."

"You said head shop? Like in dope?"

"Yeah, they been busted a few times, but all that was before Gross moved in. The guys who run the place got picked up for possession, too, but the charges were dropped. This was months ago. It was in the papers."

"Christ. What does that goddamn Grossman use for brains."

"He won't be hanging around there anymore, Nolan, not after the lecture you laid on him last night."

Nolan got out of the station wagon and crossed the street, which was almost devoid of traffic, a mere two cars passing by during his five-minute think in the car. The neighborhood was nearly soundless, too, except for the squealings of a handful of little black kids playing with a beat-up three-wheeled red wagon on the sidewalk, and the muffled blaring of a TV set down the block a house or two.

Nolan walked behind the bookstore and found a storm door, locked, and behind its glass windows was a wood door with a "No Nukes" bumper sticker on it at a slant.

He knocked.

He knocked some more.

The wood door eased part-way open and half a face with one heavy-lidded eye stared through the glass at Nolan. "Who are you, man?" His voice coming from behind the glass had a sort of underwater sound.

"Friend of Gross."

"You look a little straight for that."

"Maybe I'm his parole officer."

"Gross is kind of busy right now."

"Let me in and I'll wait. I'll find something to do. I could buy a book or something." Nolan got out a twenty and held it up for the guy to see.

"Well. Okay, man, I guess you can come in."

"Thanks."

"But you stay in the doorway, till I get Gross roused up so he can take a look at you and see if he knows you or not."

The guy let Nolan in. He was no kid, thirty if a day, short, pock-marked, greasy shoulder-length hair thinning on top. His tee-shirt commemorated the 10th anniversary of Woodstock.

The room was dark. The air hung with the smell of pot. Nolan put the twenty back in his pocket; he unbuttoned his coat. Somebody pulled the string on the overhead hanging light and Nolan took in the whole room in a glance. Half a dozen young bodies were squeezed into the cubby hole, sitting, crouching, reclining on the blanket-spread floor. A couple of rock group posters peeked out from behind boxes lining the walls.

"You know this guy, Gross?" the aging, balding hippie asked.

Before an answer came from Grossman, who wasn't yet in sight, Nolan opened his coat and let everybody look at the .38 bolstered under his left arm.

There were no screams or outbursts, not even an "Oh, shit!" Mainly just a caught-with-their-pants-down-and-don't-give-a-damn look on all the faces. Nolan couldn't help but let out a short laugh: either they were so stoned they didn't care about being busted, or they were just good and used to it.

The balding guy said, to the others in the room, "He didn't have a warrant, so don't sweat it." To Nolan he said: "If this is a rip, you might as well know we got nothing harder than pot here, and not much of that."

Nolan said nothing, glancing around, looking for Grossman.

Four guys in tee-shirts and jeans were sharing two joints and a like number of girls, one of whom had bleached blonde hair and a "Save the Whales" tee-shirt, the other a dark-haired girl wearing an old black sportcoat and a striped tee-shirt. Not bad-looking girls, but sort of skinny and not particularly clean, looking a bit tired from being passed around like another joint.

Finally Grossman stood up in the corner, where he'd been obscured by two stacks of book boxes. A third girl appeared with him, a black girl with dreadlocks and Bo Derek breasts distorting the face of Bob Marley on her sweatshirt.

"He's no pig," Grossman said, his face a mix of insolence and fear, "at least not the cop kind. Are you, old man? Of course he does steal things, but I don't think pot interests him."

"You people can go on with what you're doing," Nolan said. "Just don't get so high you're letting anybody in who asks."

A boy with a yellow caterpillar for a mustache looked up from the floor and said, "If you're looking to score some coke, I can help."

"Shut-up," said the over-age kid who'd let Nolan in, obviously not anxious to discuss a dope deal with somebody who might be there to rip them off. "Grossman, I don't know who this guy is, but I for sure don't want him in here. Or you either."

Nolan said, "Coming, Grossman?"

"Okay, old man, okay, I'm coming." He turned to the black girl and said, "See you, Naomi."

She shrugged.

Grossman came over and Nolan took him by the arm, reaching over and tugging the string on the hanging bulb, then walked out.

Nolan guided the boy away from the door and pushed him up against the side of the building.

"Grossman," Nolan said.

Grossman said, "What's the idea of cutting my runtime, old man? Don't I get Sundays off?"

"Shut up."

"Look, you won't let me see Shelly, what the hell you expect me to do with my time?"

"Try jacking off," Nolan said. "You can't get busted for that."

"You never know in Iowa," Grossman said, letting out a giggle that let Nolan know he was at least a little high. "And aw shit, man, don't you know I'm going nuts by myself up here without my old lady, what d'you expect out of me? Don't you think I'd rather be with Shelly than some fuckin', tokin' black chick?" He laughed at his own joke. "But *you* wouldn't understand about that, 'cause you're so goddamn *old*."

Nolan shoved him against the building with the heel of his hand and held him there.

"Now listen to me, clown," he said. "You been pushing my patience and I'm not patient to begin with. I told you yesterday what I'd do if I caught you doing dope, and I see you didn't take me too seriously."

"Hey, old man, tell you what, how about you eat me?"

Nolan sighed, shook his head. This kid just didn't seem to get it, but what the hell, a person had to try. He swung a sharp left into Grossman's stomach and the air emptied out

of the boy like water from a gushing hydrant; he slid down
from under Nolan's hand and sat on the ground.

"What you do that for?" Grossman said after a while, rubbing his stomach like a child with too many green apples
under his belt.

Nolan kicked him in the side and said, "Same reason I
did that."

"Goddamn you!"

"Logic fails with you, Grossman. What choice do you
leave me? There's more than just money riding on this job,
Grossman, it's not a goddamn game. Now get up."

He held his hand out for Grossman to take and pulled the
boy to his feet. Just as Grossman seemed to regain his balance, he clutched Nolan's arm and yelled, "Shit, look out!"

Two hands from behind Nolan latched onto his shoulders
and spun him to the ground. A sharp kick dug into the sore-
ness of his side and he saw some flashes of light and sank
into darkness for a while.

When his eyes opened, Nolan found himself leaned
against the side of the building with Grossman next to him.
The figure in front of him came gradually into focus, and even
then he couldn't remember who it was, who it was behind the
familiar face. Then a moment later he finally knew.

The watchdog from Werner's. The bored son of a bitch
who couldn't stay knocked out.

Calder.

He was trying to get a grip on what in the hell was going
on when Calder said, "Hello, Nolan," and kicked him in the
side again. The flashes of light returned, and the darkness.

7

Calder kept his .38 trained on the longhaired kid, but swung
his gun now and then over toward Nolan, who was still out.

Calder caught himself rubbing his left temple with his free hand; stroking the bruised area of his face had gotten to be a nervous habit with him these past several days. And now he felt a pat satisfaction in having the party responsible on the downhill end of a .38.

Calder waited for Nolan's eyes to open and said, "I'll take your gun."

Nolan handed it over.

"Who's your rock star friend, Nolan?" he said, jerking a thumb at the kid.

"Who says my name's Nolan?"

"It's Nolan. What's your name, rock star?"

The kid glanced at Nolan and got a shrug of permission. He screwed his face around sullenly and muttered, "Grossman."

"Okay, Grossman. You and your buddy Nolan get your asses up off the ground and come with me. You're taking a little walk over to my car."

The kid named Grossman turned to Nolan and asked, "He taking us for one of those one-way rides like in the movies?"

Nolan said, "Everything this guy does is like in the movies."

"Clint Eastwood, huh?"

"More Charles Bronson, I'd say."

Calder laughed softly. "Spare me, boys," he said. "Get up and get going."

Nolan pushed to his feet and Grossman followed suit. Nolan looked at the boy and said, "Watch this guy, Grossman. Study and learn. Nothing can shake him. Everything bores him."

"I'm bored with you two, all right," Calder said. He chopped the air with the .38. "Move."

Calder waited until they had walked around front of him, then motioned them to the right. He marched them carefully down the block to his car, a late-model Dodge Charger, light blue.

"Nice wheels," Grossman said.

"Don't bother buttering him up," Nolan said. "He's bored, remember?"

"Shut up and get in back, Nolan," Calder said, "and leave the door open till I get in with you. The rock star drives."

Calder waited while Grossman opened the door and got in, then joined Nolan in back. He handed the keys up to Grossman, keeping the .38 on Nolan, and said, "You know where the Maricaibo Supper Club is, kid? On the Illinois side?"

Grossman nodded. "Yeah, in Milan. Over by the Showcase Cinema."

"Head that way. Take the Centennial Bridge."

"Okay."

"And don't get cute or it's over for the funny man here. Remember, it's just him and me and my gun in the backseat behind you."

Grossman turned the key in the ignition and pulled away from the curb.

Calder said, "Keep it at twenty."

"Okay."

Calder sat with his back to the window, his right leg tucked under his left. He reached his free hand into his suit-coat pocket for a cigarette, keeping the gun leveled at Nolan. "All of a sudden you don't talk much," he said.

Nolan shrugged.

"You're going to do big things for me, Nolan, you know that?"

"Am I?"

"Yes. Some people in the Family are very interested in you."

"Oh?"

"That's right, and I wouldn't be expecting your old chum Werner to bail you out, this time."

Nolan leaned back against his window and kept silent.

Calder's soft smile stayed with him while he lit his cigarette and sucked in some smoke. Finally, he thought. Finally playing nursemaid to that pussy Werner was paying off.

The morning after his painful run-in with "prowler" Nolan, Calder had become very confused. When he'd reported the broken window to Werner, saying a neighborhood punk had tossed a rock through it, Werner had been uncharacteristically good-natured about it. And no mention of anything being disturbed in the house.

That wasn't like Werner and it confused Calder.

Because Werner's usual reaction would have been bitch bitch bitch. He was such a fucking pussy, anyway, always afraid somebody was after him, always bitching to Calder to make sure nobody got near the house.

Such a big man, Werner. Big talk, big deal. That college education cool of his, all his talk about the Family being a corporation, now; big business. Big bullshit.

The old boys who had built the Family's foundation did it with force, with violence; but those guys were almost all gone, now, replaced by the corporate types, the Werners. There was merit in both approaches, Calder admitted; but it seemed to him the next ruling faction in the Family might well be made up of men like himself, men who knew how to use both violence *and* intelligence to the best advantage.

When Werner had reacted to the broken window by brushing the incident aside, he'd set Calder to thinking. Calder came up with the theory that the guy who'd broken in was a friend of Werner's, a friend Werner didn't want anybody to know about.

The pussy was putting something over on the Family.

Calder had called his friend Nick in Jersey City and told him about what happened, and asked if he knew of anybody Werner might want to see without having the Family know.

"Werner?" Nick had said. "I doubt he'd be pulling anything. He's been around and's been considered an up-and-comer for some while. Talk is that any time now he'll be voted onto the executive council."

"All the more reason," Calder said, "for him to be careful when he sees somebody the Family wouldn't want him to see."

"True," Nick said, "but your starting point's still doubtful. Look, Calder, you're an ambitious boy, and a real thinker, but your best bet is to hang in there with Werner, get in good with him and maybe when he gets moved up, so'll you."

"Werner doesn't like me *because* I think. He's been trying to hold me down ever since I been with him. But if I could get something on him, it'd help."

"Better be careful, Calder, Werner's one of the fair-haired boys right now."

"If he's crossing the Family he won't be anybody's fair-haired anything for long."

"Well . . . what did this guy that broke in look like?"

"Six-one, or maybe only six. Dark, shaggy hair, with some gray in it, around the sideburns. Mustache. High cheekbones. Narrow eyes. Good shoulders on him, hell of a wallop for a guy his age."

"How old would you say?"

"Oh, fifty."

"Could be Nolan."

"Who?"

"Nolan. He and Werner were friends back in Chicago. The guy in the Chicago operation, this Charlie guy, is supposed to hate Nolan's guts."

"How come?"

"Charlie's brother, a guy named Gordon, a real fuck-up if there ever was one, he used to run part of the Chicago operation for Charlie. This Gordon wanted to move Nolan into the enforcer type of work, bodyguard stuff and whacking guys, too."

"What was this Nolan doing at the time?"

"He managed a nightclub. One of the Family clubs."

"Since when is a club manager tough enough to shift over into the strongarm stuff?"

"When the club is on Rush Street and he does his own bouncing. And when because of that ritzy bastards feel safe enough to come in among the seamy crowd and spread some bread around."

"He was good, I take it."

"The best."

"Well, what happened, Nick?"

"This Gordon told Nolan to kill a guy, some guy who worked in the club. Nolan didn't want nothing to do with it. He knew this guy and liked him, and besides, he was happy doing what he was doing, just managing the club. When Nolan said no, Gordon had Nolan roughed up, and the guy Nolan wouldn't whack was whacked by somebody else. The next night Nolan shot Gordon, cut out with twenty grand from the till."

"That must mean Nolan's right up there on the Family's list of open contracts."

"Well, not really, the heat's off Nolan pretty much, except with Charlie. To tell you the truth, most of the sentiment on the Family council at the time was good riddance to Gordon. And remember, it's been a long time since this happened, too, twenty years or so."

"Twenty years?"

"Fifteen maybe. More than fifteen, I think."

"You figure maybe it was Nolan who went to see Werner the other night, Nick?"

"I don't know . . . I heard . . . you keep this in strict confidence?"

"Sure, Nick."

"There's a guy that works for Werner, they call him Irish, I think . . ."

"Yeah. Herman Cavazos."

"Anyway, this guy Irish is supposed to be a friend of Nolan's. Nolan's reportedly turned into a heist artist of the first order since he split with the Family."

"How's that tie in with Cavazos?"

"Well, a friend of my brother's worked with Nolan once, and according to my brother, this Irish guy was mechanic on the job. Under the hat, okay?"

"Sure, Nick."

After that Calder spent his off hours parked near

Cavazos' warehouse, watching for Nolan. Thursday, Friday, and Saturday went by, and today, on Sunday, just when Calder was chewing himself out for wasting so much time and weighing whether or not to go in and put the squeeze on Cavazos, Nolan showed. Calder had waited till Nolan left the warehouse, not wanting to involve any of Werner's other employees if possible, and had followed him to the head shop on the hill.

In the front seat the kid said, "Who's got fifteen cents for the bridge?"

Calder dug in his pocket and tossed a dime and a nickel up to Grossman and sat back as the car eased onto the Centennial bridge.

"As you're coming down off the bridge," Calder said, as the boy slowed to toss the change into the toll basket, "there's a cut-off to a fourlane, on your right. Take it."

"What do you figure to do?" Nolan asked.

"Oh, I'll give Werner a chance to explain you."

"What?"

"I suppose I could take you to Chicago myself and deliver you to Charlie, and probably pick up some points along the way, not to mention some heavy bread. But Charlie? Charlie's on the down ride, Werner's going up. So I'll give Werner a chance to make it right by me."

"How?"

Grossman cocked his head around. "This the turn-off?"

"Yeah, kid, and don't get over thirty-five."

Nolan repeated, "Make it right, how?"

"Like I said, Werner'll be moving up, and a good man'll be needed to take over the Quad Cities operation."

"You."

"Me. Of course I'll have to keep you on ice for a while, Nolan. Wouldn't do to have you and Werner pull a little cross or anything."

"Then what?"

"Well, I'm afraid once you've served your purpose, you'll be nothing but an embarrassment to the Family, and a threat to me. Let's just say I wouldn't go planning anything for next year."

"Werner said something about you once," Nolan said, "and I guess maybe he was right."

"Oh?"

"He said you think too much."

Calder laughed. "And fucking pussies like you and Werner don't think at all."

Nolan smiled.

Calder didn't like the smile; it was disquieting, more a line than a smile, a line turning up ever so slightly at its corners.

Nolan said, "Goose it, kid."

Grossman nodded.

There was a thud as the boy punched the accelerator to the floor. The car lurched forward as the motor kicked in, and the speedometer climbed to ninety-five before Calder could get his mouth working.

"What the fuck are you doing?"

Grossman said nothing, kept the pedal to the floor. Nolan still wore the disquieting smile.

"I said what the fuck do you think you're doing?"

Neither Nolan nor Grossman spoke.

Calder grabbed a fistful of Nolan's shirt and jammed the .38 barrel to his forehead. "I'll kill him, kid!"

There was no sound other than the throb of the engine and Calder's own hard breathing.

"I'll kill him! I will, honest to Christ, kid! I'll splatter him all over the backseat if you don't slow back down!"

Grossman said, "Go ahead. I don't like him much. Do I, old man?"

"That's right," Nolan said. "We don't get along. Couldn't you see I was knocking him around when you grabbed us?"

"Goddamn it, I'm not playing with you, Nolan! I'll kill you!"

"Nothing I can do about it. Grossman doesn't like me. He doesn't give a damn if you kill me. Simple as that."

Calder's eyes went to the speedometer; the needle was

quivering near one hundred and ten.

"You let me do some work on this crate, mister," Grossman said, "and she'll *really* fly."

"I think the kid's doing a pretty fair job of driving," Nolan said, "considering he was high as a kite when I dragged him out of that head shop."

Calder abandoned Nolan and shoved the .38 barrel against the back of Grossman's neck. "Goddamnit, then, I'll shoot *you*, smart-ass!"

"I don't think you'd want to do that," Grossman said. "Going as fast as this? Shoot me and the car'll rack up bad. Ever see a car hit at this speed? Totals 'em every time. Face it, it's going to kill you, too. Shit, you don't even have your seat belt on."

"Goddamn it!"

"He's right, you know," Nolan said.

"He'll kill all of us!"

"He's a wild kid, I'll grant you that."

"*Goddamnit!*"

"How you doing, kid?"

"Fine, old man," Grossman said. "Take a look at that speedometer. Needle's buried now. Only reads to one-twenty, but we're doing better than that."

"I'd guess one-thirty," Nolan said.

Calder gripped the left side of his face with his free hand; his fingers ran up and down the bruise. "Goddamn it, *stop this car!* How can you be so goddamn calm!"

"He wants to know why we're calm," Grossman said.

"Why don't you hand me the gun," Nolan said, "then maybe I could talk Grossman into slowing down."

"No! Slow down or I'll shoot!"

"You aren't shooting anybody. Hand me the gun."

The car was vibrating, and Calder had a sudden vision of it as a mass of nuts and bolts just waiting to fly apart.

"All right!" he said. "All right." He handed the gun to Nolan, who reached over and retrieved his own .38 from Calder's belt.

"Slow down, Grossman," Nolan said.

"Okay, old man. Stop sign up ahead, anyway."

Grossman pumped the brakes and with a screeching slide the car came to a halt a few feet beyond the stop sign and the flashing yellow light beside it, a stream of traffic racing by inches away. "Where to?" he asked.

Nolan scratched his head. "Pay phone around here?"

"Yeah," Grossman said, "there's one in the Cinema parking lot. Couple blocks from here.

"Okay. I got a call to make."

Calder shut his eyes. He didn't feel good. He wanted to get his heart down out of his throat.

The car pulled into the mammoth theater lot, which was three-quarters full, stopping at the phone stall that was at its farthest and most deserted side. Nolan left the car and made his call.

Calder sat and worked at slowing his breath, stroking the left side of his face with his fingertips.

Five minutes later a gold Lincoln Continental with a black vinyl top and lettering on the side saying "Club Maricaibo" drew up next to Calder's Charger. Werner stepped out.

Nolan walked over to him. They shook hands. Nolan said, "Your boy's in the backseat."

"Okay," Werner said. "I'll handle it. You and your young friend can take my Lincoln back over to Davenport and pick up your own car. Have him drop the Lincoln off at the Concort some time tomorrow."

"Fine," Nolan said. "See you, Werner. Grossman, let's go."

Nolan and Grossman got into the Lincoln and glided away.

Werner stood outside by the window and Calder stayed in the backseat and three more minutes passed. Calder looked up and saw another car arrive, a recent-model black Ford. The door sprang open and a big black guy crawled out and ambled over to Werner.

"Tillis," Werner said, "there's a pile of garbage in the backseat of that car there. Do something about it."

The black guy yanked the door open and pulled Calder out by the arm and dragged him toward the Ford.

Just before he was pushed into the front seat of the car, Calder looked over at Werner and said, "You're still a fucking pussy."

8

Nolan crouched down by the fireplace and prodded the burning logs, studying the flames.

Jon walked in from the kitchen, shirtless, sipping a can of beer. "It's past midnight, Nolan. You going to bed pretty soon? You know what tomorrow is."

"Tomorrow's today, kid."

"Huh?"

"It's past midnight, you said. So it's Monday now."

Jon came over by where Nolan was kneeling and the reflection of flames ran up and down the boy's face. He looked very young in his new short hair, freshly cut this afternoon, the curly hair tight against his head. Nolan only hoped that now the boy wouldn't look too young.

"Butterflies, Jon?"

"Guess so."

"Go to bed."

"You know, it's just a few hours away, isn't it, Nolan? I never saw a week go so fast. Just a few hours and we'll be . . ."

"Yeah. Go to bed." Nolan stood, took the boy by the shoulders, and turned him toward the bedroom. "It'll take you a while to get to sleep, so get started."

"Good night, Nolan." The boy headed for the doorway, got half-way and looked back at Nolan. He said, "Hey, thanks for not getting pissed off about that, you know, that deal with Shelly."

"It's okay. Night."

"Night."

"Uh, Jon."

"Yeah, Nolan?"

"I might go out for a drive later. So don't worry about it if you wake up and I'm not around."

"Oh. Okay."

He disappeared into the bedroom and Nolan turned back to the fire.

Jon was right about the week going fast; a fast full week had passed since the encounter with Calder, and tonight, Sunday night again, had been Nolan's last meeting with his little task force before the Monday afternoon job.

Nolan lit a cigarette, inhaled deep, and sank into his thoughts.

Over all, things had shaped up, and not too badly.

On Monday he'd gone ahead and explained the plan in detail to each of them, making Jon, Grossman, and Shelly memorize not only every aspect of their own roles, but everyone else's, as well. They had a lot of questions, and that pleased Nolan, and all kinds of angles were explored in what turned out to be a five-and-a-half-hour discussion.

He'd done further target shooting with Jon on Tuesday, and with Grossman, too, who hadn't really needed it. Surprisingly enough, it turned out that Grossman's stepfather, his mother's third husband, had been a sheriff out in some small Eastern town, and Grossman had grown up with a pistol range in his basement, which also had been the basement of the county jail. When the target shooting was over, Nolan filled in Jon and Grossman on the rules of the use of firearms on a job.

"Never shoot on the job," Nolan said, "unless fired upon. Don't shoot in reaction to a sudden movement, or even a sudden sound. Drop to the floor in such a case, and find out what's going on. If you must shoot, shoot into a glass window and cause some confusion. And if it's absolutely necessary to *return* fire, aim for an arm or leg."

"Hey, old man," Grossman said, "what about the big talk you fed us that time about all the notches on your gun?"

"Guys I shot and killed," Nolan said, "were mostly guys on the job with me. Guys who crossed me."

Grossman said, "Oh," and got thoughtful for a while.

For the most part, Nolan was pleased with the way Grossman had come along, though he still had many of his initial doubts about him. But Grossman's outbursts of stupidity seemed on the wane, in addition to his working hard on the preparation of the job—not to mention the way he'd come through under stress in the crisis with Calder a week ago, where his handling of himself and the car was strictly pro.

On Wednesday Nolan sent Jon to Iowa City to pick up the faked credentials at Planner's, and worked with Grossman in figuring out a good route for him and Shelly to take to Canada after the hit, which would include Nolan's doubleback to Iowa strategy; only Grossman was to cross over at Fort Madison, not the Quad Cities. After that sidetrack to the south, Grossman would head back north through Iowa. It had been decided and agreed upon by all that when the four split up, Jon and Nolan would take Grossman's and Shelly's share with them, since there probably wouldn't be time to divide the money properly and because it was unlikely that Grossman and Shelly could make it to Canada without a thorough car search by some official somewhere along the line. The money would be kept by Planner in his big downstairs safe, and Jon would drive up to Canada to meet Grossman and Shelly when sufficient cooling time had elapsed, using a satisfactory smuggling method to get the money to them safely.

On Thursday Nolan had taken Grossman over to Port City and had run him over the escape route from the bank to the bridge. They did it half a dozen times, by the end of which Grossman had it down to a minute and three seconds. And Nolan had made him take it easy at that, so they wouldn't attract attention. The actual time on the job would be well under a minute.

Grossman really was a hell of a driver, Nolan had to admit. In many ways that run-in with Calder had been a good thing, not only giving Nolan a chance to see Grossman function under fire, but giving Grossman an idea of the seriousness of this kind of work.

Friday Nolan drove Jon and Grossman down to Burlington to get fitted for the business suits. They went to Burlington because an appearance of that kind in Port City or even at Iowa City at this point was out of the question, and they'd already done far too much in the Quad Cities as it was. All three purchased similar suits, dark ones with vests, and Nolan made sure everybody got a tie just loud enough to attract people to it and not the wearer's face, but not so unconventional as to be suspicious. In the suits the trio looked like two junior execs and their boss. Grossman would be light years away from his counter-culture image in the suit and short haircut.

Since Sunday would be busy, Nolan let his young co-workers have a day of rest on Saturday, doing little himself outside of a drive to Geneseo, Illinois, which was picked only because it was fairly close and was safer than Port City, Iowa City, or any of the Quad Cities. At Geneseo Nolan took care of getting some odds and ends, including three briefcases, three pairs of expensive sunglasses, two laundry bags, and the necessary tools for the Sunday haircuts due Grossman and Jon, sharp-bladed scissors and thinning shears.

Off and on throughout the week, Grossman had worked over all three cars, the Country Squire, the Chevy II, and his own Mustang, making sure they were in topnotch running order.

Sunday evening Shelly had shown up wearing her "new hair," a very natural-looking black wig that could easily pass as her own cut short. When everyone had said a word to two about the wig, she yanked it off and revealed her own long hair pinned up underneath, now colored a pale platinum blonde, which she then undid and let fall around her shoulders.

"Looks very nice," Nolan told her. "Dye it this afternoon?"

"Last night," she said.

"With your blue eyes it looks natural. And you won't have to worry about roots showing, since you just dyed it. Ought to fool your own mother."

Shelly had done a good job, and her inside information proved every day to be more and more valuable. Nolan's whole plan, in fact, revolved around specific information she'd provided.

But there were still problems, and Shelly lurked behind them.

Several hours before the meeting, Jon had come to Nolan and said, "We just got to talk, Nolan."

"What is it, kid?"

"I fucked up, Nolan, I really fucked up bad."

"Go on."

"It's . . . it's Shelly."

"Oh?"

"Remember when we talked about her, and you said you thought she had hot pants, and I said I thought you were out of your mind?"

"I remember."

"Well . . . ever since you told Grossman not to see Shelly, and since you been having me drive over to Port City to pick her up for the meetings and then drive her back again, well . . ."

"Well, well what?"

"It's just that, uh, Shelly's been making these little plays for me. You know, little things."

"Like putting her hand in your lap."

Jon made a face, nodded.

"I said she'd be a problem, Jon."

"Grossman's going to blow up if he ever finds out what a flirty little bitch she is."

"Likely."

"Nolan."

"Yeah."

"There's more."

"I figured as much."

"The other night—last night, you know? When I said I wanted to go out for a beer by myself and think?"

"Yeah."

"I, uh, went over to Port City. It was a stupid thing, I know, but Shelly said if I should happen to be around Saturday night I could, uh, stop up, and, uh . . ."

"And you did, and lost your cherry."

Jon made another face, nodded again. "That sums it up pretty good, Nolan."

"Okay," Nolan said. "Stupid? Of course. But forget about it. Even Flash Gordon gets a hard-on once in a while. The job's tomorrow, we'll be splitting up, and that'll be it. The bitch'll be Grossman's problem again. We'll just hope nobody saw you."

"Oh nobody saw us, Nolan."

"Good. But Christ, kid, stick to your comic books next time. Like you said once, it's a safe habit."

Nolan poked the burning logs again. With everything going so well, he didn't want to let this little slip of Jon's throw him. Nothing to worry about.

Nothing.

Not with Jon, anyway.

But Shelly?

During the meeting tonight she'd made her move for Nolan, starting with the knowing looks, subtle ones, but there.

Then her leg, rubbing against his under the table.

And her hand, running along his leg, then his inner thigh.

And all the time, the meeting going along smoothly, the girl an innocent child to the uninformed eye, Nolan spelling out details of the plan with his practiced calm.

So now the meeting was over, and the job hours away.

Nolan got up from the fireside, grabbed his jacket and went out to the car and got in.

9

Shelly was dreaming that she was asleep inside the bank vault, resting on a bed stuffed with thousand dollar bills, but outside the vault someone was knocking, someone was knocking very insistently and trying to pry her awake.

She jumped into a sitting position, clutched the sheets to her throat.

Not a dream?

Not all of it anyway, someone *was* outside knocking, but who?

Couldn't be Grossman, he couldn't be sex-starved enough to have waited all this time only to break his chastity pact with one night left to go. Besides, she thought, the klutz seemed almost proud of holding out so long.

And surely not Jon, the poor kid had been so sheepish and guilt-ridden the other night after his "big adventure" with her, that was out of the question.

Should she be frightened? She shrugged to herself and got out of bed, switching on the lamp next to it. She threw her short terry-cloth robe around her naked body and went to the door. Hell, if it was a rapist out there it ought at least to shape up her sex life a little bit. And as urgent as the knocking sounded, the guy needed it bad.

"Who's out there?"

"Nolan."

She cracked the door and looked out over the chain on the night latch. It was Nolan, all right.

"What do you want? Kind of late for a last minute briefing, isn't it, chief?"

"You know what I want."

"Huh?"

"The moves under the table. That beats an engraved invitation all to hell."

"Well, I'd like to let you in . . ."

"Then do."

She shrugged again and undid the nightlatch and let him in. Once in he shut the door, threw the Yale lock and put the latch back in place.

"Okay," he said, "let's go to bed."

She smiled. "That's some line you got there, Nolan."

"Yes or no?"

She touched her lips. "Uh, I'll have to go into the bathroom for a minute, and, uh, freshen up."

"All right."

When she came back he was sitting on the bed, naked, smoking a cigarette. His body was light tan in color, and leanly muscular. There was an attractive ruggedness to him that the little scars and even the red, puckered place on his side added to rather than took away. The hair on his chest was black mingled with white.

"You're beautiful, Nolan," she said.

He put out his cigarette. "Take off the robe."

She let the terry robe drop to the floor and stepped out of it and joined him on the bed, leaning over to cut the light.

She felt his arms coil around her, the possessive strength of them pleasing to her, and when his mouth covered hers the kiss was hot and almost savage. He was strong and somewhat rough, but she liked it. She was so tired of boys, so very tired of little boys, and now a man, at last a man was taking her. In spite of the heat of the act, she sensed something cold, something methodical in his lovemaking that, oddly enough, only excited her more. It seemed that for hours those strong hands of his ran up and down her body, over her breasts, cupping her buttocks, coursing up and down over the inner flesh of her upper thighs. When at last she felt his fingers twining in her pubic hair and, finally, slipping in to probe her, she said, "Oh Nolan, God I'm ready, do it now, please do it now."

The whole thing was over in less than five minutes. She lay back exhausted as he climbed off, stretching her arms out crucifix-style, feeling both used and satisfied.

She stared at the ceiling for a while and when she looked over at him again he was dressed, and she didn't even have her breath back yet.

"Aren't you . . . aren't you going to stay with me tonight?" She knew with the job so close he couldn't, but she felt she should ask.

He put on his jacket and went to the door.

"Now that you laid all three of us," Nolan said, "maybe you can get your mind on the job."

The door slammed and she sat staring at it.

•

Three

1

Half a block down from the parked station wagon, on the opposite corner of the one-way street, was the bank, two tall stories of whitestone with three fat Grecian columns chiseled out of its face. Hanging out from it over the flow of traffic was an electric sign that alternated the time with the temperature on a field of black.

Nolan sat in front on the rider's side, Grossman next to him behind the wheel, Jon in back resting chin on folded hands on the seat between the two men.

Jon said, "How much longer?"

Nolan glanced out at the electric sign. Under the red letters proclaiming "Port City Savings and Trust" the little white dots on the black field were making a 40. He waited till the white dots disbanded and regrouped as 2:10 and said, "Ten more minutes."

"They closed at two," Grossman said.

"Give them time," Nolan said. "They got customers to move out."

Grossman nodded; so did Jon, who was chewing his thumbnail. They looked like a couple of young strangers to Nolan in their clean-cut hair and light-tinted sunglasses and business suits.

He dug out a cigarette and lit.

So far so good, he thought. Nobody's wet their pants yet.

Sandy Baird smoothed her white blonde hair and looked around her and realized that even though she'd lived in Port City *all* of her nineteen years and had been inside the bank, why, probably *trillions* of times, she'd never really *seen* it before.

When she'd come in at eight that morning, her first
morning, it was like she'd just walked in for the *very first time!*

Oh, a lot of it looked familiar, the bank officers off to the
right behind a steel railing, each at his individual desk and
work area; the savings and loan people over to the left with
the same set-up as the officers but a bigger working area;
and the squared-off section that took up the whole middle
of the room, with the tellers' windows on each side of it, one
side facing the officers, the other facing savings. The last
was the only thing that had really, you know *really* looked
different to Sandy. All of a sudden that squared-off area
where the tellers worked seemed like a barricade, you know,
a fort, like they were expecting *Indians* or something.

And when she got *behind* it, actually back inside the
"fort" (she would think of it as that, call it that from now on,
she just knew) she could have almost *fainted!* All those files
and typewriters on little stands and metal trays with official
bank sacks on them and partitions and adding machines and
she just *knew* she was going to foul up, she just knew it. And
one of the first things she'd heard when she got there that
morning (it was from Anita Welch, she was that girl who had
to get married her junior year) was, "Kid, you're out of luck.
Today's the first Monday of the month, and kid, you're in for
it. We all are!" Here she'd been so hoping her first day
would be a slow one, kind of an average easy-to-get-in-the-
swing-of-it day.

She sat on the stool and watched Elaine count her money
out ("Prove up," Elaine called it), but so far Elaine hadn't
shown her much of anything, really, hardly explained a
thing. Of course, the morning had been frantic, with businesses making their deposits from weekend trade, so Sandy
figured Elaine hadn't really had the *chance* to explain anything. Maybe it was her imagination, but she had the idea
that Elaine had something on her mind, a boyfriend maybe,
or maybe it was just her time of the month (and of course
she didn't know Elaine well enough to ask about something
as personal as *that*).

Sandy had hoped to get with Anita or one of the other girls she'd known in high school, or Sally, who used to work with her at Food Mart a couple of summers back. But Sandy didn't know this Elaine Simmons at all, didn't even know where she was from, certainly not Port City, unless she'd gone to the *Catholic* school or something, or she could've just moved here recently.

Sandy guessed this Elaine was nice enough, but she'd hardly said a word, only when Sandy made a *point* of asking.

"Say," Sandy said, "at lunch I heard one of the girls say you got your hair cut and styled this weekend."

Elaine looked over her shoulder and paused in the counting of bills. "Yeah, you like it, honey?"

"Oh yes, it's really nice. You know, it's really *you*."

Elaine smiled, and Sandy thought the smile was kind of funny-strange, like her remark'd been something to *laugh* at or something.

"It's really me," Elaine said, and returned to her counting.

Shelly stacked the bills and thought to herself: ironic, today her last day and she proved to the penny in no time flat.

"Oh, Elaine," the new girl said.

Shelly turned around in the window and tried to remember the new girl's name. Uh, Sandy, yes, that was it. "What, Sandy, honey?"

"I noticed something *peculiar*."

"Oh?"

"All day long the vault's been open. You know, just *open*."

"So?"

"Don't they worry about, well, bank robbers and stuff?"

Today of all days, she thought, to be saddled with a dumb blonde recruit. She put on a pleasant smile and said, "Bonds're kept in there, honey, and we're always going in and out all the time getting them. Also sometimes a teller runs out of cash and has to go in for more. See, there's a time lock on the vault, which'd be a bitch to have to fool around with all day long. So it's left open so bank personnel like you and me can go in and out as we please."

The girl had lowered her eyes when Shelly said "bitch" and still held them down when she said, "Can you say *anything* around here and get away with it?"

"No, honey," Shelly said. "If one of the officers hears you say 'twat' you got to go in the back room and show him yours."

The girl giggled and (Shelly couldn't believe it) blushed.

Well, she thought, shaking her head, takes all kinds. She smiled to herself. And then some kinds take.

She glanced over at Mr. Rigley. How would he handle the robbery? He looked so cool sitting over there behind his big metallic bank-president's desk, his short-cut black hair with just a hint of sideburns, his nut-brown sunlamp tan, his tailor-made pinstriped banker's suit, all the components of a handcrafted, perfectly constructed machine. This year's model of the Young Exec, body by Fisher.

Every girl in the bank wanted a try at getting that in the sack, whether they'd admit it or not, and Shelly would admit it, though she had a feeling that under fire old eight-by-ten-glossy Rigley would melt down into a puddle of yellow gunk when faced with three real men. Which in spite of all their faults Gross and Jon and Nolan were.

Her mind flashed briefly to the night before.

"What'cha smiling about, Elaine?"

"Oh, nothing, honey."

"Gee, I don't mean to be nosey or anything, but you're grinning like the *cat* that ate the *canary*."

"More like the pussy that got ate."

"E-*laine!*"

The buzzer sounded, which meant someone was being let in the side door, and Shelly looked over and watched Anita Welch greet the three business-suited men to see what it was they wanted after hours. The three men were Nolan, Jon and Grossman.

"Listen, honey," Shelly said, fighting a flutter in her

stomach, "maybe I better start showing you some of the ropes." She opened her drawer. "Well, where shall we start. Oh. Okay." She picked out a packet of bills. "This, hon, is bait money."

There was nothing wrong with his desk, George Rigley thought, that couldn't be solved by its having an office around it.

That was the problem, having to sit over here along the wall with all the damn vice-presidents as if being president didn't make any difference at all.

It was the Midwest, he supposed, maybe there they feel the president has got to be where people can get to him all the time, walk in the front door and get a nice folksy down-home eyeful of the prez. A lot of bull, as far as he was concerned. He didn't work his tail to the bone to become a bank president by age forty-two just so he could sit out in the open and have farmers stroll by and say, "Hey."

But the bank was growing, bursting at the seams, really, and the future was looking bright, what with the upcoming changeover from state to federal bank and all. Pretty soon that paint store next door would be torn down and some of that additional space would finally be had, and he was going to push for an office if it was the last thing he got that damn board to put through. Privacy, gentlemen, he said to himself, going over the speech he'd had in mind for a long time now, privacy is essential to the executive banker, easy accessibility to the bank's chief officer is a liability, and not, gentlemen, *not* an asset. . . .

"Sir?"

"Uh, what is it, Anita?"

"There are three gentlemen to see you." The dark-haired girl leaned across the desk and peered over the round plastic frames of her glasses. "Examiners, sir," she whispered.

"Thank you, Anita," he said. "Show them over."

He glanced toward the steel railing a few feet away and watched as the girl took his message to the three men standing there. They wore dark suits with vests and colorful ties and carried briefcases. The man talking with Anita was considerably older than the other two; he was a mustached man with nearly white hair and an angular face. Like his young assistants, (Rigley naturally assumed the older man was in charge, head examiner and two assistants being the pattern these examining teams followed) he had on sunglasses, though after a moment he removed his and put them in his breast pocket, while the younger two left theirs on; typical of young ones, Rigley thought, to strive for an executive cool with snobbery like that, almost pitiful from glorified accountants like these.

Yes, they were examiners, all right. Damn examiners, always showing up when least expected, and a special nuisance with the damn changeover coming up (but expansion was good, that was good).

But hell, a man never had any privacy.

Jon hoped nobody noticed his trembling. He tried to steady the hand that clutched the briefcase handle. He trailed behind Nolan as the secretary led them through the little steel door in the railing over to the president's desk. Grossman didn't seem to be nervous at all, had been real close-mouthed all day. Nolan wasn't even sweating, not a bead showing; but Jon, Jon's stomach was upside down.

"Mr. Rigley," Nolan was saying.

Jon worked at getting an official look on his face.

"How do you do?" the bank president was saying, rising momentarily and sitting back down. The bank president was very handsome, a fraternity boy grown up.

"My name is Bill Leonard," Nolan said. "Sam may have mentioned me to you."

Jon swallowed. Sam was the name of one of the state examiners Shelly had met a month ago, the last time a legitimate examining team had come around the bank.

"Yes he has," the president was saying (a bullshitter from word go, Jon noted). "I didn't realize you federal boys worked out of the same office as Sam and those other fellas. I assume you're federal, since Sam told me he wouldn't be coming around anymore, what with the changeover."

"We don't work out of the same office as Sam," Nolan said, "but we keep in close touch. And as you know, with this switch from state to federal, Port City's been a common point of interest of late."

"Of course," Rigley said. "Oh, I don't believe I got the names of the other two gentlemen."

"Benton," Grossman said.

"Newman," Jon said, hoping it didn't come out a squeak.

"I think you'd better take a look at our credentials," Nolan said.

Rigley grinned. His teeth were large and white and reminded Jon of toothpaste commercials. "That's right, isn't it," he said, "you're checking up on me as much as anything today, aren't you. Let me see your papers, then."

Nolan reached in his jacket pocket and flipped open the bogus credentials; Grossman and Jon did likewise. Rigley kept the grin going, barely glancing at the credentials, waving them off.

"One must be careful," Nolan said. "In a bank a person can't take things for granted."

"Well, if you won't be hard on me in your report," Rigley said, "I think I can admit to taking you three for examiners on first look. If I can't tell an examiner on sight by now I probably never'll be able to."

"True enough," Nolan said.

"Where shall we begin, gentlemen?" Rigley rose again.

"Our main interest is to see how your employees are doing in the process of changing over to a federal bank, and, also, to proceed with an orderly and routine examination. We would, however, like to take advantage of this situation by getting all of the Port City Savings and Trust personnel together to brief them on the changes that will be taking place when you become First National Bank of Port City."

Rigley lifted his palms and said, "Shall we start with the meeting then?"

"I think it would be best."

"Fine. Our conference room's in the back of the bank, next to the vault. We ought to be able to start in just a few minutes."

"Good. That way the briefing will be out of the way and we can get to business at hand."

"Yes," Rigley agreed, "let's get it out of the way."

Nolan walked at Rigley's side with Grossman close behind and Jon trailing after. His hand was still trembling around the briefcase handle, but not as badly.

Ronnie Schmidt was giving Jeanie Day a gentle reprimand for hoarding silver when Mr. Rigley came by with three men and said, "Our first visit from federal examiners, Ronnie. Bank meeting to begin in five minutes. Help me alert the ranks, will you?"

"Yes, Mr. Rigley, glad to."

The president and the three examiners moved on toward the meeting room back by the vault, and Ronnie turned to Jeanie again and said, "Either turn in the silver coins or buy them, dear, you can't keep 'em in your drawer forever."

"Oh, Ronnie!"

"Come on now, and spread the word about the bank meeting. You heard Mr. Rigley."

Ronnie walked over to Harold Hickman, silver-haired head teller, and said, "Bank meeting right away, Harry, tell your girls. I'll, uh, go over and tell Simmons and the new girl myself."

Hickman nodded, smiling smugly.

Senile smart-ass, Ronnie thought, heading for the window Elaine Simmons was sharing with the new blonde, Sandy Baird. He ran his eyes up and down the figures of both girls as he approached them. He whistled softly to himself: a lot of sweet ass, he thought, to squeeze into one little window. He'd been trying unsuccessfully for weeks and weeks to get in that stuck-up Simmons piece, but no luck; maybe he'd do better with the blonde Simmons was breaking in. Wouldn't mind breaking that one in himself, preferably behind the door of one of the rooms out at Port City Court.

"Hiya, girls."

Sandy said, "Oh, *hello,* Mr. Schmidt."

"Ronnie, dear, all the girls around here call me that."

Simmons looked around over her shoulder. "Among other things."

The bitch didn't like him, he knew she didn't, but she still had a sweet ass. "No matter how friendly I am," Ronnie said, "you just got to give me a rough old time. How come?"

"'Cause you got a pregnant wife at home," Simmons said, "and I have no desire to be the pregnant girlfriend at work."

"That's what I like about you, Simmons," Ronnie said, starting to feel a little irritated, sweet ass or no, "you got a sense of humor as big as your, uh, heart." He cleared his throat. "Anyway, you get yourself and your pretty apprentice here together and toddle your cute rears over into the meeting room, and on the double."

Simmons arched an eyebrow. "Oh?"

"Federal bank examiners. Briefing on the changeover."

"Oh."

The room was long and narrow, most of it taken up by a huge conference table with twenty chairs on either side of it. At the far end of the table the bank president stood, arms folded. On the right side of the room, near the front, the janitor was leaning against the wall, catching some sleep, and across from him on the opposite wall, the bank's ancient guard stood at parade rest. Nolan figured the old guy was a retired cop: on his navy shirt were press creases, suspenders, and weathered badge.

Nolan went to the head of the table, with the door at his back, Rigley down at the opposite end. Grossman moved to the right, Jon to the left. Casually they spread out, Nolan staying where he was at the table, Grossman edging toward the side the janitor was sleeping on, Jon nearing the wall where the bank guard stood.

"Ladies and gentlemen," Nolan said, "the first thing we're going to cover today is what to do in case of a bank robbery." He opened his briefcase and as he did Grossman and Jon began to open theirs. "What you do in case of a robbery," Nolan continued, "is nothing."

He shut the briefcase and let them see his .38. On either side of him Grossman and Jon were doing the same.

"Freeze!" Grossman said.

Nolan stared out over forty-three open mouths (Shelly was turning in an excellent acting job) as Jon reached over and pulled the old guard's service revolver out of his hip holster. Jon stuck the gun in his belt with a show of comic-book bravado that made Nolan smile inwardly.

Grossman said, "Everybody slide your hands onto the table. Nice and easy. Okay, lay those fat pinkies of yours on the table, now, that's right, just like in Simon says, got it?"

Sighs and whispers and moans flooded over the room in one quick rush.

"Nobody make a sound," Nolan said. "It's okay you breathe, but nothing else."

Silence.

"We got any heroes here today?" Nolan said. "No? If we got any potential Audie Murphy in the audience I want to know, so I can shoot him now and get it out of the way. No? Good."

The bank president, Rigley, said, "Sir, as president of this bank . . ."

"You'll set an example by shutting up," Nolan said.

Rigley did.

"All we want," Nolan said, "is your money. Or rather the bank's money. Let us do our work and we'll leave you alone. With one exception. We're going to take some insurance out, to make sure you people act right. We're taking one of you with us."

Another rush of sighs, whispers, moans.

"Please," Nolan said.

Silence.

"The hostage won't be harmed," he said, "unless we are bothered by police. If police or FBI give us any trouble, our first move'll be to shoot the hostage."

The whites of eighty-six eyes showed all the way round.

Nolan said, "Pick somebody out, Benton."

Grossman looked at Shelly and said, "You."

Shelly made a convincing face of horror. "No . . . no, you can't . . ."

Grossman reached over and grabbed her by the wrist and hauled her to her feet. "Shut up."

Shelly somehow managed to turn her face a stark white and got her lips going in a realistic spasmodic quiver.

"Get her out of here, Benton," Nolan said, disgustedly.

Grossman dragged Shelly out of the room, she pulling away from him valiantly.

"My friend Newman is going to watch you people," Nolan said, "while I go out and help Benton make a withdrawal." Nolan snapped shut his briefcase. "Please don't anybody give him any static. Newman here's wanted on three counts of murder as it is now, and well, they can only hang you once."

Nolan left the room to Jon and the forty-two bank employees, proud he'd gotten that last line out with a straight face. He felt almost lightheaded: after all the sweat over his three young partners, this job was going as smooth as any he'd ever been on.

Shelly and Grossman were stuffing cash from all the drawers into one of the laundry bags. He walked over to them and laid his briefcase open on one of the already emptied money trays. "Shelly," he said, "be sure to put all the bait money in here. I want it kept separate."

"Okay."

"You showed Grossman where the alarm buttons are in the teller's windows? Don't want to go setting one off ourselves after taking so much trouble getting everybody else away from them."

"I showed him, Nolan," she said, and she and Grossman moved on to the next cage.

Nolan took the other laundry bag and walked into the vault, spent four minutes filling the bag three-quarters of the way. He slung it over his shoulder and joined Shelly and Grossman, who had their laundry bag over half full.

"To coin a phrase," Shelly said, "we hit the jackpot."

Nolan nodded. "Grossman, go out and pull the car around front. Go ahead and open the back up for the bags. Hustle."

Grossman turned and left.

Nolan leaned the two sacks of cash against a partition. "Where's the bait money?"

Shelly pointed to his briefcase on a nearby counter. He went over and looked in at the twenty packets, two per window, five hundred each in tens and twenties. He snapped the case shut.

"Come on, hostage."

She smiled as Nolan took her by the upper arm and hauled her into the meeting room.

"Okay," Nolan said, "file out the door past Benton here and into the vault. Make it orderly."

Rigley spoke up. "We'll suffocate in there!"

"It'll be crowded," Nolan said, "but it's got vents. You'll be able to breathe."

They moved carefully out of the room, around the corner, and into the vault. It was a tight squeeze, but there was just enough room for everybody to get in, sardine-style.

"We'll release your fellow employee when we're convinced we aren't being pursued," Nolan said.

A man in back, the one Rigley'd called Ronnie, yelled "Don't you harm her!" and Nolan shut the vault door.

He pointed at the sacks. Jon laid the guard's heavy revolver on a counter and picked up both sacks, carrying one under each arm, and headed for the door.

Nolan gripped Shelly at the elbow. "Remember not to smile," he told her.

"I'll try," she said, smiling.

2

Nolan smoothed the lather over his dampened mustache and started shaving. He took extra care not to cut himself; his upper lip would look fresh-shaven enough without nicks further encouraging suspicion. A sense of detachment washed over him as he stared into the mirror at the razor eating his mustache away, and watched as one of two selves began taking the other's place. The one with the mustache, whom he'd gotten rather used to, was making an exit, and the bare-faced bastard was putting in his first appearance in some time.

He scooped his hands down under the running tap, brought them up full of water, and splashed his face, then dipped them back for a refill, which he dumped in his hair to wash the white powder out. He toweled his head partially dry and shook some hair oil into his palms, rubbed it into his scalp. When his hair was combed and parted, its normally ungreased, dead-dry look had reversed.

Jon came into the bathroom, dressed casually now in a green banlon sweater and white jeans, his arms dangling nervously at his sides. "Hey, you really look different, Nolan. I wouldn't recognize you if I didn't know."

"That's the point."

"Say, uh, how much longer before phase two?"

"Soon. How's everybody coming?"

"Shelly's got her clothes changed. Slacks and sweater, now. She looks real different, too, with that blonde hair."

"And Grossman?"

"Yeah, he's back in tee-shirt and jeans."

"Fine."

"Something funny, though, Nolan."

"About what?"

"Shelly and Grossman."

"Go on."

"They aren't talking much."

"They're edgy, that's all."

"I don't know, Nolan. Grossman's been acting funny today."

"I don't think so."

"But he's been so quiet . . ."

"He's just been concentrating on the job."

"I don't know."

"Quit worrying, kid."

"Well, we aren't exactly home free yet, Nolan."

"That's why you shouldn't worry."

"I think I'll take some aspirin."

"Do that."

Jon's face contorted into something—a smile of sorts, Nolan guessed—and the boy turned and left. Nolan ran a wet washcloth over his face. He looked in the mirror again and frowned at the redness over his mouth and rubbed on some aftershave talc, hoping to camouflage the area. That still didn't satisfy him, but he didn't want to bother with it any longer.

He went into the bedroom and pulled a sportshirt out of his bag.

Everything was going fine, Nolan figured, just so Jon didn't spook. The boy'd been nervous on the job, but had done his part and hadn't let it show too bad. Actually, the robbery itself had gone so well it almost worried Nolan, but not much. Jon had gotten this far; it'd be a damn shame if he spooked at this point. Grossman's acting withdrawn? That didn't bother Nolan; that was the way a pro who's really into the job is supposed to act. So no sweat. Nothing left now but to go in the other room and say the goodbyes and go separate routes.

Jon stuck his head in the door and said, "Hey, Nolan, forget what I said about Gross and Shelly."

"I already did."

"Well, then, forget it again. They're out there sitting at the table together, holding hands and everything, like a couple of kids."

"I told you."

"Grossman still isn't saying much, but he's looking at her real intense. So the old love fire's still burning."

"See."

The boy smiled, this time a normal one, and disappeared.

Nolan grabbed his gray suit coat out of the closet and climbed into it. He went back over to the bed and started packing odds and ends into the travel bag.

Funny how Grossman panned out, he thought, after all the doubts. The kid had driven well on the job, he was cool behind the wheel, handled the car like a pro. Made it from the bank to the bridge in fifty seconds, and no attention-calling squeals of tire or sharp turns or anything. When they'd approached the bridge, it was he who reminded Shelly to leave on her wig until past the toll booth, as Nolan had told them they should be sure to be seen going over to Illinois, and she removed it once the "Welcome to" sign greeted them on the other side. Grossman cut the usual twenty minutes between bridge and farmhouse to fourteen; there wasn't danger of highway patrol stopping them for speeding, not on any of those country roads. Exactly fifteen minutes after he'd pulled away from Port City Savings and Trust, Grossman had returned the station wagon to its place inside the barn by the farmhouse.

Nolan lifted the travel bag with one hand and reached down with the other for his briefcase, which he'd taken time in the barn to fill with an additional ninety thousand in non-bait money. He walked out into the living room where Jon, Grossman, and Shelly were sitting around the poker table.

Shelly smiled and said, "You look different, Nolan."

"Good."

Jon got up from the table and came around to face Nolan. "What happens now?"

"It's about time we part company," he said, looking over at Grossman and Shelly. "Any last questions?"

"Yes," Shelly said. "You had us leave the bags of money in the station wagon. Are you and Jon going to take the wagon? I mean, won't there be descriptions of it on the radio?"

"Jon and I'll be taking his Chevy," Nolan said.

"Why not leave the Chevy and take the Country Squire?" Jon asked. "Nobody got a good look at the wagon."

"That's true," Nolan said, "but we can't chance leaving your car behind. Somebody'll be finding this place sooner or later, and they'll link it to the robbery. Then your Chevy would be eventually tracked to you, Jon, even if we took time now to destroy the plates and rip off the registration. We'll toss the bags of cash in the trunk. If we get stopped, you'll just say you lost your trunk key. Don't worry about it, they won't bother us, we won't fit what they'll be looking for."

Shelly said, "Any way to tell how much we got?"

Nolan shrugged. "What's your guess?"

"Seven hundred thousand. Give or take."

"Sounds right."

Jon said, "That's a big haul."

Nolan smiled. "Maybe a record, in Iowa." He turned to Grossman. "All set on your route to Canada?"

Grossman nodded.

Jon said, "Soon as you're settled, get in touch and we'll set a time for me to get the cash to you."

Grossman nodded again.

Shelly said, "Shouldn't we take *some* of it with us?"

Nolan said, "I already talked that over with Grossman. You'll be carrying around a thousand of it for expense money. That's all you can get away with carrying without somebody getting suspicious if you get stopped. And you'll be stopped once for sure, at the border."

"I just hope nothing gets fouled up," Shelly said, "and we'd never get our share."

"Don't worry," Nolan said. "Okay, that's about it . . . oh, Grossman, you'd better give me that .38 back."

"Why?" Grossman said.

"Somebody finds it on you, you'll get taken in for sure. It's best we leave all the guns behind. Jon's already given me his, it's in a drawer back in the bedroom."

"And leave them in the house for the cops to find?"

"It doesn't matter, they're untraceable. But I will rub them clean and throw them in the thicket back of the house before we go."

"So where's your gun?"

"It's in my bag here."

"We leave ours, you keep yours?"

"I'm in a little different situation than you are."

"Sure," Grossman said. "Well, let me give you mine, then."

"Fine."

Grossman moved around in the chair and reached down into his belt and came up with the .38. Nolan reached out to take the gun and Grossman batted Nolan's arm away with his free hand.

Jon said, "Don't screw around, man."

Grossman pointed the .38 at Nolan's chest.

Shelly smiled nervously and said, "Gross . . . ?"

Grossman said, "Couple things I want to talk over with you, old man."

Nolan said, "Your game."

"First let loose of that suitcase thing, just let it drop. And then hand me the briefcase."

Nolan did.

"Let's discuss a couple points," Grossman said, his voice soft and a monotone. "You said once you never shot anybody outside of guys who crossed you. Is that right?"

Nolan nodded.

"I take that to mean," Grossman said, "that you figure killing a guy that crossed you is justifiable."

Jon said, "Gross, cut it out, will you, man?"

"Shut up, Jon," Grossman said. "Nolan? How about it? Killing justifiable in such a case?"

Nolan said, "It can be."

"And you assured Shelly a minute ago that our share was safe. That we'd get paid. 'Don't worry,' you said. Right?"

"That's right."

"Well," Grossman said, "I don't see it that way. Not at all. I don't see I can trust you."

Nolan shifted his weight. "I don't know why not, Grossman."

"Don't move around," Grossman said. "Goes for you too, Jon."

"Gross," Shelly said, "what makes you think Nolan's going to cheat us?"

"Quiet," he said. "Nolan, would you trust a man who slept with his partner's woman?"

Shelly's face turned as white as it had in the bank. Only this time, Nolan noticed, no act. Jon was frozen, his mouth hanging open.

Nolan said, "You're jumping to conclusions."

"There's more," Grossman said, his voice still a matter-of-fact monotone. "How does the complexion of the situation change when still another partner comes in and sleeps with that woman? And this second partner, he was the one who told the man not to see the woman, because it was bad for the job. The one man is supposed to stay away, while his partners take turns screwing."

The monotone bothered Nolan, and so did the way Grossman's eyes wouldn't stay still, kept flicking from Nolan to Shelly to Jon and over again.

Jon thawed enough to say, "You been watching Shelly."

Grossman said, "That's right, friend. I was watching Saturday night when you went up to see her. And Sunday night when *you* went up to see her, old man."

"They just came to talk about the robbery, Gross," Shelly said, a desperate tone working its way into her voice.

"Sure, babe."

Nolan said, "There's no reason to complicate this, Grossman. We don't have the time for personal problems. Whatever happened, it's over. Take your half now, if you like. Just grab one of the bags, the one that's more full if you want. I'd appreciate it if you'd leave me the briefcase, because I have a use for the bait money. But we can't afford to fool around here any longer."

Grossman turned and looked at Shelly. "I think I understand some things about you, babe, I never understood before. All those guys that have . . ." He stopped and laughed, ". . . taken advantage of you."

Shelly looked over nervously at Jon and Nolan, then back to Grossman and said, "Are you going to kill them, Gross?"

"Wouldn't be the first time I killed for you, would it, babe? Tell me, how long after we're in Canada is it going to be before you ditch me? Will you wait a while, till Jon gets our money to us? Or have you already made arrangements to meet Jon sooner? Or Nolan? Do you get my share of the take, too, babe, or just yours? So many things make sense now. I don't know how I could have believed in you all this while. Unless it was just that I wanted to."

"If you're going to kill them," she said, her voice a sob now, "do it! Will you? I'm scared, I'm scared, I want to leave this place . . . it was all going along so nice . . . oh Gross, baby, babe, do *something!*"

Grossman touched her arm. "You were always looking for something new, weren't you, babe? A new start, a new way, a new kick. Always something new."

"Grossman," Nolan said.

"Old man," Grossman said, "I'm going now. I'm not going to kill you. I don't blame you for this, not really. Or Jon. You taught me some things, so thanks for that much. But I won't be leaving you any money, can't do that either. Now when I go, be smart and don't go sticking your head out the door. I can hit targets from about anywhere, remember. Moving targets I'm real good at."

"This is stupid, Grossman," Nolan said.

Grossman got up and stood with a hand on Shelly's shoulder. "Something new, right, babe? Try this one on, babe, it'll blow your mind."

He put the .38 barrel up against the blonde hair along her temple and squeezed the trigger.

3

Nolan dropped to the floor. As he hit he reached an arm out and knocked Jon's legs from under him, to get the boy down below the line of fire. Jon's body slapped the floor, but the immediate danger was over: the slamming door signaled Grossman's exit.

Jon's face was ashen. "Jesus, Nolan! Jesus Christ, what's happening, Nolan!" The boy pushed himself to his knees and stared over at the poker table. Shelly's lifeless figure was sprawled across its top, what remained of her face mercifully hidden by the long, now red-streaked blonde hair.

Nolan got up and pulled Jon to his feet, standing between the boy and the table.

"Oh Jesus, Nolan, what'll we do now, oh Jesus . . ."

Nolan latched onto his shoulders. "Goddamn you, kid," he said, "don't go hysterical on me."

"What's happening here? Everything was perfect, everything was fine . . ."

Nolan dug his fingers into the boy's shoulders and shook him. "Shut up and snap out of it."

"Everything's gone all to hell, Nolan, everything's . . ."

"I said snap out of it," he said, turning the boy around and facing him toward the bedroom. "We got a lot to do."

"Nolan?"

"Since there's no back door, we'll be going out a window. Go in the bedroom and wait for me. I'll be right in."

Jon nodded his head and plodded off.

Nolan bent down and opened up his bag, got out the
Smith and Wesson .38. He dug under the clothes and found
a box of shells and stuffed it in his pocket. Since Jon might
get upset at the sight of the gun, Nolan shoved it in his belt,
covered it with his coat, and headed for the bedroom.

The boy was sitting in the straight-backed chair by the
dresser, staring at his folded hands. Well, Nolan thought,
shock treatment time.

"Better take your .38 back, kid," Nolan said, pointing at
the dresser. "May need it."

Jon bent down and pulled open the bottom drawer and
took out the .38. He held it loose in his hand and looked at it
and shuddered. But that was all.

Nolan allowed himself a sigh of relief and said, "Come
on, kid." He unlocked the window and pushed it up. "Don't
jump out. Hold onto the sill and slide your feet to the
ground. And no noise."

Jon nodded and waited for Nolan to crawl out the
window first, then followed him close behind.

The farmhouse lawn did not extend to the back yard,
which was a dense thicket. The thick brush came right up to
the window and hid Nolan and Jon as they crept through it
on all fours. When they were safely behind the barn, leaning
against it, Nolan put a finger to his lips, then mouthed,
"Wait."

A few seconds later they heard the sound of a motor
starting up inside the barn, then tires spun gravel and they
knew Grossman had gone.

Jon began moving forward and Nolan grabbed his arm.
"Hold it," he said, "give him time to get out of sight." Twenty
long seconds passed and Nolan said, "Now."

They ran around to the front and inside the barn they
found the Chevy II and the Country Squire still there, the
back compartment of the station wagon open.

"Took his own," Jon said. "Figures."

"Stupid," Nolan said. "Not enough room for the bags in

the Mustang trunk. He'll have to have one, maybe both in the backseat. Out in the open. Stupid."

"What do we do?"

"Got your keys?"

"Sure."

"Give me four minutes to catch him. I'll take the wagon, then after the four minutes are gone, you come pick me up in your Chevy."

"How will I find you?"

"Same way I find him: follow the dust. Gravel roads, remember?"

"Oh. Okay."

Nolan climbed behind the wheel of the Country Squire, got out the keys. "While you're waiting, go in and get my bag. Bring it when you come for me."

"Okay."

"But after that come back out here and wait in your car. I don't want you in the house moping over that side of beef in there."

The boy swallowed and said, "Don't worry."

Nolan turned the key in the ignition.

Nothing.

"Dead?" Jon said.

"Damn," Nolan said, getting out and throwing open the hood. "Forgot the bastard knew engines."

"What'd he do to it?"

Nolan smiled. "Just lifted off one of the battery cables," he said, bending over and putting the connector back in place. "He's not as smart as I thought, and I'm not as stupid as he thought."

This time the engine jumped to life and Nolan glided out of the barn.

"Watch yourself, Nolan!"

"Four minutes, kid."

He held it to twenty going around the cinder court, then climbed to forty-five going out the narrow gravel road leading away from the farmhouse lot. If he went too fast he'd raise so much of his own dust he wouldn't be able to follow Grossman's. The ditches on each side of the road were deep, at least six feet, and if he made a sloppy turn and ended up in one of those, he might as well pitch a tent and call that ditch home.

He came to the first crossroad half a mile from the farmhouse. Grossman's dust was to the left and Nolan followed it, building a little more speed. The road widened slightly, but the ditches were just as deep, and when he came to the next crossroad a quarter mile later, Grossman's dust rising on the right, Nolan almost missed the turn as the wagon wheeled around the corner at the steady fifty-m.p.h. pace he'd set.

The next crossroad Grossman's dust trail went to the left again, and the next to the right, and still Nolan hadn't caught sight of the little yellow Mustang. Grossman was traveling fast, he thought, too fast for a narrow road like this one, much too fast for such conditions, even for as good a driver as Grossman.

The four-minute time limit he'd given himself was nearly up, and Nolan began to get a cold sensation of sinking futility. When the next crossroad came moments later, the feeling clawed at his gut: dust was freshly risen on *both* the left and right turns.

He came to a gravel-scattering halt in the center of the intersection.

Had Grossman purposely doubled back to confuse him?

Or did the dust belong to some other driver?

If that driver, should he happen to exist, got run off the road by the Mustang, or even just noticed how fast it was going and followed or reported it, things could really get tense.

He was just about ready to flip a mental coin to decide right or left when he heard the sound, a sound coming from his right, the sound of collision, of crackup. Jolting, crunching, glass-shattering, metal-tearing impact, the sound of machine eating machine.

Nolan spun the wheel, pressed the pedal to the floor, and careened around in a U and headed toward the sound's source. He had to cut his speed immediately because the dust was so thick, cut it to ten and held it there, leaning his head out the window to see better, flicking on the lights in a try at penetrating the heavy fog of dust.

Then he saw it.

The Mustang.

The front of its yellow body was twisted around the tail of a big tractor, whose two huge wheels were bent to either side of the Mustang's mutilated prow, forming a cockeyed vee. Car and tractor were melded together, one gnarled piece of obscene sculpture teetering on the edge of the deep roadside ditch.

Nolan pulled over to the opposite side and got out, leaving the motor running, went over to the Mustang, and looked in.

Grossman was leaned over the wheel, his head bloody from where it had cracked apart the windshield, his empty eyes open and staring. The bags of money and Nolan's briefcase were in the back seat.

The way the metal had twisted, it took several yanks for Nolan to get the door open, but he finally did, and the force of the action flopped Grossman over toward him, hanging out into the road. Nolan heaved him back in, noticing from the tilt of his neck that it was broken. He didn't bother checking for a pulse. He pushed forward the seat with the limp body in it and got out the two laundry bags and the briefcase from the backseat. He closed the door again, briefcase under his arm, and hauled the bags over to the wagon. He put everything into the compartment in back, in case somebody came along and he had to play innocent bystander for a while.

He returned to the coupled machines and looked up at the vacant tractor seat. In the opposite ditch, where he'd been thrown a good thirty feet away from the wreck, was the driver. He was a short man in bib overalls, around Nolan's

age, with butched white hair. Nolan leaned over the unconscious figure. Pulse normal enough. Nothing important
broken, few ribs maybe. Concussion very likely. The man
wouldn't be waking up for a while, but he would eventually.

Nolan went back to the station wagon and shifted into
drive. He pulled into a dirt inway down the road that
bridged the ditch and led into a field, then backed the
wagon out, turned around and began retracing his route.
When he reached the nearest of the crossroads he saw
another car up ahead moving through the dust, and when he
was trying to decide how to handle the situation, he recognized the car as Jon's Chevy II.

He honked and pulled over and Jon drove up alongside
him, looked out the window. "What's happened?" Jon asked.
"Is that an accident down there?"

"Never mind," Nolan said, "just get out and open your
trunk."

Jon did as told and helped Nolan transfer the two bags of
money from the wagon into the trunk of the Chevy. Nolan
slammed the trunk lid shut, tossed his briefcase in the front
seat, and said, "Wait for me here. Don't kill your motor."

"What's going on?"

"Keep your eyes open. When I come back, I'll be on
foot."

"What are you going to do?"

Nolan rolled up his window and shut the boy off. He
pulled into another dirt drive and turned around again,
headed back toward the crackup.

Nolan unlatched the door, clutched the handle with his
left hand and steered with his right. He accelerated as he
approached the mangle of car and tractor, got to thirty-five
and aimed the nose of the station wagon at the teetering
hulk of maimed machine. A quarter second before the
Country Squire smashed into its sister machines and joined
with them, Nolan pushed open the door and jumped, rolling
across the gravel and down into the ditch opposite. The
wagon shoved the car and tractor over into the other ditch

and when the three hit bottom, one of the gas tanks (Nolan wondered idly which) exploded, with the other two right behind. A big tongue of flame lashed out of the ditch and licked the air.

If the sound of the explosion didn't attract somebody, the fire would, so Nolan got himself up, brushed off as much white gravel dust as he could, crawled up out of the ditch, and started running. He'd been lucky when he dived out of the car, hadn't hurt himself at all, just the bruises and scratches on his hands and face he'd expected to get anyway. And his side was starting to burn again, as he ran, but not nearly so bad as it might've.

Jon saw him coming and started to drive down after him, but Nolan waved at him to stay put. He didn't want the boy to have to turn around again needlessly. Time would be too valuable now even for something that small. He ran up to the Chevy II, pulled open the door on the passenger side and leaped in.

"What happened to you?" Jon said. "What was the explosion all about?"

"Where are we, in relation to the route to the Cities you memorized?"

"Two turns'll get us back on."

"Good. Get going, then."

Several minutes later they were on their way, and Nolan had his breath back. He lit a cigarette and leaned back and smoked it.

Jon glanced over at him. "What happened to you?" he repeated.

"Keep your eyes on the road," Nolan said. "I jumped out of the wagon when I ran it into the accident."

"You mean you wrecked it? On purpose? What accident? That thing down the road? What was the explosion, and the flames?"

"The explosion was when I ran the wagon into the accident Grossman had."

"But . . . why'd you do that?"

"Somebody'll find the wreck soon. And the farmhouse, too. Maybe while they're trying to sort it all out they'll forget about us a little."

Another minute went by and Jon, his eyes never wavering from the road, asked, "What about Grossman? You kill him?"

"No," Nolan said. "Some farmer saved me the trouble."

4

Nolan worked the key in the lock, opened the door to the hotel room, and said, "I appreciate you sitting this out with me, kid."

Jon shrugged. "It's okay," he said, stepping in, Nolan closing the door behind them. "I don't feel like letting go of you just yet, anyway, Nolan, to tell you the truth."

Nolan glanced around the room and saw it to be a near carbon of the smaller of the two rooms he'd had last time he had been to the Concort. Only this time two single beds had been jammed in instead of one. He looked over at Jon, who was sitting on the bed closest to the window, and said, "Hungry?"

"Don't mention food."

"You haven't eaten all day, you must be hungry."

"After what's happened today? Are you kidding?" Jon puffed out his cheeks and covered his mouth with his hand.

Nolan sat on the other bed and reached over to the night-stand. He lifted the receiver off the hook. "I'll call room service anyway. You need something in your stomach."

The ride to the Quad Cities had been all but silent. Nolan stayed on watch for police cars (a state cop car passed going the other way, but its red tophat was off, as was the siren), and he didn't want any talk getting Jon's attention off the memorized route. After awhile Nolan did turn on the radio, found a station giving news on the quarter hour and heard of the "daring daylight holdup" (a phrase which caused Jon to laugh, a needed tension release) that had taken place at Port City Savings and Trust, involving a large, undisclosed amount of money. They also heard that the FBI had rushed into the case, since the "bandits," who posed as bank examiners, had kidnapped Elaine Simmons, 20, of Port City, a teller at the bank. Then the newscaster went on to his next story and Nolan switched off the radio. When the Chevy II had crossed the Centennial bridge over into Davenport, Nolan spoke for the first time in thirty minutes.

"Kid," he said, "I got some time to kill before my meeting. You want to stick with me till then, or take off?"

"Just as soon stick with you, Nolan. That okay?"

"Well, it won't matter either way for you as far as the cops go. I mean, the odds won't change better or worse if you head for Iowa City now or wait a few hours."

"Wouldn't it be better for you and me to go on to Iowa City now, though? We could stash the money with Planner and you could let things cool for a few days, and then have your meeting."

"No, it's better to take care of all of it at once. It'd be more dangerous hanging around the area for a period of days. This way, when tonight's over, I'll have my affairs settled and can clear out for good."

"Well, then, I'll keep you company, Nolan, if you'll put up with me."

"There could be some trouble."

"Why's that? You just said it didn't matter with the cops."

"It doesn't. It's the meeting I'm thinking of. If the meeting goes wrong somehow, it'd be nice to have you around. To wait outside with your car, in case I have to get out quick. In case it sours."

"Well, sure, of course, if I wasn't there you'd be without a car."

"Wouldn't that be sweet." Nolan lit up the last cigarette

off his last pack, breathed the smoke in deep, then said, "I'm sorry about this, kid."

"It's perfectly okay."

"When I called Werner yesterday, he said he needed time to set it up, two this morning was the quickest we could do it. Said it had to be that way."

"Two in the morning? It's hardly five now."

"I know. Nine hours. Still with me?"

"Sure. I just wonder what we're going to do with all that time."

"There's a hotel we can go to, real close to where I'm supposed to go for the meeting. Werner runs it."

They'd left the money in the trunk, putting the briefcase under the seat in front and locking the car, which they left parked in the Concort lot. Inside the hotel Nolan was pleased to find the clerk who'd been on duty last time behind the check-in desk again. He remembered Nolan, after struggling past the lack of mustache and the changed hairstyle, and when Nolan asked for a room overlooking the parking lot, the clerk went into his "anything for a friend of Mr. Werner" routine and gave them the room.

Nolan was on the bed stretched out when the knock at the door got him up. Instinctively he yanked his .38 from his belt, then when he heard, "Room service," stuffed it back in and put his coat on over it. He cracked the door to confirm the claim, saw it was true and let the man come in and set up his trays of food. When he was done Nolan paid him and showed him out.

Nolan lifted the little steel caps off the plates and smiled. "Prime rib," he said, "big juicy slices. Sure you won't change your mind?"

The scent of the food got Jon up off the other bed; he said, "Changed my mind," and sat behind one of the trays.

While they ate, Nolan noticed a look of concern on the boy's face and said, "What's wrong?"

"Nothing," Jon said. "Lot of things."

"Like this deal tonight?"

"That's one. How do you know this isn't a cross?"

"Don't. That's why I want you there to back me up."

"You trust these guys?"

"Don't have a choice. The guy Werner, he's a friend, or was at one time. Anyway, I trust him more than Charlie, the other guy."

"What's it all about, anyway?"

"I thought Planner told you. You heard what I told Shelly and Grossman, that's close enough."

Being reminded of Shelly and Grossman seemed to make it hard for Jon to swallow the bite of meat he was on, and Nolan looked up and watched as the boy finally got it down. "Nolan," Jon said, "all I know is that Charlie, this syndicate guy, has it in for you."

"Well, I used to run a club for him in Chicago, and he wanted me to . . ." Nolan cut a portion of fat off his meat while he tried to come up with a vague comic book term that would communicate to the boy without spoiling his supper. ". . . he wanted me to do some dirty work for him, and I wouldn't, and that's what started it."

"Oh. Is that all there is to it?"

"Yeah. Eat your food."

When they'd finished, Nolan shoved the trays and chairs up against the wall, took his coat off, and went back to the bed. He lay down, resting the .38 on the nightstand. Jon was sitting on the bed again, a blank look on his face.

"You tired, kid?"

"A little. I couldn't ever sleep, though. I'm still pretty keyed up."

"Well I can. You want to wake me in a few hours, and I'll stand watch?"

"Stand watch?"

"We really both shouldn't be asleep at the same time. If nothing else, one of us should be checking on the car out the window now and then."

"Oh. Well, you go ahead and sleep, Nolan, I'll just sit here."

Nolan shrugged. "I'll call down and have the switchboard ring us at one-thirty, if you happen to drop off."

"You don't need to, I won't."

"Better."

Nolan called down, then switched off the light and stretched out again.

A few minutes later the boy said, "Nolan?"

"Yeah, kid?"

"Why'd you save off all the marked bills like you did? Just to keep them separate? Why didn't you just leave them behind, like you had us do with the coins?"

"The bait money's my safety catch. It's in as part of my payoff to Charlie. If he and Werner cross me, I won't tell them it's in there. That way if they get me, the law will get them."

"And if they're straight with you you'll tell them?"

"I suppose. Then they can sell the bait money to a fence, at a loss."

"Won't that make this Charlie pissed that he isn't getting a hundred cents on the dollar?"

"Tough shit. Charlie made a lot of stipulations about how I was and wasn't supposed to pay him, but he didn't say anything about not using bait money."

"So if they cross you they'll get busted for being in on the bank job, like maybe for being behind it or something?"

"Or something. See, even if they manage to squirm out of the law's hands, there'll be a stink over it and they'll still have to face the Family, whose back they've been working behind."

"Works out neat." Jon smiled. "You know, Nolan, you been quite a teacher."

"If I were you," he said, "I'd stick to the comic books for my idols."

Several more minutes went by and Nolan propped himself up on one elbow and said, "Kid?"

"Yeah?"

"Remind me later to give you the list I made up the other day."

"List? What list?"

"List of people I want notified if tonight sours. Business associates of mine, who run fronts for me."

"Okay." The boy hesitated, then said, "You sweating this, Nolan?"

"I'm just careful in my old age. Oh, and also the name and address of a girl in Cicero who's supposed to get my share of the bank money—if, you know."

"Who is she?"

"Just a girl who helped me out a while back. When I got shot up. Got me on my feet again."

"That'd be a lot of money for her."

"I know, and I'd just as soon spend it myself. But if something does sour, she might as well have it as anybody."

A few more minutes went by and Nolan was nearly asleep when Jon said, "Nolan? You asleep yet?"

"No."

"I been wondering."

"What?"

"Grossman. About Grossman."

"What about him?"

"Why didn't he kill us, too, why just Shelly?"

"Getting us out of the way would've been the only reason for that. Maybe that wasn't reason enough."

"But why would he kill *her* and let us go? I mean, after all, I always figured he was crazy in love with her."

"Maybe that's why."

Jon was quiet for a while, then said, "Yeah. Yes."

Nolan shut his eyes and went to sleep.

After what seemed like an instant, the phone rang and Nolan picked it up and said, "What?"

A female voice said, "One-thirty, sir."

"Thanks."

He hung up slid off the bed and onto his feet. He looked over at Jon, who was stomach-down asleep, his face to one side, snoring softly.

He nudged him, said, "Wake up, kid."

"Huh?"

"Wake up."

"Did I fall asleep?"

"Maybe for a second. Let's go."

5

Nolan and Jon sat across from the warehouse in the Chevy II and waited. The night was dark, moonless dark, but Nolan could still make out the big red letters on the window glass that said QUAD CITY/JUKEBOX SERVICE/INCORPORATED.

"Damn it," he said, searching his pockets, "forgot to pick up cigarettes." He didn't bother asking Jon if he had any, knowing the boy didn't smoke unless somebody offered one of theirs.

Jon was staring over at the warehouse. "You know, it's funny, Nolan, really, it's funny."

"What's that?"

"It's funny, because it's *always* an old warehouse."

"What?"

"In movies, in the comics. The shoot-out, it always happens in an old abandoned warehouse."

"Well not wanting to spoil the moment for you, kid, I might point out that this warehouse isn't abandoned, it was just handy for the meeting; and let's hope there isn't any 'shoot-out.' "

Jon squirmed in the seat and made a face, as if he was trying to get up nerve to say something he'd been thinking about saying for a long time.

"Something bothering you, kid?"

"Yeah, I guess."

"Go on."

"Why don't we leave now, Nolan, and forget this? It's a

set-up to get you, I just know it is. You got plenty of money from the job. Let's take off, right now."

"Can't. If you want to go, go ahead, I'll get out here."

"No, no," he said, shaking his head. "I don't understand you, that's all. You plan so careful for a bank job, watch all the angles, rehearse, memorize, discipline yourself and your co-workers. And now you want to go walking into an obvious trap like this one."

"Get your head out of the comic books, will you."

"I will if you will."

"Look, kid, I got no choice. Nowhere to go but here. No other way." Nolan hadn't bothered trying to explain about the cover name, because he knew the boy couldn't understand what it meant to him, not only in terms of money, and time, but people running fronts for him, friends of his who'd get hurt if the cover were exposed; that this chance, however slim a chance it might be, was his only chance to regain the cover. *And if he did just say to hell with it and start over on his half of the bank take, he'd still have to live with the threat of Charlie and the Family hanging over him.*

Jon was saying, "I just don't get you," shaking his head.

"Kid. Jon."

"Yeah, Nolan?"

"I should tell you one thing."

"What's that?"

"If you get it in your head sometime to work another heist, remember what's waiting for you if you ever get connected to today's."

"What'd you mean?"

"It's more than just grand larceny is what I mean."

"Isn't grand larceny enough? What the hell else would it be?"

"Murder."

"Murder? Jesus, why?"

"Both Shelly and Grossman are dead. Any killing that takes place during the committing of a felony, even if it's somebody else in on the job with you who gets killed, is murder, under the law. No matter which finger was on what trigger, everybody left alive from the job's a candidate for a murder rap."

"Christ."

"Just thought you should know."

"Christ."

"Anyway, if we get split up here, I want you to give some thought to making this your first and last job."

"This is a hell of a time for a sermon, Nolan."

"Sermon, hell. Fact of life. You got money now, so buy your damn comic book shop, and draw your pictures, and let this cure you of living out your half-ass fantasies. There was some truth in what you said, you know . . . a lot of times it does end in an abandoned warehouse somewhere. Or in an alley, or in a cell. Or the way it did for Grossman, or Shelly."

A gold Lincoln pulled up across the street and backed into the alley, up against the triple garage doors.

Jon said, "That them?"

Nolan nodded, watching Werner and Charlie climb out of the car. Alone. Like they said they'd be. Werner unlocked the side entrance by the triple doors and he and Charlie went in.

"Drive up the block," Nolan said, "and let me out."

Jon drove out of the parking place into the empty street. A block up he swung over to the opposite corner and stopped. Nolan opened the door, reaching down under the seat for the briefcase of money.

"Go around the block," Nolan said, "then pull back into that spot you just left. Keep the car running and be ready for anything."

"Got you . . . Nolan!"

"What?"

"It means something to me, those things you said a minute ago."

"Save the sob sister stuff for later. Just make sure you got that car running in front of that warehouse if I come flying out of there with my ass-end on fire."

"Okay, Nolan."

He shut the door and headed back down the block.

He stuck the .38 down deeper in his belt, since he'd agreed not to bring a gun along, and buttoned one button on the suitcoat. If things were played out straight, he'd hand this briefcase of money over to Charlie, they'd shake hands on it and that'd be that. Werner would be around to witness the verbal agreement and would expect to answer later on if either side got shafted.

The warehouse was up ahead. Across the street Jon's parking space was still vacant, as were in fact the whole row of places on either side of the warehouse. Traffic was nearly nonexistent, though two streets down a main thoroughfare seemed active. Nolan approached the window with Irish's proud lettering on it and stopped suddenly when he noticed a round black object stuck in the lower window, on the inside.

A funeral wreath.

A black funeral wreath with a white ribbon which had gold script saying, "Beloved Provider."

An employee of Irish's had died, obviously, unless this *was* the trap Jon envisioned it to be, and the wreath was Charlie's idea of gallows humor.

Nolan ruled that out, but undid the button on his coat anyway.

He went around to the side door he'd seen Werner and Charlie go in through, and found it unlocked. He opened it and went in.

The huge room was poorly lit, one small hanging bulb over a work area at the left providing what light there was. Charlie was sitting in a folding chair over to the right, wearing an overcoat that was buttoned to the throat; in back of him was a jukebox with its wire guts hanging out. Werner stood next to him but slightly to the rear, dressed in a dark suit and dark tie.

Charlie said, "How are you, Nolan?"

Nolan shut the door, but not letting its latch click, and

stood nearby. He didn't like the feel of this. He kept the hand that was gripping the briefcase handle against the door behind him, to shove it open if necessary, and with his other hand got out his .38. "I'm fine," Nolan said, "thanks. Now how about you stand up and open the coat. Slow."

Charlie laughed and spread his hands. "When are you going to learn to trust people, Nolan? When?"

"Do it."

Charlie shrugged and stood, unbuttoned the coat, and revealed a dark suit and tie identical to Werner's.

"Conservative today, aren't we?" Nolan said.

"Business transactions," Werner said, joining the conversation for the first time, "should be entered into seriously."

Nolan didn't really know what that was supposed to mean, but he let it pass.

Charlie said, "You did well today, Nolan. Radio said a few hours ago you took in close to eight hundred thousand. Something of a record for around here."

Werner said, "We thought maybe you'd forget your deal with Charlie and just settle down with your share of the take."

"No," Nolan said, motioning to Charlie that he could sit down again if he wanted, "it's time Charlie and me got our differences out of the way."

"Look, Nolan," Werner said, "neither one of us has a gun. You can search us if you like. Why don't you put that away?"

Nolan thought it over, said, "All right," and stuck the .38 back in his belt. He walked over to Charlie, dropped the briefcase at his feet.

Charlie picked it up off the floor, set it on his lap and snapped it open. It was crammed with packets of money, each with a red band reading 500.

"Want me to wait while you count it?" Nolan asked.

Charlie said, "I trust you."

Nolan said, "That's it, then."

"Don't rush off."

"You can count me out for coffee and bagels."

"Still bitter, Nolan?"

"No. Just keep in mind that if you cross me and let the Earl Webb name leak, I'll be back for you. And I won't be after the hundred thousand."

"Such strong talk for a man who just paid another to leave him alone."

"I'll be going." Nolan began edging his way backward, toward the door.

"Wait a moment," Charlie said.

Nolan kept moving, though he slowed a shade.

"I thought you might be interested in the reason behind our . . ." Charlie smiled. ". . . conservative dress."

"Werner gave me a reason."

"I'm afraid he wasn't being entirely honest with you, Nolan."

"I'll see you around."

"We went to a funeral today, Werner and I."

Nolan stopped.

"Friend of yours."

The wreath.

Werner said, "Irish."

Nolan ran back to the chair and lifted Charlie out of it by the lapels. "What did you do to him?"

Charlie didn't answer.

Nolan squeezed his hands together, full of the cloth of Charlie's suitcoat, and picked the little man off the ground and shouted into his face: *"What did you do to him?"*

Charlie wasn't shaken. He looked back at Nolan calmly and said, "An accident. He was working late here the other night and one of his jukeboxes fell over on him. This one right here behind me, as a matter of fact. Crushed in his rib cage. Punctured a lung."

Nolan heaved him back into the folding chair, knocking it over. Charlie sat on the floor and grinned up at Nolan.

Nolan said, "I'm going to kill you, you little bastard."

"Are you?"

Nolan grabbed for the .38 and a deep voice behind him

said, "I wouldn't."

Nolan eased his hand away from the gun butt. Charlie was getting up, the grin still on his face. He reached over and plucked Nolan's gun out of his belt and tossed the .38 across the room, where it went skittering over the cement floor and into a pile of junk under a workbench.

Nolan turned his head slowly around and watched a hulking figure move out of the darkness and into the weak light.

"Hello, Tillis," Nolan said.

Tillis said nothing, his beefy hand surrounding his silenced Luger, which was pointed at Nolan's stomach.

"Tillis," Charlie said, "before you kill Nolan for me, I want to have a word with him. So you'll have to wait a bit."

Tillis nodded.

"Nolan," Charlie said, "there are some things you should know. First, I never heard of the name Earl Webb until you told me about it. I don't know who took your things out of that hotel room in Cicero, whether it was cops or FBI or some wino, but however you look at it, if your cover's blown, it's been a long time blown, and I didn't have a goddamn thing to do with it. Outside of it was my man who shot you and got people interested in you."

Nolan smiled.

He *had* to smile, because it was a joke.

Because since Charlie's men hadn't been in his hotel room in Cicero, and hadn't gotten hold of the Webb material, then from the beginning it had been a joke. The first meeting with Charlie, the payoff arrangement, the planning of the robbery, the robbery itself, all of it a joke, a right answer to a question built on a false premise. An exercise to occupy his time before this inevitable confrontation with Charlie.

But Charlie was still talking, and not paying attention to Nolan's smile. Charlie was saying, "Second, that night at the Concort, I'd given Tillis orders to hold you for me. He didn't know it, but when I got there, I was going to have him kill you. I was making sure I got to watch, that was all. But when I did show and found you'd gotten the best of Tillis, and you had a gun on me as well, I had to improvise the hundred thousand dollar payoff deal, since the pretense I was there under was to negotiate with you, anyway. I knew enough not to make it too easy, and I knew enough to restrict you from trying to use Webb money, since there was a chance you'd come through and pay me off. And a chance I might still get to see you die, after all. But mostly I just wanted to get rid of you that night without losing my skin. That was all. But you bit, oh, you bit." Charlie laughed and looked for a reaction from Nolan, but didn't get any. "No questions, Nolan?"

Nolan said, "Why kill Irish?"

"Nobody could be left around who had any inkling of what was going on between you and me and Werner. Especially not somebody working within the Family, like Irish was, who could report it to a Family council member. Tillis, here, he's been staying in Davenport with Werner these past two weeks taking care of details like Calder and Irish."

"Details."

"That's right."

"What about Tillis? You going to have him kill himself?"

Tillis stayed cement-faced and Charlie laughed again. "Don't look for a rise out of him," Charlie said, "he knows I'll play honest with him. It's guys like you, Nolan, who don't play honest with me that get screwed."

"Where does my buddy Werner fit into this?"

Werner was poking imaginary dust on the floor with his foot.

Charlie said, "He's up for promotion, didn't you know that, Nolan? Going to be a council member one of these days. And you, you're a skeleton in his closet, you might say, a goddamn thorn. See, I know you and he been keeping in touch over the years. And I got proof of it, too. Witnesses. Wiretaps. Even a couple photographs. That kind of thing could kill Werner with the Family. Not altogether, maybe, but no promotion. So Werner and me four or five months back made a deal, a goddamn deal. He helps me get to you next time you contact him, I forget about his helping you in the past."

"Who gets the hundred thousand?"

"Well, I do want to thank you for the money, Nolan," Charlie said. "I mean, it'll come in handy. I can always use a little extra retirement money. So thanks for coming here like this. Not too many men walk into suicide with a hundred thousand bucks under their arm to pay their way."

Nolan didn't say anything.

"What's wrong, Nolan?" Charlie put his hands on his hips. "Run out of goddamn questions?"

"Not quite," Nolan said, turning to Tillis. "Got a cigarette?"

Tillis looked over at Charlie, who said, "Go ahead, condemned man and all that shit."

Nolan walked closer to Tillis and the black got his cigarettes out with his free hand and let Nolan pick one out. Then he put them away and handed Nolan a book of matches. Nolan lit the cigarette, leaning close to Tillis, and whispered, "Give me a try at the door. I'll slug you, and if I'm not fast enough, go ahead and shoot me."

Charlie said, "What are you doing over there?"

Tillis looked at Nolan with large wet eyes and whispered back, "Don't do it, man."

Nolan flicked the cigarette in Tillis' face, smashed his fist into the black's jaw and ran for the door, throwing it open and running out into the alley. He heard Tillis fall behind him and Charlie's voice yelled, "Get off your ass, you black bastard, get him!"

Nolan leaned for a split second against the bricking at the mouth of the alley and saw Jon in his place, motor going, and ran toward him, out into the street.

Jon saw Nolan coming and reached around to unlatch the door in back.

The car was a few feet away and Nolan felt-heard the thunk

of a silenced slug digging into the pavement by his heels.

"Start moving, kid!"

The Chevy II began to take off gradually up the street and Nolan ran for it, reaching out for the handle on the open door. His hand touched, caressed the steel of the handle, and he got it, had hold of it, and the bullet caught him in the side, going in just above where the healed-up wound was.

He felt his hand slip away from the handle and he heard Jon braking and he said, "No! Keep moving!"

The boy kept the car going slowly ahead and Nolan could feel the handle on his fingertips again but he couldn't reach around, then he did, he had it, but his fingers wouldn't grasp, couldn't grasp. The Chevy was nearly to a halt and Nolan yelled, "Go, boy! Go on!"

"Nolan . . ."

Another bullet tore into him, his shoulder this time, and the door handle glided away from his hand. He looked up and saw dimly Jon's face looking back at him, horror, frustration, fear-pain on the boy's face, and Nolan slapped the air and yelled, "Get out of here!" and Jon's face turned away and the Chevy was gone.

Nolan rolled to the curb and lay there, a fetal ball, absorbing the warmth of his oozing wounds, clutching their damp heat in against him, protecting him from the crisp night air.

Nolan looked up after either an hour or a second and saw the three men standing in the street above him. Tillis wore a deadpan, but there was regret in his eyes. Nolan knew Tillis had done all that could be expected; he'd given Nolan a chance, Nolan had blown it, and it was over. If Werner had regrets, they weren't showing; his face was an expressionless mask. Only Charlie seemed happy. Charlie was smiling.

"Don't feel bad, Nolan," Charlie said, putting his hands on his knees and bending down by Nolan's feet. "Sometimes there isn't anything left to do but die, is there, old friend? But don't hurry yourself on my account. Take your time, you cocksucking son of a bitch, I want to enjoy this."

Nolan pushed himself up on his elbows, feeling not pain but numb throbbing, and sent his right foot flying upward and sank a deep kick into Charlie's crotch.

The kick lifted the little hood into the air and dropped him to the curb, where he sat down and buried his hands between his legs and a soundless scream hissed out of him like air rushing from a low-pitched radiator.

Nolan lay there smiling softly while Werner and Tillis went to Charlie and helped him to his feet. Charlie was wobbly but he limped over to Nolan and kicked him in the side, where both the new and old wounds were. Nolan didn't give a damn; he couldn't feel it anyway.

Charlie looked like he wanted to say something, but he couldn't verbalize the depth of hatred apparent in his face. He waved an arm toward the warehouse across the street and tried to gather the strength and dignity necessary to cross by himself.

A car came around the corner, stopped by Charlie and a man stuck his head out the window and said, "Trouble here?" and Werner told him that his friends had had a little too much to drink and the man went on. Werner rushed over to Charlie's side to offer help but Charlie, tears streaming down his face, batted him away.

Werner watched as Charlie hobbled across the street. Once Charlie was back inside, Werner turned to Nolan, leaned down by him and said, "Nolan?"

Nolan was still smiling.

"Nolan . . . hey, look, I couldn't avoid this . . . he forced me, Charlie did . . . I want you to believe me, Nolan . . . listen to me . . . I'm sorry as hell about this . . . I mean it, and I wanted you to know . . . Nolan?"

Nolan motioned him nearer and Werner bent his ear down next to the bleeding man's lips.

"Fuck off," Nolan said.

Another car rounded the corner and Werner motioned to Tillis and the two men crowded around Nolan and pretended to help him to his feet.

Nolan heard Jon's voice say, "Lay him in the back or I'll blow you apart."

He felt himself being lifted, there were hands on him, and then he was in the backseat of the Chevy II, half-sitting, half-lying, and the door was open and Jon was out there, slapping Werner with a .38, and Nolan watched Werner float to the cement and hit hard. And then Jon was slugging Tillis, a tiny white fist flying at that big black face, and Tillis went down, too. Nolan knew Jon was strong, but that strong?

He thought, *I'm dreaming*, and closed his eyes. After a while he thought he heard Charlie's voice, but then the car was moving and that was behind him.

6

"How bad?" Jon asked.

He opened his eyes. It was dark. They were on the highway, the Interstate. "Crazy bastard," Nolan said. His voice sounded strange in his ears. "Told you to leave."

"You'd better not talk, Nolan."

"Crazy asshole kid," he said, "what'd you come back for?"

"I'm taking you to Planner. He'll help you."

"Asshole kid . . ."

"You shut up, Nolan."

Nolan shook his head. "Comic books," he said. He closed his eyes.

BOOK TWO

Blood Money

One

1

The two men with guns sat in the car and waited. The man on the rider's side was young, about twenty-five, and apprehensive. The man behind the wheel was about fifty-five and his face was firmly set, as though he were very determined to do something. They were both wearing Hawaiian print sportshirts and solid color shorts. In the front seat between them was a large cardboard box full of old newspapers. Under the newspapers were the guns, two Smith and Wesson nine-millimeter automatics with silencers.

The young man was thin and had a pale complexion with some fading acne under his ears along his neck; his right arm, which was elbow bent out the window, was getting red from the sun. His dark eyes were set close together and gave him a look of naive sincerity; his eyebrows met over the bridge of his nose. His hair was brown, long but not over his ears. Beads of sweat ran down his forehead. He was slapping his left hand against his left knee in some nervous inner rhythm and didn't realize it.

The older man was thin and had a dark complexion; his skin was lined and leathered from too much sun over too many years, and his lower cheeks and neck were pockmarked. He had been handsome once. He, too, had dark eyes sitting close to each other, giving him a naturally intense look. His hair was powder white, cropped short. Though the day was hot and humid, he was bone dry. He sat motionless, staring at the building across the street.

The young man said, "How you feeling, Dad?"

"I'm feeling fine," the older man said. His voice was low. "I'm feeling fine. How are you feeling?"

"Fine," the younger man said. "Fine."

Their car, a dark blue Oldsmobile of recent vintage, was parked in the open cement area beside a Dairy Queen restaurant in Iowa City, Iowa. The car had Wisconsin license plates and air-conditioning, which the older man had rejected using while they waited, a wait that had been going on now for just over an hour. A few minutes ago they had eaten hamburgers and French fries and root beer. The food had not settled well in the young man's stomach and the root beer had gone through him at once, first teasing, then torturing his bladder, but the young man felt he shouldn't mention his condition to his father. The older man had eaten an extra hamburger and felt, as he'd said, fine.

It took several more minutes for the older man to notice his son's discomfort. He was too busy concentrating on the antique shop across the road. The shop was a two-story white clapboard structure, resembling a house more than a business establishment, and in fact marked the point where the business district trailed off into residential, the downtown and University of Iowa campus being some four blocks of filling stations and junk-food restaurants away. Directly across from the Dairy Queen was a Shell station, and next to that was the antique shop; directly across from the antique shop was a grade school, an old empty brown-brick hulk, deserted for the summer, separated from the Dairy Queen by a graveled alley. And down the street were homes, modest, aging, but well kept up, strewn along this quiet street lined with lushly green shade trees. The older man nodded to himself; yes, this was a street you could retire on, like this man Planner had.

"Dad?"

"Hmmm?"

"How's it going, Dad? How you feeling?"

"Fine," he said, still not noticing how ill at ease his son was acting.

He continued to watch the antique shop, studying it. The lower level of the building was divided in half by a recessed door set between two window displays showing assorted junk on either side: old metal advertising signs ("Coca Cola," "Chase and Sanborn," "Call for Philip Morris!") and china and kids' metal toys and tea kettles and phonograph records and mason jars and crap, just plain crap, how anyone could pay money for crap like that the older man couldn't fathom. The windows were many-paned, sectioned off with metal, like stained glass, and in the midst of each display hung a sign saying, "Antiques—Edwin Planner, proprietor." With pleasure, the older man had been noting the lack of business the antique shop was doing; it had been two o'clock when they first arrived, and now, at three-fifteen, not a soul had gone in or out.

But if this man Planner felt badly about his nonexistent customer flow, he certainly didn't show it. The older man had watched carefully as the shop's proprietor peeked outside, glancing up at the hot sun in the cloudless sky and smiling. Planner was a lanky old guy, balding, wearing baggy pants and a red tee-shirt, puffing a cigar. Twice Planner had done this, and the third time he peeked out and smiled, the older man had smiled, too, and glanced at his son to share the good cheer, and then he noticed his son's discomfort.

The boy's legs were crossed tight, like a woman afraid someone was after her privates, and he was shaking his foot. His face was bloodless pale and he was gritting his teeth. The older man sighed.

"Go get me an ice cream cone," the older man said.

His son said, "What?"

"Go get me an ice cream cone." The older man gave his son a dollar.

"Uh, how many dips?"

"Two."

"Okay, Dad. Dad?"

"Hmm?"

"Uh, what flavor?"

"Doesn't make a damn to me. Strawberry."

"I think all they got's chocolate and vanilla."

"Vanilla."

"Vanilla, okay."

"And Walter?"

"Yes, Dad?"

"Go to the can, too, why don't you, before you piss all over the front seat."

Walter let loose a shaky grin, then saw his father wasn't joking, and retracted it. He got out of the car and walked around to the back of the Dairy Queen building to the restrooms. The men's was clean, very clean, as white and wholesome as ice cream itself. He felt guilty when in his extreme need and nervousness he overshot the stool and before he flushed it, he got down on the floor with toilet paper and wiped up his mess. After he was finished doing that, he felt silly, felt he was acting irrationally, and he put the seat down and sat and held his face in his hands. Shit, he thought, I got to get my head together. Christ, he thought, don't let me make an asshole out of myself in front of him.

He went to the sink and washed his hands, then brought the cold water up and splashed it against his face. After the heat of the day, this cold water was heaven. He splashed more cold water on his face, more, more, and it felt good, then suddenly it didn't feel good, it felt lousy, and he went to the stool and frantically slapped the lid up and emptied his stomach.

Back in the car, the older man was watching a young guy walk around from behind the two-story structure. Must be a rear entrance back there, he thought, and this must be that kid they told me about. Planner's nephew. He watched the boy walk past the Shell station and head toward the Iowa City business district. The boy was short, maybe five-six or -seven, but he was strongly built, his arms muscular. His hair was curly brown and long, stopping just this side of an Afro, and the older man wondered if there was any chance in hell the boy was on his way downtown for a haircut. He was wearing worn, patched jeans and a white tee-shirt with some cartoonish thing on the front. About Walter's age, the older man thought, maybe a little younger.

"Here's your cone, Dad."

The older man turned his head and nodded to his son and took the cone. Walter came around the front of the car and got in and sat, feeling queasy as he watched his father eat the ice cream. Walter said, "Did I see a kid come out of the shop?"

"Yeah."

"I didn't see anybody go in there."

"It's the guy's nephew or something. He lives there."

"Oh. You didn't say anything about that."

"I wasn't sure whether the kid lived with him or not."

"Oh."

"Anyway, I'm glad he's left."

"How come?"

"Don't be stupid. It'll be easier with just the one guy."

"Oh. Yeah, of course."

The ice cream tasted good. And he felt good, knowing the kid wouldn't be in there. He had no compunction about what he was going to do, but killing or even hurting some kid Walter's age was something he didn't care to do. He'd gone into this knowing it would be like the old days. It had to be like the old days, like coming up in those years when brains weren't enough, you had to have balls, and balls meant shooting who you had to when you had to and the hell with manners. He had to have the right frame of mind if he expected to deal with Nolan and come out on top. So sure, this was like the old days, this was a situation where if you had to be hard, you were hard. But these last ten, fifteen soft years made it hard to be hard; it was like sex, he could still get it up, if need be, but he wasn't no tiger anymore.

He was glad the kid wouldn't be around. Some old son of a bitch, what did that matter, but some damn kid? That was something else.

2

At two o'clock, just as the two men with guns were pulling into the Dairy Queen parking lot across the street, Planner was lighting a cigar and wondering when the phone call would come. The cigar was a Garcia y Vega, at least one box of which Planner kept under the counter always; he liked cigars, Garcia y Vegas especially, and if the occasional customers who walked into his antique shop were irritated by the smoke, well, fuck 'em. The phone call he was waiting for was from Nolan, a man who played a part in Planner's other and primary occupation, which was planning jobs for professional thieves.

The antique shop, however, was more than just a front. Long before the thought of using an antique shop as a front had ever entered his mind, Planner had been a collector of antiques, though like many collectors he was a specialist and only one small branch of antiquing held a fascination for him.

Buttons.

Planner loved buttons.

Not buttons that hold your clothes together (though there were collectors of those around, too) but political buttons and advertising buttons and anything that pinned on, including sheriff's and other cop badges, if they were old enough. The mainstay of his collection was the political buttons, the pride being his Lincoln tokens and the large picture buttons of Hoover. These were in a frame upstairs, while others of lesser value and importance, but gems nonetheless, graced a display case in the front of the store.

It was that display case that let other dealers who came around know that despite the junk quality of most of the

merchandise in the shop, Planner was a dealer who knew
what he was doing, worthy of respect. It was with great pleasure that he would turn down offers from fat-cat dealers
who would drool at the generous assortment of political buttons in the airtight case, the Willkies, the Wilsons, the
Bryans. If he was feeling really generous, he might sell them
one Nixon or a Kennedy or perhaps a Goldwater, but not
often, as even recent buttons brought a pretty penny, since
during the last three or four presidential campaigns a man
had to contribute five or six bucks before the party would
give him a picture button of the candidate. And who could
guess what a McGovern/Eagleton would one day be worth?

If he was feeling particularly ornery, Planner would show
dealers the Lincoln tokens and the Hoovers upstairs and
would listen to their eager bids and pretend to consider and
then calmly refuse. Even if a dealer got down on his knees
(which had happened a couple times) Planner would shake
his head solemnly no. Back downstairs, to rub salt in the
wound, Planner would point out the barrel of buttons next
to the front display case, a barrelful of zilch buttons Planner
sold to the school kids for a quarter a throw.

Also, from dealers who came around and from stops he
made to keep his "buying trips" looking honest, Planner had
managed, over these past thirteen or fifteen years, to fill in
the gaps of his own collection, picking up damn near every
button he needed. But even before he got into the antique
trade, Planner had had one of the best goddamn button col-
lections in the U.S. of A. (if he did say so himself) and so,
when he was picking out some way to semi-retire, the
antique hustle had been a natural.

Sometimes, sitting behind the counter, smoking a Garcia
y Vega, Planner would wonder if he could actually make a
living selling antiques, you know, straight-out legitimate.
Even though he purposely filled his shop with unspectacular
horseshit, he did pretty good, better than he needed to with
a situation that was basically a front. But the little old ladies
in tennis shoes would ooo and ahh at the god-damnedest

junk, and he would constantly (three or four times a year) have to spend a day going to flea markets and yard sales and load his station wagon with more bottles and jars and furniture and china and kettles and toys and crap and more crap. When he'd bought the place, it had been jampacked with junk, which he'd thought would last for years and years. Six months, it had been, and he was out scouting flea markets to replenish his supply. Occasionally he'd run onto an honest-to-God antique for next to nothing and these he would pack carefully away in one of his backrooms. One day he might sell them, but not now. Somehow it seemed crazy to sell an antique, a real one that is, since an antique's value is its age, and tomorrow it's going to be older and hence more valuable.

In that way, and many others, the antique shop was more than a simple front. In addition to feeding Planner's button habit, and turning a nice dollar itself now and then, the antique shop was just the sort of nebulous one-man business operation that made it damn near impossible for the IRS to get to you. Just the same, Planner reported a healthy income and gave the feds their healthy share, faking his own book-keeping, which required both math skill and imagination. It was a time-consuming task, doing the books and other records, but he would find ways to amuse himself, such as inventing wild merchandise when writing up fake sales slips, his favorite being "One Afghanistan banana stand, $361." He had told that one to Nolan once, thinking he would laugh, but Nolan had said, "That's a little silly, isn't it? You're getting senile." Nolan implied that if Planner got too goddamn cute with his records, the IRS would smell something, should they go sniffing. Planner didn't think so. Anyway, the tax boys, classically, didn't care how you made your money, they just wanted their piece of your action.

Probably the best angle was that as an antique dealer, Planner could make frequent buying trips and on them gether the information that would enable him to put together "packages" for clients like Nolan. These trips aroused no suspicion whatsoever, neither locally nor wherever he chose to go.

On the trips he got his information by playing the role of a cantankerous but friendly old antique dealer, and while putting on the eccentric act had been a chore at first (fifteen, sixteen years ago when he got started) he found that now, at sixty-seven, the role was much easier to play convincingly. People weren't surprised when an old guy like him would want to talk for a while, and he could always manipulate a stranger into a lengthy and rewarding conversation. The information was easy to get: he'd act paranoid and tell about his shop and how he was afraid of being robbed and ask about alarm systems and safes and such. He'd admire the layout of, say, a jewelry store and tell about how he was thinking of remodeling his place along similar lines and just how is everything put together here, exactly. He'd express dissatisfaction with his present payroll system for his staff of ten employees (all nonexistent, of course) and ask advice. And on and on. No trick to it.

He puffed his cigar and grinned to himself. It was a damn good life. Much better than it had been for those years and years he'd spent actually working on jobs, the bank hits, the armored cars, the payroll robberies, all of it. When he was young, he'd found it stimulating, but before long (oh, even into his late twenties) his nerves had started to bother him. Planning ahead of time was one thing, but being on the job when the shit hit the proverbial fan and you got to improvise is another thing entirely. He worked things out so that at age fifty he could "sort of" retire, which he had, and a good thing too. He wouldn't like to work in the field the way things were now. He wouldn't enjoy working with the kind of people that were in the trade these days, if you could even call it a trade anymore.

Planner had been in the trade when it *was* a trade. He started young, young enough to have worked with Dillinger a few times. There wasn't anybody around today, needless to say, who could compare to Dillinger, except for Nolan, who was almost an old-timer himself, and that guy Walker, and a few others, Busch, Peters, Beckey, not many. Every string you put together these days has got somebody you can't be sure of, he thought, and one or maybe two somebodies you never heard of and got to trust what some other somebody told you about 'em. It was hard to find pros these days, people who really knew what they were doing.

Like Nolan and that bank job, a year ago November. Even with that team of amateurs, Planner thought, Nolan had managed to put together a professional score. Most people these days, when they hit a bank, clean out a teller cage or two or three (picking up mostly bait money, the marked bills every teller keeps on hand for just such occasions) and come off with a grand total of two, maybe three thousand. Shit, Planner thought, Nolan wouldn't cross the street for three thousand. Because he knew what he was doing, Nolan had knocked that bank the hell over, he'd cleaned that bank's vault out of every damn cent, choosing the day when the bank would be brimming with cash (the first Monday of the month) and got away with close to eight hundred thousand bucks.

Most of which, Planner thought, swallowing, is back there in that safe of mine. He felt suddenly uncomfortable. His cigar went out and he relit, using an old-fashioned kitchen match. He wished Nolan would call.

"Hey, Unc, I'm talking to you. Snap out of it."

"Huh?" Planner woke from his reverie and noticed his nephew Jon was standing across the counter from him, grinning. The boy had a mop of curly hair and was wearing a tee-shirt picturing a manlike pig (or piglike man) in a superhero outfit, including cape, under the words "Wonder Warthog." Planner grinned back at his crazy nephew and said, "What the hell, I didn't even see you there, Jon. I'm getting old. You say something?"

"I just wanted to know if I got any mail."

Planner nodded and reached under the counter, pulling out four wrapped packages and a long cardboard tube. Jon was always getting stuff in the mail; it was that damn fool comic book collecting of his, mostly.

Jon took the bundles in his arms and said, "Great!" His eyes were lit up like a four-year-old on his birthday. The boy nodded toward the long tube and said, "That's my EC poster, I'll bet. Made a good haul today."

"Just take that nonsense away and don't bother me."

Jon laughed. "Yeah, I can see how busy you are, Unc. Hey, has Nolan called yet?"

"No."

"Be sure to say hello to him for me."

"You know I will."

"Thanks, Unc."

The boy disappeared into the back of the store, where his room was stuck way in the back. Planner was glad Jon was living here; he felt better having someone else around what with all the cash in the safe. After all, half of that eight hundred thousand dollars from Nolan's bank job belonged to Jon. Yes, Planner thought, smiling, relighting his Garcia y Vega once again, remembering how he brought Nolan and Jon together, my nephew's a very wealthy boy, thanks to his old uncle.

But Planner wouldn't feel at ease, couldn't feel at ease, until that money was out of his safe and in some bank where it belonged. There were reasons for keeping it here, sound ones, but he would be glad, glad hell, *overjoyed,* when Nolan's call came through saying special arrangements've been made and the money can be moved.

He was used to keeping money in the safe, and large amounts of it, too. Personally, he didn't have much faith in banks, having seen too many of them fail in the Depression and having had a hand in the robbing of a goodly number as well. So he usually had twenty to fifty thousand dollars in that big old safe of his in his farthest-back backroom, as well as smaller but still substantial amounts belonging to various clients like Nolan who liked to have little nest eggs stuck here and there for emergencies. But Nolan and Jon's little nest egg—eight hundred thousand dollars—Christ! If there was such a thing as too much money, that was it; it hardly fit into the safe, all of it, between it and the other money in there, near a million all together crowded into that poor old safe, and had been for almost a year now.

When Nolan was staying there, Planner hadn't felt so nervous about the money. At first, when Jon brought Nolan in all shot up like that and that doctor trying to keep Nolan patched together, there had been too much excitement to be nervous. Then, when Nolan was healing up from the wounds, feeling pretty good and able to move around some, Planner felt fairly safe; even under the weather, Nolan was a good man to have around. And of course Jon had moved from his apartment into that room in back of the shop, and Jon was a strong, tough kid, don't let his size fool you, who'd seen Nolan through a rough spot and proved to his uncle that he could handle himself.

But near a year Nolan had been gone and all that money had been sitting in that safe, brother. Nerve-racking.

Well, Planner thought, doesn't do any good to sit and worry like some goddamn old maid. Nolan will call today and that money'll be out of here by tomorrow night. Maybe sooner.

He let out a sigh and suddenly noticed how nice and cool it was in the shop. That old air-conditioner of his was really putting out. He'd had it a long time, but it was still working like a son of a bitch. Just because a thing is old, he thought, doesn't mean it's not worth a damn. He smiled at the thought.

He got out from behind the counter and poked his nose outside the front door. The day was hot, a real scorcher, but the sun was big and yellow in the sky, and the sky was blue without any clouds at all. It was a beautiful day.

Now call, Nolan, damn you.

3

The ax was embedded in the man's head, the blood gushing down his forehead, yet somehow he was still standing, implanted there in the doorway, his eyes wide and dead but staring. The other man gasped in horror, the sweat streaming down his face, the guilt apparent in his terror-swollen eyes.

Jon grinned. He laughed out loud.

It was the most beautiful poster he'd ever seen in his life. He held it out in front of him, drinking it all in. He couldn't believe how fantastic the artwork looked blown up to this huge size; the violent scene had originally appeared as a comic book cover back in the early fifties, and blown up to a 22" by 28" poster, and in full-blooded color yet, was some trip. Almost reluctantly he allowed the poster to roll itself back up, and he tossed it on his as yet unmade bed, to be put up on the wall later that day.

Of course it wouldn't be easy finding a place to display that beautiful poster: the walls of the little room were full as it was. In its former life, the room had been one of Planner's storerooms, and after Planner and Jon had cleared and cleaned it, what remained was a dreary cubicle with four unpainted gray-wooden walls and a cement floor.

Jon had met the challenge by papering the gray-wood walls with poster after poster after poster, and the cement floor was covered by shag throw rugs and Jon's considerable collection of comic books. The comics were neatly boxed, three deep along each wall, with a filing cabinet in one corner that contained the more valuable comics. Planner had contributed a genuinely antique single bed with a carved walnut headboard, and a nonmatching walnut four-drawer chest of drawers. The room was cluttered but orderly, though against one wall was a wooden drawing easel with an expensive-looking swivel chair such as an executive might have back of his desk, easel and chair surrounded by scattered paper and pencils.

Comic art was Jon's life. It went far beyond a simple hobby, and Jon was fond of his uncle but thought Planner's button-gathering was dumb, just not sensible at all. Those precious political buttons of Planner's were artifacts of a boring and unpleasant reality, while comics were "immortal gateways to fantasy," as Jon had said in an article he was working on for submission to a fanzine.

He supposed his love for comics had something to do with his fucked-up childhood. Jon was a bastard, he hoped in the literal sense alone, and his mother had liked to think of herself as a chanteuse. What that amounted to was she sang and played piano in bars, and not very well. Because his mother was on the road most of the time, Jon's childhood had been spent here and there, with this relative and that one, Planner part of the time, and Jon hadn't lived steady with his mother until those last few years when she was serving cocktails in bars instead of singing in them. She was dead now, hit by a car some three years ago, perhaps by choice. Jon hadn't known her well enough to get properly upset, and he had occasional feelings of guilt for never having cried over her.

His childhood was a good example, Jon felt, of reality's general lack of appeal. Either it was boring—like the half dozen or so faceless relatives he'd lived with, the score of schools he'd gone to, the hundreds of kids he'd failed to get to know—or it was so goddamn tragic it was a soap opera and impossible to take seriously.

So why not comic books?

He had built his collection up carefully over the years, at first just hoarding the books he bought off the stands, then gradually, as he got into his teens, he began working on the older titles, seeking out other collectors and swapping, sending increasingly large amounts of hard-earned money through the mail for rare old issues, even trekking to New York each summer these past four years for the big comics convention. Jon read and reread the books, savoring the stories, studying the artwork. When he finished rereading one of the yellowing classics, he'd seal it back in its airtight plastic bag and carefully return it to its appropriate stack in its appropriate box.

Though he was as yet unpublished, Jon considered himself already to be a full-fledged artist in the field of the graphic story (as comics were called in the more pretentious moments of fans like himself) and he felt this way primarily because he was too old now to say, "I want to draw comics when I grow up." He *was* grown up, as much as he was going to anyway, and at twenty-one years of age, Jon was more than just serious about his artwork and comic-collecting; it was his lifestyle.

The posters on his walls reflected this. More than half of them were recreations of classic comic book and strip heroes, drawn with black marker pen and water-colored, Dick Tracy, Batman, Flash Gordon, Tarzan, Captain Marvel, Buck Rogers. The latest poster was a finely detailed face of an old witch, a withered old crone with a mostly toothless grin and a single bloodshot, popping eye, and was an indication that Jon's taste in comic art was undergoing a transition. Once the ax poster was put up, and one of the superheroes taken down, the shift from heroes to horror would become even more apparent.

He sat on the bed and began eagerly opening his other packages. One of them was from California and was filled with underground comics. Jon smiled as he examined the cover of the latest issue of Bill Griffith's "Zippy the Pinhead." Not much else of the underground art was up to Griffith's high standard of absurdity, in this batch of books anyway. He had once thought the undergrounds were where he could make his first splash, but their heyday—when Robert Crumb and Gilbert Shelton were making "Mr. Natural" and the "Freak Brothers," respectively, into household words—had passed into the ancient history that was the '70s.

Two of the other packages turned out to be rejections. Jon was very disappointed. It wasn't so much that he'd expected to sell these "graphic stories," but that he hadn't realized that this was what the packages contained. He was disappointed that their contents hadn't been more old comics or fanzines, dozens of which he'd paid for by mail order and should be showing up any day now. Both of the rejected stories were horror tales, and he was told, in a polite note from one editor, that he drew well but his style was too derivative of "Ghastly" Graham Ingels, and if he could just develop a more original style, they would be interested in seeing more. The other publisher included no note, but Jon was not surprised the story was coming back, because he'd heard through the fan grapevine that this company had gone out of business recently.

The other package perked him up considerably. It was chock-full of EC's, and he'd half expected the ad he had responded to was a hoax, since these EC's had been incredibly low in price, costing only five to six dollars a piece. There were four "Vault of Horror," two "Tales from the Crypt" and one "Crime SuspenStories." He flopped down on the bed and one by one opened each plastic bag and eased out the comic inside. He didn't read the stories, he just thumbed through the magazines, window-shopping.

He had just got into the EC horror comics in the last six months or so. He'd heard of them, of course, but had never delved into the "Vault of Horror" because the prices were stiff for books printed as recently as the early fifties. And Jon's primary interests had been the superheroes of the Golden Age of Comics, which ran roughly from 1937 to 1947, and issues reprinting newspaper strips like Dick Tracy and Buck Rogers.

But lately he'd gone sour on superheroes. They didn't seem relevant to his life anymore. He guessed it had something to do with knowing Nolan, meeting him, working with him.

He smiled, remembering the first time he and Nolan had met. He glanced at the posters over his bed, which were the only noncomic art posters in the room: photos of Leonard Nimoy as Spock, Buster Crabbe in his serial days, and Lee Van Cleef decked out in his "man in black" gun-fighter apparel. Nolan had looked over Jon's series of posters and had noticed especially the one of Lee Van Cleef, studying the black-dressed Western figure with the high cheekbones and narrow eyes and mustache, and Jon had told him who Van Cleef was, adding, "Looks something like you, don't you think?" Nolan had shaken his head no, smiled crookedly and pointed a finger at Buster Crabbe, saying "Flash Gordon's more my style."

In a way, *both* Van Cleef and Flash Gordon were Nolan's style. Nolan was the sort of man Jon had always hoped to meet but never thought he really would. The sort of man Jon had admired in fantasy. Nolan was Flash Gordon, and Bogart and Superman, too. Nolan was Dick Tracy and Clint Eastwood and Captain America. Oh, he wasn't as pretty as any of the fantasy heroes. His face was lean, hard, cruel, and his body was so scarred from bullet wounds he looked as if he'd been used for a year as some medical student's cadaver. And Nolan could be a bastard at times, could be a real bastard, really an altogether unpleasant person to be around.

Which was maybe why those fantasy guys didn't satisfy Jon anymore. Nolan was everything they were and more: he was real, both perfect and imperfect, everything. A superhero couldn't come up to Nolan's standards.

Did it matter that Nolan was a thief? Not really, Jon thought, his opinion shaded by the fact that he, too, was a thief of major proportions, since that bank job a year and a half ago. It wasn't *what* the heroes stood for, it was the *way* they stood for it that mattered. Jon remembered seeing the film *White Heat,* where the so-called good guy Edmund O'Brien double-crossed Jimmy Cagney. Cagney was a psychopathic murderer, but he had style. When they showed *White Heat* at the U of I student union last month, everybody in the house had booed that son of a bitch Edmund O'Brien.

He was picking out one of the "Vault of Horror" issues to read when he heard the phone ringing out in the store. He had the urge to jump off the bed and run out there and see if it was Nolan calling, but he repressed the urge. He'd made up his mind that he was not going to jump up and down like a spastic puppy for the chance to talk to Nolan. Besides, Jon had nothing to say, really, and Nolan just about never had anything to say.

No. This was business between Nolan and Planner (even though Jon was up to his ass involved in that business) and Jon would stay cool, the way Nolan would expect him to.

"Hey, Jon boy!"

The sound of Planner's rough voice made Jon's heart leap. Nolan had asked to talk to him! Imagine that.

Jon joined Planner out in the store and Planner said, "It's for you . . . it's that woman."

Jon didn't let the disappointment show in his voice. "Karen," he said, "Good morning, honey."

"Morning my ass, Jonny. It's two-thirty. Did you just wake up?"

"Yeah, 'bout half an hour ago."

"Me, too. I'm hung over as hell."

"Me, too. Did we have a good time last night, Kare? I can't remember it too clear."

"We had a couple good times. You had breakfast?"

"I slept through it, just like you did."

"We missed lunch, too, you know. Come on over to the apartment and I'll fix you some eggs."

"And sausage?"

"You drive a hard bargain. And sausage."

"That sounds good."

"Then maybe a little later I can refresh your memory about last night."

"That sounds better."

"Get your cute little ass over here, Jonny."

"Will do."

Jon hung up and noticed Planner's reproving gaze. Jon grinned and said, "I know, I know, she's too old for me."

"She's old enough to be your mother."

"Oh, bull. You're old enough to be my grandmother. And I don't hold it against you, do I?"

"No, but I'll bet you hold it against her," and now Planner, too, was grinning.

"What would you do in my place?"

"The same damn thing, nephew. The same damn thing."

"Thought so. All this time you've just been jealous."

"Sure, kid. That broad's just about the right age for me."

Jon walked over to the row of penny candy Planner kept along the counter for the school kids from across the street. He took a piece of bubble gum from one of the glass bowls and unwrapped the gum and tossed the pink square into his mouth. He chewed it up good and walked back to Planner and blew a healthy bubble and popped it at his uncle.

"Smartass kid," Planner said, trying not to smile.

"See you later, Unc," Jon said, and went out the back way.

4

The older man took his time eating the ice cream cone. It irritated Walter that his father could be so calm, just sitting there eating that goddamn ice cream as if they were at the beach or something. He was irritated enough to speak, and in a tone more harsh than he generally dare use when he spoke to his father. He said, "How can you just sit there and eat that goddamn stuff?"

The older man said, "What?"

"I said . . . nothing. Nothing, Dad."

"What did you say?"

"Nothing."

"Now what did I tell you? I told you don't be nervous. We're going in and do it and we'll be out and done in nothing flat. So don't be nervous, understand?"

"I'm not nervous."

The older man studied his son's face carefully. The boy was naturally pale, but he seemed to be even whiter than usual. But aside from shaking his foot on the leg crossed over one knee, the boy was showing no overt signs of tension.

"It's not going to be hard," the older man said. "I'll handle all the hard stuff. All you have to do is back me up and keep your damn wits about you."

"I know, Dad."

"But I won't lie to you. It won't be pleasant in there."

"You told me."

"It won't be pleasant in there because that's the way it has to be."

"You told me a hundred times, Dad."

"Don't smart-mouth me."

"I'm not."

"Don't. And I'm just telling you this because I look at you right now and you know what I see? I see a kid, I see a god-damn college kid who's liable to go in there and crap his pants, and I can't afford that, understand, and you can't afford it either."

"Dad . . ."

"You didn't have to be part of this. I didn't want you to be part of this, remember. But you wanted to help. You begged me to help. Fine, that's fine talk, but this is now, this is right now and we're about to go across that street and do the kind of thing they don't teach you in school, understand, so if you want out now, say so, for Christ's sake."

"Dad . . ."

"I'll drive you back to the lodge. Right now. I'll drive you back to the goddamn lodge and come back down here tomorrow and do it alone."

"Dad, you couldn't do it alone . . ."

"I could. It wouldn't be no goddamn picnic, but I could."

"I'm not nervous, Dad."

He looked at his son and saw resolve in the young face. He smiled briefly and squeezed his son's arm, reaching over the box with the newspapers and guns in it to do so.

He felt better now, now that he could have confidence in his son again. But that ice cream, which had gone down so smooth, so easy, so cool and refreshing, the damn stuff was churning in his stomach, making him feel queasy. All of a sudden *he* was nervous, and it almost made him laugh. Worrying about his son being nervous had got him that way.

Funny, Walter thought, where the hell did *that* outburst come from? His father had been sitting there for an hour, looking so calm it was unnatural, as though he were on pot or something. And then out of nowhere the old man had let go with this practically hysterical lecture. Walter was stunned; he never would have suspected that his father's placid surface was hiding such turbulent undercurrents.

Not that he hadn't had the notion that something was (how should he put it?) *wrong* with his father. Right now he was wishing he could summon courage to look at his father, to study him, observe his behavior. (Walter was a business major, but he'd taken several psychology courses as electives.) He wondered now, as he'd wondered more than once in the past few weeks, if his father was, well, sane.

Up until this uncharacteristic outburst of a moment ago, the old man seemed normal enough to Walter: quiet, self-sufficient, a hard but not unaffectionate man. But Walter knew these were superficial judgments, biased judgments from a child who desperately wanted to love and respect a father. He had never known his father all that well, really. Dad had been gone so much of the time, the business had been so demanding. Walter had felt much closer to his mother, and if she were still alive today, the situation would most certainly be different, to say the least.

The distance between Walter and his father had been

shortened only these past months, these last several weeks
especially. The old guy was no longer the aloof, godlike,
benevolent family dictator, but a human being, a *man*
willing to meet his son as an equal . . . or at least as a peer.

Walter liked that. It was a new experience and he liked it,
even now, even sitting in this car waiting to . . . to do what
they were going to.

This last week, at the lodge at Eagle's Roost, had been
wonderful and terrible. The memories the place aroused
were double-edged, pleasant this moment and painful the
next. Like a fire, nice to look at until you got too close. He at
times felt he and his father were ghosts haunting the empty
old lodge, perhaps in search of other ghosts who could share
remembrances of other, better times. He could hear the
voices, his mother, his sister, his father, too, and once he
heard himself, a high-pitched voice, prepuberty, and he
laughed; he heard all these voices, especially late at night
and early in the morning, he really heard them, but then of
course he was trying to hear them.

He sat in the main room downstairs, that huge open-
beamed, high-ceilinged room, dark wooded, dominated by
the black brick fireplace and the elk head above it. There
were three brown leather sofas arranged in a block C that
opened onto the fireplace, forming a room within the room,
an area before the hearth where throw rugs and pillows
were scattered for lounging. But the pillows and throw rugs
were gone now, and when he and his father arrived, the
sofas, like all the other furniture, were covered with sheets.
Walter had uncovered the center sofa, where he sat and
stared at the fireplace, as though it were warm and roaring
rather than cold and barren. They uncovered the long table
in the dining area to the left of the sofas, and he and his
father sat alone together at the table, eating TV dinners and
canned food and other survival rations that didn't jibe with
the memories of sumptuous feasts at this same table. On the
other side of the room, where Mother's sewing table still
stood, covered of course, and faded areas on the wood floor

where card tables had been, for playing Clue with his sister, and, later, Monopoly, was the window seat, the same plaid cushions he remembered. Once again he sat and watched the trees bend slightly in the breeze, their needles shimmering, and if he leaned close to the window, he could still get that same good view of the lake, blue and sparkling where the sun hit it, pink, bobbing swimmers close to shore, the sails of skiffs white along the horizon.

And sitting there in that window seat, his mind flooded with memories, he could not keep himself from wondering what this stranger who was his father, this stranger and guns and robbery, had to do with his life.

He'd known for a long time, of course, what his father's "business" was. No one had told him, exactly, but he'd gotten it a piece at a time, and the knowledge had been gradual, there'd been no great revelation. But the lodge seemed such an odd setting for preparing for today's possible violence. High up on that hill, overlooking the two lakes, the lodge had been the one place where his father had allowed no contact from the "business" world. Their home, in a suburb of Chicago, had seen occasionally the hard-faced men who associated with his father "at work." But the lodge was different.

He remembered the time his Uncle Harry had shown up at the lodge, with two men who wore trench coats and slouch hats and had faces like the Boogie Man. Walter had been eight at the time and had found the two men with Uncle Harry frightening, but no more so than Uncle Harry, who was himself no beauty contest winner, and Walter's sister called him Uncle Scarey behind his back. Uncle Harry had told their father there was important business at Lake Geneva that he ought to tend to personally, and to come along. Dad had been furious with Uncle Harry for bringing the two men with him, and into the lodge. Walter could still hear his father's voice: "I told you never to bring any of your goddamn goons around here! This place is for my family and myself and I don't want you or anybody contaminating it!

Now wait outside, Harry." And Dad had shoved the two Boogie Men out the door as if they were a couple of sissies.

"Are you ready?" the older man said.

"Yes," Walter said.

"One last thing," he said. "Don't be surprised at anything I do. I might have to do some things that make you sick. I might have to do some things that make you not so goddamn proud of your old man. Well, that's too bad. You're in it all the way now, and you got to go along with everything I do, and don't you flinch in there, don't you panic, don't show a thing in your face, either. Or we're liable to die. Now. Do you understand, Walter?"

He'd heard all this before, too. His father had gone over all of this, many times, during the past week at the lodge, though there he'd always seemed calm and now Walter wasn't sure. And he'd told Walter how they would go about the robbery, though he'd been vague about certain aspects. But when Walter asked him what was the purpose of the robbery, was it just money? Would they be going to Mexico or Canada or South America or something to start a new life on this money? This isn't about money, his father had said, this is a matter of blood. And that was all he would say.

"Do you understand, Walter?"

"Yes, Dad."

"Here we go then," and the older man turned the key in the ignition of the car and pulled across the street, up to the side door of the antique shop.

5

A bell was ringing. Planner sat up suddenly straight in the soft old easy chair behind the counter; he'd been dozing. The bell kept ringing. Is that the phone? Planner got up. Is that you, Nolan? Is that your call? The bell rang on and Planner said, silently, no. Somebody at the side door.

He took time out to light himself a fresh Garcia y Vega before answering the door. He had to get rid of the sour taste in his mouth. He wondered how his mouth could taste so foul from sleeping, why, not more than fifteen minutes, a half hour. You'd think he'd slept for twelve hours, as bad as the taste was. He puffed the cigar until he felt he could live with his mouth and then slowly moved toward the side door, the bell still going.

"All right, all right," Planner muttered, "hold your damn horses, Jesus almighty."

He unlocked the side door and looked through the screen at the two men standing out on the cement stoop. One of them was old, maybe fifty-five, maybe more; the other was much younger, maybe twenty, twenty-five at the most. Both of them looked like tourists, probably staying at Lake McBride. They had on bright swirling-colored shirts that almost hurt to look at; be better off looking into the sun dead on. Father and his kid, most likely. Both of them had the same dark eyes, set close together, and the same general frame.

Planner tried to say, "Yes?" but his voice cracked and it came out a croak. He cleared his throat, kicked open the screen door and shot a clot of phlegm out on the gravel to the left of where the older man was standing. He grinned. He said, "Excuse me, boys, you caught me napping. Not quite awake yet. What can I do for you?"

The older guy said, "We have some things here we'd like to have appraised."

Oh, shit. Should've known, Planner thought. Christ, what a nuisance. Sitting here waiting for Nolan to call, anxious as hell, and somebody comes around with piddling shit like this.

"I don't do much appraising," Planner said.

"We have some real nice china in the car," the older man said. "We have some real nice pieces."

"Well . . ."

"You can make us an offer, or you can just tell us what you think they're worth. We'd be much obliged."

"I usually charge for appraising," Planner said. He wondered how he could be so petty; why didn't he just tell them come on in and take a look at their damn china. But he was irritated, irritated Nolan hadn't called yet, and couldn't help himself taking it out on these nice folks.

"How much?"

The older man seemed to be getting a shade irritated himself, Planner thought, and with just cause, he supposed.

"Oh, a dollar," Planner said. "But what the hell . . . come on in and I'll tell you what I think of the stuff. Never mind the buck."

"Thank you," the older man said.

The younger one said nothing. He looked kind of pale. He wasn't the healthiest-looking kid Planner had ever seen.

"I'll get the box," the older man said, and he went to the car and got a big cardboard box out of the front seat.

What's wrong with that kid? Planner wondered. Letting his father carry that box. What was wrong with him?

Planner held the screen door open for the older man and the boy followed close on the man's heels. Planner shut the screen and locked the side door. He didn't like anyone coming in the side door, and besides, he had to keep it shut to keep the air-conditioning circulating.

Right away, the young man walked up to the front of the store and started browsing. Almost immediately he found the display case of political buttons and looked in at them. In spite of himself, Planner felt proud; no one could resist his buttons.

At the rear of the store, the older man was setting the large box on the counter, which ran from the front of the store clear back. The counter had once been used as the bar in a saloon back in Iowa City's pioneer days, and was one of the more valuable antiques in the store, though it was roughed up and scarred and chipped from daily use for a century or so. Planner let out a sigh. The sigh was one part boredom, the other part anticipation. Well, he thought, might as well see what this fella has in the box; maybe it'll take my mind off waiting for Nolan to call.

The older man was lifting some newspapers out of the box and laying them on the counter. He said to Planner, "Come take a look at this, I think you'll find it interesting," and Planner walked over to him and joined him at the end of the counter. The man reached both arms into the box and came back up holding an automatic in either hand. The automatics were good-size guns, not .45's, but good size. Nine millimeters, probably. Worst of all, Planner thought, they had silencers on them. That was bad. Very bad. It meant these guys were most likely pros of some kind. Somehow he knew. Somehow Planner knew these men knew about his safe full of money. It's all your fault, Nolan, he thought.

The older man nodded to the younger man, who was still in the front of the store. The younger man locked the front door; it was a Yale lock and was no trouble. He turned the sign around on the door so that the side reading "Closed" faced out, while the "Open" faced in. He hadn't really been interested in buttons at all. He walked back and joined the older man and Planner. The older man gave the boy one of the silenced automatics. The boy held it tight and with some effort, as though the gun were very heavy. As though it were an anvil he was holding.

The older man watched the boy for a moment to make

sure he was all right. Then he said, "Let's go in your back room and talk. I don't want nobody looking in the windows and seeing us talking. They might get suspicious, seeing we got a couple of goddamn guns."

Planner didn't like the older man. He appeared to be cool, calm, and collected, but there was a manic edge to his voice. He wasn't crazy about the nervous kid, either. He wished he was in Tahiti.

Also, he wasn't crazy about taking them into the back-room. There were two rooms directly behind where they were standing, and in the farthest one back was the safe. Planner would have liked to have been behind the counter, up by the cash register. He kept a Colt .32 automatic under the counter by the cash register. It wasn't a big gun, because he didn't want a lot of bullets flying and messing up his store, in case of a robbery; a .32 was big enough to do what-ever was needed. But right now he wished it was a .357 magnum, so he could blow these fuckers into a million bloody pieces. He didn't like either one of them at all.

"Move it," the older man said. He shoved Planner's shoulder with the heel of his hand.

Planner said, "All right," and led them into the first of the backrooms. He pulled the string on the overhead hanging bulb. The room was full of boxed and crated antiques Planner was saving for some hazy future use.

"Where's the safe?" the older man said.

Planner smiled. He'd been right! He'd been right. They knew. They did know.

The older man slapped Planner across the face with the silenced gun. The blood was salty in his mouth. The older man said, "Where's the goddamn safe?"

"This way," Planner said.

That's okay, Planner thought. He had almost forgotten, but now he fully remembered that the safe was the best place in the world to lead them. Because the twin of that .32 automatic was in the safe. Tucked behind the piles of money. Waiting.

"Okay," Planner said, tugging on the string on this room's overhead light. This room, too, was full of crates and boxes, as well as some old chairs and tables in need of repair. There was a small work area in one corner where Planner did his own mending. In the other corner was the big old gray metal safe. So old the name of the company was worn off. A good man could open it up in ten minutes. Planner had never bought a newer, more burglarproof (ha!) safe because it seemed foolish—after all, the only people who knew that he kept goodly amounts of cash in the safe were his friends, and he had the kind of friends who could open *any* safe, so why bother?

"Open it," the older man said. The younger man was standing behind him with the empty cardboard box in his arms, the silenced automatic peeking around one side of it.

That was just what Planner wanted to do. He wanted to open that safe and bring his hand out shooting that .32. But he didn't want to be obvious.

So he said, "No."

The older man slapped him across the face with the silenced gun again and Planner's upper plate flew out onto the floor. The floor was all dusty and dirty and now so was his plate. He wished Jon had cleaned this room up yesterday, as he was supposed to. Feeling silly with only half his teeth in his head, he said, "You lousy son of a bitch, put that gun away and I could whale the crap out of you."

The older man hit him again, in the stomach this time, and Planner lay down on the floor. It didn't hurt all that bad, but he figured if he acted as if it did, maybe the guy would stop hitting him. He shouldn't have got mad at the guy and sworn at him like that. That was stupid. He looked up and said, "Who the hell are you, anyway?"

"A friend of a friend," the older man said. "Now open that goddamn safe."

"What made you want to rob me for? I'm just an old feller trying to make a buck. There's nothing in there worth taking. Oh, sure, I keep a few of my prize heirlooms in there. I'll admit it. They're worth some money, sure, but they mainly just make an old man happy in his last days."

"Cut the crap," the older man said, kicking Planner in the side. "Open the goddamn safe, I said. You can keep the heirlooms, you goddamn old buzzard, and we'll take the money."

Planner just looked at him.

"That's right," the older man said. "There's a lot of goddamn money in that safe, isn't there? You know it and I know it. Forget about pretending and open it."

"Nolan will come after you," Planner said. "I feel sorry for you bastards when Nolan comes after you."

Something funny glittered in the older man's eyes. He kicked Planner again and said, "Open it. Open it."

Planner got to his feet, said, "All right, okay," and dialed the combination lock. The latch creaked as he opened the heavy door, which swung out on its hinges to reveal six shelves, lined with stacked green.

"Jesus," the younger man said, awestruck. It was the first word he'd uttered since coming into the store.

The older man said nothing. He just smiled, a grim, tight sort of smile, and nodded his head.

Planner said, "Toss that box over here and I'll help you load it up, damn it," and reached into the safe. He felt behind the stacks of money on the middle shelf, found the cold metallic surface of the automatic. He wrapped his fingers around the gun and swung his arm out, firing. Money scattered as his arm knocked stacks from the shelf, and the contact with the stacks of cash were probably what threw his aim off. The bullet splintered into the gray wood behind the older man, between him and the boy, and Planner knew he was in trouble.

He tried to drop to the floor, so he could roll and keep firing, but the room was too small, and he was too old and too slow. He was moving when he got hit by the first shot, which he didn't even hear. He was motionless when the silenced automatic snicked and the second bullet caught him in the stomach, two small bubbling holes in his gut, and the back of him felt wet, and he felt warm, he felt hot, he felt afire, and he went to sleep.

A bell was ringing. Distant. He woke up. The older man and the younger man were on their haunches, packing the money into the big cardboard box. The box was just big enough to take all of the money. The older man said, "We can lay newspaper over the top of it, and stuff it down so we don't go dropping money behind us. That'd be a hell of a goddamn trail to leave." Planner's stomach felt warm. His hand felt cold. No, something in his hand. The gun! They hadn't taken the gun away from him. The gun!

He fired and caught the older man in the thigh. It knocked both of them down, the older man knocking into the younger, and upsetting the box of money. The older man said something unintelligible, and his gun snicked and Planner felt the third bullet enter his stomach, and he thought, Christ no! Not my stomach, I've got two there already. Jesus.

A bell was ringing. Distant. The phone! Nolan! Nolan, thank God!

Relieved, he died.

Two

1

The day he turned fifty, Nolan didn't feel old anymore.

For the several years approaching this day—the day marking the start of his fiftieth year, the day he'd come to regard as the starting gun for senility—for these two long years he had become increasingly paranoid about old age. About becoming an old man: a codger; a coot. The time would've come for trading in his .38 Smith and Wesson for a cane and a spot on the bench in front of a court house in some small town somewhere.

Or in a rest home. In his nightmares he saw himself, a vegetable, a shell of a man, emaciated, sprawled on a bed in a ward full of other wrinkled husks of once men, tubes running into and out of his arms and nose and crotch, bottles of amber fluid hanging beside his bed, dangling like shrunken heads. The root of his dream came, no doubt, from the two occasions in the past two years when he'd been bedridden, the first time for three months, the second for six. Both times he'd been down with bullet wounds, the second time being the more serious, as he had been just barely healed up from the prior wound when these slugs entered his left side, the same approximate area of his body as before. It was during that second, more precarious ordeal that the rest home dream had begun, first as one of countless other feverish, delirious dreams, then as a recurring nightmare.

But that doctor had pulled him through, somehow, despite his great loss of blood. The doctor himself had said it was impossible to save him, but Nolan's whispered, almost deathbed offer of, "Five grand extra if I live," proved the trick. Money was indeed the world's most potent miracle drug.

And now today, his birthday, fifty candles on his cake, today he felt fine, just fine. Emaciated? A shell of a man? He sat up in bed, patted his pot belly and laughed like Buddha getting his feet tickled. He felt young. He felt good.

He also felt tired, even though he'd just woken up.

Well, why shouldn't he feel tired? He had a right to be tired, damn it. He ought to be hung over as hell, after all that drinking last night, and he wasn't. And he ought to be feeling physically drained, after the extended bedroom athletics with Sherry, but he didn't. The way he acted last night you'd have thought he was a soldier on his last night before shipping overseas. Well, the morrow was here and the war had been declared over and he had his discharge papers and he felt fine.

He patted the ass of the sleeping girl next to him. She was a pretty thing, a sweet thing, a pleasant and very young plaything, who had made his summer pretty, sweet, and pleasant. And young. He knew now, in a sudden flash of self-awareness, his reason for choosing a girl, how old? Twenty? Nineteen? Better be eighteen at least. That would be the crowning touch, wouldn't it? Of all the things Nolan had done in a long, enjoyable lifetime of crime, to get busted for statutory rape! He'd get laughed out of the business.

Right now, though, he was doing the laughing. At himself. For picking out a girl who was, yes, young enough to be his daughter. For all he knew she *was* his daughter; he'd never been one for keeping track of those things. He stroked her ass again and she groaned in her sleep and turned over, stretching out, her long, lithe, naked body pearled with sweat. Her legs were parted. The fountain of youth, Nolan thought, and laughed again.

He sat back in bed and listened to the girl snore. She snored like a man and he'd at first found it amusing and later it started to bug him; his present mood had him finding her snoring amusing again. She was a slender girl, with frosted hair that arced gently round a face that was all big blue eyes and pouty mouth and a semifalse look of innocence.

He thought back, with some affection, to the first time he'd seen Sherry. She was spilling coffee into a customer's lap. The customer called her a stupid bitch and Nolan asked the man to please keep his voice down and watch where he was throwing his abusive language, and the customer had said he didn't care, she was *still* a stupid bitch, and Nolan told him to get the hell out, which he did, and then Nolan took the shaken girl into his private office and sat her down and called her a stupid bitch and fired her.

She had started to cry, of course, and he'd given her a reprimand and let it go at that, since it was her first day on the job. That was his problem, Nolan knew. He was just too damn softhearted. Once on a bank job, a guy whom Nolan had jumped on for roughing up employees needlessly, had said to him, "Shit, man, you probably cry at Disney pitchers," and though the remark wasn't true, it had struck home. Also, Nolan had struck the guy.

But for the next week the reports continued. She spilled coffee, tea, and milk, and plates and trays of food constantly into customer laps. If just once she could have landed the crap on the floor, even, but no . . . into lap after lap after lap, and soon she was on the carpet again, getting one of Nolan's lectures, and then she was crying and suddenly was on Nolan's lap. Which was certainly an improvement over drinks and food, and as the tears welled out, so did a sob story about how much she needed this summer's job to pay for her college. This was patently untrue, Nolan knew. She had dropped out of college, according to the data on her application form, and as far as he knew, her main reason for taking a summer job at the Tropical was to get a nice tan.

However, he liked the feel of her in his lap, and before long Sherry was back on the carpet, but in a different sense, and out of her waitress uniform both temporarily and permanently. By that afternoon her name was listed on the payroll as "Social Consultant." And so began a relationship that was clearly immoral, entirely corrupt and wholly enjoyable.

"Unnngghhh," she said. Her eyes were still closed.

Nolan said, "Did you say something?"

"Ungh . . . what time is it, honey?"

Nolan looked at his wristwatch. "Five after two."

"Morning or afternoon?"

"Afternoon."

"We miss breakfast?"

"And lunch."

"I'm hungry, honey." Her eyes were open now; half open, anyway.

"That's understandable," Nolan said.

"What do they call it when you mix breakfast and lunch together?"

"A goddamn mess."

"Don't tease me, honey."

"You call it brunch."

"That's right. Brunch. Let's have brunch."

"Good idea. Scrambled eggs and bacon and toast?"

"Good idea, honey."

He sat on the edge of the bed and used the phone. "This is Logan. Put Brooks on."

Logan was the name Nolan was using right now.

"Good afternoon, Mr. Logan."

"Good morning, Brooks. Send my usual breakfast over, will you?"

"For two?"

"I said my usual breakfast, didn't I? And Brooks?"

"Yes, Mr. Logan?"

"*You* scramble the damn things, this time. With milk and some grated cheese the way you do. Don't put one of those half-ass college kids on it, for Christ's sake."

"When did I ever do that to you, Mr. Logan?"

"Yesterday."

"I'll get right on it, Mr. Logan."

Sherry was getting out of bed, jiggling over to the dresser where she'd left her bikini. He watched her get into it. The bikini was innocence-white and Sherry was berry-brown.

Happy birthday, you bastard, he said to himself, grinning.

You're finally getting there. He was really enjoying this job, even though it was only temporary, only a trial run. The place was called the Tropical Motel, and consisted of one building, half restaurant and half bar-with-entertainment, and four buildings with sixteen motel units in each. There were also two swimming pools, both heated, one indoor, one out. The Tropical was located ten miles outside of Sycamore, Illinois, and was devoted to serving newlyweds of all ages, regardless of race, creed, or actual marital status. Nolan had known nothing about running the hotel end of it, but had been given sufficient help, so no sweat. What he was good at was running nightclubs and restaurants, that was something he'd done for years, though admittedly it had been years since he'd done it.

Seventeen, eighteen years, in fact, since the trouble with Charlie put an end to his career as a nitery manager. Nolan had managed several Chicago clubs to great success, but those clubs were owned by the Family. Of the many Families around the country (loosely united and known by various names—Syndicate, Mafia, Cosa Nostra, etc.), the Chicago outfit was the single biggest, most powerful Family of them all, and was in a very real sense *the* Family. And Charlie was one of the most powerful men in *the* Family.

It was after a violent clash with Charlie that Nolan had turned professional thief, using his organizational ability to put together strings of specialists who under his command pulled off one successful robbery after another. The world of organized crime and professional thievery don't intersect as often as you might think, and Nolan steered clear of his old enemy Charlie for many years, without much trouble, just by staying away from places owned or controlled by the Family, avoiding Chicago itself altogether. Besides, a pro thief generally shied away from hitting any Syndicate operations, anyway, out of interprofessional courtesy.

Last year, though, Nolan had returned to the Chicago area, thinking that after sixteen years the feud with Charlie was past history. That led to the first of his two injuries: one of Charlie's men had spotted Nolan in Cicero and tagged him with a bullet. Later, Nolan and Charlie met for a meeting of truce, in which Nolan agreed to pay Charlie a set amount of money to repay past damages. The treaty was signed but broken by Charlie, and that had led to Nolan's second and near-fatal trial by gunfire.

And then, after months holed-up recuperating, word filtered down to Nolan that the Family wanted to send a representative to meet with him. The representative was to be Felix, counselor in the Family, a lawyer with a single client. Sending the legal arm of the Family meant reconciliation was not only possible, but imminent.

Which was beautiful, because Nolan had nearly four hundred thousand dollars and the inclination to set himself up in business with a restaurant or nightclub or both, but he wanted all past wounds with the Family to be healed before making a move.

Nolan had conferred with the man named Felix in a room in a motel at the LaSalle-Peru exit on Interstate 80. Felix had said, "We want to thank you, Mr. Nolan."

"You're welcome," he said. "What for?"

"For exposing that idiot for the idiot he was."

"Charlie, you mean."

"Yes," Felix had said. Felix was a small man, about five-four. His hair was gray and modishly long and his face was gray and he wore a well-cut gray suit and a tie the color of peaches. Felix could have been thirty or he could have been fifty or anywhere along the road between.

"You said 'was,' " Nolan said.

"That's right. Charlie is no longer a problem."

"You mean Charlie's dead."

"Excuse my euphemism. Force of habit. Charlie is most certainly dead."

"Maybe we ought to have a moment of silence or something."

"The news hasn't broken yet," Felix said, pleasantly, "but you should be seeing something about the tragic event in the papers and on television this evening and tomorrow morning . . . though a 'gangland leader' who dies in an automobile mishap does not make nearly as good copy as one who dies by the gun."

Nolan began to understand Felix's friendly attitude. Nolan knew that the Family in Chicago had been much torn with political maneuvering within ranks, as for several years now the Chicago Boss of All Bosses had been living in Argentina in self-imposed exile to avoid prosecution on a narcotics charge. With the top seat vacant but still unattainable, underboss Charlie was the man with most authority, though even he was not wholly in command, as the exiled overlord had (perhaps unwisely) spread his authority out among a number of men, unwilling to see anyone gain total control. Nolan looked at Felix and realized that the lawyer was representing an anti-Charlie faction, which had apparently won their power struggle, having just pulled a relatively bloodless coup.

Which was no doubt supported by members on the executive council of the national organization of Families, who sympathized with these younger, anti-Charlie forces in the Chicago outfit. The sympathy was a chauvinistic one, as the other Families throughout the nation weren't nearly as strong as Chicago. New York alone had five weaker, sometimes warring Families to Chicago's powerful, monolithic one. Dumping Charlie would further destroy the strong center of power in the windy city, spreading the biggest Family in the country out among younger, less dominant gang leaders. It was all very similar to chess, or Cold War politics.

"I think we could find a place for you in the Family, Mr. Nolan," Felix was saying.

"Like you found a place for Charlie?"

"Please. I would hope we're here in mutual friendship, and good will."

"Anybody who tells me Charlie is dead is a friend of mine."

"I must say you exposed him ingeniously, and I'm sure if I knew all the details, every twist and turn of the scheme, I'd be all the more impressed."

What Felix was referring to was something Nolan had done to countercheck Charlie in case of a double cross. When Charlie had agreed to make peace with Nolan—for a price—Nolan had included "bait money" in with the payoff, that being the marked bills from a recent bank job. Nolan's intention had been to see if Charlie stuck by his word, and then if so, tell him about the marked bills. Charlie hadn't, and months later, when one of the Family fences had tried to circulate those bills for Charlie, bad things started happening. Lawyers and judges-on-the-take got the trouble cleared up, but the anti-Charlie forces in the Family (with the support of the national Executive Council of Families, no doubt) had evidently seized upon the incident to depose the longtime underboss, since Charlie's dealings with Nolan had been behind Family backs and in violation of several council rulings. It had all worked pretty much as Nolan had intended it to.

"What about the others?" Nolan asked. "Werner? Tillis?"

These were two other men involved in Charlie's plotting. Werner was a major cog in the wheel; Tillis was a black gunman Nolan rather liked.

"Werner is no longer a problem. And Tillis has proved helpful in Charlie's removal. He's working in Milwaukee now."

"Tillis is a good man. I'm glad he's still around."

"And what are *your* plans?"

Nolan told Felix of his vague notions to start something up . . . a nightclub, a restaurant, something.

"We have several openings along those lines ourselves."

"Strictly legitimate or I'm not interested. I'm retiring. I'm an old man."

"Old? You're scarcely fifty."

"I'm forty-nine and I feel eighty. You ought to see my fucking side. I'd show it to you only I got to keep the bandage on because it's draining pus. It's a twisted bunch of stitched purple skin from where I took three bullets that by all rights should've killed me. Sometimes I think I did die and was resurrected and I'm Jesus Christ. But I'm not. What I am is skinny and sick and I want out of that life."

"Strictly legitimate. We have some big openings." Felix mentioned several of them; one was a major resort, a multi-million-dollar operation; another was a huge, beautiful, fantastically successful combination restaurant and nightclub.

"I was thinking something smaller," Nolan said. He was stunned but he kept it inside. "Why would you put me into something as major as those places?"

"It would require an investment on your part. An investment as major as those places I mentioned."

And then it was down-to-brass-tacks time. After much further conversation, the bottom line was this: if Nolan would invest $250,000 in the operation of his choice, he would gain twenty percent ownership and a managerial salary of $60,000 per annum with a five-year ironclad contract. It was the dream of his life, but he held back his enthusiasm. He insisted on some assurance of the Family's good faith and intentions; perhaps a period of time during which he could prove himself to them, in some managerial capacity, while they in turn proved their trust in him. Felix said that not only did he concur with Nolan's suggestion, but that such an arrangement was a stipulation of the agreement. Nolan would take over management of the Tropical Motel for one year, as a trial run.

"Are you tired of this bikini?" Sherry was saying.

"No," Nolan said.

"You've been looking at it all summer."

"I'm not tired of it. It's terrific."

"Well, if you're tired of it, I'll have to go get a new one. That's all there is to it."

The phone rang on the nightstand and Nolan picked off the receiver and said, "Yeah?"

"Mr. Logan. Good afternoon."

It was Felix.

"When did you get in?" Nolan said.

"Half an hour ago. Are things in order for the switch?"

"I'll just want to get together with you and see what you have in mind."

"Fine. Is the man in Iowa ready?"

"I'm sure he is. I've been waiting for your call, so I can call him."

"Good. I'm in building three, room one. Come over in ten minutes and we'll make final arrangements."

Nolan said fine and thumbed down the button on the phone, let it up and got the switchboard girl. He asked her to get him long distance and had a call put through to Planner. He listened as the phone rang and rang. He waited a long time. The store is long, he thought, and Planner is old; he could have customers. He waited and waited, then finally gave up. The old guy probably just stepped out for something. Across the street for an ice cream cone, maybe. And that damn Jon's probably buried in his room reading comic books, Nolan thought, gone to the world. He smiled in spite of himself. He hung up the phone.

Sherry said, "Brunch is at the door, honey."

"Let it in," he said, grabbing his trousers off a chair and pulling them on. He would have his breakfast now and phone Planner again later.

2

Greer hadn't killed anybody for two years now. He sat on the edge of the bed, arms dangling at his sides, and looked at the snub-nosed .38 Colt in his lap. He studied the gun, regarded it curiously, as though he expected the object to speak. "I wonder," he said aloud. He was wondering if he was losing his edge.

He was a small, dark, babyfaced man. He'd been told by more than one woman that he looked like the late Audie Murphy, famous war hero and actor, the main difference being Greer was balding and his chin was sort of weak. He had the build of a fullback, scaled down somewhat, and the arms hanging loose at his sides were heavy with veined muscle.

He was wearing a short-sleeved white shirt and a dark green tie and white trousers. Under his arms were sweat stains and the loops of his shoulder holster, which X'ed across the back of the white shirt. On the bed beside him was a light green sportcoat, cut especially to accommodate a shoulder-bolstered gun. He had never gotten used to this year-round, constant wearing of suits and sportcoats, though he'd been doing so since starting with Felix two summers ago. He was glad the motel room was air-conditioned, and even the blue stucco walls were cool, cooling to the sight, as was the light blue shag carpet.

The door opened and Angello came in, carrying the room key in one hand and two ice-cold Pabsts by their necks in the other. He was six feet tall, a thin man with a round lumpy face; it was a fat man's face, because up until recent months Angello had been fat, and while he was trim everywhere else, he still had his double chin, puffy cheeks, and a bumpy, thick nose that all the dieting in the world wouldn't do anything about. Angello kicked the door shut. He was wearing a pink sportcoat and white shirt and red tie and white trousers.

"Just two beers, Ange?"

"Hey, baby, we're on call, right? Just wet the whistles, that's all. Never mind the good time."

"Toss one here. Where's the opener?"

"Don't need one. Twist-off caps."

"Ain't science grand."

Angello sat on the twin bed opposite Greer's. Angello looked strange, fat head on skinny body, as if one person's face was being superimposed somehow over the body of another.

Greer twisted off the cap and swigged. So did Angello.

Angello said, "Hey, Greer."

"Hey, what?"

"What d'you think of these clothes we're wearing?"

"What d'you think?"

"I think I feel like a fairy."

"You look like one."

"Shit, cut it out. What d'you suppose people think when they see a couple guys dressed like us going into a motel room together?"

"I don't know what they think. They think to each his own, I suppose."

"Well, I feel like a fairy. Why does Felix dress us up like this, I want to know."

"Why don't you ask him?"

"Funny man. I'll tell you why, it's because he thinks we look less conspicuous dressed like this. Because we got to wear coats to cover up our guns and since it's summer he doesn't want us to look like pallbearers in black or something, so we walk around instead like a couple of fairies."

"Golf pros dress like this," Greer said. "Golf pros are athletes, aren't they? You know any fairy athletes?"

"Golf pros aren't athletes. *Football* players are athletes. *Hockey* players are athletes."

"Drink your beer, fairy."

"Yeah, yeah, okay. Just next time you go into the bar after it, okay? Greer."

"Huh?"

"Greer, what you doing with your gun in your lap?"

"Nothing."

"Beating it off, or what?" Angello laughed and swallowed at the same time and it sounded like something going down a drain.

"You're funny as a crutch, Ange."

"Hey, you uptight today? Something on your mind today, Greer? Your forehead's all wrinkled up. You been thinking again?"

"Look," Greer said, "quit being cute long enough to tell me something. How long you been doing this bodyguard thing for Felix, anyway?"

"I don't know. Maybe three years. Yeah, three years, a year longer than you."

"What were you doing before that?"

Angello smiled. "People borrow money they sometimes forget to pay back and somebody's got to remind them of their obligation. You know." Angello laughed and swallowed again.

"Backing up the shylocks," Greer said. "Pretty tough work. You have to kill guys sometimes doing work like that."

Angello nodded. "Not often, though. It's bad business. How you going to get money out of a dead guy?"

"I used to hit guys," Greer said.

"Yeah, you told me before. You were a real scary guy."

"I used to do hits for Tony Action."

"Sure, Tony Action. Mr. Machismo. They say he tied his wife to a chair in the kitchen and poured gas on her and gave her a light. That's one way to duck divorce. Now me, my wife ties *me* up in the kitchen and feeds me her food and I get gas." Angello thought that was pretty funny. This time he devoted all his attention to laughing, no swallowing at all.

"Tony Action was really something," Greer said. "You can laugh, but man, I mean to tell you. Really something."

"Well, Tony is dead now, and I for one am never sorry to see one of those flashy tough asses get their ass shot off, they attract attention and give the rest of us a bad name, and you ought to be glad you had a reputation for being good help. Most of Tony's guys got stepped down. You're the only one who got fucking promoted."

"I was lucky," Greer said. "Don't get me wrong. Working for Felix is good. It's a good job. It's just . . ."

"It's just what?"

"I feel I'm getting soft in this job," Greer said.

"What do you mean?"

"I mean it's like you say . . . we wear pink coats and

follow a lawyer around, that's what I mean."

"You rather lay your balls on the chopping block every day? You're a fucking nut."

"No, no . . . it's just that even though we're following a lawyer around, we're carrying guns, and that means we're here because there's some chance something might happen. And when it happens, I don't want to be out of shape, you know?"

"Hey, Greer, tell you what . . . let's go sit in the bar and wait till some fruits pick us up and bring them back here and you can beat the fuck out of 'em. How does that sound?" Angello laughed-swallowed. He couldn't have been having a better time at a party.

"You got a warped sense of humor, Ange. You really do."

"What is it? You think maybe something's going to happen on that overnight hike you're going on tonight? Don't worry, that guy Nolan will be along to protect you. Or is that it? Is that who you're nervous about?"

"Bullshit."

"Say, Felix isn't going to try and cross this guy Nolan, is he? Is that why you're nervous, baby?"

"Why don't you just finish your beer, Angello."

"They tell stories about Nolan. He never burned up any women in the kitchen, but they tell stories about him."

"Look," Greer said, "all Felix said was I'd be going along. My understanding is that the guy has some money stashed somewhere, and that I'm supposed to escort him and the cash to one of our Chicago banks. If I'm worried about anything, it's that money. All that money's a big responsibility."

"How much is it, anyway?"

"Felix wasn't specific. I'd guess a couple hundred thousand, at least."

"That's probably right," Angello nodded. "You know I heard Felix say Nolan was behind that bank heist in Iowa a year or two back. The one that came close to eight hundred thousand. There were three or four men in on the job, I think. So he ought to have a couple hundred thousand at least is right."

"Should," Greer said. He sipped the beer. "Uh, what kind of stories you heard about him?"

"You ever hear how the thing between him and Charlie got going?"

"That's before my time."

"Mine, too. But my older brother Vinnie . . . you know Vinnie?"

"Yeah."

"That's in his era. Told me all about it. Charlie had a brother name of Gordon, an asshole from way back, and Charlie set this asshole Gordon up with part of the Chicago action. A bigger part than Gordon could handle, according to Vinnie. Anyway, Nolan is managing nightclubs and making quite a rep. He takes over a loser on Rush Street and turns it into a moneymaker in two months. And he does his own bouncing, I might add. So this Gordon, not content to leave ride a good thing, tries to move Nolan out of the club racket into strongarm, of all things. Nolan doesn't want no part of enforcer stuff, and tells Gordon so. Now Gordon was a lot like Charlie, see, only less brains. All the pride, but lots less brains. And so Gordon tells Nolan, look, he doesn't care, if he says crap, Nolan is supposed to ask how high, and that line of garbage. He tells Nolan to kill a guy, some guy who's a friend of Nolan's who works in his club. Nolan says no way. A few days go by and this guy, this friend of Nolan's, turns up in Lake Michigan and he isn't swimming. Nolan gets mad. He goes to Gordon and shoots the asshole and splits with twenty grand of the Family's money."

Greer smiled. He put his gun in his shoulder holster. "So that's why Charlie hated Nolan so much. Nolan killed his brother."

Angello smirked, batted a hand at the air, "Oh, hell, Gordon was no loss to anybody. Not even Charlie. It was pride. Keep in mind Charlie's pride, Greer. That was one puffed-up son of a bitch. Nolan's play made a fool out of Charlie. He killed Charlie's brother, right? *And* he stole Charlie's money. *And* he got away clean. Worst of all, he got away clean. For years Charlie had an open contract out on Nolan. Nobody collected. Made Charlie look bad. Real bad. When all this happened, nearly twenty years ago, Charlie was underboss in Chicago. The day Charlie died he was still the same damn thing."

Greer nodded. "And he probably died blaming that on Nolan."

"Probably," Angello agreed. He sighed. "I could use another beer."

"Me, too."

"But we're on call, better not. And besides, I'm not about to go walking into that bar again. A guy practically whistled at me last time." Angello grinned, tried to drain one last drop out of the Pabst.

The phone on the nightstand rang. Angello reached over and answered it. He said, "Yes, sir . . . yes, sir . . . right away, sir." He hung up.

Greer said, "Felix?"

"Felix," Angello said. "I think we're about to get a nice close look at this guy Nolan. Come on."

Greer put on his coat.

3

After brunch, Nolan called the bar and had them send over some beer in a cooler to Felix's room. A few bottles each of Schlitz, Heineken, and one can of Point Special. Nolan didn't know if Felix drank beer but it seemed early in the day for anything else, and if Felix did drink beer, it'd have to be something imported, like Heineken. The Point Special, a Wisconsin brew, was for Nolan.

He pushed the tray of dishes aside, got up from the edge of the bed where he'd been sitting and eating, and went to the bureau where he took out a dark yellow short-sleeve

Banlon and pulled it on. He got a brown sports jacket out of the closet and put it on.

"Doesn't go with your slacks," Sherry said.

His slacks were black.

Nolan nodded, took off the coat, and hung it back in the closet. He found a charcoal gray sports jacket and climbed into it. He turned to Sherry, who was still eating her eggs, for approval.

"That's better," she said.

"One thing," he said, "I can't figure out."

"Oh, yeah?"

"What are you, my mother, sister, or daughter?"

She grinned, cheeks puffed with food. "Whichever's dirtiest," she said, not too distinctly.

He grinned at her, feeling affection for her against his best judgment. "See you later," he said.

"How long you going to be?"

"I don't know."

"I'll be at the pool."

"I kind of figured that."

"Oh, yeah?"

"Your bikini."

"Oh, yeah. Well, I'm not going to swim, just going to sun."

"You get much more sun you're going to have to ride in the back of the bus."

"I will? Why?"

"That was a joke."

"Really? Must've been before my time or something."

He sighed. "Everything's before your time."

"Don't belittle me, Logan. I wasn't born yesterday, you know."

"Yes you were. Yesterday. Just yesterday."

"Give us a kiss."

He went over and pecked her forehead.

"A *kiss*, dammit."

"You got egg on your mouth."

"I'll wipe it off."

She did, and he kissed her, but it still tasted like eggs. Maybe it was just his imagination. He kissed her again. No, he thought, eggs, all right.

"Sorry I didn't get your joke," she said.

"It wasn't much of a joke," he said.

"Well, you can't expect me to be looking for jokes from you. You don't make jokes that often. Next time tell me first."

"Are you saying I don't have a sense of humor?"

"Let's just say it wasn't what attracted me to you."

"I must have a sense of humor."

"Why?"

"I put up with you, don't I?"

She made a mock-angry face and said, "Happy birthday, you S.O.B."

"How'd you know it was my birthday?"

"You told me last night, or I mean this morning. You were pretty drunk. You sang yourself the 'Happy Birthday' song."

"Told you I had a sense of humor. Did I really do that? After a certain point things get a little hazy. Did I do it in front of anybody, for Christ's sake?"

"Just me. We were back in the room by then, with the champagne."

"I don't remember any of that."

She pointed toward the corner by her side of the bed and sure enough, there was an empty bottle of champagne, lying on its side like a casualty of war. Two water glasses had in them each a quarter of an inch or so of by now very flat champagne. It was, unfortunately, all coming back to him.

"Do me a favor," he said.

"Sure."

"Don't ever tell me what else I did. I got a certain self-image to maintain."

"Yeah, I know. You're a tough guy. You told me that, too."

"Please," he said. "You're twisting the knife."

"Okay, okay. Logan?"

"What?"

"Are you?"

"Are I what?"

"A tough guy?"

"Sure. I eat babies."

"I hope that's another joke."

"Well, it is. Sort of."

"I been wanting to ask you something for a long time."

"Ask."

"Where'd you get all the funny scars?"

"Don't ask."

She accepted that graciously, taking a swallow of milk and smiling at him with a milk mustache. "See you later, Logan. I'll be sunning."

"At the pool."

"Right."

They said good-bye to each other.

When Nolan knocked at Felix's door, somebody else answered. It was a balding, babyface guy in a light green coat with a dark green tie. There was a dull hardness to the guy's matching light green eyes, and he was packing a gun under his left arm, though the coat was cut to hide it. The guy looked familiar but Nolan couldn't place him.

"Come in, come in," Felix's silky voice said, from somewhere behind the gunman.

Nolan came in and found Felix sitting on the edge of the big double bed, at its foot. Felix was wearing a lemon sports coat and lemonade tie. His trousers were tan. His face wasn't gray this time, but brown, as brown as Sherry's. Felix had evidently been to Miami recently. His graying hair was styled, covering one fourth of his ears, and he looked overall very with it. Beside him on the bed was an ashtray and a pack of Gauloises Disque Bleu and the ashtray had half a dozen of the cigarettes stubbed out in it. Though Felix wasn't smoking at the moment, chainsmoking probably explained the flaw in Felix's well-groomed looks: his teeth were as yellow as his sports coat.

To Felix's left, sitting on a straightback chair, was another bodyguard, a tall guy with a round face that didn't quite go with the rest of him. The tall gunman was wearing a pink coat and red tie, which made him look like a fag or something. Felix's idea of class, probably.

"Shut the door and sit down, Greer," Felix told the baby-face. Greer did as he was told. "Nolan, my friend, make yourself comfortable. Angello, give Mr. Nolan your chair."

Angello did so.

"And thank you, Nolan," Felix continued, "for being kind enough to send over some refreshment. Very thoughtful. Would you like something to cool yourself off, Nolan?"

Nolan said, "The Point Special's mine," to Angello.

Felix said, "Heineken, Angello."

"And," Nolan said, "crack open a couple Schlitz for you and what's-his-name, Angello."

Angello looked to Felix for approval. He got it.

"Thanks," Angello said to Nolan. He had a gruff voice that didn't fit the red coat and tie, as his head didn't fit his body.

Nolan waited till everybody had beers and then figured all the bullshit preliminaries were over and said, "What's the word, Felix?"

Felix smiled, turned to Angello and said, "Bring me a glass," and Angello brought him a bathroom glass still wrapped in paper. Felix waited for Angello to tear off the wrapping and hand him the glass. Then Felix poured the golden liquid out of the green bottle and sipped it and said, "Have you heard from your friend in Iowa?"

"I'm having trouble getting through to him."

"Trouble?"

"I've tried twice. Nothing to worry about. He may try to call me. I told the switchboard girl to route the call to me here in this room if he does."

"Do you think there could be a problem on his end?"

"No. It's nothing. You got to understand he's an eccentric old guy with a mind of his own. He feels like stepping out for a while, he steps out for a while."

"I see. I hope everything is all right."

"Everything's cool. The money's safe where it is, like it has been for almost a year now. Nothing's going to happen."

"I wish I could share your confidence," Felix said, wagging his head gravely. "I won't feel safe until the money is in that bank of ours."

"Me, too, but no sweat. I can't see how anybody could know where the cash is. Do you know where it is?"

"No," Felix said.

"Maybe you're telling the truth," Nolan said, "I don't know." He took a gulp of his beer, giving Felix a chance to say something, then went on. "You know enough to find out, that's for sure. You know about the bank job, and I went so far as to tell you the money's stashed in Iowa someplace. Send some boys snooping to find out about me, you could figure where the stuff is, easy enough. Charlie could've figured it out, if he wasn't dead."

Felix smiled meaninglessly, like a sphinx.

"But nobody else could," Nolan said. "Unless you leaked what you know about me. Or unless you talked as loose as I am now in front of bodyguard clowns like these two." Nolan caught out of the corner of his eye Greer narrowing his. "Nobody in my field knows I'm the one who pulled that particular job, and if they did, they sure wouldn't figure I'd leave the money sit where I did. For this long especially."

"What you're saying," Felix said, taking a genteel sip from his glass of beer, "is this hiding place is so stupid it's smart."

Nolan shrugged, took another gulp of beer. They'd been over all of this before, a lot of times. Nolan had resisted handing the money over to the Family immediately because he didn't trust them, he wanted to fully understand their intentions before making any final steps. Now, after these months at the Tropical, he felt assured that the offer Felix had made in that other room in the motel at the LaSalle-Peru exit on Interstate 80 was legitimate. Of course, even by

Family standards the amount of money involved was a sizable one, but it didn't seem logical that they'd try to get at it through so elaborate a double cross. And why *should* they double-cross him? Nolan was convinced that the Chicago Family was grateful to him, glad to be rid of Charlie. After all, they had entrusted Nolan with the reins of the Tropical, an expensive bauble for even the Family to be tossing casually around, and had been paying him well for this "trial run." But still he'd waited until recently to tell Felix he was ready to transfer the money, and it was only yesterday that he'd mentioned to the lawyer that Iowa was where he had to go to get it.

Felix said, "What I had in mind was this . . . you will leave here this evening, around eight or nine, and arrive in Iowa, wherever in Iowa it is, sometime after midnight, depending on how far you're going. We have a car for you with a specially rigged trunk compartment, so that you can get stopped by the police, for God knows what reason, and still get by even a fairly thorough search. You will deliver the money to our bank in Riverside an hour and a half before opening . . . that's seven-thirty, Daylight Savings Time . . . and the bank president, a Mr. Shepler, will be waiting for you."

"Fine. What's the name of the bank in Riverside and how do I get there?"

"Just leave that to Greer."

"To who?"

"Greer," he said, nodding toward the babyface gunman.

"Why should I leave it to him, Felix?"

"He'll be accompanying you, Nolan. You wouldn't want all that money to go unguarded."

Nolan sighed. He took two long swallows from the Point Special, set the half-empty can on the floor beside his chair and got up. Felix was starting to get on his nerves. Felix was starting to be a pompous ass. Nolan paced for a moment, till the urge to tell Felix those things went away. Then he said, "I don't like muscle, Felix."

"Nolan . . ."

"What do I need muscle for? I can take care of myself."

"It's a big responsibility for one man."

"I'll pick up somebody else when I get there."

"Who?"

"Never mind who. The other guy who has a say in where this money is going, that's who."

"A partner of yours? Is he capable?"

"All my partners are capable," he said, but that wasn't quite true. It was Jon he was talking about, and Jon was just a kid, hardly a seasoned veteran. But Jon was who he wanted, not some mindless strongarm. And he didn't want any Family accompaniment at all.

Nolan sat back down and finished his beer in one long swig. He was getting surly and he knew it. He supposed he ought to stay nice and businesslike around Felix, but the pompous little prick was getting to him. Nolan put the empty can on the floor. He said, "Greer? Is that your name?"

Greer nodded, sitting forward in his chair. Greer sensed Nolan's hostility and unbuttoned his green sportcoat.

"You good for anything, Greer?" Nolan asked.

Nolan watched the hood bristle, then he said, "Greer, get me a Schlitz."

Greer got up slowly, a pained look on the babyface, and went over to the cooler of ice and beer and got one.

Nolan said, "Well, Felix, I suppose if you insist he go along . . ."

Greer handed Nolan the beer and Nolan reached inside Greer's coat and took the .38 from out of the underarm holster and pushed the snub-nose up under Greer's Andy Gump chin.

"You son of a bitch," Greer hissed.

"Shut up," Nolan said, pushing him backward, toward the straightback chair. Greer crouched and got a fierce expression on his face, as if he was thinking of doing something. Nolan gave him a look and the hood sat down. Over on the other side of the room Angello was smiling.

Nolan said, "Felix, is that who you want to go along and protect me?"

Greer waved his hands and said, "I wasn't expecting . . ."

"You weren't expecting," Nolan said. "I suppose if somebody wants to hit us en route, they'll announce it."

Greer said, "You fucking son of a bitch . . ."

Felix said, "Greer."

And Greer got quiet.

Nolan examined the gun. "I got no respect for a man who carries a snub-nose," he said, tossing the gun back to Greer, hard. "You can't aim the damn things, they shoot different every time. And all that damn fire coming out of the muzzle, and noisy, shit. What kind of bodyguard are you, anyway, carrying a snub-nose?"

"You've made your point," Felix said. "You'll go alone."

"Fine," Nolan said.

Felix was explaining to Nolan how to get to the Riverside bank, drawing a little map on note paper, when the phone rang. Felix told Angello to answer it and Angello did, then said, "It's for somebody named Logan."

"That's my name here," Nolan explained, and went to the phone.

"Nolan?" the phone said. "Nolan, Christ, Nolan, is it you?"

"Jon?" Nolan said. "Calm down, Jon, what's wrong?"

"It's Planner, Nolan . . ."

"What about him?"

"They killed him, Nolan, somebody killed him."

"Jesus, kid. Stay calm. Don't go hysterical on me. Jon?"

"Yes. I'm okay."

"Now tell me about it."

"He's dead, Nolan. Planner's dead."

"You said that already. He's dead. Go on."

"He's dead, and the money . . ."

"Yes?"

"It's gone. All of it."

Nolan drew a deep breath, let it out.

"Nolan? You okay?"

Suddenly he felt old again.

"Yeah, kid. Go on."

4

Joey ordered lobster. He sipped his white wine as he watched the waitress sway away, a college girl in a yellow and orange Polynesian-print sarong. Nice ass on the kid, Joey thought, nice ass.

He was a fat, dark little man in a two hundred-and-fifty-dollar suit, a dollar for every pound he weighed. The suit was tan, its coat wide-lapeled, trousers flared. His shirt was rust color and his tie was white and wide and thickly knotted. His hair was black, brought forward to disguise a receding forehead, but skillfully so, by a barber who had shaped the hair well, leaving it long on the sides, partially covering Joey's flat, splayed ears. Lamb-dropping eyes crowded the bridge of his narrow, hooking nose, and his teeth were white as porcelain. He wore a one-carat diamond pinkie ring on his left hand, and a two-carat diamond ring on the third finger of his right hand.

The wine was calming him down. This was his third glass and his stomach felt pleasantly warm. Not fluttering, as it had when he'd gotten Felix's call, asking (demanding) in that soft Felix voice for Joey to come down to the Tropical for the evening. Joey'd been angry and afraid, but had shown neither emotion to Felix (hope to God!) and of course had said, yes, yes, sure. He was pissed off, but he said yes, Felix. He was pissless scared, but he said, what time should I be there, Felix?

He'd been angry because it was four o'clock in the damn afternoon when Felix called to say come spend the evening with me. It was what, sixty some miles to the Tropical from the city, and all the rush-hour traffic to contend with on the expressway. And what kind of notice was that, anyway, four fucking o'clock in the afternoon, come down tonight, Jesus.

He'd been afraid because his life had taken on a constant undercurrent of fear since the fall of Charlie, and it took very little to bring that fear bobbing to the surface. He knew he shouldn't feel that way, but there it was. He knew he was secure in his position. So what if he got his start with the Family because he was Charlie's cousin, that didn't mean there was anything to worry about now. He was too high, too big, too important, too valuable. It was unthinkable, Jesus.

After all, think of how much money he'd made for the Chicago Family these past years. How many millions had the housing project shuffle brought the Family coffers? He smiled, sipped the wine. And that was nothing next to the cigarette stamp dodge. When he was fronting that tobacco distributing company, the boys must've made fifteen million on the counterfeit tax stamp angle, and when it did fall through and went to court, the judge, being a Family judge, dismissed the case for lack of evidence.

And now, why, shit, he was a public figure. You can't do nothing to a public figure. He was *Joey,* for Christ's sake, not just any Joey, but *the* Joey, his name up in glittering lights for the whole goddamn town to see. The opening, last year, had been fabulous, greatest day of his life. All the big-name stars and the TV cameras and the reporters, it was something. One of the columnists had said, "Mannheim Road, the West Side's answer to Rush Street, was the scene of Chicago's biggest happening since the Fire: the opening of reputed gangland protege Joey Metrano's $11-million-plus hostelry, *Joey Metrano's Riviera.*" And that famous one, Kupcinet (Kup himself!) said, "Joey Metrano, called by some a 'cheap braggart of a hoodlum,' has brought Vegas to Chicagoland with his *Riviera.*"

The lobster came, two nice tails surrounding a butter pot. And speaking of nice tails, that waitress was giving him a honey of a smile as she put the food in front of him. He smiled right back at her, getting mileage out of the caps. She was blonde, or sort of blonde, having kind of light brunette hair streaked or tipped or whatever the hell they called it. When she served his iced tea, she spilled some of it in his lap, and be damned if she didn't dab it up with a napkin, oh, sweet Jesus. "I'm so sorry, sir," she said, and he told her the pleasure was all his. When she gave him the baked potato, she brushed a pert breast against his shoulder, and Joey couldn't help but wonder if it was an invitation, especially the sexy damn way she said, "Sour cream on your potato, sir?"

Jesus, Jesus, what he'd give for some of that stuff tonight. The little broad had a fresh look to her, not like the Chicago meat—lookers, sure, but it seemed like every one of them been giving head since they was ten and humping since eight, and it would be something to get a piece of something that wasn't up the ass with experience.

But he had little hope for any action in this dump. In fact, using college girl help was just one sign of this being a half-ass operation. Look at the place, just fucking look at it. The room was so tasteless, with fishnet on the phony-bamboo walls, and Hawaiian and Caribbean and African and Oriental and all sorts of mishmash goddamn stuff hanging on the walls. What'd they do, bring in some guy from Nebraska who saw a travelog once and give him fifty bucks and say, "Do it up exotic." Tropical, my ass, he thought. No taste.

Now *his* place, *Joey Metrano's Riviera,* that was a different story. (About $10 million different!) Take just one of the things he had going there. Take, for example, the lounge, the Chez Joey (just like in Sinatra's movie) with its gold-brocade walls and the plush gold carpet, and the gold chairs and gold tablecloths and gold drapes and the girls dressed in Rome-type minitogas, gold also. Now there was class. Take the food, for instance. He forked a bite of lobster and studied it. This lobster was good, but the lobster *he* served, why, it made these suckers look like shrimps. What did Nolan know about running a restaurant, anyway.

The bit of lobster went down the wrong way, and, for a moment, he choked.

Nolan.

He shivered. (It was cold in here, damn air-conditioning.) Joey hadn't wanted to think about Nolan, about Nolan being under the wing of the Family, about Nolan running this place here, this Tropical, for the Family. Word had it Nolan was going to move up, and fast. It was spooky, after Charlie and Nolan hating each other for so long, and an open Family contract out on Nolan for all those years. But times change, and Charlie the powerful underboss was now Charlie the deposed underboss.

And Joey? Joey was Charlie's cousin.

Nothing to worry about, shit. Not a thing. Felix wouldn't let Nolan do anything. Nolan was nothing to the Family, and Joey was so much.

Like the *Riviera*. Think how much money the Family made off just building the place, never mind the profit it was turning now. And he, Joey, was the one who wined and dined the various savings and loan guys, one firm anteing up $6 million (for an under-the-table inducement of a mere hundred grand). The rake-off for the Family from these multimillion buck loans was simple and immense. Family construction and supply outfits handed in inflated estimates of cost, and so *Joey Metrano's Riviera* (which an appraiser today might put at, say $5 million) had had a provable projected cost of over $11 million.

After dinner he copped a few more feels from the waitress with the nice ass, then settled back with one last glass of wine. He was just starting the second one last glass of wine when Nolan came out of somewhere and approached Joey's table.

"Hope you enjoyed your dinner, Joe," Nolan said.

Why did Nolan look so tall, Joey wondered, when he couldn't have been more than six foot or so? He supposed it was the long, hard lines in his face, the prominent cheekbones, the narrow, almost chink-looking eyes.

"How you doing?" Joey asked, motioning for Nolan to sit down.

Nolan sat.

"What are they calling you here?" Joey asked, in a whisper. "Felix told me but I forgot."

"Logan," Nolan said.

"Listen," Joey said, "where is Felix, anyway?"

"Felix got called back to the city," Nolan said. "He said I should put you up for the night. He'll be back early tomorrow morning."

"Aw, shit," Joey said, unable to keep the infuriated feeling down inside him. "Aw, shit, goddamn shit. I come all the way down here, I cancel my goddamn evening, and aw, shit."

"It's not my fault, Joe," Nolan said. "I'll make you as comfortable as possible."

"I know it's not your fault, No . . . Logan. And listen, I want you to know something. Just because I was Charlie's cousin, well, it doesn't mean, you know."

"Sure," Nolan said. "No reason for hard feelings between us. You weren't your cousin's keeper."

"Ha, that's a good one. Uh, Logan, nobody was Charlie's keeper, all right. He had a mind of his own, all right."

"Too bad how he died."

Joey swallowed. "Uh, yeah, real tragic is what it was."

What was Nolan fishing for? Joey could feel beads of sweat forming on his forehead. Surely Nolan knew Charlie's "death" was a Family coverup. Surely Nolan knew Charlie was spared the usual blow-him-apart-and-stuff-him-in-the-trunk-of-a-car gangland execution, because Charlie was too high up for that. Charlie was a goddamn underboss.

Nolan said, "He was disfigured in the accident, wasn't he?"

"Yeah . . . yes," Joey said. "Burnt up. Both burnt up. He and . . . his son. They were in the car together."

"Was quite a dropoff, wasn't it?"

"Yeah . . . yeah, it sure was."

"Not much left of the bodies."

"No . . . burnt to a crisp, like I said. No doubt it was Charlie, though."

Did he know? Did Nolan know?

"I never doubted it was Charlie," Nolan said.

"They could check it out through Charlie's bridgework, through his dentist, you know. And rings and other identifying things like that."

"Well, Joe, it's not really a pleasant after-dinner topic, is it? Let's let it pass. Let me just assure you I hold you no grudge, just for being blood kin of an old enemy . . . and let me say, too, that I hold no grudge for that old enemy, either. I'm not one to speak bad of the dead. Rest in peace, I always say."

"R—right. Some wine, Logan?"

"No thanks." Nolan bent close, like a conspirator. "Listen. I saw you flirting with Janey."

"Janey?"

"The waitress."

"Well, hey, I mean Christ, uh, I didn't mean anything by . . ."

"Cool it," Nolan said. "Don't worry about it."

"Well, then, uh, why . . ."

"Why mention it? Now listen, Joe, just between the two of us, I mean, we're two of a kind, right? You run a hotel; I run a motel. The only difference is you're in the city and I'm in the country, right?"

"Uh, right."

"Now tell me, you have some pretty foxy chicks working in that *Riviera* of yours, don't you?"

"Well, sure, sure I do."

"And sometimes you, you know, dip into the old private stock, know what I mean?" Nolan grinned, the grin of lech.

"I know what you mean," Joey said, returning the grin.

"So if you like Janey, I think maybe I can work something out for you."

"Oh . . . terrific, I mean, Christ, would you do that for me, Nolan? Er, Logan? I never expected . . ."

"Forget it. You just return the favor for me sometime, okay? Next time I'm in the city for an overnight, just fix me up with one of those foxy ladies in a Roman toga."

"Hey, you scratch my back, I'll scratch yours, right?"

"Right, Joe."

"Listen, I'm not checked in or anything."

"I already took care of that," Nolan said. "I sent your driver, Brown, back to the city to get a change of clothes for you."

"Oh . . . well, Brown is . . ."

"Yeah, he's sort of a bodyguard, too, I know, but don't worry. You're on vacation here. Nobody's going to hurt you." Nolan grinned again and whispered. "Unless some foxy chick bites you on the ass, you know what I mean?"

"I know what you mean."

Nolan got up. "Enjoy yourself, Joe."

Half an hour later, Joey was in bed under the covers in his room. He was naked. He was waiting.

Too good to be true, he thought. He'd really misjudged Nolan. Back in the old days Nolan had been a tough customer, but the years must've softened him up. All those stories about Nolan being such a hardass, why, shit. He was friendly, would you believe it, and not just a little naive. If Nolan really thought Charlie could die accidentally, in a car crash, well . . .

A knock at the door.

"It's open," he said.

She came in.

"Lock it, will you, sugar?" he said.

She did.

"It's dark," she said.

"I'm over here."

"Don't you want to see me?" she said.

"I . . . I don't know if you'll want to see me. I . . . I could stand to lose some weight, sugar."

"I don't care about that," she said.

"Turn on the light then."

She was in a flowing red silk robe, tied at the waist, brushing the floor. She undid the belt. The robe fell in a red silk puddle at her feet.

"My God," Joey said. "You're beautiful."

She was beautiful. She had brown skin, coffee-skin, ivory white where some wisp of a bikini had done its enviable job. Her nipples were large and copper-colored and as yet soft, but he would see to that; they would soon be as erect as he was. Her legs were long, muscular, tapering. She smiled at his appreciation. She turned in a circle, like a model, saying, "See anything you like?"

Her ass was perfection. Oh, that dimpled ass! Oh my God.

She stood at the foot of the bed, hands on her hips, legs spread, that tangle of hair between them open and inviting and she said, "Anything I can do for you?" and she pulled the covers off him.

Joey patted the bed beside him. She crawled onto the bed like a cat, and wiggled into his arms, and he turned her on her side and he eased himself up against her, gently ever gently, saying, you sweetheart, oh honey, oh sugar, and the guy with the camera came in and the flashbulbs started popping.

"Jesus fuck!" Joey said. Spots in front of his eyes.

Blinking, Joey reached for her. She was gone. Where was she?

She had the robe on again, how could she have the robe on again so fast? She was standing back beside the door, which was closed, and Nolan was there.

Nolan was there.

Oh, God. Nolan was there and some guy with a camera. Oh God, some guy with a camera and . . .

And so what? Joey wasn't married. Joey never had time for that. So, so what? What did he care? Scandal? A damn laugh. Nolan was an asshole.

"You're an asshole, Nolan," Joey said, "if you think those pictures are worth a goddamn."

Nolan said, "How many shots did you get?"

The guy with the camera said, "Six. Six good ones. I got more than butts, too. I got faces plain as day."

"Okay," Nolan said. "Now get out of here."

The guy with the camera did.

Joey got out of bed and pulled on his trousers. His dignity was ruffled, and he was a little confused, flustered, but that was all. He said, "Nolan . . ."

"Joe," Nolan said, "allow me to introduce you to Felicia Colletta."

Colletta?

"Who?" Joey said. "Colletta?"

"Colletta. That's right. You know the name."

He knew the name if it was *that* Colletta, the *Family* Colletta.

"You know how Mr. Colletta feels about his daughters," Nolan said.

Colletta. Boss of the biggest New York Family. Colletta, with four beautiful daughters from age fourteen to twenty-two. Four beautiful daughters Colletta loved with an Old World paternal passion.

"You probably heard about his older daughter Angella," Nolan was saying, "who is married now. You probably heard about the college kid who screwed Angella when she was fifteen."

Colletta had a guy use acid on the kid, Joey didn't want to think about where.

"Felicia's going to turn eighteen this summer, aren't you, Felicia? Mr. Colletta sent her here to the middle West where she could breathe some clean country air."

This wasn't happening.

"All right, Felicia," Nolan was saying, "thank you so much. Don't say a word about this to anyone, you hear?"

And she was nodding and leaving.

Joey sat down on the bed.

Nolan came and joined him.

Nolan said, "I want you to tell me about Charlie."

Joey said, "No."

"The pictures will be destroyed. I'll bring you the camera and let you take the film out and expose it yourself."

"This is a goddamn hoax."

"Okay."

"That isn't Felicia Colletta."

"Okay. See you, Joey."

Nolan got up.

Joey grabbed Nolan's sleeve. "That . . . that isn't Felicia Colletta, is it?"

"If you say so, Joe. See you."

Nolan walked to the door and put his hand on the knob.

"Nolan!"

"Yes?"

"I'll tell you."

"All right."

"Charlie's death . . . Charlie's death wasn't an accident. The Family did it."

And Nolan started to laugh. "I'll have the best shot blown up to poster size and send it to you, Joe."

"You bastard."

"See you, Joe."

"Come back, you fucker!"

"What do you want, Joe?"

"Nolan . . . you *know*, Nolan. You *know*, don't you?"

"I think so," Nolan said, nodding. "But I want to hear it from you."

Joey put his head in his hands. Sobbing was coming up out of him, out of his gut somewhere. It was hard to talk through it.

"Charlie," Joey said, chest heaving, "Charlie is still alive."

5

There was no moon and you could count the stars on your

fingers. Nolan lay on his back on the rubber raft, floating around the deep end of the pool, studying the sky. He was having a hard time deciding whether the sky was black or dark blue, and finally compromised on Smith and Wesson blue-black. He found watching the lustreless sky soothed him, and after a while he noticed he could make out some clouds up there and figured they were probably responsible for his problem pinning down the sky's color. The clouds were like charcoal smoke clinging to the sky, blending with it, making the sky look light in places, as though it were wearing out.

It was restful, drifting around the pool, the easy movement of the water lulling him. There was no one to bother him, as it was eleven-thirty now, and at eleven the pool was closed to Tropical guests. The gas torches that surrounded the pool flickered and danced on the water's surface, and Nolan watched and enjoyed the reflecting flames when he wasn't looking at the sky.

He needed this interlude, needed it to drain away what tension he had left from the preceding hours of rant and rush. The news of the robbery at Planner's had led to a frantic afternoon and evening, beginning with an hour of heated, involved conversation with Felix and ending with the preparations for having Joey Metrano down for a chat. But now that Nolan's theory about Charlie had been proved correct, there was no need for everybody to run around like a bunch of idiots in heat. What there was a need for was rest for Nolan, time for him to relax, sort things out, calm himself before setting out for his money.

He hadn't thought about Planner being dead. Now that he was feeling good again, he wouldn't allow such thoughts to push forward in his mind and spoil his mood. He wasn't good at sorrow anyway, and it didn't occur to him to feel in any way guilty about the old man's death. Nolan figured Planner knew the rules and risks of the game. Besides, most of Nolan's friends didn't get to be as old as Planner had.

Sherry's head bobbed up out of the water beside him and

she arose wet and grinning, the water splashing up and around and on her as if it was having as good a time as she was. "Hey, this is fun!" she sputtered, treading water. "I ought to go swimming more often!"

Nolan shook his head. This was probably the first time she'd been swimming this summer, though she'd spent most of every day at the pool. Sunning. Just now Nolan had convinced her to go to the pool with him and she'd found nothing else to do there but swim.

Nolan said, "How you doing, Felicia Colletta, child of the underworld?"

Sherry giggled, paddling hands and feet to stay above water. She said, "I just hope you keep me in mind come Academy Award time."

"Don't know about that," Nolan told her, "but if I ever cast a stag film, you're the first one I'll call."

She made a face and slapped at the water to get him wet, then decided that wasn't enough and overturned the raft and dumped him, arms flailing, into the deep. "Don't be afraid of the water," he heard her say, "it won't bite!" Which struck him as a very hypocritical thing for this queen of suntan lotions to say.

The pool was heated, so the water was luxuriously warm, like a lazy bath, and Nolan stayed down under for a while, waiting for her to come looking for him. She did, and he grabbed for her, and she slipped away from him, swimming down toward the shallow section, underwater all the way, stroking like a frog. He caught up with her just as she was getting on her feet at the far end of the pool, and he pinched her ass just as her head cleared the water. She was still squealing as he got to his feet laughing and saw Felix standing there, back far enough to keep from getting wet, but standing there just the same, looking vaguely annoyed.

"Hello, Felix," Nolan said.

"What are you doing?" Felix said.

"Right now I'm getting out of the swimming pool," he said, and did, giving Sherry his hand and helping her out, too.

Felix said, "I hope you're enjoying yourself."

"I am," Nolan said.

Nolan went to the lounge chair where he'd left his towel and dried off. There was a small round metal table next to the chair, a canopied table with a pitcher of martinis and ice on it. Nolan poured three glasses from the pitcher and gave one to Sherry and one to Felix and kept the third.

"Thank you," Felix said. His tone was almost friendly now; evidently he was dropping the reproving manner, having gotten nowhere with it. He sipped the drink and said, "What sort of martini is this?"

"Vodka," Nolan said.

"Oh," Felix nodded, and took a seat beside Nolan's lounge chair, checking it first for moisture.

"How's Joey doing?" Nolan asked.

Sherry had finished her drink already and was diving back into the pool.

Felix said, "Pretty girl. We should do something for her for helping out."

"I'll do something for her," Nolan said. "What about Joey?"

"Well, he's not pleased that you've taken his clothes away from him."

"It's one way to keep him in his room."

"And he doesn't like my sending Greer in to watch him all the time, either."

"That's another way." Nolan was beginning to get quietly pissed off at this smug little lawyer.

Earlier, Nolan had assured Joey that the Family would hear nothing of their conversation, and Joey had talked easier that way, but after Nolan was finished with him, Felix and the two bodyguards had shouldered into the room to find things out for themselves. Nolan hadn't stayed around to watch, as redundant violence irritated him, but it wasn't his show anymore, so he'd let it pass.

"Other than that," Felix was saying, "Joey Metrano's turned into a humble, quiet little guy. He's full of apologies and bowing and scraping. He knows that his life is hanging by the slenderest of threads now that he's admitted helping Charlie hoax the Family." Felix said the word "Charlie" as though he were spitting out a seed. "He'll be taken back to the city tomorrow morning and kept under close watch. I don't need to go over what Joey told us, do I? He probably told you much the same. Says all he was doing was keeping some of his cousin's money in a bank account, and knows he's one of several doing that for Charlie, though he insists he doesn't know who any of the others are. Claims he had nothing to do with helping Charlie pull off the phony death, other than knowledge of the fact, and says he doesn't know who did. Well, what do you think, Nolan? Is he lying or not? You think there's any chance he knows where Charlie is?"

"No," Nolan said. Charlie was too smart to tell Joey much, and it figured he wouldn't let his different co-conspirators know each other either. Less you know, less you can tell under duress. "I figure Joey's telling the truth. I questioned him pretty thorough."

Felix said, "I questioned him rather thoroughly myself, or I should say Greer and Angello did. So I have to agree with you. It would seem Joey's told us everything he knows."

Nolan said, "No wonder he's a humble, quiet little guy. It's been a bitch of a night for him."

Felix leaned close, like a quarterback giving the signals. "We better come to some kind of mutual understanding, Nolan, about how we're going about handling this affair. I can't be sure how many people were involved in helping Charlie put over his little charade, but I think it should be obvious to you that there is going to be some, shall we say, extensive inter-Family housecleaning."

"Give me two days."

"What can you do in two days?"

"Try me."

"What are you asking?"

"Leave me alone for two days. Give me that long before you start weeding out your bad stock."

"Where will you start?"

"I have some people in mind to see."

"What sort of people?"

"Family people. Some people who seem likely bedfellows for Charlie."

"Such as?"

Nolan told him.

Felix nodded. "They're well insulated, you know. Not that easy to get at."

"Don't worry about it."

"You'll be needing some information from me, addresses, telephone numbers, that sort of thing."

"Yes."

Felix thought for a moment. Then he said, "Is there a phone I could use?"

Nolan pointed across the pool, where there was a snack bar, closed now, of course, but with a phone on the counter. Felix got up and walked over to the counter and used the phone. Nolan watched Sherry swim. She was graceful.

Ten minutes later Felix was back. "Two days," he said.

"Thanks," Nolan said.

"You know, I still don't understand how you guessed Charlie." Felix laughed, "I mean a dead man, my God. I would have assumed it was someone from *your* field."

They'd been over that this afternoon and Nolan didn't want to go into it again.

"Call it a hunch," Nolan said.

It was, of course, much more than a hunch. Nolan knew it was possible that a pro thief had pulled the job, some heistman down on his luck who needed ready cash and knew Planner's safe in the backroom usually had a good piece of change in it. But it was unlikely as hell. Maybe in sheer desperation, but otherwise Nolan couldn't see a professional hitting Planner: you don't hit one of your own. The old guy had virtually no enemies in the trade, and was a valued friend of everyone who knew him and made use of him.

And right there was another reason: Planner had too

many friends to risk stealing from him. Whoever pulled this had ripped off not only Planner, but maybe a dozen professionals who'd entrusted emergency money to Planner's safekeeping. What it came down to was this: let it leak you were the one who wasted Planner, a hundred guys would drop the hammer on you.

An amateur, then?

No. Someone outside the trade was even more unlikely. Why would some amateur pick an antique shop to knock over, and a shabby one at that? If he did, how would he know about that safe, way back in the second of two storerooms? No, an amateur would probably just empty the cash register and run.

Most important, nobody—nobody outside of Nolan, Jon and Planner—knew an eight-hundred-thousand-buck haul from a bank job was nestled in that safe. Very few people knew for sure Nolan had pulled that particular job, and no one would likely figure he'd leave the money with Planner.

Except maybe Charlie.

Charlie might've figured it.

Charlie not only knew that Nolan had pulled the bank heist, he also knew Nolan had been wounded after the robbery and wounded badly, because it was Charlie and his people who shot Nolan, in that fucking double cross Charlie pulled. He would've known Nolan would have to hole up close by. He would've known Nolan hadn't had the time or health to get properly rid of the money; he could've figured that the money had stayed right there where Nolan was holing up. Charlie could've used his vast Family resources to investigate Nolan's working habits, his associates, especially in the immediate area, to determine precisely where Nolan was hiding, sooner or later coming up with Planner.

When the Family started negotiating with Nolan, a Nolan who was still just getting on his feet, Charlie's inside sources (the same people within the Family who helped Charlie "die") could've relayed word to him that Nolan was resisting transfer of the money. And Nolan had told Felix and others who pressed moving the money to a Family bank, "I'm not sweating the money's safety. It's been okay where it is this long and a while longer won't make a difference." Perhaps these words of Nolan's (foolish words, he knew now) had gotten back to Charlie.

But Charlie was dead.

Sure.

That auto-wreck business had smelled to Nolan from word go, but he'd wanted Charlie to be dead so bad he'd accepted it. Even then he'd questioned Felix, who had told him that this pretense of an accident was a necessity, that Charlie was simply too high in the Family to die anything but a "natural" death.

Sure.

That was where the hunch part did come in. Deep down in Nolan's gut, Charlie didn't *feel* dead. Nolan had ignored the tingle in his gut, chalking it up to all that time the feud with Charlie had lasted, figuring there was bound to be mental residue left after all the emotional and physical violence Charlie had caused him over the years. But now with Planner dead and the money, all that money stolen, Nolan was listening to everything his gut had to say.

So how could Felix be expected to understand? This was a complex chain of logic intertwined with instinct and was something an attorney in a tailored suit could never comprehend.

"When are you going to get started?" Felix was asking.

"Tomorrow morning."

"Not tonight?"

"Tomorrow morning. Tonight I'm going to get some sleep."

"Whatever you think is best, I suppose. Nolan?"

"What?"

"Why is it you haven't told me just where the hell in Iowa the scene was of this afternoon's fiasco?"

"Because you already checked with the switchboard to see where the long distance call was from."

"Oh. Well. Don't you think it would be wise to get to Iowa City as soon as possible and start investigating?"

"Felix."

"What?"

"I asked for two days and you said I could have them."

"Right, but that doesn't mean . . ."

"Felix."

"What?"

"How can I put this? Felix. You're full of shit."

Felix drew a breath. "Am I really?"

"Yeah. You are. You're a lawyer, Felix. Don't tell me how to handle the sort of thing you know nothing about, okay? I get married and want a divorce, I'll come to you."

"You're tense, Nolan," Felix said tensely. "I'm going to forget you've said this."

"I don't give a damn what you do. You're just a goddamn lawyer."

"Just a goddamn lawyer . . ."

"Okay, so you represent the Family. That powerful organization that clutches the city of Chicago by its very balls. That powerful organization that let one balding old hood named Charlie turn it into the world's biggest asshole. But don't feel bad. Look what that guy Nader did to General Motors."

Felix smiled and wagged his head. "By God, you're right. Pour me another vodka martini."

"Sure, Felix." Nolan did.

Felix took the martini and nibbled it, then said, "Why don't you take one of my men with you? Take Angello if you don't like Greer."

"Felix . . ."

"Now this is one thing I'm going to have to insist on. This is not the lawyer talking now, this is from upstairs, as they say. The Family has a big interest in this affair. You have to understand. It's more than just money now that Charlie's turned up."

"Suppose you're right," Nolan said. "Give me Greer then.

He'll need to take a car for himself, by the way."

"Why?"

"Why don't I just explain that to Greer."

"Well, all right, whatever it takes to make your investigation a success."

"Look, you said that before, that word 'investigate' . . . I'm not going to investigate, Felix. I don't know how to do that. I'm not the goddamn FBI. I'm not going to Iowa City and snoop around, because all the action there is over and I got a friend there covering things for me. What I'm going to do is go around knocking heads together, Family heads, because that's who was involved in faking Charlie's sendoff. Right?"

"Correct," Felix said, his smile damn near feeble.

Nolan said, "It's not that I don't appreciate your help. You deserve credit for thinking of Joey Metrano. We'd been in trouble if we picked the wrong guy to work over."

Nolan had said that to unruffle Felix's feathers, and it worked nicely, sparking Felix into a rambling, self-glorifying explanation of how he had known that if Charlie were alive, Joey would know, and of Charlie's friends and relatives in the Family, Joey would be easiest to break, and so on. Nolan tried not to fall asleep. Across the pool, the phone on the snack bar counter began to ring during the closing moments of Felix's oration.

Nolan said, "That'll be for me," and went after it.

The switchboard girl said, "I've got a long-distance call from Iowa City for you," and Nolan said, "Put him on," hoping Jon had better tidings this time around than last.

"Hello?" a voice said. Not Jon's. A female voice.

"Yes? This is Logan."

"Uh, is your name Logan or Nolan or what? Jon says Nolan and then tells me ask for Logan and . . . oh, Christ, I suppose that's unimportant, I mean . . ."

She was almost crying.

"Hey!" Nolan said. "Who is this? What's wrong?"

"I suppose I shouldn't be upset. Jon said if I got worried,

really got worried, I should call you. He explained that this was . . . a dangerous situation. That men with guns were involved."

"Settle down. My name is Nolan. All right? I'm Jon's friend. All right? And I'm your friend, too. Now tell me your name."

"Karen."

"All right, Karen. Now what's the problem?"

"I'm sorry to bother you, I really am, I shouldn't be bothering you, I'm just easily upset, I guess."

"Why are you upset, Karen?"

"It's Jon. He said he'd be back by eight, and, well, you know what time it is now."

That was bad.

"It's nothing to worry about, Karen."

"There was something else . . ."

"What?"

"Well, he gave me a number to call. I was supposed to try him there, before bothering you. He said don't bother you unless I was really upset or worried or something."

"Do you know whose number it was?"

"Jon said it was a doctor he was going to see."

That made sense, Nolan thought. "Go on, Karen."

"Well, I called the doctor a half hour ago and he said . . . he said he hadn't seen Jon. He doesn't even know Jon, he says. Didn't understand what the hell I was talking about."

Shit.

"Okay," Nolan said. "Don't worry. You did right calling, Karen. You'll hear from me soon."

Her sigh of relief came over clear on the phone. "Thanks," she said. "I mean it, thanks. Whatever the hell your name is."

"Now give me your address and phone number."

She did, and Nolan found a note pad to jot them down.

After he'd hung up, he went over to where Sherry was swimming and told her to go back to the room and wait for him. She nodded yes, grabbed up her towel, and scooted off. Nolan walked over to Felix and said, "Looks like you get your wish after all."

Felix looked up from his third martini and said, "How's that?"

"My friend in Iowa City is in trouble, I think. You go get Greer and have him ready to go in the parking lot within fifteen minutes or I'm leaving without him."

Three

1

The sun was hot and high in a practically cloud-free sky and Jon was feeling lousy. It was Tuesday afternoon, just an hour and a half after he'd left his uncle at the antique shop to join Karen at her apartment, and he was on his way back already. The late breakfast at Karen's had been fine; she was a good cook and Jon enjoyed that side of her as much as anything. But her ten-year-old pride and joy, Larry, had a dentist's appointment at four, and, of course, Karen had to drive the kid there and be by his side throughout the great ordeal. And so Jon had been rushed through the breakfast, forced into throwing those delicious eggs and sausage down his throat as if he was shoveling coal into a boiler.

"Why," Jon had asked her, through a mouthful of eggs, "did you ask me over if you were in such a goddamn hurry? You didn't say anything about the kid's teeth on the phone."

"What're you bitching about?" she had said. "The price is right, isn't it? I thought maybe you'd lower yourself to go along with me when I take Larry to his dental appointment."

"That's my idea of a good time," he'd said.

"Oh," she'd said angrily, "go read a comic book."

Larry had been sitting at the table the whole time and the kid would flash an innocent smile now and then, batting his lashes at Jon. Larry had red hair and freckles and big brown eyes, like the kids in paintings you can buy prints of by sending in three toilet paper wrappers and a dollar-fifty. Jon hated Larry.

Jon supposed he was jealous of the kid. It was hard getting used to going with a girl—woman—who was the mother of a ten-year-old kid. Karen looked younger than thirty, and was very pretty, with long, wild, dark hair and the same brown eyes as the kid, only on her they looked good. She also had a body that wouldn't quit.

But still it was odd, strange getting used to. Karen's apartment was large enough that privacy wasn't a real problem, and Larry kept pretty much to himself, having a stamp collection or some silly such thing he played around with all the time, shut tight in his room. When Larry did decide to intrude, however, he intruded big, and could, with his big-brown-eyes coaxing, dictate the course of an evening's activities. The new Brian DePalma film they had planned to attend could be turned into the latest revival of "Son of Flubber"; a night of Cantonese dining at Ming Gardens could be transformed easily into greasy take-out tacos; and on television the educational channel's showing of "The Maltese Falcon" on the Bogart Festival would lose out to a made-for-TV movie with someone who used to be on "Laugh-In." When a need of Jon's was balanced against a need of Larry's, no contest, Larry won every time.

So Jon hated Larry, and felt quite sure that the feeling was reciprocal, even though the kid rarely said a word. But with those shit-eating big brown eyes, who needed the power of speech?

Jon had met Karen in her candle shop, which catered to a head crowd, selling incense and Zig-Zag papers and hash pipes and posters and the like, in addition to countless candles, most of which Karen made herself. He went there to buy underground comics and posters, and after a while he was haunting the place, checking for new stuff (which was ridiculous, since he bought so much mail order) but mostly just getting to know Karen. At first it was just that he was fascinated watching her boobs act as a bouncing billboard for various causes, in tee-shirts ranging from NO NUKES to SAVE THE WHALES. Later he found out she was funny and bright and crazy, when she got politics off her chest.

Jon realized that probably the primary reason he and Karen got together was because both of them were straighter than they appeared to be: Jon with his frizzy hair and Wonder Warthog tee-shirts, Karen with her equally frizzy, longer hair and ERA slogans. The turning point in their relationship was that day in the Airliner when they had been sitting drinking beers and Jon had made a confession. He told Karen sheepishly that he was not into the dope scene, in spite of his looks and certain bullshit comments he'd from time to time made. Karen had grinned and admitted the same thing, that despite her latter-day hippie appearance, she was a painfully straight, divorced woman of thirty with a ten-year-old child.

Which was the first Jon heard of her age, her broken marriage, and her kid, but he hadn't minded, as the shared confessions had played like a scene in a movie and fantasy was something he could really get into, so they had laughed, toasted beers and joined forces.

Jon never got the details of her marriage. He did know that her husband was an attorney who lived in Des Moines and came from a long line of attorneys. Jon gathered that the marriage had come out of those prehistoric times when the pill was not so common and have-to marriages were, and Karen had dropped out as an undergrad to play wife and mother while her hubby was put through law school by his wealthy family. Later on, she proved a burden to her husband, mostly because she was "intellectually inferior" (she hadn't even made it through college, after all). Her husband may have been a hypocritical bastard, but he was no dummy: he'd let Karen have pride-and-joy Larry and asked next-to-no-visitation rights.

And his alimony and child-support payments were generous, too. Karen's monetary situation was such that she could hold a long-term lease on the building, which had as a bottom floor her candle shop and above that the five-room, remodeled apartment she and Larry lived in; another apartment above that she rented out. The building was in the heart of Iowa City's shopping district, on the back side of a block that faced the U of I Quadrangle, the candle shop bookended by a pair of busy record stores. The setup provided her a lucrative source of income.

That was all Jon knew about the former daddy of Larry, picked up here and there from bits and pieces of conversation. Jon didn't know the guy's name (the bitterness ran so deep in Karen she'd reverted to her maiden name) but Jon hoped one day to look up the (he assumed) red-haired, freckle-faced butthole and punch him out.

These were the things that Jon reflected on as he walked the six blocks from Karen's downtown apartment to Planner's antique shop. The beautiful breakfast that had been rammed down his throat was showing no signs of settling in his stomach, and he was generally disturbed over the unkind words he and Karen had tossed back and forth at one another.

He walked around to the side of the antique shop and as he was crossing the cement porch, his right foot hit something wet and he slipped and fell. He landed on his ass but broke his fall with the heels of his hands, which slid off the cement and skidded back across the gravel surrounding the porch.

"Oh, shit," he said, after the fact, and just sat there for a moment, half on porch, half on gravel. Then he got up, slowly, and examined his scraped but not badly bleeding palms, deciding the injury wouldn't impair his drawing too much. He dusted himself off with the untenderized sides of his hands.

He went over to the porch to see what had made him slip and saw a trickle of red, smeared where his foot had hit it, a stream trailing from the door across the cement stoop onto the gravel. He touched the red wetness and smelled his fingertips, looked at them, rubbed them together. What the hell was this, he wondered. Not paint; it's too thin.

"What the hell," he said aloud, shrugged, wiped the damp stuff off his fingertips onto his Wonder Warthog tee-shirt and tried the door.

Locked.

Jesus, how many times had he asked his uncle not to lock

the side door? But the old guy kept on doing it, anyway, wanting to keep the air-conditioning inside. It was a nuisance to Jon because his uncle had the only key to the side door and wouldn't let it out of his keeping for Jon to have a duplicate made. Jon had a key to the front and that was enough, his uncle reasoned. Yet his uncle was always complaining about Jon coming through the front way and scaring off the customers with his bushy hair and crazy tee-shirts.

This was the last straw, Jon thought. He and Planner got along, got along famously, but there were certain things that, dammit, just required an argument. And this locked-door business was one of those things.

He walked around to the front. The "Closed" sign was turned facing out for some reason, and he couldn't see Planner when he peeked in. The old guy probably stepped out for a sandwich, Jon thought. Probably over at the Dairy Queen right now.

Or maybe Nolan called, and Planner had to leave to make some kind of preparations for Nolan. That was it. Nolan called.

He dug the key out of his pocket and opened the front door. "Planner?" he said. He repeated his uncle's name three more times, each progressively louder, and getting no response, he locked the door again. If Planner wanted the place closed, then closed it would be.

The air hung with traces of smoke from one of Planner's Garcia y Vegas, which didn't do Jon's still-churning stomach any good. The air-conditioning kept it from getting too damn stale in there, but nothing known to man could completely wipe out the memory of those potent cee-gars of Planner's.

Jon got behind the counter and sat down in Planner's soft old easy chair. His stomach continued to grind away in its attempt to digest breakfast; his conscience nagged him slightly about the semi-arguments he'd had with Karen. He found himself staring at the phone on the counter.

"What was that dentist's name?" he muttered to himself. "Paulson? Paulsen?" He picked up the phone book and tried to find the listing and couldn't. Finally he looked in the yellow pages under "Dentists-Orthodontists" and found it: Povlsen. Odd damn spelling. He dialed the number and asked the girl who answered if Karen was there and was told just a moment.

"Yes?" the voice said.

"Hi, Kare."

"Hi, Jon." Her voice was neutral; she couldn't make up her mind whether she was mad or not.

"Listen. I want to tell you something."

"I'm listening."

"I mean, you can talk, can't you? Has Larry had his teeth worked on yet?"

"Yes. That is, the doctor's working on him right now."

"Well, why aren't you . . . ?"

"The doctor said I . . . I shouldn't be in there . . . said Larry was too old for that sort of thing."

Good man, Jon thought.

"Kare?"

"Yes, Jon?"

"Thanks for breakfast. Thanks for asking me over."

"You're welcome," she said, and he could hear the smile in her voice.

He got out of the chair and sat up on the counter. "And listen, something else . . ."

"What?"

"When are you going to be done at the dentist's?"

"Why?"

"Maybe I want to fill *your* cavity."

She laughed and said, "That's medicine I'll gladly take. I'll be home in half an hour."

"Good," he said, and suddenly noticed the trail of red across the floor down at the end of the counter. "Hey, Kare, hold on, will you?"

"Sure, Jonny."

The thin red streak led from the side door across the floor and around into the first backroom. What the hell was it, anyway? It wasn't . . . blood?

He followed the red trail into the second backroom.

And found the slumped shell of his uncle.

Jon started to shake.

He approached his uncle tentatively, bent down saying, "Unc? Uh . . . Planner?"

He shook his uncle's shoulder and could feel how slack the body was, and turned him off his side and saw Planner's face, saw the queer smile, saw how white the face was, saw the blood his uncle was soaking in, and ran back to the phone.

"Je . . . jesus," he sputtered into the receiver.

"Jonny?"

"Listen . . . something . . . something terrible's happened."

"What should I do, Jonny?"

"Nothing. Go . . . go home when . . . Larry's through and . . . I'll call you in an hour. O . . . okay?"

"Are you all right?"

"I . . . will be."

He hung up.

Shaking, he felt the cramp buckle him over, overpower him, and he heaved his breakfast onto the old wooden floor of his uncle's antique shop.

2

The housing addition had a vaguely English look to it, rough wood, watered-down Tudor architecture, occasional stone. It was more plush than your run-of-the-mill housing addition, carefully laid out on gently rolling hills, each lawn spacious and immaculately tended, though the spread-out nature of the addition and the lack of trees made it look barren and lonely and cold against the clear sky. It was on the edge of Iowa City, on one of the less-traveled routes out of town, just beyond a modest commercial area dominated by a Giant grocery store, Colonel Sanders Chicken, and filling stations. On the other side it was surrounded by sprawling farmland, and at that very moment a farmer was on a tractor working slow and hard along the horizon, making the cluster of houses seem out of place and somehow irrelevant, to the farmer's life at least. Though the houses were not crackerbox identical, there was still a housing addition sameness to them, which was only emphasized by the contrived effort to avoid repetition that amounted mainly to alternating one-story homes with split-levels. Walter slowed as he approached one of the one-story homes, focusing his vision on the number on the door, making sure this was the one he was after.

This particular house was dark wood with light stone and sat on a corner next door to a house that was light wood with dark stone. It was just another house in another (if elite) housing addition, with the only noticeable difference being that this had a red Mercedes Benz in the driveway instead of a Ford LTD or a Cadillac. The house was a surprise to Walter, as the whole addition had been. It was not the sort of neighborhood where he'd expected to find the home of a dope peddler.

Of course Sturms was more than a dope peddler, Walter supposed, though he didn't know what else you'd call him, really. Supplier, maybe. From the looks of the housing addition Sturms evidently thought of himself as a district sales manager or something.

Walter had a low regard for people who dealt in drugs, and knew his father, Charlie, shared that low regard. Once they had discussed the subject and his father had told him that the Chicago Family was only into drugs because they had to be, and they were in it mainly as financeers, not fucking around with diddly-shit pushers and such.

Walter guessed that in Iowa City circles Sturms was probably considered to be "the Man," which wasn't particularly impressive, since most towns have one. Just the same, Charlie had assured his son that Sturms *was* important, in a small-time way, because he was the dope guy in Iowa City, and Iowa City was one of the big drug centers in that part of the midwest.

And Sturms was important for another reason.

He was important to this Iowa City trip, because if Walter and Charlie ran into any trouble, Sturms was someone they could turn to.

"Doesn't he know you?" Walter had asked, on the drive down from Wisconsin that morning. "Doesn't he know you're supposed to be dead?"

"He'd know me by name, sure," his father had said, "but not by sight. And we sure as hell won't be handing him no goddamn calling card. Look, I just mentioned him 'cause if we get in a tight squeeze, we can call on the guy, see, just drop a few of the right names and he'll jump for us, is all."

It made sense that Sturms wouldn't know Charlie. Walter knew that his father had been high up enough in the Family to make it unlikely for a nobody like Sturms, stuck clear out here in Iowa, to know him personally. And, too, his father looked different now, since his "death." Walter figured an old friend could easily pass Charlie on the street without recognizing him. Charlie had lost weight, was damn near skinny. And there was the work that plastic surgeon did, too, changing Charlie's bumpy, several-times-broken nose into something small and straight, right off a movie star's face.

All of this floated down Walter's mental stream, but he wasn't thinking about any of it, really; these were non-thoughts, passing quickly, skimming across the surface of his mind, part reflex action, part Walter's semiconscious attempt to stay calm. He had driven slowly through the housing addition, noting the children on bicycles, the teenaged boys mowing lawns, a husband or wife hosing down family cars in drives, none of it making any impression on him, no more than a boring sermon in church, though all this middle-class straight life reminded him to keep calm, to drive slow, to make as if the man sitting next to him was just taking a nap.

Walter thought about a lot of things, but the only thing he really thought about was his father, because his father was hurt and his father's being hurt was the only thing that was really on Walter's mind.

They'd come out of the antique shop awkwardly, with Walter trying to keep his one arm under the huge cardboard box of money, while looping his other arm around his wounded father's waist. It was like being in one of those races at a picnic where they strap your leg and somebody else's together and tell you to run. It was like that, only with blood.

Walter's father had trailed blood out of there and Walter had been very worried. He knew that his father had high blood pressure and also knew that having high blood pressure could make a wound worse for a person, maybe make him bleed more, maybe make him more prone to shock. In the car he had looked at the wound in his father's leg, exposed as it was just below the line of the Bermuda shorts, and Walter was stunned by the realization of how frail his father's legs looked, how skinny they were, how the flesh just hung helpless on the bone. Walter was surprised, too, that such a small wound could leak so much blood. His father had stopped the bleeding by ramming a wadded handkerchief in against the hole in his bare thigh, but the wadded handkerchief hadn't stopped Walter's worrying.

Charlie would say, "Don't worry, just get out of here," whenever Walter asked him about the leg. Charlie had said it while Walter helped him out the antique shop door, and he said it while Walter helped him into the car, and he said it as Walter drove out Dubuque Street toward the Interstate 80 approach. And then Charlie passed out.

Walter had pulled into a driveway that led down to a tree-sheltered fraternity house and backed out and headed back on Dubuque toward the downtown. He stopped at a Standard station to use the pay phone. He found Sturms's number in the phone book and dialed.

"Yes," a voice had said. A bored tenor voice.

"Mr. Sturms?"

"Yes. What is it?"

"You don't know me, but we have mutual friends."

"Really."

"I was told you could help out in a pinch. I have a man with me who needs help. He needs a doctor."

"Who is this?"

"We have mutual friends."

"You said that before. What kind of mutual friends?"

"Chicago friends. Milwaukee friends."

"Name one."

"Harry in Milwaukee. Now listen, I'm not screwing around. We need some help here."

"How bad do you need the doctor?"

"I don't know. Not bad I hope. But bad enough to bother you when I rather wouldn't."

"The guy isn't dying or anything, is he?"

"Not unless it's from old age, waiting on you to make up your mind if you're going to help us or not."

"Shit. I guess you better bring him out to my place. Where are you now?"

Walter told him. Sturms gave Walter directions.

And so now Walter was pulling into the oversize driveway of the house that was dark wood with light stone. He stopped the blue Olds alongside the red Mercedes, his foot on the brake, the car still in gear. He stared at the dark rough wood of the double garage doors and after ten seconds honked the horn once. He reached a hand over and patted his father's shoulder, as if to reassure the unconscious man.

The garage door swung suddenly up and out of view and a man motioned at Walter to pull the Oldsmobile inside and

Walter did. The man shut the garage door and walked over to meet Walter as he got out of the car.

The man was in his vague thirties, with the build of a linebacker, and had light brown hair that was neither long nor short and had been expensively styled to look natural. He wore a long-sleeve rust-color shirt and white slacks and was tanned and handsome in a standard sort of a way, except for a broad, flat nose.

Walter said, "Is the doctor here?"

Sturms said, "I haven't been able to get him."

"Jesus. What's the problem?"

"Out on a house call. What happened anyway?"

"My father's been shot."

"How?"

"Never mind how. You don't really want to know how, do you?"

"I guess not. How bad is he?"

"Caught a bullet in his thigh. He's unconscious."

"Let me take a look at him."

Walter led Sturms around to the other side of the car. Sturms just peeked in the window, then turned to Walter and said, "Let's go inside."

"You going to help me move my father?"

"He's all right where he is."

"Well . . ."

"Moving him inside won't help him any. Come on. We'll try the doctor again."

Walter followed Sturms into the house. The first room was the kitchen, where all the appliances were pastel green and the wood was maple brown. Dozens of bottles of pills sat on the counter. Walter's surprise registered on his face.

Sturms grinned, said, "Wondering why I'd leave my stock out in the open like that, kid?"

"Yes, as a matter of fact."

"That's not merchandise. Those are vitamins I take. I wouldn't touch that shit I sell. Haven't even touched grass in years."

Walter was led into a large living room with an open-beam ceiling of the same dark rough wood as the outside and pebbled plaster walls the same rust color as Sturms's shirt. The carpet was burnt umber, and thick and fluffy like whipped egg whites. There was a sofa, a recliner and a chair with an ottoman, all dark brown imitation leather with button-tufted seats and backs. Cocktail table, end tables, even the stereo and television complex were dark Spanish-style hand-carved wood, looking lush and expensive. It was an attractive room, only slightly marred by two out of place abstract paintings over the sofa, a red spattered on a field of white, and a white spattered on a field of red. Sturms told Walter to sit, and Walter went to the sofa so he could sit with his back to the paintings. Air whooshed out of the cushion as Walter settled his ass uneasily down.

Sturms left the room momentarily and came back with a yellow telephone, which he plugged into a jack behind one of the sofa's end tables. He brought the phone around in front of Walter and sat it in front of him, on the cocktail table, next to a bowl of artificial fruit.

"Now call Harry in Milwaukee," Sturms said. "I want some proof of who you are."

"You haven't even called the doctor yet," Walter said.

"I'll get you something to drink while you're doing that. What would you like? A beer? Maybe a Pepsi?"

"You haven't even called the doctor yet, have you?"

"You call Harry. Then I'll call the doctor."

"You son of a bitch," Walter said, and jumped up off the sofa.

Sturms showed Walter the gun. Walter didn't know where the gun had come from, but Sturms most certainly did have it. It was an automatic, silenced, smaller than the ones Walter and his father had carried earlier that day. Those nine millimeters were under the seat of the Olds right now, not doing Walter a hell of a lot of good.

"What's going on, honey?" a female voice said.

A tall brunette with a short haircut and dark tan skin was

standing in the background. Like Sturms's gun, she'd popped up from nowhere. She was wearing a warmup outfit, a trimmed-in-brown beige tee-shirt and matching short shorts, breasts bobbling under the skimpy top. Walter sat down again.

"Nothing, baby," Sturms said. "Go get my friend and me a couple of beers, will you?"

"Sure thing, honey."

"My wife," Sturms explained, as she took her time bobbling out. "Sweet kid. She painted those pictures there, on the wall, behind you."

"Talented," Walter said.

"Now why don't you call Harry?"

"I don't know his number."

"I thought he was a friend of yours."

"He's a friend of that man bleeding out there in your fucking garage."

"All right," Sturms said, sticking the gun down in his waistband. "I'll call him and let you talk to him."

He crouched and dialed the number from memory. It took a few seconds for the direct-dialing long-distance wheels to turn, and then he said, "Could I speak to Harry, please . . . Mr. Sturms in Iowa City is calling. I'll hold . . . Hello, Harry, it's good to hear your voice. No, everything was fine with the last shipment, no problem, everything's terrific. No, it's something else . . . I have a guy here says he's a friend of yours, wants some help from me. I'll put him on."

Walter took the phone and said, "This is Walter."

"Walter?" The connection was good; Walter's Uncle Harry was coming through fine. "Walter, something didn't go wrong today, did it?"

"I'm afraid so. Dad's been hurt."

"Oh, Christ. How bad is it?"

"Just his thigh, took one in the thigh. But he's unconscious, and you know his high blood pressure trouble. You can't die from a thigh wound, can you?"

"Depends on what gets hit. How bad's he bleeding?"

"Bad at first, but we stopped it. I don't think some major artery got hit or anything, if that's what you mean."

"Listen, you tell Sturms get a doctor for you, and get your father patched up and hit the road. Did things go okay otherwise?"

Walter hadn't even thought about that. He hadn't even thought about the old guy at the antique shop his father had shot.

"It could've gone smoother," Walter said.

"What about the money?"

"We got it."

"Good. Well, then, have Sturms get a doctor for you straight away and . . ."

"Sturms won't do it till he gets the word from you that I'm worth helping."

"Put the cocksucker on."

Walter said, "He says put the cocksucker on."

Sturms flinched and took the phone. Walter could hear his uncle yelling, but couldn't make out the exact words. Sturms said, "You bet, Harry . . . Right away . . . Good-bye, sir."

He hung up.

"Look," Sturms said, "sorry I hassled you. Let's forget it and start over."

"Never mind trying to get in good with me," Walter said. "Get your ass on that phone and get a doctor for my father."

Sturms nodded.

The brunette bounced back in and gave Walter a Pabst in a bottle. She gave her husband one, too, but he was busy on the phone and just set the bottle down. She smiled at Walter and said, "Do you really think I'm talented?"

3

"Easy now, Planner," Jon soothed, "easy now, this isn't going to hurt a bit." He lowered Planner's blanket-wrapped body into the empty wooden crate. He'd felt lucky to find the crate, which was six feet long and a bit wider than necessary, but it sufficed. It had held an antique chest of drawers Planner had stored away. Jon had liberated the crate for this present purpose, the probably valuable antique shoved into a storeroom corner.

"There now," Jon said softly, whispering, "there now, Unc, that'll be fine, won't it?" The blanket-wrapped body was comfortably settled in a soft bed of excelsior lining the crate's bottom. Jon replaced the lid on the crate and said, "Good-bye, Planner, 'bye."

Maybe he was an asshole, talking to Planner like that. But he just couldn't think of his uncle's body as some cold chunk of meat, even though he knew that was what it was. The body was *Planner*, for God's sake, and looked as much like Planner as it had when there hadn't been bullet holes in it, and the only way Jon could deal with the situation was to keep talking to Planner. It seemed natural to keep talking to Planner.

And when he'd lifted the body, it had seemed light and heavy all at once. Could this featherlight bundle of flesh have walked and breathed? Could this granite-heavy load of bulk be the body of a frail old man? He held the body like a baby in his arms, and he felt as though he were parodying that famous statue at the Vatican, the one that got defaced, and he gave out a nervous little laugh that wasn't really a laugh at all, and said, "Aw, shit, Planner, you can't be dead."

But he was, of course, and there was work to be done. Work for the living. Nolan had said so.

After throwing up, Jon had grabbed for the phone and dialed Nolan direct. It took a while to get through, what with the switchboard operator at that motel or whatever it was trying to track Nolan down. It'd seemed an hour before Nolan came on, and Jon's bladder was about to burst.

"Jon?" Nolan had said. "Calm down, Jon, what's wrong?"

And Jon had told Nolan about Planner, about Planner being dead.

"Jesus, kid. Stay calm," Nolan had said, his voice as soft, as sure of itself as ever. "Don't go hysterical on me."

Don't go hysterical on me . . . Nolan had told him that once before, after the bank job, when everything had exploded into blood and death, and Jon had been able to hang on, because Nolan was there. He'd been able to make it because Nolan was a rock and Nolan was there, and now Nolan's voice was coming over that hunk of plastic, disembodied but here just the same, reassuring him, calming him, enabling him to survive, for the moment anyway.

"Go on," Nolan was saying.

"He's dead, and the money . . ."

Jon hadn't realized yet what it meant, but he could remember seeing the safe door swung open and the shelves empty.

The money. Good God, the money.

"It's gone," he told Nolan. "All of it."

Nolan was silent for a moment. A long moment.

"Nolan?" Jon asked, panic rising in his chest, catching in his throat.

"Yeah, kid," the steady voice said. A rock again. "Go on."

"The money's gone. I just came in and . . . and found Planner and it must've all just happened."

"How do you know?"

"Hell, I wasn't gone more than an hour, and the . . . blood . . . it's still wet, uh, fresh." He remembered slipping in the stream of it on the back stoop. "You know, Nolan, you wouldn't think Planner had so much blood in him. You wouldn't think it could seep all the way back to the porch like that."

"How do you mean?"

"I mean somehow it ran from the backroom, where the safe was cleaned out, back onto the porch and . . . shit, that couldn't be Planner's blood, could it? What do you figure . . . ?"

"I figure Planner got a shot off at whoever shot him."

"Of course. Bad, you suppose?"

"Bad enough he left some blood behind."

"Nolan, should I call the police or what? I mean, we were robbed and Planner was murdered and . . ."

"Christ no! Use your damn head."

"That was stupid. I'm sorry I even said it, Nolan."

"Never mind that. Did Planner have a gun in his hand?"

"I . . . I haven't really looked that close yet. If you want to know the truth, all I've done so far is spot Planner's body, puke out my guts, and call you on the phone."

"You go look the backroom over. I'll hold on."

Jon set the receiver on the counter and went back for a look. He found one of his uncle's two .32 automatics clutched in an already stiffening hand, and he found across from Planner the place in the wall where one of the bullets had gone in. And the beginning of the trail of blood was at the safe, where the guy would've been crouched down, emptying the shelves. He went back to the phone and reported what he'd found to Nolan.

"Okay," Nolan said. "Now listen to me. Are you pulled together? Are you settled down?"

"Yes. I'm settled down."

And Nolan told him what to do. Told him to contact that doctor, Ainsworth, the one that patched Nolan up and treated him while he was holed up at Planner's. Contact the doctor and pay him to make out a false death certificate, verifying Planner's demise as by natural causes. Pay him plenty, to fill out the forms and such and help keep the cops from coming and having a close posthumous peek into Planner's setup. Then clean the place up, get rid of the gun Planner fired at whoever shot him. Put Planner in a box and arrange to have him cremated. Do all of that, and then ask around at the places in the neighborhood, that Dairy Queen, the filling station next door, ask if they saw anybody leaving Planner's around that time. But don't act suspicious in asking. Make something up, like whoever it was was going to sell you something and didn't leave an address, something like that.

"About that doctor," Jon said.

"What about him?" Nolan said.

"What'll I pay him with?"

"There should be eight thousand or so in the wall safe upstairs."

"Oh, yeah, behind his framed Hoover buttons. Planner keeps . . . kept . . . the combination in the kitchen, in the silverware drawer."

"Good. Pay Ainsworth, oh, four thousand. I know that sounds high, kid, but remember, as far as the doc knows, you could've murdered your uncle yourself and're asking him to cover up. So he'll be expecting a fat reward."

"What then?"

"Sit tight. I'll call you there at Planner's when I get a chance. I have a notion of who maybe pulled this piece of shit."

"You do? Who, for Christ's sake?"

"Charlie."

"That Mafia guy? *That* guy? He's dead, how can . . ."

"He's supposed to be dead. We'll see. I'll be looking into it."

"Okay. When can I expect your call?"

"Just stay there at the shop. Get those things done I told you and otherwise sit tight. Got it?"

"Got it."

"Jon."

"Yes, Nolan?"

"You're doing fine."

And Nolan had hung up.

Now that Planner was wrapped in a blanket and lain to temporary rest, Jon began to get the place in shape. He went into the adjoining storeroom and got the box of sawdust, which was used to clean up various sorts of messes, mostly wet. He poured the sawdust first onto the pile of vomit, and his half-digested, stinking breakfast soaked the stuff up. He swept the gunk up, and it took several dustpan loads to do so, and dumped the rancid mess into a big empty heavy-cardboard barrel. He then did the same with the blood, pouring sawdust onto the trail of it and the pool where his uncle had been lying, and some of it had started to dry, getting dark, almost black. After he'd dumped the several dustpans of bloody sawdust, he got out a can of Ajax and a bucket of water and a scrub-brush and worked on the wooden floor till all visible traces of blood were gone. He thought, rather absurdly, that it was a good thing he hadn't cleaned the storerooms yesterday, as today's work would've been needless double duty. He ran across his uncle's false teeth, his upper plate, and gagged, but his stomach was empty now, fortunately. He held the plate by two trembling fingers and went over to the crate and lifted the lid an inch or two and pushed the teeth inside.

Afterward he went upstairs and sat at the kitchen table and poured a water glass half full with vodka and the rest with Seven-Up. He stirred the mixture with a spoon and threw it quickly down. He wasn't a drinking man, so he soon found himself gagging again, but by the third glass he was doing fine.

God, what an awful experience, he thought. People died so easily in the movies and the comics. Real life was such a gruesome fucking mess. The movies never showed the poor slobs who had to clean up after the hero's carnage; think of all the trouble Clint Eastwood was causing for people; think of what off-screen horror was happening to the survivors of a film like *Halloween*.

And even when death was portrayed as bloody and awful,

it was nothing like this. Jon had had only one other close experience with violent death (not counting Nolan's near bout with the grim reaper, thanks to that Syndicate guy, Charlie) and that had been after the Port City bank job year and a half ago. The robbery had gone flawlessly, but afterward some jealousy within ranks had caused an outburst of insane violence, and Nolan and Jon had ended up sole survivors. Witnessing the head getting blown off someone he'd been friend to had been the single most traumatic incident in his life, and he wondered now if he hadn't countered that trauma by turning from his superheroes to horror comics, where the blood was bright red and sickly humorous, where he might try to learn to live with gore, get used to it, even laugh at it. He didn't know.

He heard the sound of hard pounding and jumped off his chair. Where was it coming from? He got hold of himself and listened close and it was someone knocking at the back door, and it scared him shitless.

He got up and went to the window and drew back the curtain.

The doctor.

That was all. It was Ainsworth, the doctor, and he let out a sigh and went downstairs to let Ainsworth in.

Ainsworth was the standard country doctor image come to life. He was fifty-five, slightly chubby, and had a mustached, lined, wise and friendly old face. He was Iowa City's longest practicing abortionist, once-and-future aider-and-abetter of draft-dodgers and doer of sundry other medically shady deeds.

"What's the problem?" Ainsworth said, locking the door behind him. He was wearing a blue long-sleeve sweater, over a white Banlon, and yellow pants: golf clothes. Jon had caught him at the country club, where he'd learned to look in previous dealings with Ainsworth.

"My uncle's been shot," Jon said.

"What's his condition?" the doctor asked.

"Dead," Jon said.

"Oh. I see."

"Why don't you come upstairs and have some vodka and Seven-Up and we'll talk."

They did.

"I fully understand your position," he said. "Your uncle's, shall we say, sideline, would make it desirable to prevent the police from taking an active interest in his death."

"That's it exactly."

"Your uncle has a long history of heart trouble, and . . ."

"I didn't know that."

"Well, let's say he will have a history of heart trouble, when I finish rewriting his records."

"Oh."

"And so, his death by coronary came as no surprise to me, I can assure you."

"What else needs to be done?"

"Can you come by around seven? I'll have the necessary papers and forms ready for you to sign."

"Where? At your house?"

"Heavens, no. My office, of course. And I think I can have your uncle's remains disposed of for you, as well. There's a crematorium in West Liberty that does good work. They can pick your uncle up tomorrow afternoon, I'm sure."

"Won't they notice Planner had his 'coronary' in a rather peculiar way?" Jon asked, on his fourth glass of vodka and pop.

"Well, perhaps I'd best go downstairs now and bandage your uncle. That way anyone glancing in won't see anything, even if the poor man gets stripped of his clothes . . . though that shouldn't happen, as these West Liberty folks do good, discreet work, mind you."

"Whatever you think."

"And have you a nice suit of your uncle's? You and I had probably best put one of his suits on him."

"Oh, Christ. That won't be pleasant."

"A tragedy like this one rarely is. And as for me, well, I was a friend of your uncle's, and you've both done a lot of business with me, you and your uncle and that friend Mr. Nolan of yours as well, so you do whatever you think is fair."

Jon got up and went to the silverware drawer to get the combination to Planner's wall safe.

4

The doctor put two pillows under Charlie's feet. He took the pulse of his unconscious patient, casting a cursory glance at the wounded thigh. Then he gave Walter a brief smile—one of those meaningless smiles doled out by doctors like another pill—and walked to a sink across the room to wash up.

Walter stood at his father's upraised feet, wishing he could do something to help, watching the doctor's every action, wondering why the man moved so damn slow.

Or maybe it was just him. Maybe the doctor wasn't slow at all. Walter couldn't be sure. His sense of time was fouled up. Was that business at the antique shop just this afternoon? It seemed years ago.

Moments earlier—or was it hours?—the doctor had offered to give Walter a hand carrying Charlie, but Walter had refused, wanting to bear both the weight and responsibility of his father in his own arms, following the doctor through the darkened waiting room and down a short narrow hall and into a closet of a room, where Walter had eased his father onto a padded examining table that sat high off the floor, like a sacrificial altar. The table was white porcelain with its padded, contoured surface black but mostly covered by white crinkly tissue paper. In fact, almost everything in the room was white: stucco walls, mosaic stone floor, ceiling tile overhead, counters, cabinets, sink, everything.

Except the doctor's clothes. Walter thought the blue

sweater and yellow slacks were grossly inappropriate. He would've felt more secure if his father's welfare were in the hands of a man in traditional white; he had the feeling this guy wouldn't know the Hippocratic oath if he tripped over it.

The doctor removed his sweater and folded it neatly and deposited it on a chair by the sink and began ceremoniously to wash his hands. Jesus, Walter thought, what does he think he is, a damn brain surgeon? The shirt beneath the sweater turned out to be white, but that was no consolation to Walter, as it was an off-white, sporty Banlon, with rings of sweat under the arms and wrinkled from eighteen holes of golf.

The doctor dried his hands and moved from the sink to a counter, where he filled a modest-sized hypo from a small bottle of something.

"What's that?" Walter said.

"Morphine," the doctor said cheerfully, beaming at Walter with all the sincerity of a politician. "Why don't you have a seat?"

"All right," Walter said. There was a chair directly behind him and he backed into it and sat.

The doctor administered the hypo, then went back to the counter and unscrewed the cap on a bottle of cloudy liquid. He dabbed some of the liquid onto a folded strip of gauze.

"Ammonia," the doctor said, anticipating Walter's question. He walked across the room and held the gauze under Charlie's nose and Charlie came around quickly, thrashing his arms like a man waking from a nightmare, finally pushing himself to a sitting position with the heels of his hands.

"Goddamn shit," he said to the doctor, "what'd you hold under my nose? Who . . . who the hell are you? Where the hell am I? What's going on?"

The doctor smiled again. He did that a lot. He said, "You'll have to ask your young friend here about that."

Walter got up and came around the other side of the table and squeezed his father's shoulder. "You're going to be all right, Dad."

"Of course I'm going to be all right," Charlie said, his speech slightly muddy. "I'm all right *now*. I feel just fine."

"You should," the doctor said, "you're full of morphine."

Suddenly Charlie noticed his wound, said, "Jesus," and settled back down on the table.

The doctor continued to work while Charlie talked to Walter. What the doctor did was give Charlie several shots— a tetanus toxid, some Novocain around the wound—and proceeded to debride the wound, stripping away the flesh that had died of shock on the bullet's impact. What Charlie said to Walter was, "You stupid goddamn kid, we should be long gone from here by now, what the hell you doing dragging me to a doctor for, Christ, a little goddamn scratch on the leg and you're dragging me to a doctor, what the hell you use for brains, boy," and more along those lines.

After the doctor was through debriding the wound, and his father was through sermonizing, Walter said, "Dad, you were unconscious and I felt I should get you to a doctor. I don't want to talk about it anymore.

Then Walter turned away and walked to the window and separated two blades of the white Venetian blinds and stared out into the street. It was twilight and a few seconds after he started looking, the streetlights came on. The doctor's office was on the back edge of the Iowa City downtown, where the businesses trailed off into the residential district. The street was quiet, right now anyway, and almost peaceful to watch. The traffic ran mostly to kids of all ages sliding by on bikes, with only an occasional car, and every now and then a bird would cut from this tree to that one. Walter felt better now. He was relieved that his father was coming out of it. His father yelling at him for staying in town and going to a doctor was a disappointment, but to be expected, he supposed. It wasn't worth brooding over.

While Walter stared out at the quiet street, the doctor applied a pressure dressing to the wound and explained to Charlie that carrying that bullet in his leg wasn't going to hurt him any, and going in after the slug just wasn't worth the time and trouble. Charlie said he knew that, that a lot of his friends had bullets in them.

"Hey," Charlie said.

"Yeah?" Walter said.

"Listen. Listen, thanks."

"It's okay."

"Come here a minute."

"Okay."

Walter joined his father. The doctor said that he was going across the hall to get some pills for Charlie and left the room. Charlie asked Walter to tell him what had been happening.

Walter explained about going to see Sturms, and calling Uncle Harry, and then having trouble getting hold of the doctor. Seemed the doctor's wife was out of town and it wasn't till Sturms thought of the country club that they got a lead on the guy. Unfortunately, the doctor had left the club on an emergency call and hadn't told anyone what or where the emergency was. They had continued calling the man's home, and finally someone at the country club called back and said the doctor had returned to the club for supper and cocktails and Sturms had got him on the line and set things up.

"What's the doc's name?" Charlie said.

"Ainsworth," Walter said. "Sturms says he'll do anything for a buck. Built his practice on abortions and draft dodge. Still helps Sturms out, with O.D. situations, different drug things. I guess the reason Ainsworth stays out of trouble is he's done work for important people in the area and has too much on too many of them for anybody to bother him."

There was the sound of talking outside the room and Charlie jerked up into a sitting position. "What the hell's that? Who the hell's that goddamn quack talking to? You bring Sturms along or something?"

"No, I told you, Dad, he just set it up and never left his house."

"You got a gun?"

"Right here," he said, pulling the silenced nine-millimeter from his waistband. After getting caught by Sturms he wasn't taking chances.

"Go out and see what the hell's happening."

"Okay."

"And watch your ass."

"Okay."

Walter peeked out into the hall. Ainsworth was talking to a young guy, a guy about Walter's age, maybe a year or so younger. He was short with a headful of curly hair and a well-muscled frame. He was wearing jeans and a tee-shirt with the words "Wonder Warthog" above a cartoon, caped hog. Ainsworth was saying, "You're a little early, Jon," standing by the entrance to a room that Walter assumed was the doctor's private office. Walter shut the door.

"I think it's just some thing about drugs he's doing for Sturms," Walter told his father.

"Help me up," Charlie said.

"Dad . . ."

"Help me up, goddammit."

Walter guided his father off the high table, put an arm around his waist and moved him over to the door. Charlie shook free of his son and stood on one leg.

"Give me the gun," he ordered.

Walter gave it to him.

Charlie cracked the door and looked out.

"It's the goddamn kid," Charlie said to himself.

"Who?"

"The kid, it's the goddamn kid who lives with that old guy at the antique shop. His nephew or something." Charlie's eyes narrowed and his lips were drawn back tight. "I smell a cross."

Charlie pushed through the door, slammed against the wall, lost his balance momentarily, got it back quick. He hobbled forward, nearing the doctor and Jon, the gun as steady in his hand as his legs under him weren't.

"What the hell's going on here?" Charlie demanded.

The doctor started pushing the air with his palms. "Put that gun away! Put that gun away!"

Jon had a puzzled look on his face that rapidly dissolved into a knowing one. He pointed his finger at Charlie, as if he was aiming back another gun. "You," he said. "I know you." A red sheet of rage flashed across his face and Jon leaped at Charlie, like an animal jumping out of a tree.

And Charlie slapped Jon across the forehead with the heavy gun. The kid folded up and dropped hard to the floor. Charlie didn't even lose his balance.

"Why . . . why in heaven's name did you do that?" the doctor sputtered.

Charlie looked at the doctor and so did Charlie's gun.

"Are you pulling a double cross, Ainsworth? Do you know who this kid is?"

"Why, that's . . . that's just Jon, Ed Planner's nephew. He's only here to . . ."

Charlie limped painfully up to the doctor and held the gun against the man's throat, right along his Adam's apple. "Why is he here?"

"His . . . his uncle passed away today and I was helping him with the funeral arrangements, death certificate, and so on. Jon and his uncle're like you people . . . have to steer clear of the authorities."

"And do you know how his uncle 'happened' to pass away?"

"He was . . . shot."

"And who the fuck do you think shot him?"

"Oh, my God."

Charlie stepped back a pace, said, "Walter."

"Yes?"

"Help the doc here carry the kid in that room."

Walter and Ainsworth carried Jon into the examining room, Charlie following them in on wobbly legs.

"No, not on the table," Charlie said. "Just drop him on the floor there."

They did.

The jolt seemed to rouse Jon. He stirred, shook his head, looked up. He raised a middle finger to Charlie and said, "Nolan knows you're alive. Kiss your ass good-bye, big shot."

Charlie slapped Jon with the gun and put him to sleep again.

Walter said, "What are you going to do, Dad?"

"I don't know. Let me think. Help me up on the table. I want to sit down."

Walter helped his father.

He watched his father sitting there, the close-set eyes narrowing, the lips moving ever so slightly. Was his father deciding to go ahead with the next phase of some secret master plan? Or just throwing together some spur-of-the-moment piece of strategy? Walter didn't know and couldn't guess. But a full minute went by before the eyes softened, the lips settled into a tight grin and a false calm washed across the tan, lined face and Charlie said, "We'll take the little bastard with us."

Why? Walter wanted to ask it, but knew he shouldn't. He was glad of his father's decision, in a way. He had a feeling the alternative would've been to kill the kid named Jon.

"Come here, Ainsworth," Charlie said.

The doctor shuffled over. The room was air-conditioned and near-cold, but the doctor was sweating profusely.

"Where's the stuff you were going to get for me?"

The doctor looked down at his right hand, which was clenched in a nervous fist. He opened it and revealed two little white packets. "Antibiotic," the doctor said, handing one of the little envelopes to Charlie, "and painkiller," handing him the other one. "Instructions are written on the packets."

Charlie told the doctor about his high blood pressure and asked if it made any difference about anything. The doctor said no, but that the high blood pressure probably added to Charlie's passing out from the wound, perhaps had made him bleed somewhat more than the average person might.

"Okay, Doc," Charlie said, "you're doing fine. You getting more relaxed now? Not so nervous anymore?"

Ainsworth nodded.

"Good. You don't need to be nervous. Nothing's going to happen to you. You're a friend of Sturms and Sturms is a friend of a friend of mine, so we're all friends and nothing's going to happen to you. But I want your help. Give that kid something that'll keep him out for a while."

"How long?" Ainsworth asked.

"Oh, four hours maybe. Can do?"

"Yes."

Walter watched the doctor go to the counter and fill a big hypo with clear fluid. It seemed to Walter that the doctor was moving faster than before.

Walter sat down and swallowed and looked at what was going on in front of him. A doctor in a golf outfit was giving a horse-size hypo to a curly-haired kid in a weird tee-shirt who was slumped unconscious on the floor. And a man in a bright Hawaiian-print shirt and Bermuda shorts, thigh bandaged, hand squeezed tight around a cannon of a gun, was sitting high on an examining table, seeming to tower over the rest of the room, ruling over the insanity and violence that hung in the air of this white, unpadded cell.

Walter closed his eyes and wished it would all go away.

5

Jon woke to darkness.

He was hot. He was sticky. He hurt.

For the first few moments he was aware of nothing else: just the saunalike heat of the room, his shirt and jeans damp, clinging to his body; the staleness of the air, like some musty old museum; the overall pain, a sluggish doped aching that coursed through his arms and legs and seemed to culminate in the throbbing between his temples; and the extreme darkness of the room, the lack of any light at all, making him think for one awful half-awake moment that he had gone blind.

Or had been blinded.

Maybe he was in hell. Maybe this was the end of an EC horror comic and he was trapped in some ironic hell for robbing that bank last year. The thought made him laugh, but the laugh got caught in his throat and came out as something else, something that smacked more of despair than amusement.

"All right," he said aloud, but not loudly. "Okay." Just a whisper. He was telling himself that he was alive. Assess the situation, he told himself, his head foggy. Take your time. Slowly now.

He was on his back. He could feel something hard and metallic under him, but circular, like large rings, and springy. Springs? Bedsprings? He moved his body slightly, jiggled the surface beneath him. Yes. He was on a bed. On the exposed springs of an old-fashioned bed.

He smiled and the sweat running down his face got into his mouth and tasted salty. He didn't mind. He was on a bed somewhere, alive, and that beat being in hell by a long shot.

He tried to get up off the bed and found he couldn't. He wasn't paralyzed, he knew that. He could lift the trunk of his body several inches off the bed, maybe half a foot. He wasn't paralyzed.

What, then?

He lay there and breathed deep, slow, trying to let his mind clear, which it did, gradually. The fuzziness went away and he realized he was bound, he could feel the rope around his wrists, around his ankles. Rope was looped around ankles and wrists, not tight, but secure. His circulation wasn't cut off or anything, but working with his fingers he found the chance of slipping the loops up around over his hands was nonexistent. The rope he was bound with was not thick and coarse, but more on the order of clothesline, and didn't scrape his skin or make him particularly uncomfortable. There was a lot of leeway in the rope, which he'd decided was tied to the bedposts, and he actually had his arms free at his sides and could lift them or his legs in the air and do just about anything with them except push himself up and walk off—without taking the bed with him, anyway.

So. His situation was this: on his back, on a bed, tied to the bedposts, God knew where.

Where? Was he in Ainsworth's office? That was where he last remembered being. Not likely, unless Ainsworth had taken to collecting antique beds. Antiques! He'd been taken back to Planner's and tied to an old antique bed! But the only one in the shop was Jon's, and it was small, with a box spring. Planner didn't have any other antique beds.

Planner.

Planner was dead. Planner was more than dead. Planner was murdered. Murdered by that son of a bitch Charlie.

Charlie.

Jon hadn't recognized Charlie immediately. Jon'd come to Ainsworth's office early, but not by design; he was just walking by on his way to grab a quick sandwich at the Hamburg Inn and saw Ainsworth's lights on and thought what the hell and stopped. He'd just been standing there saying hello to Ainsworth and Ainsworth had been getting ready to show him into the private office to fill out some forms and such and that madman had come tumbling out into the hall, waving an automatic that looked like the Gun of Navarone. It took Jon a few seconds to recognize the man, but the pieces had fallen together quickly: gun and bandaged thigh had gelled with Nolan's mention of Charlie, and Jon had known.

He had only seen Charlie one time before—that night when Nolan got shot up by Charlie and his men—and then only for moments and not close up, but the image of the wild little man had stuck in Jon's mind: short and dark with powder-white hair and two black little eyes stuck together close like beads on the face of a cheap rag doll.

And so Jon had jumped at the crazy gun-waving madman in the hallway at Ainsworth's office, leaped at him, mind full of Nolan bleeding and Planner dead and got knocked cold to the floor by a backhand blow from Charlie's gun-in-hand.

He had come to twice after that, both times in Ainsworth's examining room. The first time he'd come out of it, he'd looked up at Charlie and fingered the sucker and told him what Nolan would do to him. And Charlie had whacked him to the floor again. The second time he woke up, just half woke, and saw Ainsworth coming down on him, and it was like some fish-eye camera angle in a monster movie, distorted, out of focus, Ainsworth as Dr. Frankenstein bug-eyed and sweaty above a hypo the size of Cleveland. And as the needle jammed into his arm, he glanced up and saw that little asshole Charlie sitting, sitting way up there like some court jester who'd made his way to the throne by poisoning the king and queen.

That was the last thing he could remember, and it wasn't a pleasant memory to dwell on, though it was vivid enough. How much time had passed since then? He could feel his watch on his wrist, right under where the rope was looped, but in all the knocking about the thing had probably conked out on him. Why couldn't he be a normal person and have a Bulova with a luminous dial? But no, he had to be different—he had to wear an antique Dick Tracy watch that ran when it felt like it.

Never mind that, he told himself. Never mind superfluous thoughts. Think. What could have happened? Where was he? Why had Ainsworth stuck a needle in his arm?

To put him out, of course. He'd been doped. But why? Getting knocked out, or just tied up, would keep him indisposed long enough for Charlie to get away. Why dope him *and* tie him up *and* clobber him? Just for the sheer hell of it? Why not just kill him?

Jon tried to make sense of it, tried to develop logical theories about where he was and who had put him there, but all he came up with was questions, more questions. He had the feeling that Charlie had not only done all this to him, but was still around, that Charlie had taken him off somewhere and was keeping him captive. He even remembered, vaguely, delirious, strange dreams of travel, a ride, dreams of an ocean voyage that might have been a drive in a car.

But there was no sense in it, none at all. Why would Charlie have any interest in Jon?

Fuck it, he thought. He decided to concentrate his efforts on getting loose. Prospects were dim, but he had to try, didn't he? He started out slowly, tugging first at his right wrist, then moving to the left, then each foot got a prolonged effort. He spent a good while at it, kicking, tugging, struggling, making absolutely no progress at all. Finally he heaved up off the bed, came down hard, repeated the process, again, and again, at the same time thrusting his legs upward and outward and every way, flailing his arms, pounding his butt on the springs, hoping to break the bed if nothing else and maybe, somehow, slip rope over broken bent bedpost and . . .

But in the end all he got was tired. Very tired, and he found himself getting drowsy, and found also that after staring up at the darkness for a time there was little else to do but sleep. So he did.

"Wake up."

Jon's eyes opened. Light. It was light in the room now.

"Hey, wake up."

Jon's eyes focused. He saw a young guy of maybe twenty, twenty-two years, about his age, sitting on a chair by the bed. He was thin and pale and had the same close-set eyes as Charlie.

"Who the hell are you?" Jon said. "Some relative of Charlie's?"

"I'm his son."

"You got my sympathy."

"I brought some food for you. You want some food?"

Jon sat up.

"Hey," he said. "I sat up." He shook his hands; they were free. His legs had been freed, too. The ropes hung untied on the bedposts of, yes, an old antique bed, a brass one, and quite attractive; the nicest bed Jon had ever been tied to. The room was still dim, but light was creeping under the drawn shade on a window directly across from the foot of the bed.

"Look," Charlie's son said, "I'm sorry about the ropes and everything. I didn't know he'd tied you up like this. Dad has a tendency to be overdramatic. He's . . . he's been acting a little strange lately."

"Like killing my uncle, you mean," Jon said. "What's he going to do to me? What's going on? Where the hell am I?"

"Do you want this food?"

The guy had set up a tray by the bed and on it was a plate of scrambled eggs and bacon and some milk.

"Sure I want the food," Jon said. "I feel like I haven't eaten for hours."

"You haven't. You been out fifteen hours. First five or six hours you were unconscious, from the stuff that doctor gave you. I suppose you woke up sometime in the night and squirmed a while, then fell back asleep."

Jon frowned at the guy. "Give me the food."

"Okay," he said. "I'll be back in half an hour and take the dishes off your hands and see how you're doing. I'm not going to tie you up."

"Aren't you afraid I'll get away?"

"Take a look at the two-story drop out that window and decide for yourself. And I don't think you'll be breaking down the door, either. The wood's four inches thick and the lock's pretty firm."

"Let me eat, why don't you."

"See you later."

The guy left and Jon started in on the food. It tasted good to him, but wasn't as good as the last meal he'd eaten, which had also been a breakfast of scrambled eggs. Hell, right now he wouldn't even have minded the company of Larry, that wide-eyed brat of Karen's.

Karen.

His gut ached with the thought of her. He put down his fork and rubbed a spot over his left eye.

She'd be worried as hell. She'd have spent a miserable night. He'd called her and told her a little about the situation, not much, but enough to worry her to death, goddammit. Mentioned she should watch her step about whom she let into the apartment. "There's a guy with a gun involved," he'd told her. When he'd told her that, she'd insisted on having a number to call for help, if she couldn't find him or he didn't show up or something. Jon had given her Nolan's number at the Tropical and while he hadn't liked doing that, he'd supposed an emergency *might* come up, requiring that sort of thing, and he sure as hell didn't want her phoning the police. He'd also given her the doctor's number, and he wondered what Ainsworth had said when she called him, as she must've. The good doctor would've lied through the teeth, no doubt. But would he tell Karen a soothing lie, or one that would upset her? Would she then have called Nolan? If so, would it do any good? How in hell could Nolan find him? Shit, *he* didn't know where he was. He could have a phone fall out of the sky, plop down in his lap, a direct line to Nolan and what would he say? "Help, save me! And while you're at it, tell me where I am."

Fuck.

Jon ate. As he did he glanced around the room. All the furniture had been covered up with sheets, but he could tell this was a girl's room, or had been once; one of the pieces of furniture had the shape of a make-up table with tall mirror, and the walls were papered in pink with blue bells on it. The rest of the room was rugged, running to rough, barnlike wood, from the unvarnished floor to the open-beamed ceiling that followed the slant of the roof. If a girl's room could be so rustic, Jon figured, the place must be a large cabin or cottage of some kind.

He had just finished his milk when the guy came back in.

"How was breakfast?"

"It was swell. Now if I could just have a cake with a file in it."

"Listen, I don't blame you for being bitter."

"No shit."

The guy sat wearily down, frustration obvious on his face. For some reason he seemed to want Jon to like him, or approve of his actions. Jesus. Jon studied him.

He wasn't particularly big; in fact, he was slender, his arms thin. He was wearing a tank-top tee-shirt, blue, and white jeans. He had a college boy look to him, as if he should be out hazing some pledges for a fraternity somewhere.

Jon made his decision. He would watch the guy and find an opening and go with it. Take the guy down and get the hell out. It would be easy. Find an opening and cream the guy. Easy.

"I'd like to tell you what's going on," the guy was saying, "but I don't know myself, really. I'm just as scared as you are, believe it or not, maybe more. I'm in this situation because I wanted to stand beside my father and I guess I didn't realize just exactly who my father was."

"That he's a maniac, you mean."

"That's your point of view. He's still my father, and I'm in this with him, to the end. Whether I like it or not, at this point. I guess I could go to jail a long time."

"If Nolan finds you, don't sweat jail."

"Who is this Nolan?"

"You don't know?"

"No."

"Wait. Just wait."

"Look. I'm trying to tell you I'm going to help you, if I can."

"Oh?"

"I won't let Dad, uh, do anything . . . extreme."

"Like kill me?"

He shrugged. "Like kill you," he admitted.

"Get me out of here, then."

"I can't."

"You won't."

"All right I won't. But stay cool. It'll be all right."

"You're crazier than your father."

"Could be. Anyway, can I get you something? We got some beer. Something to read maybe?"

"Not unless it's your old man's obituary."

"I try to help you and you hassle me."

"Ungrateful me."

"I noticed your watch."

"What?"

"Your watch. I noticed it. What kind of watch is that?"

"It's just a watch."

"You some kind of comic book nut or something?"

"Why do you ask that?"

"That watch has, who? Dick Tracy on it? And the tee-shirt you're wearing is some other cartoon character. Thought it followed, your being a comic book nut."

"All right, so I like comic books. What of it?"

"Christ. Take it easy. Just thought you might like to look through the box of old comics we got in the attic, up in the other house. At least I think they're still up there, if they haven't been thrown in the trash or something."

Jon perked, getting interested in spite of himself. "How . . . how old are these comics?"

"I don't know. They were my cousin's, and he's older than I am. My sister and I used to read them when we were kids, coming up here summers."

"Well, I guess I wouldn't mind taking a look at them."

"Okay. Your name's Jon, right? Mine's Walter. Walt."

"It's a pleasure."

Walt ignored the sarcasm and said, "I'll go over and get them for you."

Jon watched him leave, the door shut and lock behind him. He sat on the bed and wondered if there would be any good books in the box. You never knew when you were going to luck onto a find. If that cousin was older than Walter, why

those comics could be early fifties or before, and that meant
there could be some good shit in . . .

Jesus Christ Almighty!

Goddamn comic book fever! He slammed a fist into his
thigh. It was a blindness that came over him; all collectors
feel it, he supposed, but he felt it deep. No logic to it, or
reason. Just the fever.

You're an asshole, he told himself, meaning it. *Your
uncle's dead, murdered by this creep and his old man, and
you're all of a sudden grateful to him, you're his buddy, just
because he's got some moldy old comic books he's going to
show you. You're trapped in a room somewhere, held prisoner by a senile old Mafiosi and his loving kid, probably
going to get your balls shot off any minute, and all you can
do is slobber at the mouth over the chance of seeing some old
comics. You goddamn idiot. Shape the fuck up.*

"Okay," he said aloud, after a moment.

He was okay. The fever was in check. He was sane again.

He formed his plan. He would sit on the edge of the bed,
wait for his buddy Walter to stroll in with the box in his
hands, and as the guy was putting the box down on the bed,
Jon would kick him in the side of the head. That would do
the trick.

Get ready, he told himself.

He got ready.

The door opened and in Walter came, arms full of an
aging cardboard box, falling apart at the sides. *Now's your
chance,* Jon told himself, *don't blow it, asshole.*

"Here they are," Walter said, coming over to the bed with
the box.

Jon braced himself, his leg was tensed and ready to kick,
and he noticed the comic on top of the stack in the box.

An EC.

"Vault of Horror" number 18.

What a beautiful cover! A couple kissing by a wishing
well, out of which was crawling an oozing, decomposing
ghoul. What an artist that Johnny Craig was. Jon didn't have

that issue; it was an early one, kind of hard to find.

He grabbed hold of the box and settled it in his lap and started flipping through titles. They weren't all EC's, but many of them were; there was an early one, "Crypt of Terror" 17, worth probably sixty bucks, and some rare science-fiction titles like "Weird Fantasy" and "Weird Science." Jesus, here was a "White Indian" with Frazetta art! What a find! The box was a treasure chest. This was fantastic.

"Enjoy yourself," Walter said.

And was out the door.

Four

Nolan got out of the car. He moved slowly, but he was alert, and his movements were both deliberate and fluid. You would never guess he'd just driven well over two hundred miles in under three hours. He stood and looked in the window of the shop; a hanging wooden sign, with the words "Karen's Candle Corner" spelled out in red melted wax, dominated a display case of candles and knicknacks, while in the background faces on posters seemed to stare out of the dim shop like disinterested observers.

He watched in the reflection of the window as the black Chevy pulled in behind his tan Ford, and wondered if anyone in the world besides cops and hoods still drove black Chevys.

Greer got out of the car, made a real effort to shut the door silently but it made a noise that echoed in the empty street. It was three o'clock in the morning (a bank time-and-temperature sign spelled it out just down the street) and downtown Iowa City could have been a deserted backlot at some bankrupt Hollywood studio. The sky overhead was a washed-out gray and the streetlamps provided pale, artificial light.

Nolan watched Greer approach in the reflection. The dark little man yawned, stretched his arms, scratched his belly. Greer had discarded the Felix-dictated sporty ensemble and now had on an ordinary, rumpled brown suit, such as a fertilizer salesman might wear. A common sense outfit, Nolan thought, encouraged; maybe Greer wasn't such a hopeless schmuck after all.

As for Nolan, he was wearing the same clothes he'd worn all day: yellow turtleneck, gray sports jacket, black slacks.

The only wardrobe change he'd made before leaving the Tropical was taking his jacket off long enough to sling on his worn leather shoulder rig. Like Nolan, the holster was old but dependable, and he felt good having a Smith and Wesson .38 with four-inch barrel snuggled under his arm.

Greer walked up to Nolan and they looked at each other in the reflection.

Greer said, "You move right along, don't you?"

Nolan shrugged.

Greer said, "What were you trying to do, lose me?"

Nolan said, "If I was trying to lose you, you'd be lost."

Greer yawned again, said, "Wish to hell you'd've stopped for coffee."

"Well, I didn't."

"Listen, what's happening? What are we doing in Iowa City, for Chrissake?"

"I'm going to talk to a woman. This is her place." He pointed to the floor above the shop, where the lights were on. "She's a civilian, so don't go waving guns around."

"What do you take me for?"

Nolan said nothing.

"Hey, why don't you go fuck yourself, Nolan? I don't like being here any more than . . ."

"Shut up. Don't be so goddamn defensive. Are you still pissed off because I made a fool of you this afternoon?"

"Well, I . . ."

"I did that because I didn't want Felix sending anybody with me, I wanted to be left alone with this. But Felix sent you anyway, so let's forget about that."

Greer sighed, grinned, said, "Okay. I'll just stay in the background and do what you tell me to."

"Good."

Between the candle shop and a record store was a doorway, beyond which were steps. Nolan and Greer went up them. When they got to the landing, they found two doors; one was labeled "Karen Hastings," the other was blank. Nolan knocked on the labelled door.

A voice from behind the door said, "Who is it?" The voice was female and firm, masking the fear pretty well.

"Nolan. Jon's friend."

The door opened tentatively, the night-latch chain still hooked. The face that peeked out was haggard but pretty, framed by long, curly brunette hair. "You're Nolan?"

"Yes."

"How . . . how do I know that?"

"You don't; unless you recognize my voice from the phone."

"Prove you're Nolan."

"How?"

"What's Jon's hobby?"

"Pardon?"

"Jon's hobby, what is it?"

"He collects funny books."

She unlatched the door. She was a little startled by seeing Greer in the background. Nolan glanced back over his shoulder at Greer, who in the darkness of the stairwell looked somewhat like the gunman he was.

"Don't worry about him," Nolan said. "He's here to help, too."

"Okay, come in, both of you."

They stepped in and were hit by the coolness of the air-conditioned apartment. Nolan looked the woman over quickly: she was nicely built, kind of busty, pretty face accented by a large but sensual mouth; she wore a clinging black dress with cream-color sandals. Her clothes and free-flowing hair were styles befitting a girl twenty or younger, though she was thirty or more. A singularly attractive woman, Nolan summed her up as, though too old for a kid like Jon.

"Heard anything from Jon?"

"No," she said, regret in her face. "Not a word. What do you think happened?"

"I don't know. I'll find out."

"You got here fast. That was an Illinois area code, wasn't

it? I looked it up. What'd you do, drive it straight?"

Nolan nodded, exchanging a brief smile with Greer.

"Well, sit down, I'll get you some coffee."

"We've got some things to do, maybe you shouldn't waste time . . ."

"It's already ready. I'll just go in the kitchen and pour it out. Besides, both of you look dead on your feet. Excuse me."

She left and Nolan and Greer took seats on the sofa. The walls were paneled in deep rich brown, and cluttered with paintings and such; the theme of the wall opposite them was Camelot: brass knight's heads, crossed broadswords, an oil painting of a surreal castle in blues and grays. The furniture ran to antiques, with thick, colorful candles stuck on everything that wasn't moving. Nolan had two immediate impressions: first, she got stuff wholesale as a shopkeeper and consequently had more decorative shit than any ten people needed; and second, she had a very feminine idea of how to make a room look masculine. He wondered why she was trying to compensate for the lack of a live-in male.

She came back with coffee, which was strong and black. Greer sipped it and smiled and said, "Thanks, ma'am," like a shy cowboy in an old movie.

She sat next to Nolan on the sofa and said, "Can we do anything? I'll do whatever you want me to. I feel I can . . . trust you. You're the man Jon speaks about, aren't you? He never mentioned your name, until tonight, anyway . . . but you're the man he talks about, the older man he looks up to, respects. Am I right?"

Nolan felt strangely touched, both by the woman's open concern for Jon, and her telling of Jon's affection for him. He was having trouble fighting the notion that Jon was dead, and the woman's small emotional outburst chipped at his personal wall.

"I thought you were," she said, nodding, though he hadn't replied.

"Are you willing to take some risks?" Nolan asked her.

"Of course, anything . . . but I have a child here, my son

Larry, and . . . I wouldn't want anything to happen to him."

"Could you send him to a friend's place?"

"It's three o'clock in the morning."

"I know. Could you do it?"

She nodded. "I'll have to make a phone call."

"Make it."

She left again.

Greer said, "Nice-looking woman."

Nolan said, "Yeah."

"No bra," Greer said.

"No kidding," Nolan said.

That ended that line of conversation.

"Good coffee," Greer said.

"Good coffee," Nolan said.

She came back and said, "I'll have to get Larry ready."

"How old is he?"

"Ten."

"Is he a cripple?"

"No."

"Tell him to get himself ready. Can he walk where he's going?"

"I . . . I think so. It's just two blocks."

"Good. Go tell him and come back."

This time she was gone thirty seconds, no longer.

"Now what?" she said.

"I want you to make another phone call."

"All right."

"I want you to call that doctor back. Do you think he'll recognize your voice?"

"Not if I don't want him to."

"Good. Do you know his name?"

"No. Jon didn't leave me his name, just the number."

"Get the phone book."

She did.

"Now look up the number of a Dr. Ainsworth. Okay? Got it? Now, is that the number Jon left you to call?"

She nodded.

"Good. Have you heard of Ainsworth? Know him?"

"I don't know him," she said. "Know of him. Girl friend of mine got a nice, quiet abortion from him. I heard he'll help you if you get into a drug jam, and without reporting anything to the cops. He does valuable work, but word is he's a real pirate."

"Where's your phone?"

"I can plug it into a jack right here in the living room, if you like."

"Do that."

She did, and Nolan told her what to say.

She was excellent. She did better than Nolan had hoped, weaving his basic material into a piece of drama fit for stage or screen. Her voice was best of all, a pleading, whining thing that sounded like the voice of a girl far younger than this mother of a ten-year-old boy. She said, "Is this Dr. Ainsworth? . . . It is? Oh, wow, thank God, thank God, I got you, mister . . . I mean, Jesus, I'm sorry I woke you, but I need you, Christ, we need you bad . . . I'll try to calm down, but it isn't easy, you know, I mean my boyfriend, I'm afraid he's OD'ed, Jesus, can you help? . . . Bad shape, he's really bad, I mean I'm fucked up myself, you know? But I know he's bad, really bad and you got to help, I heard from a girl friend of mine you're okay, you'll help out and keep the trouble down as much as possible . . . I mean, I got money, we both got money, that's no problem, we just don't want any hassle with cops, but if you won't help I'll call whoever I have to to get help, I mean you got to get here fast . . . oh, Christ, hurry, mister, please . . . You're beautiful. Bless your soul, man." She gave him her address, blessed him again, and hung up.

"Nice going," Nolan said.

"Really good," Greer said.

"Thanks," she said, almost blushing, "I just hope I didn't overdo. I was a little nervous."

"That probably helped," Nolan said.

"Either of you guys want more coffee? I know I do."

Nolan said, "Yeah." So did Greer.

She got up and went after it.

While she was gone, a small boy not much over five feet tall walked into the room, an overnight case in his hand. He was wearing blue jeans and a red-and-white striped tee-shirt and he had big brown eyes and a headful of red hair and more freckles than Doris Day.

"I'm going now, Mom!" he hollered.

She rushed into the living room, kissed him on the forehead and said, "Be a good boy, Larry, don't cause Mrs. Murphy any trouble."

"I won't, Mom."

"Be sure to thank her for letting you stay with Tommy, and apologize for bothering them so late."

"I will, Mom."

"You're a good boy." She kissed him on the head again and went back to the kitchen.

"How ya doin', sonny?" Greer asked the kid.

"Bite my ass," the boy said, and went out the front door, slamming it behind him.

"Little bastard," Greer said.

"I kind of like him," Nolan said.

The boy's mother came back and refilled their coffee cups. They waited for Ainsworth.

2

Fifteen minutes later, the knock came at the door. They had had time to drink their cups of coffee and bring a chair in from the kitchen and Karen had found the rope Nolan had asked for.

Nolan said, "Let him in," and Karen nodded yes.

Greer had his gun out, on Nolan's request. Nolan had both big hands unencumbered. Greer stood behind the door, so that he would be hidden when Karen opened it. Nolan stood to the other side, flat against the wall.

Karen freed the night latch, opened the door.

Behind Karen was a bureau with mirror and in it Nolan could see Ainsworth in the doorway; he hoped Ainsworth wouldn't notice him in the mirror, but wasn't worried, as things would be moving faster than that. Ainsworth was standing there with a pompous, fatherly smile on his face; he was wearing a dark suit and green tie. What an asshole, Nolan thought; an emergency phone call and he still takes time to put on his country doctor outfit.

"I came as soon as I could," Ainsworth was saying, "what's the problem, young lady?"

Nolan grabbed the doctor by the arm and yanked him into the apartment. Behind him, Karen shut the door, locked it, refastened the night latch. Greer got into full view, holding the .38 in his right hand with that casual but controlled grasp that only a professional knows how to master.

Ainsworth said, "Oh, my God!" and his pudgy face looked very white around the brown mustache.

Nolan slammed him into the kitchen chair and tied him up. Ainsworth still had his black doctor's bag in hand as he sat roped to the chair. Nolan knocked the bag out of his hand and glass things rattled and maybe broke. Ainsworth repeated what he'd said before, though this time it sounded more a prayer and less an expression of surprise.

Nolan put both his hands on the doctor's shoulders and said, "How's it going, Ainsworth?"

"Oh . . . oh . . . oh . . ."

"Try not to shit. This lady has an expensive carpet down and if you shit, I'm going to make you clean it up."

"No . . . No . . . No . . ."

He wasn't saying no; he was trying to say Nolan.

"I'm glad you remember me," Nolan said. "I put on weight since you saw me last. And believe I'd let my beard grow out. How've you been, Doc?"

Ainsworth began to make a whimpering sound.

Nolan turned to Greer and Karen. "Ainsworth here is a good old friend of mine. I owe him a lot. Don't I, Ainsworth?"

"I . . . I helped you," he said. "Don't . . . don't forget I helped you."

"Saved my life is what you did," Nolan said. He grinned. Nolan didn't grin often and when he did, it wasn't pleasant. Knowing that, he reserved the grin for special occasions. "I'll never forget what all you did for me. And it only cost me, what was it? A paltry seven thousand bucks. Why, hell. You must've been running a special that day, Ainsworth."

"What . . . what do you want with me?"

Nolan's grin disappeared. "Don't fuck around."

"I'm . . . I'm not . . . oh Lord, good Lord, man!"

"You know why I'm here."

"They . . . they made me do it."

"Who made you do what?"

"Your friend . . . Jon . . . the boy . . ." The doctor closed his mouth, his eyes.

"Ainsworth," Nolan said, his voice flat, nothing in it at all, "I'm the one who advised Jon to go to you. To help him about his uncle. So I share the guilt I'm sure you feel right now. Why don't you get that guilt off your shoulders? Pretend this is confession and I'm a priest. Pretend you're face to face with Christ himself and you can't lie, because the consequences are too goddamn great."

"I was helping Jon," Ainsworth said, his face tight with sincerity, "believe me. I *like* the boy. You know that, you believe that, don't you, Nolan? I like him, and Planner, too. He came for help and . . . so did these other men. I didn't . . . didn't know, didn't guess there was any relation between these other men and Planner's . . . death."

"What did these men look like?"

"One of them was old, the other was young. Father and son, I think they were. Sure of it, from . . . from their conversation. The father was short and thin, had a dark tan. His hair was white and cut in a butch. He was maybe sixty years old. His eyes, I noticed his eyes especially . . . they were set close together, and dark. His son had the same eyes, but not so . . . so frightening. The son was light-complected, skinny, his hair was sort of long, and, brown, I think. His hair wasn't as long as . . . as Jon's, but it was longer than his father's."

"Did they use any names?"

"The son's name was Walter. I think. I only heard the name used once, and I can't be positive about it. The father's name was . . . it was Charlie. At least that was what . . . what Jon called him."

Nolan sighed. "You better tell it all."

"The older man had been shot in the thigh. It wasn't a bad wound, but he passed out from it and that scared his kid enough to bring him to me. While I was treating the older man, Jon showed up . . . we had some papers to fill out, regarding Planner's death, you see, and . . . well, he just showed up. It was a coincidence that they were here at the same time, you have to believe that! I didn't . . . betray Jon, you have to believe that! I like the boy."

Nolan put his hand on Ainsworth's throat. He didn't squeeze, or grip the flesh; he just laid his hand alongside the doctor's throat and said, "What happened to Jon? What did they do to him?"

"They . . . they took him with them."

Nolan removed his hand. He took a step back, then another. He began to pace for a moment. He was stunned by what the doctor had told him. He was also somewhat relieved, as it meant Jon was maybe still alive. But it made no sense. Charlie should have shot Jon, should kill him, and then take right off. Get the hell out of the country. Now.

But this was no ordinary man. No sane, reasoning mind. This was Charlie.

Nolan walked back over to Ainsworth and slapped him hard. "Is that the truth?"

Ainsworth's eyes teared, and his tongue licked feebly at blood in the corner of his mouth. "Why . . . why'd you hit me?"

"Is it the truth?"

Ainsworth nodded and kept nodding until Nolan took Ainsworth's chin in one hand and looked at him, like an archeologist studying a skull.

"Was Jon all right when you saw him last?"

"Yes. Yes he was. Well, he *was* unconscious, but . . ."

"Unconscious?"

"Yes, you see I gave the boy something to put him out, so he wouldn't be any trouble to them in the car. The older man . . . Charlie? The older man, Charlie, said he wanted me to give Jon something that would keep him out for four hours . . . which I assume was the approximate length of time they had to travel."

"You saw them put Jon in their car? What kind of car was it?"

"I . . . I helped them. We wrapped him in a blanket and put him on the floor in the backseat. Of an Oldsmobile, last year's model, I believe, blue, dark blue. It . . . it was a good thing that I gave him a shot and put him out, you know."

"Why's that?"

"Because that . . . that older man, Charlie, he . . . didn't seem to like Jon much. Jon . . . sassed him. And the one named Charlie was . . . was rough with the boy."

Nolan heard Karen make a noise behind him. He turned and she was crying. He should have thought about that before, should have known her emotional attachment to the boy would make this hard for her. He should've had her leave the room. But he hadn't. He hadn't thought of anything, really. Just get to Ainsworth and shake the truth out of him.

"Are you . . . are you going to let me go, now?" The doctor was much more calm now; his face had returned to its natural color.

"Not just yet," Nolan said.

Greer was lighting up a cigarette. "You want one, Nolan?"

"No thanks, I gave it up."

Greer shrugged. "Thought you might have some other use for it."

Ainsworth's face turned pale again.

Nolan said, "No. I can do fine with just my hands."

All at once the doctor began to shake and sweat, as though he were going into a dance routine. "I told you everything, Nolan! Those men forced me to help them, at gun point! I wouldn't . . ."

"How much did they pay you?"

"Nothing. I assume I'll be paid through . . . nothing."

"You assume *what*?"

"Nothing . . . nothing. I just meant to say I . . . assumed I was lucky to get off with my life."

"You said you assumed you'd be paid through somebody. Who?"

"Nolan, please . . ."

"I don't want to hit you, Ainsworth. I'm not the sort of guy that gets his rocks off hurting people. Don't make me do something I find distasteful. That'll just make me mad and you're the only one around I'd have to take it out on. So tell me who."

"His name is Sturms."

Karen said, "There's a Sturms in town who has an insurance agency. I've heard some rumors about him. Having to do with drugs."

Nolan turned to Ainsworth. "Well?"

"It's true," he admitted. "Sturms is . . . important in town. I help him out with things. He's the one that sent those two men to me."

Nolan turned to Greer. "Untie him."

Greer nodded and went over to Ainsworth and did so.

Nolan said, "Karen, how you doing?"

She smiled and said, "At least Jon is alive."

"That's how I look at it."

"Do you think you can find him?"

"Yes." He went over to Ainsworth and picked him up by the lapels. He dragged him over to the couch and plopped him down, kicking the kitchen chair to one side. He picked up the phone from off the end table and tossed it on Ainsworth's lap. "Call your Sturms. Get him over here."

"I . . . I can't do that."

"Ainsworth."

"Okay. Okay, okay, just give me a moment to . . . compose myself."

"If you try anything, I'm going to feed that phone to you."

"Listen, I'm scared of you, all right? Does that satisfy you, Nolan? I'm scared to death of you, is your ego satisfied? I'm scared to death and I'm going to do whatever you say so . . . so don't worry."

"I'm not worried."

Ainsworth swallowed. He picked up the receiver and dialed. It took a while to get an answer, but finally the doctor said, "Sturms? Ainsworth . . . I'm sorry, really I'm sorry, but we got a problem . . . you got to get over here right away, I can't talk about it on the phone . . . I can't . . . I can't handle it, I don't have my bag with me. Okay." He told him the address and hung up.

Ainsworth smiled and Nolan said, "What did you tell him?"

"What?"

"What did you tell him?"

"What do you mean, what did I tell him? You were right here, you *heard* what I told him!"

"You said, 'I don't have my bag with me.' What's that, some kind of signal, some goddamn code, what?"

"I . . . I . . . I just meant, I couldn't handle it, I mean, you, uh . . ."

"Do you remember when you were treating me?"

He swallowed again, touched his face where Nolan hit him, his mouth where the blood had been. "Sure I remember."

"What d'you treat me for?"

"You'd been shot. I . . . I took care of you after you were shot."

"And what did you do for Charlie?"

"For Charlie? I . . . patched him up. Patched up a bullet wound."

"Let me ask you a question, then. You're a man of science, you're a man of logic. What do you suppose happens to people who fuck around with people like Charlie and me?"

Ainsworth said, "I told Sturms he should bring a gun with him."

"You asshole," Nolan said, and hit him in the face.

"My nose," Ainsworth sputtered. "My nose, you broke it, I think you broke my nose, I told you and you hit me anyway, broke my nose. What am I going to do?"

"Heal yourself," Nolan said. "Karen, get him a towel or something. Greer, get that bag of his, look in it."

Greer went after the bag, fished around inside, held up a small low-caliber automatic, the sort a woman might carry in her purse.

"Toss it here," Nolan said.

Greer did, and Nolan caught it in his left hand, without looking. He dropped the little gun into his sports coat pocket.

The doctor's self-diagnosis proved incorrect; a simple nosebleed was all it was, and after it subsided, Nolan tied Ainsworth back up to the chair and dragged him into the kitchen, where Karen found herself a carving knife and sat watch over him.

Nolan and Greer positioned themselves the same way as before, except this time Nolan had his .38 in hand, and when the knock came at the door, Karen did as she'd been told and held the knife to her charge's throat and Ainsworth yelled from the kitchen, "Come on in, it's open!"

He may have been important in Iowa City, but Sturms wouldn't have been shit elsewhere. His arm, extended awkwardly, came in first. He had the silenced automatic clutched tight in a whitening hand, his gun arm held straight out in front of him, elbow locked, like a man groping through the dark, trying not to bump into furniture. All but smiling, Nolan grabbed Sturms by the wrist and shook gun from hand and held the four-inch barrel of the .38 against the man's temple.

"I'll do whatever you say," Sturms said.

3

Nolan bit into the cheeseburger.

Angello said, "Why be pissed at me? It's not my idea."

Of course not. It was Felix's idea. But that didn't make it any more palatable. Nolan chewed the bite of cheeseburger, dragged a French fry through ketchup.

Angello sat across from him in the booth, wearing a light blue sports jacket and dark blue shirt and light blue tie, also Felix's idea. The thin gunman with the fat face sat and stuffed himself with a big plate of pancakes, saying, "My wife'd kill me if she found out I gone off my diet." It was nearly dawn, and breakfast had seemed in order to Angello, though Nolan had gone for cheeseburger-in-the-basket. They were in a truck-stop restaurant on the tollway, not far from Milwaukee.

Angello said, "Anyway, here are the addresses Felix sent for you. He said you'd be needing them."

Nolan put down the sandwich and took the piece of paper. He looked over the names, addresses, and phone numbers and thought, well, at least Felix did a good thorough job of it. He folded the paper and slipped it in his sports coat pocket and said thanks to Angello.

"You're welcome. And look, I'm as sorry as you are I got to tag the hell along."

"You're not tagging along."

"An order is an order, Nolan."

"An order is a bunch of words."

"And those words got meaning, and this order means I

got to stick to you like batshit, Nolan, like it or not."

"Angello, it's a shame you lost all that weight."

"Why's that?"

"It's good to have some weight on you when you're trying to get over a bad injury."

"What's that supposed to mean?"

Nolan shrugged.

Angello's round face showed irritation, his big bump of a nose twitching like an animated lump of clay. "Hey, you make me tired, all that tough-guy stuff. How do you keep it up, all day long, the tough-guy stuff? Don't you know some of us go home to the wife and kids, and live, you know, pretty normal lives, and all this tough-guy stuff just doesn't make it, it isn't real life, you know?"

Nolan leaned close to the chubby face and pointed with a French fry. "You want to hear about real life? I'll tell you about it. Real life is you in a ditch with your arms broken if you think you're coming with me."

Angello grinned suddenly, scooped a tall bite of pancakes into his mouth and chewed while he said, "You don't frighten me. I don't pee my pants when you say boo, Nolan. I'm not a fucking kid like Greer. You shook him up with all that taking his gun away nonsense, back with Felix at the Tropical yesterday, but your show, it doesn't move me. That's what it is, you know, a show, a act, and I know it, so drop it already. Your type, Nolan, your type talks a hell of a show but you die like everybody else."

"I'm alive," Nolan said.

"Today. How'd you do with Greer, anyway? You slap the kid around and make yourself feel like a champ, or what? Jeez."

"We got along okay," Nolan said, softly, not knowing quite how to react to this guy. "I'd trade you in for him gladly."

"I bet you would. Rather have somebody you can push around, right?"

No, Nolan thought; that wasn't it, not quite. Maybe

Angello wasn't scared of Nolan, but the reverse was equally true. But Nolan did prefer dealing with someone more predictable. He didn't know what to make of this chubby-faced thin man, who talked about the wife and kids and hinted at guns and death out on the edges of his conversation.

Nolan liked known quantities. He didn't like the idea of taking *any* Family man along on the very delicate calls he was planning to make in Milwaukee these next few hours, but at least with Greer he would have been able to depend on unquestioning workmanship. Greer had shown himself to be an unobtrusive pro back at Iowa City, with Karen, Ainsworth, and Sturms.

Sturms had been no problem, none at all. He came in and, in spite of a slight case of nerves because of the guns pointed at him, the well-groomed glorified drug peddler told Nolan everything he knew of Charlie's trip to Iowa City. Told Nolan about the phone calls from Charlie's son, and how cautious he, Sturms, had been about helping the pair, insisting on the son calling Harry in Milwaukee for confirmation.

Nolan felt now that his initial appraisal of Greer had been hasty. Greer hadn't done anything especially noteworthy in Iowa City, but he'd provided good solid backup, and when Nolan suggested that Greer stay behind to watch over Sturms and Ainsworth, there'd been no smartass arguments or indignant refusals. Greer had just accepted it, without making necessary Nolan's going into the obvious need for keeping the two men from getting to a telephone to warn Harry that Nolan was on his way to Milwaukee. Greer had only said that he'd have to call and check first with Felix, and Nolan had said go ahead.

But Felix hadn't taken Nolan's leaving Greer behind as graciously as had Greer himself.

"You knew this before you left," the shrill voice had said from over the phone, "you knew then that you'd be leaving my man behind. That's why you insisted on his taking a separate car, isn't it? You want to shake loose from the Family on this, don't you, Nolan? You see this only as a personal vendetta, and insist on ignoring the more far-reaching consequences."

Nolan had denied the charges, but allowed Felix to carry on with his summation to the jury a while longer before interrupting to remind the lawyer that that list of addresses and phone numbers promised earlier would come in handy now. Felix had agreed and set up this meeting at the tollway truck stop, where Angello was to deliver the list.

Nolan sipped his coffee, his second cup, and hoped things would be okay in Iowa City. He had confidence in Greer, now, but soon Greer would be leaving Karen's apartment, releasing the two men, and Karen would be left to live in Iowa City, where Ainsworth and Sturms both resided, and the two of them might bear the girl a grudge.

But they wouldn't do anything about it. Before he'd gone Nolan had explained to them that after their release they would be expected to stay out of Karen's hair. If, in fact, *one* hair on her head was touched, Nolan promised he'd come around and cut their balls off. Whether they were responsible or not.

"If you don't think I'm serious," Nolan had said, "check with Charlie's brother Gordon."

And Sturms had said, "I thought Charlie's brother Gordon was dead."

And Nolan hadn't said anything.

Reflecting on that, he smiled a little, and thought that perhaps this Angello was right about the hardnose routine; maybe it was just a routine, which he'd put into use now that he was getting old—fifty!—and perhaps didn't have the stuff to back himself up anymore. An aging hoodlum, propped up on verbal crutches.

But that wasn't right either, because he'd always found that saying things for effect was a powerful tool, when used with restraint, and he'd handled that tool long and well. If people think you're hard, they'll leave you be, and save you needless grief—not to mention energy and ammunition.

Not that he was the melodramatic son of a bitch Charlie was.

The old bastard. Now there was a guy who talked tough, always had, and was no fake: Charlie backed it up, every time. Nolan had never feared Charlie—but he knew enough to respect him. Not his word, which Charlie kept only when it was to his advantage to do so, but respect his threats, no matter how ridiculous they might seem. Charlie would hang a man by the ass from the ceiling of a warehouse with a meathook, in a day when such tactics were thought to be long dead and almost quaint memories of the Prohibition era. Charlie would have a man taken to a basement somewhere and tied to a stool and a dead bird shoved in his mouth and two men shooting behind either ear of the "stool pigeon" in a ritual that in being a cliché was no less terrifying and, well, efficient. Charlie might lie to you, but never in his threats, because Charlie was a melodramatic son of a bitch, who took delight in seeing his melodramatic notions brought into play, and that was probably part of why he snatched Jon.

Nolan got up from the booth without excusing himself and felt Angello's eyes on his back as he headed for the cash register where a girl broke several of his dollars into change. He headed for the phone booth in the recession between two facing restrooms and closed himself inside the booth. A light and a fan went on and Nolan sat and looked over the list, though he knew already the best place to start.

Tillis.

Tillis was an enforcer who had worked for Charlie for the last five years or so, and was presently working for Charlie's late wife's brother Harry in Milwaukee. Tillis was one of a select few blacks serving the upper echelon of the Chicago Family, and had broken the racial barrier in a time-honored American way: he was an athlete, and a good one. The six-three, two-seventy black had played pro ball in the NFL, but left early in a promising career because of a bum knee, and it was long-time football buff Charlie who gave the ex-guard a new team to play for—the mob.

Nolan and Tillis had met last year, in the flare-up of the long-smoldering feud with Charlie. Being soldiers in opposing armies didn't keep the two men from liking each other, and Tillis had, in fact, secretly helped Nolan in a tight spot with Charlie, and without Tillis, Nolan might not have been alive today.

But Tillis's loyalty to Charlie was something to contend with, as Nolan had little doubt that without Tillis, *Charlie* might not have been alive today, either.

Four of the telephone numbers on the list pertained to Tillis. Two were work-oriented: Harry's office and a Family-owned restaurant; the others were apartments: one was in Tillis's name, the other in a woman's. Nolan tried the woman and got Tillis on the line in ten rings.

There was a rumble, as a throat was cleared and a mind struggled to uncloud, and Tillis finally said, "Uh, yeah . . . yes, what is it?"

"How you doing, Tillis?"

"Is that you, Corio? Is something up? Am I suppose to come down or something?"

"No, it's not Corio."

"Well, Jesus Christ, fuck, who is this, do you know what time it is? Shit, it's so goddamn late it's early."

"This is Nolan. Remember me?"

"Nolan! You crazy motherfuck, are *you* still alive? Man, never thought I'd be hearing your voice again. What's happening?"

"Want to talk to you, Tillis. You going to be where you are for a while?"

"All day, unless I get a call from the Man, saying do some work. Got the day off and I'm planning on spending it in bed with my woman."

"I'll come talk to you, then."

"Okay. You know how to get here?"

"I'll find it."

"When should I expect you?"

"Well, I'm calling long distance, never mind from where. I'm about three hours, maybe four from Milwaukee. Look for me late morning, early afternoon."

"Okay, man. What's this about?"

"Don't you know?"

"Maybe."

"Yeah. Well, do me a favor and don't call your present employer, okay? I want to talk to you, not a roomful of Harry's button men."

"We were always straight with each other, Nolan."

"Right. You're the straightest guy that ever shot me, Tillis. You're my pal."

"Same old mouthy motherfuck, ain't you, Nolan? See you round noon and my woman'll whip up some soul food for you."

"What kind of soul food?"

"Your people's kind, man. Irish stew." Tillis's laugh was booming even over the phone. "Can you get into that?"

"I can dig it," Nolan said, smiling.

Nolan hung up the phone, checked his watch. He could make it to Tillis's place in forty minutes or so from here. Being five or six hours early should help avoid any problems that could come if Tillis decided to call Harry and some of the boys. He liked Tillis, but didn't particularly trust him.

Phoning Tillis was risky, but it saved time. Going around to the various places on the list looking for him would have been a lengthy pain in the ass, and besides, nobody could shoot you over the phone. Now he had Tillis nailed down in one spot, and by lying about when he'd be there, Nolan was as protected in the situation as he could hope to be.

On his way back he ordered his third cup of coffee, then sat down in the booth, not even glancing at Angello. He knew he should be moving faster, and that the twenty minutes he'd have spent in this truck stop could prove decisive. But he also knew that unless he got some caffeine and food in him, he wasn't going to last. He'd been up all night, crisscrossing the damn Interstate, first to Iowa and now back to

Illinois and Wisconsin, and he hadn't had a meal since the scrambled egg breakfast he'd shared with Sherry some sixteen hours ago. A few years back all of this would have rolled off him; now was a different story. Happy birthday, he thought, with as much humor as bitterness.

He wasn't thinking about Jon. He wouldn't. Couldn't. If the boy was alive, Nolan would find him. If the boy was dead, Nolan would see some people suffer.

"I'm talking to you, Nolan," Angello was saying.

"I'm not listening," Nolan said. He looked down and realized he'd finished his cheeseburger and fries; he didn't remember doing it.

Angello said, "I'm willing to give you a sort of a break, you know?"

"No. I don't know."

"You don't want me along, right? You seem to take one look at me and your mouth fills up with rotten things to say. And me, I don't relish spending the day in the company of a sour would-be hardass like you."

"We don't like each other. Agreed."

Angello smiled, his pudgy face almost cherubic. "You see, it's like this . . . I got this lady friend in Milwaukee, and when I found out I was going to be in town today I called her up and she was free. And, well, I wouldn't mind spending the morning with this lady friend, you know what I mean?"

"What about your wife you're always talking about?"

"She's at home with the kids where she belongs, what d'you mean what about my wife? Anyway, the only reason I'm insisting on staying with you is I got to stay in tight with Felix. I mean, I want to hang onto my job, you can understand that, it pays good, keeps my family in nice clothes and their stomachs filled, you know?"

Nolan nodded.

"So here's what I thought. I'll kind of let you go your own way, but I'll leave the number for you to call. It's a greasy spoon on the north side of Milwaukee, my lady friend lives up above. The guy'll relay whatever message you got for me upstairs. I think it would work out okay, but you worry me a little. I mean, Jesus, if you go and get killed you'll put me in a very sticky situation."

"I wasn't planning on getting killed."

"That's just it, who does? And you, you're due to get it one of these times, I mean, I heard the stories about you. But I'm willing, if you'll promise to cover for me with Felix, and call that number I'll give you every half hour or so, to let me know things are going okay, and give me some idea of where you're going to be. And we'll have to meet someplace afterward and get our stories together. I don't know. Jeez. What d'you think?"

"I think I like you better now," Nolan said. He waved at a waitress, to get one last cup of coffee. "Let me buy you some more pancakes."

"Okay," Angello said, "but my wife is going to kill me."

4

When he got there, Nolan thought he'd screwed up. Or maybe that kid at the filling station told him wrong. The neighborhood was upper middle class, full of big two-story white houses, old but with good gothic lines and well kept up. The streets were wide and lined with shade trees and two cars per family. The lawns sloped away from sidewalks and were well tended, green trimmed hedges crowding porches, separating this yard from that one. What the hell was Tillis doing here?

Balling some white chick, most likely, Nolan mused, allowing himself a small smile. He got out of the tan Ford and walked up onto the porch of this particular house, the one in which Tillis's woman supposedly lived. The porch was screened in and had an old-fashioned swing on it and the paper was here but hadn't been brought in yet. He noticed he was standing on a rubber mat that said the Stillwell family. Before he knocked, he thought it over and backed down off the porch and took a look around. This was the right number, all right. Because the porch was roofed, the second floor seemed to sit way back, emphasizing the gothic shape of the house, its gingerbread trimming. Some of the windows up there were stained glass and it was an absurd obsolete old house that Nolan would have liked to live in, in another life, and only reaffirmed his thoughts about the neighborhood being wrong for Tillis—what's a rotten guy like you doing in a nice place like this?

Inside a doorway in back, he went up a spastic stairway that required three right turns of him and finally deposited him on an over-size landing in front of a white door. On the door was a slot with a card in it saying Phyllis Watson. Nolan knocked. He had his .38 out, which he didn't think he'd need, but caution never hurt anybody; he also stood to one side of the door, back to the wall.

A pretty white girl, with puffy brown eyes and long brown hair that was tousled and a little bit greasy, opened the door and stepped out on the landing, wearing a shortie terrycloth robe, belted at the waist, not too securely. Nolan thought Tillis ought to train his women a little better, she certainly had no hesitation about answering the door (which didn't seem to have a night latch on it, as far as Nolan could tell) and coming out to say hello with most of her skin showing. She was a tall girl, which made sense with Tillis being so big, and she had great legs, and Nolan put his hand over her mouth and dragged her back inside the apartment, nudging the door shut with his foot.

The kitchen was ordinary, tidy. He showed her the gun and whispered into her ear, "Don't scream," and marched her into the next room, his one arm around her waist with the gun poking her side, the other arm reached up across melony breasts to cover her mouth. They walked in step together, clumsily, as though doing a dance they just learned together.

The room was high ceilinged, trimmed in carved wood-working that isn't done these days, and had once been the house library, judging from the walls of bookcases on either side of the room. They moved quickly through the library, which with lounging pillows and shag carpet and couch and easy chairs and TV had been reconverted into a living room, and on to the bedroom, where an air conditioner stuck in a window was cooling Tillis, who was asleep on his stomach, on top of the covers, naked.

Carefully, like a contortionist, without moving the arm across melony breasts or the one around her waist, Nolan stretched out a foot and kicked the bed.

Tillis roused, rolled over, sat up in bed, said, "What the fuck," rubbed sleep from his eyes.

Nolan said, "Surprise."

Tillis said, "Nolan?"

"Tell this girl I'm a friend and not to scream when I let her go."

"Phyllis, honey, he's my friend, don't go screaming, honey."

"And tell her not to jab me in the balls or anything."

"Don't go jabbing him in the balls or nothing, honey."

He let her go and she squirmed onto the bed and put her arms around Tillis. She was whiter than usual, being scared, and up against the big naked black man she made quite a contrast. Her eyes were full of confusion and hate, and she twisted up her face at Nolan.

"Racist motherfucker," she said.

"You forgot 'sexist,' " Nolan said.

"Cool it, Phyllis honey," Tillis said laughing, patting her backside, "He really is a friend. Sorta. He just got reason to play things a little close to the vest. He's a little more cautious than some people I know."

Phyllis said, "You mean I should have been more careful about just opening the door for him like I did?"

"We talked about that before, honey. I ain't no goddamn plumber, you know."

"I'm sorry, Tillie."

"It's okay. You gonna put the gun down, Nolan?"

"Down," Nolan said, lowering it. "Not away."

Tillis grinned, his white smile flashing in the darkened room; he looked like a sinister Louis Armstrong. He turned to Phyllis, said, "Be a good girl and get me some pants."

"Just pants," Nolan told her as she crossed in front of him, going to a dresser.

"What makes you so goddamn paranoid, man?" Tillis wanted to know.

"Old age," Nolan said, watching Tillis climb into his trousers.

"I thought you'd be in one of those homes by now," Tillis said, "boppin' round the grounds in a wheelchair with a shawl around your shoulders."

"Last time you told me that, I just finished knocking you on your black ass."

"And this time you caught me cold, with my black ass *really* hangin' out. Yeah, you're old all right, but you're good."

Nolan grinned back at him, said, "This time I thought we'd skip the preliminaries. My ribs hurt for a week last time we tangled."

"Must be that arthritis gettin' to you."

"Must be. Let's go talk in the other room. How about your friend getting us some coffee?"

"Good idea. Phyllis, honey, do what the man says."

"Is there a phone in the kitchen?" Nolan asked.

"No," Tillis said, pointing to the nightstand phone. "Only one in the apartment's here."

"Okay," Nolan told the girl, "go make the coffee."

"Get fucked," she told him.

"Start without me," he said.

She started to spit back a reply, but saw that Tillis was laughing at what Nolan said, and she shrugged helplessly and went off to the kitchen.

Nolan and Tillis took seats in the library-living room.

Tillis sat on the couch, Nolan on an easy chair across. He glanced at the books in the case behind him and recognized only one author; he hadn't heard of James Baldwin, Leroi Jones, Germaine Greer or Joyce Carol Oates, but he knew Harold Robbins.

Tillis said, "You're early, man."

"I made good time on the tollway."

"I wouldn't've called Harry in on you, you know."

"Thought crossed your mind, though, didn't it?"

Tillis grinned, then got serious fast. "What's this about, anyway?"

"You asked me that on the phone."

"Want you to tell me, man. Want to hear you say it."

"It's Charlie, Tillis."

"Charlie's dead."

"Yeah. And you helped crucify him. Only on the seventh day he rose."

"What makes you think he's alive?"

"Nothing much. Just that yesterday he murdered a friend of mine, stole around a million dollars from me, and kidnapped a kid I know. That's all."

"Shit. You jivin' me? You're a shifty motherfuck, I know that much. You shitin' me?"

"No shit at all. He's alive and I know it. If I wasn't sitting on this, the boys from Chicago would be coming around and checking out all Charlie's friends."

Tillis leaned over, hands folded, and thought for several long moments. When he looked up, his dark eyes were big and solemn and brimming with honesty. "All right, man. I'm gonna tell it. Gonna tell it all to you. You got to help me save my ass is all I ask. Whew. Jesus. The shit hit the fan this time, right? Shit, man."

"Tillis, you're going to be in trouble. I'm your only hope."

"The Great White Hope, that's my old buddy Nolan. Jesus Christ. Let me catch my breath. My whole fuckin' world's crashing down in my head. This is bad news for the big shitter, Nolan. Christ all fuckin' mighty."

"You started to tell me."

"Okay. Now you know about Charlie and me. I didn't love the sucker, but he helped me out, stayed by me. I didn't go to college first to play ball like most of the dudes, and I didn't play ball long enough to have a name that was gonna make me a goddamn announcer with Howard Cosell on the tube or nothin'. My football career, shit, when that fuckin' knee went, I mean maybe I coulda got a job selling tires or something . . . right here, folks, here's our boy Tillis, he'll show you the tires, he played ball with the pros, shook hands with Joe Namath, this boy did."

"Tillis."

"Yeah. Anyway, Charlie. He did right by me. Paid me good, treated me with respect, unless he got real mad or something. I didn't love him, but who do you think I was gonna love in the goddamn Family? Wasn't exactly a truck-load of soul brothers around me. I had to develop a god-damn taste for pasta, let me tell you. Charlie did me right, and then you come along and fucked him in the ear with those marked bills you passed him, and then this political thing started happening, only it was going on all the time, I guess, but this trouble you brought Charlie brought it to a head. The younger bunch was buckin' the old regime, Charlie bein' the main one, you know. It was a political deal, power play, like General Motors or the court of some fuckin' king or the goddamn Democratic Party. So those of us lined up with Charlie were maybe gonna get chopped when he did. Wasn't no *if*—just *when*. There was a bunch of us. Anyway, me and some other guys took a hand in helping the people against Charlie in the Family get rid of him. Only, as you guessed, I guess, we faked it. It was a couple of bums off skid row who got roasted in that fire when Charlie's car acci-dent'ly on purpose cracked up. We just used some stuff to make it look like Charlie. See, Charlie knew he didn't have a chance, so him and his kid were going to like *pretend* to die in this crash and take off somewhere, South America, I don't know where really . . . Charlie had plenty of money put in other people's accounts, people he trusted, so money was no hassle."

"Hold it. Why'd he include his kid in the crash?"

"The kid was workin' in the Family. Just an overblowed accountant, but Charlie was afraid the kid would get wasted along with him. Guess the kid always wanted to work with his father, wanted to be a part of the Family, saw it as . . . I don't know, adventure, I guess. Or a family tradition or some goddamn thing. Charlie never went for it, really, that business about working your kids into the Family ain't so true anymore. But this kid of his insisted, and when the boy got out of college Charlie gave him this token desk thing, away from the guns and that side of it. Charlie was like a lot of guys, wanted his kids to get an education, be respectable. I think his daughter was in the fuckin' Peace Corps, can you get into that?"

"Why didn't Charlie leave, like he was supposed to?"

"Nolan, I swear to God I thought that sucker was in Argentina or someplace, with his buddy the Boss of the Bosses. Swear to shit, I thought that's where he was. But Nolan, I'm no fuckin' wheel, remember . . . I'm a cog, man, and Charlie was pretty foxy about who he had help him, well, die . . . and just as foxy about how much each of us knew exactly. Like, I know *some* of the people involved, but not all."

Nolan got out of the chair, walked over and sat on the couch next to Tillis. He handed Tillis the list Felix had made up. "How many of those people were in this with Charlie?"

Tillis studied the list. The girl in the terrycloth robe came in and gave them cups of coffee. Tillis told her to go back out to the kitchen and she did.

"I see Charlie's daughter is on this list," Tillis said.

"Yeah."

"You gonna bother her?"

"No."

"Good."

"Well?"

"I'm not going to tell you any names."

"What?"

"Listen. My ass is grass because of this. I gotta move slow on this, think it through. You're in pretty good with the Family, now, right? I heard you made the peace with that tightass lawyer, Felix what's-his-name."

"Yeah, the Family's behind me. I already admitted that. But they're going to sit on this till I say go. You got my word. I can save your damn ass. You maybe aren't going to get a pension out of the deal, and a penthouse overlooking Lake Michigan, but you'll be alive."

"Maybe I can get that job selling tires," Tillis said, with a rueful grin. "God. I got about as much chance to get outa this as a turd in a toilet."

"Mine's the only hand can stop the guy from flushing it."

"I know, man."

"Listen to me, Tillis. Charlie's fucking nuts. He's out of his mind. He wants to hurt me and I got to stop him. He's got my money, Tillis. Worse than that, he's got this kid. I like this kid, Tillis."

"You don't like anybody."

"Hell, I like *you*. I must be capable of liking any damn body."

"What do you mean, a kid?"

"Well, he's about twenty. He was in on that last job of mine."

"That bank number?"

"Yeah."

"Then you're talking about a man, not a kid."

"Compared to you and me, he's a kid, Tillis. And compared to Charlie." Nolan sipped his coffee; it was weak. "Maybe he's dead."

"Charlie?"

"The kid. Jon's his name. If Charlie killed that kid, I'm nailing the bastard to the wall. That bastard is a cancer that's got to be cut out of the human race."

Tillis shook his head, said, "I can't imagine him messing

around with a young kid, especially somebody you're fond of, Nolan. Too much like his own son, you know? Charlie wouldn't want anybody hurting *his* kid, and that's what you might do to get back at him, so I can't . . ."

"Charlie's capable of anything, as long as it's insane. As far as his own precious kid is concerned, Charlie's got his pride'n'joy at his side, the kid's been in it with him from word go."

"What? Momma, that man *has* flipped out."

The phone rang in the bedroom. Tillis said, "Phyllis, honey, go get that!"

Tillis said, "You'll want to get to Harry, right? That's the next step."

"Right. I figure he knows what's happening."

"You probably figure right, man. Maybe I'm a cog, but ol' Harry's a wheel."

Phyllis trudged through the room, all but pouting, plodding along toward the trilling phone.

Tillis said, "I think maybe I know the best way to handle it."

"Let's hear it."

"Let me go pump him."

"Oh, sure."

"Now listen, you go down there, try to see Harry downtown, you're gonna have to break some people in half. Maybe you get busted in half yourself, and that kid, and that money, ain't never gonna be found. You be better off trust me in this."

"Come on."

"Tillie!" Phyllis yelled.

"Hey, I'm not stupid, man. I know how close those Chicago dudes are, I can feel 'em on my neck, breathing hot and hard, man. Shit. Remember, I used to work with those boys in the windy town, and I know how tough some of them mothers are. This town is nothin'. We're a suburb of Chicago that got outa hand and that's all. Those guys, they think it's 1927 or something."

"Tillie!" the girl called again. "Guy says it's urgent!"

Nolan followed him into the bedroom. Tillis took the phone and said, "Yeah? . . . What? . . . What? . . . Jesus fuck . . . How long ago? . . . Where do we go from here, man? . . . No, I'll come to you . . . Downtown I guess, be cops at the house . . . Yeah." Tillis hung the phone up, said, "Somebody shot Harry."

Nolan sat on the bed. "Say again."

"Somebody killed him. He was coming out of his house. He was in his goddamn pajamas, gettin' the paper off the porch. Some guy came by, in a car it must've been, and shot him. You know what with?"

"No."

"A grease gun, they think. A fuckin' grease gun. I don't believe it."

"Harry lives in a kind of nice neighborhood, doesn't he? Didn't that cause a scene? Didn't everybody see the guy that did it, his car at least?"

"That fuckin' grease gun must've been silenced. He laid there ten minutes before his wife found him. Can you put a silencer on a fuckin' grease gun, a submachine gun like that?"

"Sure could. It wouldn't make any more noise than somebody shuffling cards."

"Who? The Family? They do it, Nolan? You been shittin' me all along? Settin' me up?"

"No. But it *could* be the Family. It could be that bastard Felix using me. Or it could be Charlie, killing everybody who helped him, anybody who could lead somebody to him."

"Jesus. I got to get downtown. Jesus."

"Is there anybody else who could tell you something?"

"Huh?"

"About Charlie. Anybody else in Harry's regime here you can pump? Who's second in command? Vito?"

Tillis nodded.

"Isn't Vito Harry's cousin, makes him some kind of half-ass relative of Charlie's, then, too, right?"

"Yeah. Well. Nolan, Jesus. Okay, I guess my head's straight. Yeah. You want, you can stay here, I'll call the information to you if I can get it. If I can't get nothin', I'll call you and you can try some of the other people on that list. But I suggest you move on to the Chicago names, man, because this town's gonna be a fuckin' funny farm for a while."

"If I stay here, and wait for you to call, am I an asshole?"

"I'm not going to screw you, Nolan. I helped you before."

"Yeah. I'll show you the scars."

Tillis mustered a weary grin. "Well, you want to watch me get dressed?"

"I don't want to, but I'm going to."

Before he left, dressed in his brown suit and black shoulder holster, the Luger in it unloaded at present, Tillis kissed Phyllis good-bye and said, "Later," to Nolan, adding, "Take care of this girl while I'm gone, Nolan, I like her," and Nolan knew what he meant, felt better about trusting Tillis.

Nolan and Phyllis retired to the living room. Nolan took Tillis's place on the couch and Phyllis took the easy chair across. She stared sullenly at him, unaware that her spread legs were giving Nolan a view worthy of *Hustler* magazine.

"What do you do?" Nolan said.

"What Tillis tells me to," she said, still sullen.

"For a living, I mean."

"I'm a grad student."

"You go to college, you mean? What do you study?"

"I'm in the Afro-American Studies program."

Nolan looked at her thighs and got ready to ask her what the hell she meant, but the scream broke in.

He jumped up, and so did the girl.

The noise, the scream had come from outside. He pressed up against the clear glass and looked down and saw Tillis sprawled across the tan Ford, his unloaded Luger in his hand, a ribbon of blood across his chest. Even from the second floor, Nolan could see the wide white rolled-back eyes, the bulging tongue.

Didn't take a college education to tell Tillis was dead.

5

The modern buildings of Northern Illinois University rose to the left like the set of a science fiction film with a big budget. The rich Illinois farmland dissolved into a blur of plastic college-town shopping center, apartment building and franchise restaurant living; the highway became a shaded street along which kids of both sexes wearing tee-shirts and cut-off jeans walked and pedaled bikes. Then, after blocks of pizza places and boutiques and McDonald's hamburgers and dormitories, a wide, off-center intersection appeared from nowhere, as if to separate one half of Dekalb from the other. That seemed only right, as this other part of town was so different it was like passing through to another dimension; the business district beyond the intersection had no doubt been much the same for many years, the narrow main street lined with one- and two-story buildings, drug stores, dress shops, five and dime, hardware stores and only rare indications ("Adult Books in Rear" and "Water Bed Sale") that this was a college town and not just a congre-gating point for area farmers and sedately middle class townspeople. Dekalb was a schizophrenic town. Even Nolan noticed it.

"Hey, look at the jugs on that one," Angello said, pointing to a tall blonde girl with a short haircut, cut-off jeans and green tee-shirt. "Bouncy bouncy."

"Just drive," Nolan said.

"Sour ass," Angello said.

Nolan still wasn't happy about being with Angello, though he supposed he should've been grateful to his chubby-faced companion. It was just an hour and half ago that Nolan had been looking out the window and watching the crowd form, a crowd of briefcase-carrying men ready to leave for work and curlered women in housewifely robes and gleeful little kids in bright summer shirts, all looking on in fascinated horror at the big black dead man sprawled across the tan Ford. Nolan's tan Ford, and at that moment of no damn use at all, as far as transportation went. Nolan hadn't bothered trying to calm the hysterical Phyllis Watson, who had started to scream, pummeling him with hard little fists. Instead, he had knocked her cold with a solid right cross, sincerely hoping he hadn't broken the girl's jaw, and went down the stairs and out of the house, cutting through the backyards of houses behind, moving away from the scene of Tillis's death as quickly as possible. He'd gone to a filling station, called the number Angello had left, and after fifteen minutes and two cups of coffee in the station's adjacent cafe, Nolan had gladly hopped in a car beside Angello and got the hell out of Milwaukee. Somebody would have to go back for the tan Ford, which belonged to the Tropical Motel and could conceivably cause some problems, but that was one of those details that would have to be ironed out later. Some asshole like Felix could sweat over that.

And so now Nolan was with Angello in a black Chevy (naturally) in Dekalb, Illinois. Nolan wasn't happy about being in Dekalb, for several reasons. For one thing, Dekalb was only fifteen miles from the Tropical, his starting point on this largely fruitless trip, which already had lasted some nine or ten hours. Being so close to home served to remind him of how far he hadn't gotten; he sensed he was going around in a big circle that included all of Illinois, Iowa, and Wisconsin. He felt like a traveling salesman with nothing to sell.

Another reason for his discontent was that he was in Dekalb to do something he would rather not do. Something he had told Tillis he wouldn't do.

He was going to bother Charlie's daughter.

And he was, in fact, probably going to kidnap her.

Angello said, "What should I do, stop at a filling station and ask, or what?" They jostled across the railroad tracks that slanted across Dekalb's main street, announcing the decline of the business district.

"No," Nolan said, "we're already on the right street. She must live over one of these stores downtown here." He checked the street number on the list of names, checked it against the numbers they were passing. "Yeah, just another couple blocks. Keep it slow."

Back on the Interstate they had stopped long enough to call Felix. Nolan had questioned the lawyer, hard, about the violent doings in Milwaukee, and Felix had said, "Do you really think we would do *that* to people who could lead us to the man we *really* want?" The man they really wanted being Charlie, of course. Felix was careful about what words he used on the phone.

"I don't know," Nolan had answered. "I been dealing with crazy people so much I'm feeling that way myself."

"Nolan, be reasonable. We're fighting the same battle, for Christ's sake."

"But who is on what side, is what I want to know."

"Let me send some people to help you out. This is getting big."

"I already got your Angello along, and that's one man too many. Oh, and you can call your man Greer and take him off those people in Iowa City. Not much chance of anybody warning Harry about anything anymore."

"If you're through making your ridiculous accusations, Nolan, I have something to tell you. Something important. We have a lead on Charlie."

That had pleased Nolan, but still he said, "I thought this was my show."

"I told you, it's bigger than that now. We won't get in your way, but we have interests in this affair far wider than your own, and resources at our disposal that a single man—even a most competent one, like yourself—could not hope to match."

"So what have you got?"

"We've located a pilot who'd been chartered by Harry.

He was to fly up to a private air field in the Lake Geneva area and take a passenger to Mexico."

Felix paused, for applause Nolan guessed.

When he didn't get any, Felix continued. "The guy, the pilot, has done some work for us before . . . has picked up merchandise of ours in Mexico, occasionally, if you get my meaning."

"Go on."

"Harry's death was reported on the radio and television about half an hour ago, and this pilot heard it and immediately called Vito up and asked him if this chartered plane thing was still on. Vito knew nothing about it, but thought it smelled funny and called Chicago to see what we made of it."

"What you made of it was the plane was for Charlie."

"Naturally. I told Vito to tell the pilot to go ahead and be where he was supposed to be at the proper time. We'll have our men waiting there, at the private field."

"If the field's near Lake Geneva, odds are Charlie's holed up someplace close by."

"I would think so. Seems to me he used to have a lodge or summer home of some kind in that neck of the woods. We're running a check on it now, trying to see exactly where it was."

"What time was that meeting at the airfield supposed to be?"

"It was set for last night but the 'passenger' ran into some difficulty and they'd rescheduled the next possible time. Which was one o'clock today."

"Tonight, you mean?"

"This afternoon, I mean."

"Jesus. Not much time. Where is this air field, anyway?"

Felix gave Nolan directions; they were complicated and Nolan had to write them down. He knew the Lake Geneva area fairly well, but there were a hell of a lot of country roads around there to confuse things.

"You don't really think Charlie will go ahead with the flight, do you, Felix? He's pretty likely to've heard the news about Harry and Tillis by now and figure something's up."

"Nolan, it's pretty likely, too, that Charlie was responsible for what happened to Harry and Tillis. Tidying up after himself. He's certainly ruthless enough to handle things that way. If our people aren't responsible for what happened in Milwaukee . . . and Nolan, I assure you we aren't . . . then who else could it be but Charlie?"

That was a good question, and it was still on Nolan's mind even as Angello wheeled the black Chevy down a side street and slid into a diagonal parking stall next to the cycle shop over which Charlie's daughter lived.

"Don't tell me," Angello grunted. "You want me to keep my ass in the car, right?"

Nolan nodded. "And if somebody comes at you with a silenced grease gun, try to get out of the way."

"I'll do my best."

"But if you can't, fall on the horn and warn me before you breathe your last, okay, Angello?"

"Nolan, what the fuck makes you such a nice guy?"

"The company I keep."

To the left of the row of motorcycles and the window full of Yamaha signs was a doorless doorway, beyond that a stairway. At the bottom of the stairs were two mailboxes: apartment one had somebody called Barry West in it; apartment two had Joyce Walters. Walters wasn't Charlie's name, and Joyce wasn't married, but she was Charlie's kid just the same.

Nolan didn't like this. It gave him a bad taste in his mouth. Charlie was a crazy man, and that made anyone who chose to play by Charlie's rules a crazy man, as well.

But shit. What else was there to do? Where else could he turn? Milwaukee was out; it was a madhouse at the moment, and the two men he needed to talk to were both dead. Chicago? Might be a few people there worth seeing, but he doubted it, doubted he'd find out anything he hadn't found out already, from Joey Metrano. No, it was obvious Charlie had done his most recent arranging through Harry, in

Milwaukee, so Chicago was no good, and besides, Felix would have Family men poking around the city, and as for that meeting at the air field, that was the same damn thing: Family people would be in control there, too. And Charlie wasn't likely to show anyway; he'd much more likely be holed up, trying to regroup, trying to find some new way to get out of the country, now that the plane was out. Unless Felix was right and Charlie *was* going around shooting those who'd helped him. But Nolan simply couldn't believe that, even though there was a cockeyed Charlie-like logic to it.

There was only one name on that list worth talking to. Only one person he could try.

The daughter.

And he knew that the best thing for him to do would be grab her, take her with him and try to work out a trade with Charlie—the girl for Jon and the money. If anyone would know where Charlie was, the daughter would, and if Nolan kidnapped her and worked out a swap, the whole damn problem could be solved in one easy stroke. Nolan wouldn't even have to kill the old bastard; he could leave that to Charlie's Family friends.

So it was easy. Just take the girl. Exchange of prisoners. Simple.

But he'd be playing Charlie's game, doing what Charlie had done to Jon, and that gave him a bad taste in his mouth.

He knocked. A voice from within said, "One moment," a girl's voice, medium-range, firm.

She opened the door a crack and peered out at Nolan, looked him over, said, "Oh. You're a friend of my father's, I suppose." She gave out a heavy sigh. "I imagine you want to come in and talk to me."

"If I could," Nolan said.

She let him in, with another sigh, as if she'd known he was coming and was resigned to the fact. "Come in," she said, though he already was, "if you feel you have to."

Nolan walked over to a worn green couch, sat. The apartment was spare but spotless; the furniture old but serviceable. The only concession to luxury was a tiny portable TV that sat in a corner so low that your neck would have to ache no matter where you chose to watch, perhaps as punishment for doing so. The floor was hard varnished wood, scrubbed but too old to shine. The walls were flat, unpebbled plaster, white and very clean; they were bare except for a wooden carved thing over the couch, from some culture Nolan couldn't conceive of, and three posters, all on the wall directly across from him. One poster had an abstract drawing and the words "War Is Not Healthy for Children and Other Living Things," while the other two showed photographs of starving children, one labeled Biafra, the other Cambodia. It wasn't the most cheerful apartment Nolan had ever been in.

"Excuse me if I was rude before," she said. "Would you care for something to drink?"

He shrugged. "Coffee," he said.

"I have a pot of tea in the kitchen."

"Fine."

She wasn't gone long. She gave him the tea and on the saucer next to the cup was a single cookie, a vanilla Hydrox. Nolan bit the Hydrox in half and a hungry-eyed kid from Biafra caught his attention; the mouthful went down hard.

"I don't believe this is necessary," she said. "But I suppose you people mean well doing it."

She was a girl who might have been pretty, had she a mind to. She was small and had those same dark, close-set eyes her father had, though on her the effect was much different; there was a softness in the eyes that outer layers of strength couldn't mask. She sat in a straightback chair across from him, right by the Cambodia poster, and crossed her legs, tugging down her long skirt. She wasn't bad-looking, really, he thought, considering she was Charlie's kid and dressed like a goddamn nun, black skirt and short-sleeve white blouse, tucked neatly in. Her dark hair probably looked good when it hung loose to her shoulders; right now it was in a tight bun, pulled back from attractive features that had been totally denied make-up.

"I said, I don't believe this is necessary," she repeated, "but I suppose you people mean well doing it."

"Pardon?"

"Believe me, I know this is awkward for you. But I do understand what this is all about. As you must know, when Daddy died, Uncle Harry came down and talked to me, to try to soothe me, calm me. What upset Uncle Harry was I wasn't upset. I wish he could have understood that as far as I was concerned my father had died long before that stupid crash, and that my brother's death was of a far greater importance to me, because I had . . . I had hope for Walter. But Walter was . . . stubborn. Stubborn as hell, and he wanted to walk in his father's footsteps, God alone knows why. So I could accept his death, too."

Nolan sipped his tea. He felt uncomfortable. He wished he'd thought this out better, planned exactly how he was going to handle the daughter. But who could have planned for a girl like this, anyway? Nothing to do but sit here and let her talk.

"So, as I said, this is entirely unnecessary. I heard the news on the television, and I was saddened for a moment, but I must admit that while Uncle Harry was a nice man in his way, I feel the world will be a better place without him. People like my uncle . . . and my father . . . are destructive, to themselves and to their society. My family had long been a part of organized corruption, our family history is long and illustrious in that regard. My mother's father, my grandfather, why they write books about him! Famous people played him in the movies, I was a celebrity as a little girl because of it . . . the only kid on the block whose grandpa was on 'The Untouchables'! No, I won't miss Uncle Harry, just like I won't miss my father. You want to know who I miss? Walter, sure, Walt, but mostly, I miss my mother, I wish I could sit and talk to my mother. She was ten years older than Daddy, she was a good woman and always pretended she didn't realize Daddy married her because she was somebody's daughter. She was young when she died, in her early sixties, and she died more of neglect than anything else, but she was too much in love with Daddy ever to complain . . . at least she never complained loud enough for me to hear. My whole family was caught up in that other Family, it drained the life out of all of us, and so please tell your people not to come bother me anymore. It's so ridiculous now, there's not a close blood relative left and yet still they feel obliged to send you, out of some insane, archaic sense of duty or custom or something. Excuse me. I hope I haven't offended you. But you must understand. My father was dead long before he was killed in that crash. He was morally dead. My uncle, too. Can you understand that?"

Nolan nodded. He cleared his throat, said, "Uh, you were in the Peace Corps, weren't you?"

"Yes. Guatemala. I was in the Central American jungle, with very primitive people, who believe in evil spirits and that sort of thing. We built them a school. It was a good experience, but it was as much escape as service, and I realize now that my joining the Peace Corps was somewhat hypocritical. I'm back in college again, taking a degree in English this time, because I want to help where I'm needed most, and where my own moral need is greatest. I hope to teach in the slums, the ghettos. In Chicago, if at all possible. Do you understand what I'm saying?"

He did.

"No," he said.

"I want to go into the jungle where it's my father's kind who are the evil spirits. His kind who need warding off. With education, with patience, with love, maybe a person like me can teach the underfed, the underprivileged, educate them into understanding that hell is what the heroin dealers offer, to realize the absurdity of spending five dollars a day on a game of chance when your family is starving, to know what it is to . . ."

He stopped listening to her. Bleeding-heart liberals gave him a pain in the butt. She was doing her best, he supposed, but she was starting to sound like the naive, condescending child she was.

"I'm sorry Uncle Harry is dead," she said after a while, "and please thank whoever it was that sent you. But that part of me is gone now. I won't miss Uncle Harry. I'll admit . . . I miss my mother. My brother, too. And I miss the father of my childhood."

"I knew you when you were little," Nolan said. It was a shot in the dark, untrue, of course. But he tried it.

"You did?"

"I came around to your summer place once. On business."

She found a smile somewhere and showed it to him. "I won't lie and say I remember you, but I guess you could've seen me when I was a child. I can remember that Daddy was secretive about that place, about Eagle's Roost." She grinned, forgetting herself. "He bawled Uncle Harry out one time, bawled him out terrible, for bringing business people around to the lodge . . . I can remember it so clearly. Maybe you were one of the men with Uncle Scarey, uh, Harry that time. Maybe that was the time you saw me."

"I think it was," Nolan said. "I remember how mad your father got."

"Oh, he could get mad all right, but we had good times at the lakes. My best memories are there, at Eagle's Roost, we were a family there more than anywhere else. Up so high, away from everything, where we could look down at both those pretty blue lakes. We had a sailboat, a little one, for two people, you know? And Daddy and I would . . ." She stopped. "That was a long time ago."

"Your lodge was up around Lake Geneva, wasn't it?"

"Well, the lakes, Twin Lakes, actually, but in that area, yes. It's kind of a unique place, sort of a shame no one's using it now, been all shut up for several years. Got the best view in the whole area, up on that hill on that little piece of land between the two lakes. Eagle's Roost . . . a beautiful place, but just a memory now, *one* pleasant one I have, anyway." She got up. "Would you like another cup of tea before you go?"

"Yes, please. Never mind the Hydrox."

They drank the second cup of tea quickly, in silence.

Finally she said, "Did you wonder about my name, on the mailbox?"

"Not really," he said.

"I changed it. Legally. I'm not a part of that family anymore. I'd been meaning to change it for years, but always thought I'd be getting married one day, and, well . . ." She touched her hair. "I've other things to do for the time being. Do you think it odd, me changing my name?"

"No," Nolan smiled. "I've done it a few times myself."

He rose, handed her his empty cup and left.

6

It was no problem finding Eagle's Roost. The narrow strip of land between Lake Mary and Lake Elizabeth had only the one, steep hill. Standing at the bottom and looking up, Nolan thought the hill looked like the Matterhorn, but in reality it was only a hundred some feet, going up at an eighty-degree angle, flattening out level on top. From the foot of the hill all you could see of what was up there was the tall row of pines lining the edge and sheltering the lodge from view, the breeze riffling through their needles. But it was there, Nolan knew, Eagle's Roost was up there.

Nolan and Angello left the black Chevy a quarter of a mile away, back behind a bend on the blacktop road. Both men were carrying Smith and Wesson .38's; Angello's was a Bodyguard model, a five-shot revolver with a two-inch barrel, good for shooting people close up, but not much else; the four-inch barrel on Nolan's revolver assured far greater accuracy and he didn't like working with supposed professionals who didn't observe such simple facts. But he felt he could use some support, so he'd let Angello come along anyway. They circled the bottom of the hill, staying down low, moving carefully through dense foliage like soldiers in a jungle.

It was noon, but the sun overhead was under a cover of clouds, so the heat was modest, tempered by gentle lake winds. The sun would come out now and then, but mostly the day was pleasantly overcast, a day of floating shadows that rolled cool and blue and gray across the green Wisconsin landscape. Nolan could smell the lake in the air and envied, for a moment, the people out boating, skiing, swimming. Then he squeezed the .38 in his hand, as if to reassure the weapon of his intent, and pressed on.

"Fucking bugs," Angello said, swatting.

Nolan hadn't noticed them. He pointed, said, "Over there."

They could see the lake now, as well as smell it. This was Lake Mary and Elizabeth was over on the other side of the steep hill. A combination boathouse and garage, possibly with sleeping rooms on the upper floor, was maybe twenty yards from the bottom of the hill, some hundred yards from the lake front. But what Nolan was pointing to was the driveway extending from the boathouse and cutting through the thick foliage to a big wrought-iron gate that opened onto a road that ran through a subdivision of summerhouses nearby. The big padlocked gate was the most awesome feature of a five-foot brick wall that separated the grounds of Eagle's Roost (which even from this distance could be seen spelled out backward in wrought-iron on the gate) from those of the subdivision.

"Go back to the car," Nolan said. "Drive down through that bunch of houses and wait by the gate. If I screw up and Charlie gets away from me somehow, he's probably going to come tearing out through there."

Angello nodded. "No other way out?"

"Just those steps we saw on the other side of the hill. If

Charlie's wounded, and I think he is, he won't be coming down an incline like that. Besides, a car'd have to be waiting to pick him up, and where would that come from?"

"Maybe he's got people helping him."

"Risk it."

"Okay, then. I'm on my way."

"Angello."

"Yeah?"

"Family guys are probably going to start showing up, and I'd appreciate you keeping them away, for a while. I want time with Charlie alone."

"I'll do my best, Nolan. But it's not you I work for, remember."

"Do it for the sake of our friendship."

A grin split Angello's chubby face and he said, "Well, since you put it that way . . ." And he trudged off through the high grass and weeds toward the blacktop.

Down in front of the subdivision was a beach, where girls and women sunned, and swimmers, kids mostly, romped close to shore. Out on the lake, sailboats and motorboats of various sizes and shapes skimmed across the water. The cool breeze was soothing, and Nolan could have dropped down into a soft bed of grass and fallen asleep, had this been another time.

But it wasn't.

He moved toward the boathouse, which was two stories of yellow stucco trimmed with brown wood, Swiss chalet-style. Wooden stairs on either side met in a balcony that came across the front of the building and faced the lake, but not around the back. Trees and bushes and out-of-hand weeds crowded the boathouse; it had been some good time since a gardener tended these grounds.

He approached slowly, keeping down, pushing through the heavy bushes around the house, keeping under their cover. On his haunches, he moved along the side of the stucco wall, then eased carefully out onto the graveled drive, the balcony overhead shading him as he edged along the garage door. The brown wood of the garage door didn't quite match the wood trim and stairs and balcony, being more modern than the rest of this twenties vintage building; the door had windows strung across it that allowed Nolan to peek in at the blue Oldsmobile inside. One half of the garage had been meant for boat storage, but no boat was there now, just a dirty, long-discarded tarp that lay slumped across the spot where a boat had once rested. The garage was empty of people and, except for the Olds and the tarp, any sign of human life. Not a rake or a saw or a carjack or a pile of old newspapers, nothing. People didn't live here anymore.

The garage took up half of the lower floor; next to it was a large games room, dartboard still on the wall, chairs and tables covered, one of them big and round and obviously a poker table, with the back wall taken up by a bar, stocked with nothing. The outside door that led into this room was unlocked, and Nolan went silently in, taking his time, opening the door so that it hardly creaked a bit, even though it surely hadn't had much use lately.

To the left of the bar area was a stairway. Nolan crossed the room like an Indian and started up the stairs, at the top of which was the light of an open doorway. As he climbed he noticed the tightness of his facial muscles, how tense his neck was, and consciously loosened himself, fanning his .38 out in front of him in a fluid, almost graceful motion. Nolan stepped into the hallway on the balls of his feet. The hall was narrow, three doors on each side, all of them shut tight. One by one he stood before the doors and listened, not opening any of them, only listening, pressing an ear tenderly against the heavy wood, searching for a sound. A dripping faucet behind one door told him he'd found the can, but he heard nothing else until he'd worked his way down both sides of the hall. This final door was to one of the rooms that faced the hill; the rooms on this side were more likely for holding a prisoner than those with views of the lake and a balcony running by. He listened and then he heard it, a voice, a man's voice, a young man perhaps.

He stood to the left of the door, back to the wall, and reached across and turned the knob and nudged the door barely open. Then with a quick kick he knocked it open all the way and flattened back against the wall and heard the snick of a silenced gun and watched the slug splinter into the door opposite. Still flat to the wall, he peered around between fully open door and doorjamb, hopefully to fire through the crack into the room at whoever shot at him, and saw Jon standing there, holding an automatic in one trembling hand.

"It's Nolan," Nolan said softly, and stepped into the doorway.

"Nolan!"

"Quiet," he said, walking into the room.

"I could've killed you."

"Well, you didn't."

The room had pink wallpaper, a big bed with open springs and sheet-covered furniture. On the bed was a young guy in his early twenties, wearing a blue tee-shirt and white jeans and tied to the bed. One of his feet was bare; this was explained by the sock stuffed in his mouth, as a make-do gag.

"I bet that tastes sweet," Nolan said. "Charlie's kid?"

"Charlie's kid. His name is Walt. God, am I glad to see you, Nolan."

"Where'd you get the gun and the ropes?"

"From him. Those are the ropes I was tied up with for longer than I'd care to talk about."

"How long you been in control here?"

"Five minutes maybe. Had a chance earlier, but I blew it. Anyway, he came around a while ago to see if I had to take a piss or anything and I kicked him in the nuts."

"You're learning."

"He's really a pretty decent guy, for a kidnapper. He was going to help me."

"Then why'd you feel it necessary to kick his balls in?"

"He kept *talking* about helping me, but he never got around to doing it."

"I see. Where's Charlie?"

"Up on that hill there, I guess. In that house up there. You can see the place from the window." He walked over to the window and Nolan came along. Jon pointed out and said, "See?"

This side of the hill was just as steep, but there was no row of pines blocking the view. The house was two stories of yellow stucco, like the boathouse, but was much bigger and of that pseudo-Spanish architecture so common in the twenties. With its turrets and archways, it was a genuine relic, the castle of latter-day robber barons, built during the blood-and-booze era by the father of Charlie's late wife. Someday people would pay fifty cents to hear a tour guide tell about it. Maybe today would provide a sock finish for the guide's line of patter.

"Somewhere down in those bushes," Jon said, "is an underground elevator or something. Or maybe a hidden stairway. Over to the right of those cobblestone steps, see? I watched Walt last time he came back from the house and he came out of those bushes."

Nolan scratched his chin with the hand the .38 was in. "Kind of figured there was some other, easy way up there, besides steps. There's steps in front and back both, but with Charlie wounded . . . he *is* wounded, isn't he?"

"Yeah," Jon nodded, "his thigh. I saw him back in Ainsworth's office, his thigh was all bandaged. That's the last time I saw Charlie, was back there in Iowa City. Christ, that reminds me, how's Karen? How the hell is she? Did you see her?"

"Yes. She's fine. How about you? You all right?"

"I am now that you're here. How'd you find me, anyway?"

"We can shoot the bull later, kid. Right now we got things to do."

"Listen, why don't we just . . . no. Forget it."

"Something on your mind?"

"No, nothing, forget it."

"You were going to say, why don't we just take off while we got our asses in one piece?"

"Well, yes. Being alive sounds pretty damn good to me at the moment."

"Do what you want. I'm staying."

"Yeah, well, me too, of course. And I understand how you feel about this guy Charlie, it's a real thing between you two, been going on a lot of years and . . ."

"Fuck that. The money's what I care about. That son of a bitch has three quarters of a million dollars, *our* three quarters of a million dollars, Jon. And all that money sounds pretty damn good to me. That's what I call being alive."

"I'd . . . almost forgotten about the money . . . how could I forget that much money. Seems so long since yesterday . . . yesterday Planner was alive, Nolan, do you realize that?" Jon's hand whitened around the nine-millimeter automatic. "I'm glad we're going to do something about . . . about what they did to Planner."

"Look. One thing we don't need to be is emotional. We got no time for revenge. That's for the crazy assholes, like Charlie. I want that bastard breathing, for the time being anyway. I got to shake our money out of him. God knows what he's done with it."

"The money," Jon said, nodding, loosening up. "That's what's important."

Nolan pointed at Walter, whose close-set eyes were big from listening intently to the conversation. "What about him? Have you gotten anything out of him?"

"We hadn't got very far in our conversation when you got here. I was asking him yes and no questions so he could shake his head and answer, and he claimed he wouldn't scream or anything if I ungagged him, but I wasn't convinced yet."

"It's just the two of them, then, right? Charlie and the kid?"

"Far as I know. Why not ask Walt, here?"

"Take the sock out of his mouth."

Jon did.

Walter tried to spit the taste out of his mouth, didn't quite get the job done.

"This is Nolan," Jon said. "The guy I told you about."

Walter said nothing. He had a blank expression, as though he couldn't make up his mind whether to be outraged or scared shitless.

"How about it, Walt?" Nolan asked. "Just you and your dad?"

Walter said nothing.

Jon said, "I don't think he's going to say anything."

Nolan said, "Well. I'm going up the hill."

"Wait," Walter said. "Don't hurt him! He's just a poor old man!"

Nolan said nothing.

Jon said, "What do I do?"

Nolan stuffed the sock back into Walter's mouth and said, "Stay here and guard Junior. If Charlie comes out on top, you'll have good bargaining power."

"Don't talk that way! How could that old bastard come out on top over you?"

"Oh, I don't know. Maybe shoot me, like the other two times."

"Jesus, Nolan."

"Come on, I'll help you take him downstairs. Ground floor'll be better for you and if you set up behind the bar you'll have a decent vantage point, and you'll be right by the garage. He didn't have car keys on him, by any chance?"

"No."

"Can you hotwire a car, kid?"

"My J.D. days pay off at last. Sure I can hotwire a car, can't everybody?"

"Good man. Come on."

They dragged Walter down the stairs into the gameroom.

"See you kid," Nolan said.

"See you, Nolan," Jon said. But he didn't quite sound sure.

7

The elevator hadn't seen regular use for years, having only recently been brought back into service for Charlie's homecoming to Eagle's Roost. Nolan stood inside the cramped, steel-frame cage, finger poised over a button that said UP. Should he press the damn thing?

He didn't know.

All he knew was the elevator would deliver him *somewhere* inside that yellow stucco dinosaur up there. But *somewhere* covered a lot of unchartered territory. Still, it would be an easy, quick way inside the place; he would avoid that steep, out-in-the-open climb, wouldn't have to worry about approaching the many-windowed house on all that flat surrounding ground. And there was surprise in it, too: no way in hell Charlie would figure Nolan for coming up the damn elevator.

But the cage was doorless, and gave him absolutely no place to hide, nowhere to shoot from behind, nothing to help him work out a defense in case he was dropped into a waiting Charlie's lap. And as basic as this elevator system was, Nolan expected no sliding door to await him at the end of his upward ride.

Chances were good, however, that the elevator would open onto an entryway of some kind, with coatracks and such, a vestibule type of thing. Or perhaps somewhere in or near the kitchen, since anyone coming to a summer place like this for a stay would surely come bearing groceries. Neither kitchen or vestibule seemed highly likely places for Charlie to be hanging around.

He pressed the button.

The motor wheezed and coughed, the cable groaned as it

lifted the cage. That was okay. He had known there'd be
noise, especially with an elevator as old as this. Charlie
would be expecting his son to be coming back and the sound
of the elevator wouldn't surprise him. And if Charlie was
waiting for Walter by where the elevator came up, no
problem either, as long as the old man was expecting the kid
and not Nolan, he'd be easy to overcome.

To get to the underground elevator, Nolan had had to
shove his way through the brush and weeds that had over-
taken what had once been a well-worn pathway, and sure
enough, just in that area Jon had pointed out from the
boathouse window, Nolan found an entrance. A heavy
wrought-iron gate, which was being choked to death by ugly,
clinging weeds, had been swung open to one side and a rock
shoved against it to keep it open. He had then entered a
narrow, low-ceilinged passageway, with plywood walls and a
gravel floor; the air was dank and stale, the atmosphere
falling somewhere between dungeon and cattle shed.

The passageway, and the elevator itself, said something
about the mobster mentality, or at least first-generation
mobster mentality, and this, as much as the obvious age of
everything, dated it all back to Capone days, in Nolan's
mind. After going to the fantastic expense of tunneling a
hundred feet down through a hill, and then out thirty or
forty feet more through the side of the hill to make the passageway, the first owner of Eagle's Roost had then spared
all expense, getting the most fundamental, bare-ass elevator system he could, and putting in a passageway that
could've been the gateway to Shanty Town. Those old mob-
sters betrayed their beginnings every time; they reverted to
the penny-squeezing of poverty-stricken upbringings,
whenever given half a chance. Those bastards knew how to
suck up the money, Nolan thought, but they never learned
how to spend it.

And that none of it had ever been extensively revamped
said something about Charlie, a first-generation mobster
himself, who hadn't been born into the Family, he'd married

into it. Like his wife's father, Charlie had known hard times, and like Nolan, he was a product of Depression years. While the elevator had apparently been kept in good working order and minor renovations made (electric motor replacing hydraulic, perhaps), Charlie had never put a new elevator in, or modernized the rustic passageway. Nolan could understand the psychology of it, because he shared Charlie's inability to enjoy money, had never really been good at spending it, afraid somehow to get accustomed to luxury, as if getting ready for the next Depression. With it came a tendency to hoard your money for a rosy retirement, which wasn't the best policy for men in high-risk fields, like Nolan and Charlie.

In fact, this wasn't the first time Nolan had lost all his money in one fell swoop, wasn't even the first time Charlie had been responsible. Not long ago Charlie had exposed Nolan's well-established cover name and cost him his hoarder's life savings. And Nolan had done the same for Charlie, hadn't he? Exposing him to the Family and ending a lifelong career?

And so now they were down to this. Two men who hadn't been young for a long time, who for reasons obscured by the years had done their best to wreck one another's lives (and with considerable success), two men alone in a house, with guns.

Going up in that elevator, impressions of the long conflict with Charlie flashing through his mind, Nolan might have felt a sense of destiny, a feeling that here at last would be an end to the struggle, an answer to a question long ago forgotten, an end to the senseless waste of each other's lives. But he didn't. His mind was full of one thing: the money. He had squeezed the need for revenge out of his perception. Charlie was just a man who had taken Nolan's money, and Nolan had to get that money back.

The elevator chugged to a halt.

Nolan had been right, on two counts: no door, sliding or otherwise, greeted him, just a metal safety gate that creaked unmercifully when he folded it back, and yes, he was in a vestibule, to the right of which he could see the shelves of a pantry, to the left the white walls of a kitchen.

But he was wrong, too, on just about everything else.

Charlie was in the kitchen.

Charlie was sitting on one of four plastic-covered chairs at a gray-speckled-formica-top table in the surprisingly small kitchen, its walls crowded with appliances, sink, cabinets, with one small counter strewn with Schlitz beer cans and empty TV dinner cartons.

In front of Charlie, on the table, was a silenced nine-millimeter automatic. Also in front of him were six more Schlitz cans. Charlie was wearing his underwear, a sleeveless tee-shirt and gray boxer shorts. The flesh of his limbs looked as gray as the shorts, a tan that had sickened, and flaccid; his right thigh was bandaged; on his upper left arm was a tattoo of a rose, nicely done. Charlie had a new nose; it was pink, unlike the gray-tan skin surrounding it. He was sleeping.

He was, in fact, snoring, quite loudly, contentedly, even drunkenly. His head was resting on folded arms and he looked both very young and very old.

Nolan took a chair next to him at the Formica-top table. He picked up the gun and stuffed it in his belt. Charlie didn't stir. Nolan sat and studied his old enemy, the adversary who'd given him so much hell for so many years, tried to see the maniac he'd come looking for, and saw only a frail old sleeping drunken man.

It was all disappointing somehow. An anticlimax that turned years of running, hating, fighting into an absurd, unfunny joke. He felt foolish, a little. And vaguely sad.

But this wasn't a time for reflection; there was money to find, and Nolan grabbed the tattooed gray arm and shook the sleeping man and said, "Come on, Charlie, wake up."

Like the curtain of a play, the lids on the close-set eyes raised slowly, and Charlie lifted head from folded arms and gradually got himself into a sitting position. He yawned. He smiled. He said, "Hello, Nolan."

"Well, hello Charlie."

"It's been a long time."

"Yeah. We got to quit meeting like this."

"I see you took my gun, Nolan."

Charlie's speech was thick but clear, each word let out after careful consideration.

Nolan shook his head. "Why'd you have to get drunk on your ass like this, Charlie?"

He shrugged, looked almost embarrassed. "A hell of a thing, I know. I guess I wanted to be numb for the goddamn bullets."

"I won't kill you, Charlie, not if you give my money back."

The laughter came rumbling out of Charlie's gut and he touched his forehead to the Formica top and cackled. When he looked up at Nolan he had tears in his eyes from laughing. "You stupid goddamn asshole, you think I'm afraid of you, afraid you're going to kill me? Get away, get away, you silly bastard."

"Charlie."

"You can't kill *me,* Nolan. Not you or the whole goddamn fucking Family. Nobody can kill me, I died a long time ago; don't you read the goddamn papers? How can you kill a goddamn dead man? You tell me! I'm getting another beer."

Charlie got up and weaved toward the refrigerator and Nolan was up and on him, latched onto his arm and dragged him out into the adjacent room.

They were in the big main room of the lodge now, a high-ceilinged hall with open beams and much dark wood and lots of doors and windows. The bulk of Eagle's Roost was right here in this one big room, the ceiling coming down on the back third, indicating the partial second floor; everything but sleeping and cooking had been done in this hall, or so the covered furniture all around would indicate; a few pieces were uncovered, the sofas, the long dining table that was over to the left, as you faced the black-brick fireplace with its elk's head above. In spite of the coolness of the day, it was rather warm in the hall, almost as if the fireplace had been going or the heat'd been on. Nolan dragged Charlie over to the semicircle of sofas facing the fireplace. Nolan tossed the little man onto one of the sofas, sat opposite him. Between them was a large round marble coffee table with a radio on it. Charlie had started to laugh again and was rocking side to side, holding his stomach, buckling with laughter.

Charlie's laughter subsided and he looked at Nolan and grinned. "I won, Nolan. I beat you. For years I've hated your fucking guts, for months all I've done is think about seeing you die. And now I don't even hate you anymore. I forgive you, Nolan. I forgive you for shooting my brother eighteen years ago and stealing my money and making a fool out of me in the Family. Yeah, that's right, I told you before, remember? How you wrecked my goddamn life, how I never moved an inch with the Family after you killed my brother Gordon and made me look stupid. But, Nolan, I forgive you. No shit, I forgive you. I even forgive you for passing me those marked bills, and look what *that* did to me. I don't hate you, anymore, Nolan, now that I've won. Now that I've won I can look at you and just not give a goddamn."

"Where's my money, Charlie? I'll knock it out of you if I have to."

Charlie waved his hands at Nolan, gave him a Bronx cheer. "No way, I'm too far gone to feel it, you'd have to knock me out before you hurt me and *then* what would I tell you?"

Nolan closed his eyes. Well, Nolan thought, he wants to talk, so humor him, sneak up on him that way.

"Did you kill Harry, Charlie? Did you kill Tillis?"

"Hell, no. Did you?" Charlie's grin disappeared and he got suddenly somber. He rubbed his cheek. "I shouldn't talk lightly of that. Harry was . . . he was my friend and he was my wife's brother, you know. I liked him and he helped me. He did a lot. He's the one who helped me get the bead on you, for one thing, he was bankrolling jobs for people like you, ripoff guys, and had the connections it took to run down your friends and the people you work with. We even knew you stayed with that guy Planner for a while, but we weren't sure that was where you left the money, not until I heard you were going to go to Iowa to move it."

"How did you find that out?"

"One of Felix's boys was working for me. Right under that goddamn pimp lawyer's nose. We knew all about you planning to switch the money to a Family bank, but you were pretty goddamn careful about telling where you were hiding it, weren't you? Waited until the last minute to tell Felix where it was, and even then all you said was 'Iowa,' though it wasn't any goddamn trick figuring out *where* in Iowa."

Charlie glanced slowly around the high-ceilinged hall. "Walter and me were just waiting at the lodge here to get the word where the money was, to know where to go to get it. It was good staying here with my boy, Nolan. I wish now he wasn't involved in this, but just the same it was good being with him, in this place. This place has a lot of memories for me, a lot of my good hours were spent at the Roost, and I don't mind ending it here, even though I always wanted to keep that part of my life outside. But you can't do that, can you, Nolan, you can't get away from what you are and you might as well come face to goddamn face with it."

He slammed his fist down on the marble of the coffee table in front of him. "Jesus! It was so fucking perfect, had it all worked out, just come back here with that money and hop on that goddamn plane to Mexico and fly down to Argentina like we had set up and Walter and me, we could've built a new life together . . . Walter's so goddamn smart, I can't believe it, you know he's a college man . . . but then I got hit in the leg, that old bastard Planner hit me in the goddamn leg and made me kill him, and we got stuck in goddamn Iowa City and lost time there and messed up the flight and had to put it off till today and then Jesus, you were onto me and the Family was onto me, and then I hear on the radio they're killing off everybody who helped me . . . Harry . . . Tillis . . . Jesus."

"You think the Family killed those guys?"

"Who else? I knew they'd be on me, when that kid, that friend of yours Jon, told me back in that doctor's office, told me *you* knew I was the one that took the money, told me *you* were coming after me. I knew about you and your new ties with the Family. That if you knew I was alive, so did they. They're coming today, aren't they? Are they outside now, Nolan?"

"If they are, they got here on their own. They know you're alive, yes, but they gave me two days to find you and get my money back."

"Don't shit me, not with Harry and Tillis shot all to shit." He bent over and looked very sober. "Nolan, I want to work out a trade with you. Listen to me. You take care of Walter, get him out of here before the Family comes. You see that he stays alive."

"What do I get in return?"

"That kid friend of yours, that Jon. Walter's holding him down at the boathouse right now. Why the hell else would I take that kid Jon with me? I knew you were coming after me, that if you caught up with me, I could use the kid as a buffer. He's your friend, saved your life once, I know, I was there."

"Sorry. Jon is holding a gun to your son's head right this minute. You don't have the edge you thought you had, Charlie."

"I don't believe you."

"I don't have time to lie to you, Charlie. We got to get on with this before those people you mentioned start showing up."

"No, no," Charlie said, whimpering, his eyes filling with tears. "Walter's got to get out, nothing to happen to Walter, not Walter, he's the only thing left. Please God."

"Tell me what you did with the money, Charlie, and I'll help your kid get out of this."

"Do . . . do I get your word on that?"

"Sure."

"You always called me a melodramatic bastard, remember?"

"I still do, Charlie."

"Well, that's true, I guess it's true but you . . . you got your own quirk. You're straight, in your crooked way. You give your word and you keep it. So I know if you give me your word, you're going to stand behind it, Nolan. I'm sure of it."

That wasn't particularly true, but Nolan let it slide by. Charlie was saying all that in order to convince himself he could trust Nolan, and Nolan knew it.

"What did you do with the money, Charlie?"

"You *promise,* you *promise* you'll help Walter?"

"Sure."

Charlie let out a relieved sigh. He smiled on one side of his face and said, "A funny goddamn way for us to finish it up, Nolan. Me turning to you to save my kid's ass. My God. You know something else funny? I didn't even *need* that goddamn money of yours. I got all kinds of money, in this guy's account and that one, money to live a couple goddamn lifetimes, if I had 'em. No, I took that money because I hated you, I wanted you to bleed, I wanted to hurt you the one place you could feel it, in your goddamn pocketbook. It was for blood, not money, and now neither one means a goddamn thing. Why'd we do it to each other? What the hell was the goddamn point?"

From behind them came a sound—*bup bup bup bup bup bup*—no louder than someone giving a deck of cards a hard shuffle, and Charlie screamed, "Mother of God!" and jumped behind the sofa. Nolan dove under the coffee table, turned it on its side and held it in front of him like a shield, while the slugs ate up the room, tearing into the dark wood walls, ripping apart the leather sofas, knocking down furniture, their white sheets flying in the air, like dancing ghosts. Charlie went scrambling over to the dining area, got behind the big long table and tipped it over with a crash, got sheltered behind its thick wood while the slugs splintered away at its surface, *bup bup bup bup bup.*

Silence.

Nolan peeked out from behind the table and the *bup bup bup* started in again, but not before Nolan saw the gun and the man behind it. The gun was a grease gun, a submachine gun that fired .45 slugs and looked as if it had been put together with discarded tin cans; the barrel had been screwed off and a tubular silencer put on its place; two magazines had been taped together so the guy could flip it around and shove in a fresh round without missing more than a half-second of action.

The guy behind the grease gun had a chubby face and a skinny body and all of a sudden Nolan knew who Charlie's pipeline to Felix was. All of a sudden Nolan knew who killed Tillis and Harry and why.

Nolan had his .38 in one hand and the silenced automatic of Charlie's in the other and started firing at Angello, shooting haphazardly, firing both guns like some two-gun kid in a Western. With that grease gun out there, aiming was out of the question, even though the guy was standing out in the open, over by a side door directly behind where Nolan had been sitting.

Charlie dove from behind the table, pitched himself into the kitchen, caught one in the gut just as he went through the doorway. Nolan could see the little man in underwear crawling off through the kitchen, out toward the elevator. Somehow Nolan sensed that Charlie was not so much trying to get away as making an attempt to get to Walter and warn him. Well, luck to you, Charlie, Nolan thought.

Angello yanked the magazine out, flipped it around and shoved it in place and Nolan blew Angello's kneecap apart with a .38 slug. Angello fell on his face, like a pratfalling clown, but much harder, and on his side started in firing the grease gun again and the room was splintering, chunks of the marble top started to fly and Nolan held his breath, hoping Angello's pain and rage and reflex would empty that damn, damn gun.

It did. The *bup bup bup* trailed away and Nolan spun out

and pointed the .38 at Angello's head and Angello threw the empty grease gun, whipped it at Nolan. The metal of the gun smashed into his head, slashed a red crease across his forehead, and he fired the .38 wildly, missed, and blacked out.

When he came to a second later, he looked up, blinked the blood from his eyes, saw Angello kneeling on his good knee in front of him. "Are you awake, Nolan?"

Nolan nodded.

"Good," Angello said. "I want you awake, you overrated bastard. Some fucking tough guy," and Angello lifted the Bodyguard Smith and Wesson .38 and let Nolan look into its short snub-nose, let him wait for the blossom of fire and smoke.

"Hold it!"

The voice came from behind them.

"What the hell's happening here?"

It was Greer.

The babyfaced man was standing in the doorway over where moments before Angello had been firing the grease gun. Greer had his own snub-nose .38 in his right hand.

"Greer," Angello said, his eyes moving back and forth.

"What you doing, Ange?"

"I'm going to kill this son of a bitch, Greer," Angello said. "He tried to pull a cross, tried to team up with Charlie and cross the Family."

"I don't believe you," Greer said, and shot Angello through the throat.

Angello's .38 went off, but Nolan had had sense to duck and roll as Greer fired, and Angello's gun clattered to the floor and he clutched with both hands under his double chin and flopped onto his back and gurgled and died.

Nolan said, "Jesus."

Greer came over and helped him up. "Where's Charlie?"

"Shit," Nolan said, and headed for the kitchen.

When he got there the elevator had gone to the bottom. Charlie had somehow found strength to punch DOWN. Nolan pressed the button and heard the elevator whine and moan and start its ascent. When it got back up, Charlie was still inside the cage.

He was sitting against the steel wall, his lower tee-shirt and shorts soaked with red. His eyes were shut.

Nolan crouched down beside the little man and yelled as though Charlie were a hundred yards away. "Charlie! For Christ's sake, Charlie!"

The close-set eyes flickered.

"Charlie," Nolan said, putting a hand on the little man's shoulder. "Thank God you're alive."

"Never thought I'd live to . . . hear you . . . say that, Nolan."

"Where is it, Charlie? What did you do with my money?"

"I won, Nolan. I beat you."

"You want me to help your boy, don't you? Well, where's the money, what'd you do with it?"

"You promise . . . promise you'll . . . help Walter?"

"I'll do whatever you want, just what did you do with my money!"

"You'll keep your word . . . if I tell you what I did with it?"

"Yes, dammit! Don't die on me, you son of a bitch!"

"All right," Charlie said, and he told Nolan what he'd done with the money. The look of dismayed surprise on Nolan's face tickled Charlie's ass and Charlie let out one big, raucous belly laugh and held his bleeding belly and died that way.

8

Nolan got to his feet unsteadily. He felt as if he, too, had been ripped into by Angello's grease gun. He stepped out of the elevator and wandered into the kitchen, took a seat at the Formica-top table, sat and stared at the cluster of empty Schlitz cans in front of him, pressed his hands against his temples.

Greer said, "What's going on?"

Nolan pointed toward the vestibule and Greer went over and saw Charlie and came back.

"That's a nasty gash on your forehead," Greer said.

Nolan said, "Get me a beer, will you? Should be some in that refrigerator."

Greer brought Nolan a Schlitz, got one for himself and sat with Nolan at the table.

"You okay, Nolan?"

"I don't know yet." He gulped down the beer. He belched. "That was nice shooting in there. I take back what I said about snub-nose .38's."

Greer grinned. "How do you know I was aiming at Ange?"

Nolan managed to return the grin, said, "Where'd you come from, anyway? I didn't expect you to show up like the fucking marines."

"Came straight from Iowa City. Felix called me and said to get my butt up to this place."

It hadn't taken Felix long to track down Eagle's Roost. "How'd you beat Felix's boys up here?"

"I didn't. Not the first wave anyway. Two Family guys, friends of mine, are lying back in those pine trees with their guts shot out of them. Didn't you hear gunfire?"

Nolan shook his head no. "Angello was using a grease gun with a silencer. You make more noise breathing than it makes shooting."

"What was he up to, anyway?"

"Covering his tracks. He was in with Charlie."

"Shit. Wait'll Felix finds out."

"That's what Angello must've been thinking. He knew he was up shit crick when the Family got onto Charlie. I figure he killed Tillis and Harry because they were his fellow conspirators and could implicate him. Same goes for killing Charlie. He probably hoped to make it look like I was going around shooting the guys responsible for taking my money, and leave it looking like Charlie and me killed each other in a crossfire."

"Maybe he was after the money, too."

"I don't know. Maybe."

"What *about* the money?"

"Gone. All of it. Gone."

"How, for Christ's sake?"

Nolan told Greer what Charlie did with the money. Greer shook his head, said, "Old bastard must've been crazy."

"Yeah," Nolan agreed. "Like the rest of us."

Nolan told Greer to relay word to Felix about the money, told him he'd be at the Tropical waiting for Felix to come talk. There would be plans to cancel, new arrangements to be made.

Jon had the Olds hotwired and ready to go in the boathouse garage, but it was unnecessary, because Nolan had found Charlie's keys on the kitchen counter. Nolan and Jon laid Walter in the backseat; somewhere along the line the sock had been taken out of his mouth, but he wasn't saying much anyway. Nolan didn't answer any of Jon's questions about what had happened or where the money was. Finally Jon asked if he could run upstairs and get something before they left, and Nolan said okay. When Jon came back with a box full of comic books, Nolan didn't even say anything; he just opened the trunk for the boy and thought, well, at least somebody got something out of this.

They drove out of the garage, stopped to unlock the gate, where Nolan told Jon to get in the backseat with Walter and untie him.

Nolan started driving again and talked to Walter in the rearview mirror. "Your father is dead."

Walter made a move to grab Nolan and Jon stopped him.

"Easy," Nolan said. "I didn't kill your old man, one of his own cohorts did. What I'm doing now is answering his dying request, God knows why, and hauling your ass away from that place before more Family people show up."

"Where . . . where are you taking me?" Walter said.

"I'm going to drop you off at your sister's apartment in

Dekalb. She'll be glad to see you, I think, if she isn't off feeding the world's hungry."

They were passing through the subdivision of summer homes now. Nolan slowed the Olds and let a little boy and girl in swimming suits cross in front of him.

Walter said, "Won't they . . . they be coming after me?"

"I don't think so. You're no threat to anybody. I'll do some talking for you."

"But . . . I'm supposed to be *dead* . . ."

"It's not your fault they mistook some poor bastard in a car crash for you."

"I don't know . . . I don't know . . ."

Nolan glanced back at the kid. "It'll work out. Get yourself a job in an office."

"Nolan," Jon said.

"Yeah?"

"Are you going to say anything about the money, or aren't you?"

"Forget about it."

"What do you mean, forget about it?"

"It's gone, kid. Up in smoke. Let it go." He pulled off the subdivision drive onto the blacktop. He was thinking about Sherry, about climbing in the sack with Sherry and forgetting things for a while.

"Nolan," Jon said, getting pissed, "what the hell happened to our money?"

Walter knew. Walter was smiling.

"Charlie burned it," Nolan said.

THE
END

First And (Not) Last Time
An Afterword by Max Allan Collins

I'm grateful to Charles Ardai and Hard Case Crime for choosing these two novels—collected here as one book, for the first time—as part of their new noir line. I believe Charles would have put them out individually, but I see them as one big novel now, and requested their publication in this manner.

Bait Money was my first published book, written during 1969 and '70, when I was attending the University of Iowa. Its sequel, *Blood Money*, was actually written several years later, in between two other novels of mine (*No Cure for Death*, the first Mallory—though the second published—and *The Broker*, in which hired killer Quarry was introduced). When Curtis Books bought *Bait Money* (the news came on Christmas Eve, 1971), I almost immediately began a sequel. I did *Blood Money* so quickly, and it sold so quickly, the books came out simultaneously, as a matched pair.

Two interesting things about the Curtis Books publication, both having to do with names.

The books had been submitted as by Allan Collins. As a "junior," I grew up using my middle name, to avoid confusion with my father (Max), which is why if you see me at a mystery or comic con, you may hear me called "Al" or "Allan" by my closer pals and my wife Barb. But when I signed the contracts with Curtis, I used my full legal name: Max Allan Collins Jr. Then, when advance copies of the books arrived (around Christmas of '72), the byline was suddenly MAX COLLINS. No one had told me of this decision (later I heard an editor correctly thought "Max Collins" sounded more like a mystery writer) and I first learned of it when I saw the published novels. "Max Collins" was my father's name, and he seemed delighted. I was not.

Neither was mystery writer Michael Collins, whose real name is Dennis Lynds. He called and requested I stop using that name. I offered to use a pen name—Dennis Lynds— which he didn't find very funny. A few years later, both of us wrote novels called *The Slasher* and the two "M. Collins" mystery writers caused all sorts of bibliographic nightmares. That was when I added "Allan" into the byline: to better set myself apart from the other Collins (who is now a good friend of mine), and to reclaim my byline, at least in part. I guess I'm the only writer in history whose pseudonym is his real name.

The other name problem was with Nolan himself. Nolan was originally conceived as a pastiche of Richard Stark's Parker, also a mono-named thief (more of this later). But again, someone at Curtis Books—an editor, or perhaps someone in the art department—decided that Nolan needed a first name. So they gave him one—Frank—in all of the cover copy.

Frank is not Nolan's first name. I don't know what his real first name is, but it's not Frank . . . though you'll find "Frank Nolan" listed as one of my series characters in scads of reference books. Yet another bibliographic nightmare. . . .

The Richard Stark "Parker" novels and the comic mystery fiction of Donald E. Westlake were the last two enthusiasms of my pre-professional life. Stark and Westlake were the final writers I discovered before turning pro, in the sense of authors who would influence me. I read both these guys for a good year or two before I found out these seeming opposites were one man (had their books side by side on the shelf already, and merely removed a bookend and slid them all together).

My previous heroes had been Mickey Spillane, Dashiell Hammett, Raymond Chandler, Jim Thompson and James M. Cain . . . plus many writers of paperback originals for Gold Medal, Lion Books, and other pulp publishers of the

'50s and '60s (I didn't start reading this stuff till the early
'60s, but haunted used bookstores). My first novels, written
in high school, were Spillane pastiches; I attempted to
market these, and of course failed, but along the way
learned to write. When I hit my late teens, the Richard Stark
books hit me hard—the idea that a "bad guy" could be the
lead character, that a man with a code could be a crook, not
a cop.

Now I'd already shelved (temporarily, as it turned out)
my desire to write private eye novels in the Mike
Hammer/Shell Scott mode. Already private eyes were
seeming quaint to me, rooted in another era, and I didn't
feel like writing about cops. I was a long-haired hippie
(according to my father, anyway) and was disillusioned by
cops clubbing kids in Chicago at the Democratic convention, among other outrages of the day. So the anti-establish-
ment notion of Stark's Parker appealed.

I played catch-up, reading other writers of "crook
books," in particular W.R. Burnett and Horace McCoy
(whose *Kiss Tomorrow Goodbye* remains one of my half
dozen favorite novels). And soon I set about to write my own
Stark-like novel, with the notion of hitting the contemporary
scene as hard as I could—no crime writers were dealing
with my long-haired hippie generation. The result was a
novel called *Mourn the Living*, which ended up being serial-
ized long after the fact in *Hardboiled* magazine and in
recent years has been collected into hardcover form by Five
Star. The Nolan character was called Cord in that book (I
changed it to Nolan many years later, since the character
really was the same, down to the backstory).

The book did not find a publisher, though it was good
enough to get me into the Writers Workshop (undergrad) at
Iowa City, where I began to work with my mentor, the fine
mainstream novelist and short story writer, Richard Yates.
Dick Yates had a lot to do with pushing me across the line
from imitator into creator, and helped me understand the
needs of character over plot, though he was highly compli-

mentary about several minor characters in *Mourn the Living*. He paid me the best compliment of my career: "You're a real writer." (This, he believed, in spite of my genre leanings.)

I had taken a tentative step toward writing about the midwest in *Mourn*, and took a greater leap with *Bait Money*, which was initially called *First and Last Time*. I set the story in my own home area—Muscatine, Iowa (Port City) and the Quad Cities (home of John Looney, *Road to Perdition*'s real-life gangster). Essentially, my wife Barb helped me rob the bank where she worked; I in fact used the bank's own security plan as a guide (it's quoted at the front of the book). The book is called *Bait Money* because I loved the sound of this real banking term my bride shared with me.

The Nolan-esque character in *Mourn* had been presented as in his thirties and a sort of Robin Hood who hit only the mob. I aged him almost to 50 and threw out the Robin Hood notion; the concept was to take a Parker-like character who has reached the ancient age of 48 and wants badly to retire, and of course needs one last heist to do so. My thinking was, if anybody lived like Steve McQueen did in the movies, in real life, he'd be dead by 50. (McQueen later pretty much proved my point.)

The second notion was to partner this "old" man with a young kid who represented my generation, those long-haired hippies previously mentioned—to put the traditional hardboiled hero in contact with youth of the late '60s/early '70s. I believe I was one of the first writers in the genre to do this. Further, the heist in the novel would be Nolan's last and Jon's first (and last). I figured Jon was a basically honest kid, not cut out for this life, who got caught up in crime naively and because of his heister uncle, Planner.

Because of this first-and-last theme, and since I knew the book was at least partially a Richard Stark rip-off, I killed Nolan at the end. My then-agent Knox Burger—who Dick Yates had found for me—did not like the ending. Rather prophetically, he said, "Robin does not leave Batman to die."

I was stubborn, because . . . because I'm stubborn. I felt this was a novel about the death of the American tough guy . . . which seemed to require the American tough guy dying.

And so the book was sent out with that bleak ending. It was rejected perhaps ten times over the course of a year or two. Then an editor did me an unintentional favor: a cup of coffee was spilled on the manuscript. In those ancient, type-written days, this meant preparing a new manuscript—retyping the sucker; couldn't even submit carbons in those days. And Burger said, "Why don't you take this opportunity to put on a better ending?"

So I unkilled Nolan, writing an extra couple of paragraphs, and Burger sold the book next try. And immediately the editor asked for a sequel.

Now I was nervous. One Parker pastiche was an homage; a series really did seem a rip-off. . . .

By this time I was corresponding with Don Westlake, who had read *Bait Money* in manuscript and said nice things about it to Burger, which may be why Knox kept trying with it after so many rejections. And I asked Don what he thought—did he mind if I kept writing Nolan novels?

He did not. He was extremely gracious, saying that the Jon aspect of the books humanized Nolan in a manner that made these books wholly different animals (never mind that I even mimicked his point of view method and time-shifting chapters) (we were both way ahead of Quentin Tarantino, but behind Kubrick).

And with Don's blessing, I went forward. There were seven Nolans . . . eight, counting *Mourn the Living* . . . and that was where my career began, thanks to Dick Yates and Don Westlake and Knox Burger. They were the collective Nolan to my Jon, and I'll always be grateful to them.

But I've stayed with my life of crime.

MAX ALLAN COLLINS
Muscatine, Iowa AKA Port City
November 2003